AFRICAN WRITERS SERIES

PETER ABRAHAMS
6 *Mine Boy*

CHINUA ACHEBE
✳ *Things Fall Apart*
✳ *No Longer at Ease*
✳ *Arrow of God*
31 *A Man of the People*
100 *Girls at War* *
120 *Beware Soul Brother* †

THOMAS AKARE
241 *The Slums*

T. M. ALUKO
30 *One Man, One Wife*
32 *Kinsman and Foreman*
70 *Chief, the Honourable Minister*
130 *His Worshipful Majesty*
242 *Wrong Ones in the Dock*

ELECHI AMADI
25 *The Concubine*
44 *The Great Ponds*
210 *The Slave*
✳ *Estrangement*

I. N. C. ANIEBO
206 *The Journey Within*
253 *Of Wives, Talismans and the Dead* *

KOFI ANYIDOHO
261 *A Harvest of Our Dreams* †

AYI KWEI ARMAH
43 *The Beautyful Ones Are Not Yet Born*
154 *Fragments*
155 *Why Are We So Blest?*
194 *The Healers*
218 *Two Thousand Seasons*

BEDIAKO ASARE
59 *Rebel*

KOFI AWOONOR
108 *This Earth, My Brother*
260 *Until the Morning After* †

MARIAMA BÂ
248 *So Long a Letter*

FRANCIS BEBEY
205 *The Ashanti Doll*

MONGO BETI
13 *Mission to Kala*
77 *King Lazarus*
88 *The Poor Christ of Bomba*
181 *Perpetua and the Habit of Unhappiness*
214 *Remember Ruben*

STEVE BIKO
✳ *I Write What I Like* §

OKOT P'BITEK
147 *The Horn of My Love* †
193 *Hare and Hornbill* *
266 *Song of Lawino & Song of Ocol* †

YAW M. BOATENG
186 *The Return*

✳ Four colour tra...
* Short Stories
† Poetry
‡ Plays
§ Biography/Politics

DENNIS BRUTUS
46 *Letters to Martha* †
115 *A Simple Lust* †
208 *Stubborn Hope* †

SYL CHENEY-COKER
221 *The Graveyard Also Has Teeth* †

DRISS CHRAIBI
79 *Heirs to the Past*

J. P. CLARK
50 *America, Their America* §

WILLIAM CONTON
12 *The African*

BERNARD B. DADIE
87 *Climbié*

DANIACHEW WORKU
125 *The Thirteenth Sun*

MODIKWE DIKOBE
124 *The Marabi Dance*

MBELLA SONNE DIPOKO
57 *Because of Women*
107 *Black and White in Love* †

AMU DJOLETO
41 *The Strange Man*

T. OBINKARAM ECHEWA
✳ *The Crippled Dancer*

CYPRIAN EKWENSI
2 *Burning Grass*
5 *People of the City*
19 *Lokotown* *
84 *Beautiful Feathers*
✳ *Jagua Nana*
172 *Restless City* *
185 *Survive the Peace*

BUCHI EMECHETA
227 *The Joys of Motherhood*

OLAUDAH EQUIANO
10 *Equiano's Travels* §

NURUDDIN FARAH
80 *From a Crooked Rib*
184 *A Naked Needle*
252 *Sardines*

FATHY GHANEM
223 *The Man Who Lost His Shadow*

NADINE GORDIMER
177 *Some Monday for Sure* *

JOE DE GRAFT
166 *Beneath the Jazz and Brass* †
264 *Muntu* ‡

...Sarowe: Village of the Rain Wind §
✳ *When Rain Clouds Gather*

LUIS BERNARDO HONWANA
60 *We Killed Mangy-Dog* *

TAHA HUSSEIN
228 *An Egyptian Childhood*

YUSUF IDRIS
209 *The Cheapest Nights* *
267 *Rings of Burnished Brass* *

OBOTUNDE IJIMÈRE
18 *The Imprisonment of Obatala* ‡

EDDIE IROH
189 *Forty-Eight Guns for the General*
213 *Toads of War*
255 *The Siren in the Night*

KENJO JUMBAM
231 *The White Man of God*

AUBREY KACHINGWE
24 *No Easy Task*

SAMUEL KAHIGA
158 *The Girl from Abroad*

CHEIKH HAMIDOU KANE
119 *Ambiguous Adventure*

KENNETH KAUNDA
4 *Zambia Shall Be Free* §

LEGSON KAYIRA
162 *The Detainee*

A. W. KAYPER-MENSAH
157 *The Drummer in Our Time* †

JOMO KENYATTA
219 *Facing Mount Kenya* §

ASARE KONADU
40 *A Woman in her Prime*
55 *Ordained by the Oracle*

AHMADOU KOUROUMA
239 *The Suns of Independence*

MAZISI KUNENE
211 *Emperor Shaka the Great* †
234 *Anthem of the Decades* †
235 *The Ancestors* †

ALEX LA GUMA
✳ *A Walk in the Night* *
110 *In the Fog of the Seasons' End*
✳ *Time of the Butcherbird*

HUGH LEWIN
251 *Bandiet*

TABAN LO LIYONG
69 *Fixions* *
74 *Eating Chiefs* *

NAGUIB MAHFOUZ
225 Children of Gebelawi

NELSON MANDELA
✷ No Easy Walk to Freedom§

JACK MAPANJE
236 Of Chameleons and Gods†

DAMBUDZO MARECHERA
207 The House of Hunger*
237 Black Sunlight

ALI A MAZRUI
97 The Trial of Christopher
    Okigbo

TOM MBOYA
81 The Challenge of Nationhood
    (Speeches) §

THOMAS MOFOLO
229 Chaka

DOMINIC MULAISHO
98 The Tongue of the Dumb
204 The Smoke that Thunders

JOHN MUNONYE
21 The Only Son
45 Obi
94 Oil Man of Obange
153 A Dancer of Fortune
195 Bridge to a Wedding

MARTHA MVUNGI
159 Thee Solid Stones*

MEJA MWANGI
143 Kill Me Quick
145 Carcase for Hounds
176 Gang Down River Road

GEORGE SIMEON MWASE
160 Strike a Blow and Die§

JOHN NAGENDA
✷ The Seasons of Thomas Tebo

NGUGI WA THIONG O
7 Weep Not Child
17 The River Between
✷ A Grain of Wheat
51 The Black Hermit‡
150 Secret Lives*
✷ Petals of Blood
✷ Devil on the Cross
240 Detained§

NGUGI & MICERE MUGO
191 The Trial of Dedan Kimathi‡

NGUGI & NGUGI WA MIRII
246 I Will Marry When I Want‡

REBEKA NJAU
203 Ripples in the Pool

NKEM NWANKWO
67 Danda
173 My Mercedes is Bigger Than
    Yours

FLORA NWAPA
26 Efuru
56 Idu

S NYAMFUKUDZA
233 The Non-Believer's Journey

ONUORA NZEKWU
85 Wand of Noble Wood

OGINGA ODINGA
38 Not Yet Uhuru §

GABRIEL OKARA
68 The Voice
183 The Fisherman's Invocation†

CHRISTOPHER OKIGBO
62 Labyrinths†

KOLE OMOTOSO
122 The Combat

SEMBENE OUSMANE
✷ God's Bits of Wood
✷ The Money-Order
175 Xala
250 The Last of the Empire
✷ Black Docker

YAMBO OUOLOGUEM
99 Bound to Violence

FERDINANDO OYONO
29 Houseboy
39 The Old Man and the Medal

SOL T. PLAATJE
201 Mhudi

PEPETELA
269 Mayombe

R. L. PETENI
178 Hill of Fools

LENRIE PETERS
22 The Second Round
37 Satellites†
238 Selected Poetry†

MOLEFE PHETO
258 And Night Fell§

ALIFA RIFAAT
✷ Distant View of a Minaret

RICHARD RIVE
✷ Buckingham Palace: District
    Six

MWANGI RUHENI
156 The Minister's Daughter

TAYEB SALIH
47 The Wedding of Zein*
66 Season of Migration to the
    North

STANLAKE SAMKANGE
33 On Trial for my Country
169 The Mourned One
190 Year of the Uprising

WILLIAMS SASSINE
199 Wirriyamu

KOBINA SEKYI
136 The Blinkards‡

FRANCIS SELORMEY
27 The Narrow Path

L. S. SENGHOR
71 Nocturnes†
180 Prose and Poetry

SIPHO SEPAMLA
268 A Ride on the Whirlwind

MONGANE SEROTE
263 To Every Birth Its Blood

WOLE SOYINKA
76 The Interpreters

OLIVER TAMBO
✷ Oliver Tambo Speaks

TCHICAYA U TAM'SI
72 Selected Poems†

CAN THEMBA
104 The Will to Die*

REMS NNA UMEASIEGBU
61 The Way We Lived*

J. L. VIEIRA
202 The Real Life of Domingos
    Xavier
222 Luuanda

JOHN YA-OTTO
244 Battlefront Namibia§

ASIEDU YIRENKYI
216 Kivuli and Other Plays†

D. M. ZWELONKE
128 Robben Island

COLLECTIONS OF PROSE
14 Quartet
23 The Origin of Life and Death
48 Not Even God is Ripe Enough
83 Myths and Legends of the
    Congo
118 Amadu's Bundle
132 Two Centuries of African
    English
243 Africa South Contemporary
    Writings
254 Stories from Central and
    Southern Africa
256 Unwinding Threads
270 African Short Stories

ANTHOLOGIES OF POETRY
93 A Choice of Flowers
96 Poems from East Africa
129 Igbo Traditional Verse
164 Black Poets in South Africa
171 Poems of Black Africa
192 Anthology of Swahili Poetry
215 Poems from Angola
230 Poets to the People
257 New Poetry from Africa

COLLECTIONS OF PLAYS
34 Ten One-Act Plays
127 Nine African Plays for Radio
165 African Plays for Playing 1
179 African Plays for Playing 2
232 Egyptian One-Act Plays

AFRICAN WRITERS SERIES

263

To Every Birth Its Blood

TO EVERY BIRTH ITS BLOOD

Mongane Serote

LONDON

HEINEMANN

IBADAN   NAIROBI

Heinemann International Publishing
a division of Heinemann Educational Books Ltd,
Halley Court, Jordan Hill, Oxford OX2 8EJ
Heinemann Educational Books (Nigeria) Ltd
PMB 5205, Ibadan
Heinemann Educational Books Inc.
70 Court Street, Portsmouth, New Hampshire, 03801, USA

OXFORD LONDON EDINBURGH
MELBOURNE SYDNEY AUCKLAND
SINGAPORE MADRID IBADAN
NAIROBI GABORONE HARARE
KINGSTON PORTSMOUTH (NH)

British Library Cataloguing in Publication Data

Serote, Mongane W.
  To every birth its blood.—(African writers series; v. 263)
  I. Title II. Series
  823[F]   PR9368.4.S/

  ISBN 0-435-90263-6

Set in 10pt Times by Performance Typesetting Limited, Milton Keynes,
Buckinghamshire
Printed in Great Britain by Richard Clay Limited, Bungay, Suffolk

Part I

One

So, when she and I walked into the house after we had been in the street so long, I knew that another time was coming when we would have to be in the street again. That moment, as she went about the house opening the windows, taking off her shoes, unbuttoning her blouse, looking calm and more friendly, I wanted to weep. I did not know how I was going to tell her, 'Baby, most things about this earth want you to run, want to make you weary, want you to faint.'

So I sat back on the chair. I said, 'Honey, why don't you play Nina Simone?'

She was smiling as she came softly towards me and, hugging me, asked whether I wanted tea or whether she must send a kid to the shebeen for beer. I said beer. Beer makes things easy, I thought to myself. 'Streets full of people all alone,' Nina was saying.

Yes, when Lily and I were walking, coming home, I was in a good loving mood. I felt very close to her. I knew she was one person I could say I knew. Lily can enjoy a person like a child enjoys a peach. You see the juice flowing down her tender, strong fingers, towards her smooth arms. Her teeth dig in, right into the flesh; you can see her thick, warm lips embrace the peach, tasting its flesh. Something about her laughter, when she really laughs, not when she laughs instead of crying, has made me discover many things, even about myself.

I was looking at her legs. Long legs which give her a tall, steady gait as her thigh muscles thrust and relax. I watched her walk from the wardrobe to the table, where she took out the money from her bag. Then she moved to the door. I heard her call our little friend's name. My mother has called me that way, so many times, in that long dragging way, as if my name were spaghetti threads. Her lips tasting the name, something about the voice becoming tender. They spoke at the door, I heard the little footsteps run and fade. Lily, almost talking to herself, said, 'While you have your beer I will have my tea.'

I took off my shoes. I took off my socks. I unbuttoned my shirt and sat back. It felt so good, really, so good to know I was not going to faint. I had been running, oh, I was weary, but now I knew I was not going to faint. The noise of the primus stove started. She put the kettle on, placed a glass and a cup on the table, and came over to sit next to me and enjoy me.

'Do you feel good about the theatre now?'

'I do not know, Baby,' I said.

'What do you think is going to happen?'

'The worst,' I said, 'is that we could all get arrested. At the least, we could be banned.' There was silence. I could feel her thinking, her mind fidgeting with the future.

'Don't faint Baby, please child, don't faint,' I said.

'No, I won't,' she said. Our eyes met. I waited for her to kiss me. But I could feel her waiting for me to kiss her. I was not about to do that. Her eyes were digging into mine. There was silence. I thought, God, something is going to break. I waited.

There was a knock on the door. Our little friend walked in, put the beer bottle on the table. He saw me.

'Ah, Abuti-Tsi, was that your car you came in yesterday?'

'No, it belongs to some white people,' I said.

'Where you work?'

'No, Vusi, I do not work for white people,' I said. I watched Lily wiping the glass. She brought the beer and the glass next to me. Her face told me things were happening now.

'Who do you work for?'

'Vusi, I will tell you tomorrow,' I said. 'Look, take five cents, buy yourself something, we will talk tomorrow.'

'Not five cents,' Lily snapped. I retreated. She gave Vusi two cents. Vusi looked at me, was about to say something, but walked out after saying bye bye to me and then to Lily. She poured out some tea and sat at the table.

'Lily, do you think if things came to the worst, you would be all right?' I knew I could never bear to see Lily break down. I looked at her. Her eyes, ever so gentle, made me want to protect her: her face, gentle, beautiful, stormy like the many journeys we had had together; those brutal gentle journeys which every time took us into a deep sleep, a dream in which we would be locked into each other; and when we broke, we would realise we were trying to be one.

'Are you sure?'

'I am,' she said.

'Are you sure?'

'What do you want me to say?' she asked. I sensed anger in her voice.

'I am not assured.'

'I will never be able to reassure you.' How true, I thought. But still, something was not in line; God, something was missing. I put on a record. The guitar started screaming, the humming voice, like the ocean, vast, troubled in its calm, came in: 'Be on my side I will be on your side, Baby.' I thought wow, Buddy Miles, what is going to happen now, what are we going to do? 'I shot my Baby.'

I was riding on the wings of the beer now. I went out to get another one. When I came back, Lily was in her house mood. She was peeling potatoes. A pot was dancing on the stove. The room was hot. Miriam Makeba's voice had filled the room. Everything in the house made me fall in love.

'Baby, let's save this boat today,' I said. 'It's not going for the storm.'

'Stop being smart,' she said. Her voice told me we were, after all, heading for the storm. I have always tried to talk to my Baby with music. So, I thought, Ausi Miriam has her way about this. I pushed the button to reject. Flipped the record and put on 'Woza'. And Miriam's voice and Hugh's trumpet took over the house, I could smell curry. The room was hot. My Baby never looked at me. Something about the record, the house, everything, maybe also the beer, made me sad now. I started to long for things I did not know. Hugh's trumpet and Miriam's voice held each other as if they were fire and wind, ready to drown everything around them. I wondered where Hugh was, where Miriam was, when would they come back home. I thought, both of them know Alexandra so well. I began to put my shoes on. I was also thinking how I was going to put it to my Baby. My Baby, my feather has broken, I can't fly, I want to hide? No. My Baby, I will be back? No. What was I going to say?

'Where are you going?' She took me by surprise. I stood up, lost in thought, and played with my beard.

'I want to see the boys out there,' I said.

'Take your key, I won't wake up to open for you.' I looked at her. I kissed her. She pushed me back.

'Don't over-drink,' she said. 'You know that you fight when you are drunk, and that breaks my heart.'

'Drunk!'

'Put on your jersey, it's going to be cold outside,' she said. I took my jersey and stood around.

'I can only give you two rands, no more,' she said.

'Baby, you know those boys have been buying beer for me all this week. Be proud of your man!'

She looked at me with her mischievous eyes. She fought her laughter. 'We have to pay permit tomorrow,' she said, almost pleading.

'I will go dig the heap for that. Okay, give me five.'

'Five?' she said, 'Tsi, five?'

'I should be saying ten, you know.' She looked at me with eyes saying, you are mad, ten? Never! I got four.

I left my Baby and went out. The sun was setting and the sky was yellow. The air was busy with sounds of buses, cars, scooters, footsteps, playing children. Something about all this made me sad. I went on. Thinking about me and my Baby. As usual, I was walking into crowds. I have never walked with crowds. I walk into them. Where was I going with four rands in my pocket? I stopped an old man and asked him for time. 'Five,' he said. Most of the boys would still be on their way home. I turned up Hofmeyr Street, into Sixth Avenue. I walked into crowds flooding from the bus terminus, people, many people stopping now and then to talk to one another, and moving on.

I went up Selborne Street. The river was in flood; footsteps, eyes, flesh flowing down. I walked into it. Someone called my name. Oh, I was happy to see him.

'Fucker, howzit?'

'Our man, I'm all right,' I said. He started laughing loudly, pointing at me.

'But you, you are mad,' he said, still laughing. 'Why is your hair unkempt?' He took me by surprise. I felt like saying – fuck you. But I did not say anything. We talked about things. I told him I had been to his place two or three days ago, but he had not been there. He laughed. He said he had been in the street. Got home drunk that night. He looked into the crowd.

'My Baby, hey my Baby, come here sweetheart,' he said. A girl ran across the street and came towards us. The way she was jumping made her look like a little girl. They kissed and he held her arm. Then his hand went for her stomach. She blocked it; it was automatic the way she did it.

'Moipone, what will people say?' she asked. I think I was embarrassed. Moipone laughed.

'They will say, hoo, that man wants the thing,' he said, 'And they will be jealous.' He held her round the waist. Both her hands were between her thighs.

'Tsi, where are you going?'

'To see John, then maybe to George Steel.'

'Baby, you want to come along?'

'No, I have to go home.' He started to pull her. Everybody was looking at us. She tried to resist, then gave in. The sun was gone. We walked up Selborne Street. The girl slipped and ran down Selborne. Moipone ran after her. He picked up a brick, screaming stop! stop! and was about to throw the brick when she stopped. I waited under the light. They talked for a while and he came back alone.

'Hey Moipone, what shit is this man. By the way, I am a married man.'

'Ah, my brother, me too I'm married. No, don't worry, no trouble, my brother.'

We walked on in silence. I wanted to talk but knew it would mean nothing. So we were left to the settling shadows of the night. We walked, both of us, in silence.

Our eyes paved the darkness that caught up with us. Friday is a bad day. When Friday night flies away, it has bloody wings. We saw someone get killed. We watched, silently. We walked on and the man's scream kept snatching our scruffs. My heart was knocking rather too loudly. We heard footsteps, running and running and running, and the night was quiet and the darkness resisted the street lights. The scream had stopped. We took quick glances over our shoulders. The footsteps were running away from us, into the dark night.

'They killed him,' Moipone said at last. 'Let's go see.'

'You want to eat him?' I said, becoming angry.

'No, but maybe we know him.'

'Fuck it, if we knew him, we should have gone to him before they killed him.' I walked on. I could not bear to think about what had happened. I preferred to walk on, covered in the dark. Moipone stopped. Then ran back. I heard his footsteps in the dark. Silence. I saw a match flame feebly struggling against the knowing night wind; a shadow. Footsteps started coming towards me. He was breathing heavily.

'Hey my brother, the nights show us things,' Moipone said. I could not see his face. The darkness took it away. I said nothing. I could not say anything.

We walked on. We walked into a door. There were many people, all from work. They needed clothes, for the following day was going to be Saturday. On Saturday people dress well. John was giving them their clothes. I have often wondered what made John run a dry-cleaning shop. He was wrapping clothes. The till rang now and then. People went out into the dark, others came in. What's the colour of your trousers?

John's 'One Day Service Dry Cleaners' is a busy place on Friday. People come and go, and the shop is crammed until late at night. John, going to and from the horizontal rail on which the trousers, skirts and jackets are hung, manages to do business quietly. In and out people go, the buses roar, the taxis hoot, people talk and laugh; all you see of John is his quiet face, his up and down. Now and then he smiles, or answers a question.

We left John at his shop. When he is that busy, there is very little you can say to him about plans for the evening. Moipone and I walked back into the night. People were flowing in from the bus stop into the shebeen. George Steel's house was slowly getting crowded. It was buzzing with voices; coming in from outside, you met the buzz and the curls of cigarette smoke climbing to the ceiling, hanging around the bulbs as you entered the house. The lounge, its air a mixture of Sanpic disinfectant spray, beer, cigarettes and all types of deodorants and perfumes, invoked a mixture of feelings. There is very little one has not seen in this lounge. There is very little one has not heard in this lounge. In a sense, one becomes numb on entering it, in preparation for the unknown yet also with the hope of fulfilment.

When Moipone and I arrived, there were many women and men, already washed and soaking in the smelly fumes of the lounge. We joined them. We sat at a table which was unoccupied, near the window. There were four or five other tables, the occupants engrossed in their talk. Our first round came and went. Round after round came and went. My head was beginning to buzz and go in circles.

'When is John coming?' I asked Moipone.

'I don't know. Look, I want to talk to that woman there,' he said, pointing at a lady, wig, lipstick and all. I must have fallen asleep on the chair while Moipone was talking to the lady.

There was a great noise and I was being shaken when I woke up. I saw Moipone, staggering backwards and forwards, looking down at me and saying something.

'I want to go home now,' I said, and began to stand up.

Two

The sun, its rays clinging to the trees, was rising up over Jukskei river. The sky was yellow where the sun was peeping, and becoming silver as the rays moved, spreading further into the vast sky. The sky is an empty hole? That is disappointing! I walked on. Somewhere a dog was barking, dogs were barking. I thought, they may be chasing a horse, a donkey or a cow. I could also hear drums and whistles. I walked on, down Vasco da Gama Street; past Seventeenth Avenue. The heat of the sun hit me straight on the forehead. An old lady wearing a sombrero which almost obscured her view passed, carrying a spade and a bucket. Her legs carried her as if they were creaking. She was bent forward, miraculously managing not to crash down on her face. Slowly she trod on, and this took her away on her journey, away from the dead.

I went through the gate. Ah, if graves could talk! There they were, spread throughout this vast field, their number-plates sticking up in the air, as if they were hands waving bye-bye. The tombstones looked like miniature sky-scrapers. Some said something about wealth, others were ordinary, and some graves had no tombstones at all. Birds were singing. A cow mooed. Cars roared. But the silence was stubborn. It stuck in the air, looming over the heaps of soil and those who could still walk. Somewhere in an empty patch, a car without wheels, if we could still call it a car, had turned colourless: its seats were ashes, smoke still rose from somewhere around its bowels. The car stood there, proclaiming its death too. As I approached it, I realised it was that year's Valiant. They took what they wanted from it, and left it there. The owner, probably white, will talk to the dead about it. I went along the road.

There are always many people, children, women, men, families, widows, widowers, all of them busy, busy with the graves, silent, weeding, putting fresh flowers into vases; many people, scattered throughout the cemetery early on a Sunday morning. The silence here is graceful. The silence sounds like the song of the birds, of the trees, of the wind; something about the silence of this place suggests, makes one suspect that God, or maybe the dead, are looking at one, listening to one, about to talk to one, just about to do it – but they never do. Women, some in fresh black mourning clothes; all of us, for some reason, wearing casual clothes – men trying to walk straight, holding spades and rakes; children, forever children, now and then playing, now having to follow the elders, now being scolded; families, holding to each other by freshening the graves of their beloved, weeding the sides of the graves; a hymn, a desperate prayer, whispers, the wind, the silence of the dead.

I was sitting on the grave of my grandfather. I fought the thought that nagged me, which wanted to know whether he heard me when I asked about Fix; and also, when I told him that I was getting tired of going to the shebeen; and that I wouldn't go to church. I fought this thought. I will fight, fight it forever. By coming here, every Sunday, I will fight it; I know he is listening, and asking whether I was willing to change. That is where the trouble started – was I willing to change?

I stood up to go.

I was washing my hands near the gate, when I saw him. The water wet my trousers. I thought shit, people will think I peed on my trousers. Where had I seen this old man? He was walking slowly towards the gate. His backside swung left-right-left-right, and now and then he stood to look at the field of tombstones and number-plates. As I got closer I recognised him.

'I see you, Daddy,' I said.

'Yes.' He stopped and looked at me. He was breathing heavily. His eyes were fixed on me, searching. His hat, flipped over to the back of his head, revealed white, white hair, which in turn joined the white, white beard. His eyes were wet and grey. They sure revealed how weary he was. I could not tell whether he was frowning or whether those were permanent old-age folds on his face. He kept staring at me, in silence, then he looked away.

'You boys have no sense,' he said. He looked away and with his stick pointed at the car, which was still smoking.

'Why don't you throw that thing in the street? We want to rest here, not to be burdened with your foolishness. Look at that!' He looked at me.

'Huh?' I was still trying to search for something to say.

'They burn the grass when they clean the rest place, and then you come and throw stolen cars here? What a curse!' He began to walk. I walked next to him, slowly. He stopped.

'You see that tall tombstone?'

'Yes,' I said.

'Nkabinde is resting there.' He began to walk again. 'You know Nkabinde? He used to own a shop near Eighth Avenue. He died last year, they say he had bad lungs or something. He had a big funeral. Yes, he was a good man, a man of the people.' He stopped to take a look again. 'I never used to understand why he said we should buy properties from the old ladies and from anyone else who wanted to sell. You know, I used to think he was greedy, but no, he had a head. If we did that, that time, these Boers would not have taken our place so easily, like they have. Look at all that!' He pointed with his stick towards Alexandra. For some reason or other, every time I looked at Alexandra from the graveyard, it looked like a graveyard.

'Every time I look at all that, my heart bleeds. It breaks. We worked very hard to build this place.' He stopped walking and looked at me.

'Whose child are you?'

'Molope.'

'Molope at 11th, up the street?'

'Yes, father,' I said. He began to walk, now and then looking at me. He was silent for a long time. Then —

'How are you living, man?'

'All right,' I said, shrugging my shoulders.

'Where is your father?'

'He is there.'

'How is his health?'

'He is living.'

'Your mother?'

'She is living too.'

'That is good to hear. I am still living too, but age is telling now, we are going.'

'Yes, I hear you father.'

'Have you heard anything about your brother?'

'No.'

'Nothing?' He sighed.

'Nothing.'

'This is Mokonyama's property,' he said, pointing at the yard where many men were sitting outside in the sun. He stopped to look at the yard. 'Looks like he has sold it,' he said.

'I think so, because those are the men of the Hostel.'

'We can't get water to drink from there anymore,' he said.

'Ja, we have been defeated.'

He stopped to look again. 'I hear you. You say your father is still alive?'

'Yes, he is still going on.'

'He is still going on, eh?' he laughed. 'Yes, your father is a good man. We used to drink our brandy together. We used to talk for a long time with him, and then go away to sleep. He is a good man.' He stopped to take a look at another yard. His face, folded as it was, curious as it was, still glimmered with something which seemed to get out from the eyes and spread throughout the face. He murmured something to himself and starting walking again.

'Ja, I hear you. I had gone to visit the old lady,' he said. 'I took her flowers. You know, she used to love roses. We have beautiful roses in the garden, I took her some.' The sun was blazing, almost as if to roast our scalps. Sweat ran down the old man's face — the tired, weary, old face; the strong, defiant, fearstricken face, glittering now and then with a bright smile and soon becoming a sad shadow, eyes cold like marble.

'So they are still holding your brother?'

'Yes,' I said.

'It will be some time before we hear anything. How is your mother taking it?'

'Well . . .'

'Ja, I know, I know, when I came back, the old lady was weary. She was tired. It was only the heart which kept her, her body had long given in, she was tired. Two weeks after I came back, when they brought my banning order, she died.' He was breathing heavily, he stopped to wipe his face and to take a breath. 'Man, those men are fighting, yes, they are fighting,' he said, and, suddenly he looked very, very old. I thought any time I was going to see tears flowing down his face. His eyes grazed the earth, where there were tins, broken bottles, bricks, dirty water running freely on the street; from where dust rose up to the sky, taking along with it bits and pieces of paper. Something was smelling. I knew what it was, a dead dog or cat lying somewhere in the donga. The children as usual, were playing, swearing, running across the street, chasing balls or each other — and like the children of other places like Alexandra, they were on the look-out, while running, for speeding cars.

When I looked back, I saw the steep hill which we had climbed at that slow pace, stopping to ponder, at times almost beginning to cry, laughing, walking on, thinking about the past, the future. He unbuttoned his shirt, right to the stomach: a snow-white vest showed. I wondered who washed for him. Yes, maybe his daughter Thula. I had not see her for a long, long time then.

Maybe the last time I saw her was when I was still at school. She had a friend, Noni. She and Thula, then young, innocent, if ever there is such a thing in a place like Alexandra, were close friends. It was difficult to see one without the other. I got used to them both when I went to see Noni. It was with some longing that I thought of Noni and the things we used to do.

'Ja, those were really bad days, but then we were good men too,' the old man said. 'I stayed in jail for thirteen months, all alone in my cell. But then, it is a goat only which screams when it is in trouble.' He stopped again to look at another yard. He murmured something to himself, and then looking at me he said, 'Son, your brother is in great trouble, he must be a man to be able to meet the demands of that place. They will break him, many were broken there, young men, their heads were broken forever. Children should not play there.'

'What happens there?' I became curious.

'No, leave that alone, leave it alone, I will tell you all that some day.' He sneezed. 'I am going to have a cold,' he said. 'Ja, your brother is in trouble, he must be a man. Tell your father I will come and see him, tell him if my legs allow me, I will come and see him soon, tell him that.'

'I will.'

'You know Thula?'

'Yes, she was my classmate.'

'Yes, yes, she is a mother now,' he said and looked at me. 'But I cannot understand you boys, you love the meat with hair, but you don't realise that that thing makes people, who eat, who cry, who get sick. When it comes you run away!' He had a mischievous smile on his face, then laughed. 'How old are you?'

'I am thirty.'

He took a careful look at me.

'You even have a little beard,' he said and laughed. 'No, you are grown-up now, Molope has men now, he has worked, he had grown-up men.' He raised his stick to greet someone.

'Hey, where are you?'

'We are here!'

'The sun, hey, the sun.' He pointed to the heavens with his stick and began to walk again. 'You know,' he said, 'I can't understand that man, he is in love with the church,' he laughed. 'Your father loves the church too, but your father is a man. That one has been made a woman by the church.' I let out a groan; I meant it to be laughter. He looked at me.

'Boy, don't laugh at your elders,' he said, trying to look serious, suppressing laughter. He stopped. 'Oh, they are building a bridge there?' He sighed. 'Why did I not see it when I was going to the place of rest, I must have been dreaming, or is it old age?'

I said nothing.

'They are building bridges, hostels, beerhalls in our place, without even asking us.' He was talking to himself. 'To be defeated is a very painful thing,' he said. His face was bright, he was like a farmer looking at his crops. 'But, you know, when you defeat someone and while he is lying on the ground, you continue to beat him, it just shows you are not a man. Men don't fight like that. That is fear. And I don't blame them, they must fear, they don't know us, you see. Where they come from, when they fight, they burn everything up. You must have read about Hitler. He wiped villages and villages out, that is the way they fight,' he said, wiping his forehead. 'Hitler put people in an oven, hundreds and hundreds of people and cooked them us, you would have thought he was going to eat them, but no, he threw them away. How can a man fight like that?' He laughed lightly, 'That is why I don't respect their god. We talked a lot about it with your father, he knows me on that one.' He began to walk again in silence. He seemed to be deep in thought. I could hear his struggling footsteps, dragging slowly, but also something about them said a lot about strength, or the will to go on and on, no matter how hard things were.

Someone's voice was flying in the sky, singing about potatoes, how they were fresh, how mothers needed them because their children needed them, how the meat needed his fresh potatoes to make a tasty stew. Now and then dogs barked at him. Now and then you could hear children singing his song, about potatoes, oranges, carrots, beetroots, about Sunday when you should have good food because it is the only day you are with your family, so why not cook them something good. Good food makes children happy, makes them lick their fingers.

We approached the horse-drawn cart. The old man stopped. He was looking at the huge, healthy-looking horses, with bright, happy eyes. Then he began to touch the vegetables on the cart.

'Hey, Machipisa, I see you, man!'

'Our old man, Zola, where are you?'

'I am here, looking at you, where are you?'

'I am here, my old man. The sun and work. That is all.'

'That is right, a man must work. Otherwise your family dies. I like your vegetables, they look fresh.'

'You know, you must know old man, I try hard,' Machipisa said.

'I think I must buy some,' the old man Zola said, looking at me.

'Yes,' I said. He bought cabbage, carrots, potatoes, onions and oranges.

'Chew this,' he said, and gave me a huge orange. 'It must be sweet, oranges are good for your health.' I took it and thanked him. We started walking again. At the corner of Fifteenth and John Brandt, the old man stopped, looked at me and said I should give my father his greetings, he had to turn there. I shook his hand, again thanked him for the orange and asked him to give my greetings to Thula and her daughter. I saw the old man Zola walk away, slowly, carrying the bag of vegetables and his jacket. He began to lean on his stick. His gait was weary indeed, perhaps defeated. Slowly he went away, and I went away thinking, I must see him some day.

I walked up John Brandt Street. I got home. My baby was not home yet. I put on John Coltrane. I lit the primus stove and put the kettle on. I made up the bed.

My brother came to see me. His eyes told me where he had been. He sat down on the chair and said he wanted coffee.

'Is that Coltrane?'

'Ja,' I said. He began to sing along with Coltrane, tapping his shoe and clapping hands. His head was bowed, as the branch of a tree, loaded with fruit. He began to murmur something to himself. Then he continued to sing with the record again.

'Ja, all this means that I am a coward,' he said at last. I said nothing. I knew now what was on his mind. The storm. His eyes were bloodshot, his hair unkempt, and something in his face said he was angry. A twist on the forehead, or was it a combination of the eyes, the twist, and the words that kept leaping out of his lips.

'When last were you home?'

'Must be a week now,' I said.

'I am from there now,' he said, 'Mama says they came and asked about Fix.'

'What?'

'All sorts of things,' he said. He was silent, sipping his coffee, unsteady on his chair, murmuring.

'When did they come?'

'On Wednesday and on Friday.'

'Did they say where Fix is?'

'No, no one is allowed to see him or know where he is.'

'You know, I was talking about Fix with old man Zola today, when I came back from the graveyard.'

'I have not been to the graveyard for a long time now,' he said. 'What did the old man say?'

'No, he asked me if we had heard where Fix is.'

'Maybe they killed him, my brother, they killed him, otherwise why are they so secretive about him? Why? They killed him. You see, I knew what Fix was doing. I knew, and I told him he was foolish to think he could get away with it, but then, he knows better. What better things does he know? Now, look where he is . . . look what is happening to my mother!' He spread his arms.

'Bra Ndo . . .'

'Bra Ndo, Bra Ndo, you are next, why don't you bastards listen?' He looked at me with his red eyes, and the twist on his forehead which he must have got from my father. 'Bra Ndo, shit Bra Ndo, and quit your shit, don't say Bra Ndo, say Ndo. What matters? Nothing!' I could hear voices of women and men and children singing a hymn, they were clapping hands to the accompaniment of a drum which beat on and on, in a thick, slow monotonous sound.

'Play Dollar Brand,' Ndo said. 'If Fix knew as much as he wanted to make us believe, why could he not know that is where he would end? The security police have a wide, efficient information network, did he know this?'

'What's the point of talking like that?'

'Shut up!'

'No, I want to know, what is the point? You forget about him or we try to help him. Your talking like that won't help,' I said. I said to hell with everything now, I knew this was coming, so let it be. He stared at me.

'You are my younger brother,' he said, still staring at me.

'So what?'

'So shut up.'

'I am not going to sit here and listen to you talking that type of nonsense. Fix is my brother too!'

He stared at me, looking hurt.

'Is he not my brother?'

'I did not say that . . . watch out, you are spilling your coffee,' I said.

'Fuck it!' He threw the cup on the floor and it went shattering across the room. He stood up and left the room.

I could hear him talking to someone outside. I could not hear the words. But I knew that he was still talking about Fix, about me, he was still angry. I thought of his wife. Wherever she was now, she was expecting it, she was expecting him to come home, angry, full of shit. Somehow, she had learnt to live with it, or maybe she was still trying to find alternatives. That frightens me, for I have often wondered what she will do the day she gets tired, the day she decides she has had enough. Many a time, so many times, she has come to my door, finished, having travelled deep into despair, tears in her eyes, her face stricken with a desperate pain, a pain so desperate, even the tears refused to swallow it. She would be there at the door, her baby held closely in her arms. It clung to its mother as if afraid to fall, its eyes shot out, as if they were about to burst. Its mother, Ausi-Pule, what is it, strength? Despair? Love? What is it? Ausi-Pule would sit there on the chair, her boy on her lap suckling, and she, in terrible calmness, would relate what had happened. Sometimes tears began to flow, sometimes she would stare straight at me as if to say, now you know what your brother is about, what do you say?

Ah, what could I say? I loved Ausi-Pule, I loved my brother. All I wished was that they live together like they thought they could. But, even as this ran through my mind, I knew it was unreal. I knew that her life was a terrible, brutal pain. She must have felt, many a time, trapped by this thing called marriage. She must have, many a time, regretted ever meeting Ndo; must have, many a time, wished herself into the day when she would be single again. But what was it that made her endure, that made her think that there was, after all, still hope? I knew by now, that every time she heard that word, it was like she was skinless, her nerves scraped. Her eyes, which could shoot defiance, anger, love and hatred straight into your heart with one stare, said it; they said how weary she was, how bewildered, and how she was at the verge of anything, be it to kill, or to make love until it hurt, or to pour methylated spirits over her body, set herself alight and laugh at you. It could be done.

It could be done, so her eyes said, and Alexandra, in ever so many ways, never hesitates to show one how it could be done. Her face, which all the time registered her experience and sometimes seemed indifferent, had frowns that

18

ran deep into her flesh. And right there, on whatever it is we have come to call a face, you could feel her listening carefully, watching, always ready for self-protection.

Ausi-Pule had a beautiful body. When she was happy, she carried it as though she were doing a teasing dance – on legs which bulged forwards, her shoulders firm, and her face, while clinging to its bewilderment, let go a smile, through the eyes, and her bright white teeth flashed. She walked . . . and her firm shoulders were like a teasing dance. She walked upright, flashing her smile, her eyes bright and running, sometimes mischievously, also at times so innocent, you felt like being very protective. That was the time when I knew she enjoyed cooking for us, looking after the children, wanting us to rest, dominating everything, as she moved from the stove to the table, to the other rooms, talking to the children and to us, mocking and teasing about what had happened. Then it was amazing how she would be mother to all of us, the children, us, the house, be a sister to me, and to her husband be a wife. All the time, he would be saying, 'Mama, you don't mind me playing Dollar Brand?' and Ausi-Pule, 'No, I love him too, I could go on and on with him.' Dollar would stalk the house, bombard it, rise high and high, go low and low, in that journey which Dollar takes, sometimes as an ant moving, moving, on and on, climbing on thin grass as if it were a huge fallen tree trunk, moving back and forwards as if seeking something which he himself does not know, moving on and on, at times like a tiger, agile, beautiful, ferocious, stalking, knowing, planning and ready for the final attack. Yes, Dollar would dominate the silence and my brother now and then, in his quiet way, would talk to his wife, to his child, to me, saying how futile it was to be himself, to be a man, to love, saying sometimes everything is so beautiful it frightens. Sometimes I would read poetry to them. I would feel them as we moved together, Ausi-Pule holding her son by the hand, trying to keep him quiet as he demanded attention. She would kiss him, lift him up, hold him to her bosom, and suddenly we would all be aware again of Dollar, pacing, paving all sorts of things, and when the record ended, it would be like the house was sighing.

This has happened on many occasions. Sometimes it made us sleep well, through many treacherous nights. Sometimes it caused us trouble, for we tossed and turned in the bed, and in the morning, when we met again, the trouble would still be written on our faces. Sometimes it was just too hard to listen to Dollar. There would be no nerve, no courage to even suggest that we start to listen. Everything would be like a load, pressing down. Every word that our lips formed would be like a force pushing everything away from us.

It was when I heard Ndo talk outside that I wondered about Ausi-Pule. He was gone now. It was painful to try and picture what was happening wherever he was now. The coffee and the shattering of china, still held me hostage. Fix. I wondered where he was as all this was happening. I wondered. I began to clean the floor, and the smell of coffee came to my nostrils, and the shattering sound ran through my ears. I wondered where Fix was. Where Ndo was, where my mother, my father, were. I decided I was not going to tell Lily anything about what had happened. She needed rest.

Strange. But it is true. I have been in this house, room, for four years now, and I have done many many things in here. I have broken cups with coffee myself. I have fought, wept, got furiously angry, right in this room, so many many times. I have lived in this room, my house, but suddenly, as I moved in it, cleaning the floor, washing the dishes, cleaning the stove, I began to find out that I was a stranger in it. It had taken me a long time to know where to put things, like cups and dishes, it took me a long time to make up the bed.

When I finished cleaning the house — what was it — I felt exhausted. Suddenly, Nina Simone's voice became a hammer, pounding and pounding on my head, shoulders, pounding and pounding me to pulp. I dared not listen to it, I dared not lie down to rest. The walls of the room began to stalk me, to crowd me. I knew that I must try to get some rest, but there was no way I could come round to doing it.

I was in the street. The Sunday afternoon street. Alexandra makes its peculiar Sunday mornings, afternoons and nights. The sun, the smell of food, music; the women, in their brand new Sunday skirts — something about the way they walk, they smile. They are loud when they talk or laugh — the women, lovers, mothers, sisters of some people, hug the sun, the light, in their gestures; and walk, with their bibles, and their children, some dragging their men with them; and make a Sunday afternoon. There is a Sunday noise in Alexandra. It purrs and buzzes in the air, in the sun, in the wind, in the eyes of men, in the bodies of women, it purrs and purrs and purrs.

A funeral procession went by. Lovers, hand in hand, walked the streets, like the children of this place. Men sat under trees, drinking, talking and laughing. Music. Drums. A trumpet in the distance. A song, sung by a group of men and women of the church. Selborne Street, the Alexandra bus, taxi street, was deserted, except for lone lovers, hand in hand, walking to the stadium.

I saw the light gleaming through the curtains. The sun had long set. There were many people now in the yard. They were still drinking and laughing. I entered the yard. The light from my window, our window, told me that Lily had come back from work.

'How was your day?' she asked, leaning against the table, looking me in the eye.

'Okay,' I said. 'Yours?'

'Okay, I was tired though, when I came.' She looked at me.

'I waited for you to come, but after some time, I could not take being in the house.'

'Where did you go?'

'Spent some time with Mama, then I went to see John, and he and I went for a drive. When he went to Pretoria I came home.'

'How's mama?'

'She's okay,' I said. 'I think the old lady is a bit weary now.' Silence fell. Lily was washing her pots, dishes, cups, spoons and all that. I went to the record player. 'Members don't get weary . . .' Max Roach was saying.

'Have they heard anything about Fix?'

'Ja.' I thought of Mama. 'Ja, they have only heard that the security police wanted to know how many brothers Fix had.'

She looked at me. What could I say. 'Members don't get weary . . .' Roach kept saying. Otherwise, there was absolute silence. A comfortable silence, for I knew Lily and I, at that point, were tossed about, in search of what that question from the security police meant. 'Members don't get weary . . .' the singer kept saying.

In our silence, Lily and I became closer. No, it was not silence at all. It was a knowing. Lily knew Fix through me. I came to know Fix more through Lily. He used to talk to me about her. I know he used to talk to her about me. We used to talk, all of us, laugh, fear, cry, love together. How many brothers or sisters does Fix have. My mother had asked: 'What has that to do with you?' They had said, 'We want to know and we have to know.' And they wrote the number down. My mother had said to me, 'What have you all been doing?' She said it, or asked that question as if she had never known me, had never seen me before, would never ever guess what I could do. She had carried her arms folded on her bosom, looked at me, as if watching me carefully, every step, so she could protect her life, protect herself from me. She did not want to hurt. She asked me, 'What have you all been doing?' That was a hard question. I tried to think what we had been doing. What had I been doing, at least. I did not know. She had stared at me, with her eyes and her face. In silence, she had stared at me. At last I said, 'Mama, truly I do not know what I have been doing.' We had tea. Did not talk. I had to go, because the weight of the silence was too heavy for me. She had barely managed to say bye, when I shut the door behind me.

Lily gave me food. We ate in silence. The food was good. I did not know I was so hungry. After food, we had tea. We went to bed in silence. I remember how I clung to her.

Three

Alexandra is one of the oldest townships in South Africa. It is closely related to Johannesburg. From the centre of the Golden City to the centre of the Dark City is a mere nine miles. Where one starts the other ends, and where one ends, the other begins. The difference between the two is like day and night. Everything that says anything about the progress of man, the distance which man has made in terms of technology, efficiency and comfort: the Golden City says it well; the Dark City, by contrast, is dirty and deathly. The Golden City belongs to the white people of South Africa, and the Dark City to the black people. The Saturdays and Sundays of Alexandra roar, groan and rumble, like a troubled stomach. The same days in Johannesburg are as silent as the stomach of a dead person. The weekdays of Alexandra are those of a place which has been erased; in Johannesburg, week days are like a time when thousands of people arrive in a place at the end of their pilgrimage – nothing is still, the streets buzz.

I don't know which village it was: I know though, that it was somewhere in Natal — I was born there. 'I was born there': that is, the biological act of my birth took place there. That is all. I grew up in Alexandra. I am a curious and dangerous combination, if we are to take Verwoerd's dream of South Africa seriously. We have not taken it seriously, but that does not mean we do not have to deal with it, in blood, in tears — and even at the expense of our lives. My mother was born in Natal, my father in Lesotho. Verwoerd's dream of South Africa defines this as immoral. A moSotho should not marry an umZulu. My mother and father did get married. My elder brothers, Fix and Ndo, were born in Lesotho, I in Natal, and Mary in Alexandra. This is a terrible stew in terms of the influx laws of South Africa, but then that is another story entirely. Alexandra is just that — a terrible stew. The stew bubbles, usually on Saturdays and Sundays. Everyone is in Alexandra. The grace of the dances, the variety of both the dances and the traditional garb, the many, many languages of the people of South Africa, all these, are packed and piled into the pot, Alexandra, and they bubble and bubble and bubble. And then there is the fact that this is not Natal, nor Lesotho, nor a village.

Alexandra is a creation of schizophrenics like Jan Smuts; it is a makeshift place of abode, a township — that is, black people live here. Live here only if the whims of the Verwoerds are still stable to that end.

Memory can be an unreliable mirror. It shifts and shifts, now and then emphasizing the dramatic, now and then leaving out detail, now and then flushing out detail at surprising moments. My memory of Alexandra, as I knew when I was very young, is sharp and blunt and blunt and sharp. In those days there were brand new houses, in all sorts of shapes, popping out of the ground like mushrooms; but then, also, there were the frightening houses, of mud, of corrugated zinc; there were pipes in which other people chose to live, or broken cars where some of my friends lived and which they called home.

There were people: some went to church in suits, some in dresses, whether men or women; some went to the houses where the guitar wailed and wailed, the drum boomed and boomed; some people owned mules, cattle and donkeys, some Cadillacs; some had nothing but the pipe and the broken car and children.

Alexandra was pitch dark at night in those days. And there were the Spoilers who made sleeping a terrible inconvenience. I do not know how the Spoilers broke down doors, but they did, and then they took everything: wardrobes and the clothes in them, tables, money, even lives. They were feared. There were the Msomis, equally brutal, more efficient and better organised. The Spoilers and the Msomis brought the movies out of the movie houses into the streets of Alexandra, for real, guns, blood and all.

There were the police. They came on horseback, in fast cars, in huge trucks, and shot for real; they came in Saracens and with machine guns and banged on doors, shouting 'Afrika, Afrika'. Alexandra met them in song, rallies and demonstrations. There were the beer raids. The pass raids. One day the Verwoerd schools were closed and the 'Afrika' schools opened. The police came, we ran away and came back to school the next day. One day the police shot a girl in the leg and she lost it. It was during the days of the stay-home strikes. There was Chief Albert Luthuli – rallies, demonstrations, potato boycott – 'Afrika! Afrika! Afrika!' and 'Mayibuye iAfrika!'

My wife, Lily, comes from Evaton, but her father and mother come from Northern Transvaal, they are ba-Venda. Lily says Mphephu is mad. When she comes back from Northern Transvaal, she brings pawpaws, mangoes and bananas. I must go there one day. Anka also comes from there, a proud and stubborn man whose friendship Lily and I share. He named our theatre – Takalane Black Theatre. Onalenna, whose father is a Motswana and her mother a Mochankane, said that Takalane means 'be happy' in her mother's language. Takalane Black Theatre floats like a canoe in the middle of a stormy ocean. I came to it when it was no longer possible to be a journalist. But that is another story. In Takalane, we rehearse every Monday, Wednesday and Friday.

Today is a Monday. It was a Monday night. There was, what was it? There was smoke coming out of the hundreds and hundreds of chimneys of Alexandra. There were the crowds of people, flowing out of the buses. There were the hasty footsteps. The faintly-lit streets. The many, many voices, sailing in the semi-darkness of the streets. It felt like Mondays always do, as if it were the beginning of the world. There was energy. I heard it in the voice of a mother who was calling her child to come home. I saw it in the silhouettes which now leaped and leaped in the dark, homeward bound – silhouettes of men and women, young girls and boys, who have rendered Johannesburg a stomach of a dead person. And now Alexandra, rumbling, groaning, roaring like a troubled stomach. It is late, it is night, time ticks and ticks and ticks – tomorrow, Tuesday, is a working day – so says Monday night. What was it? It was a winter night, chasing everyone home, with its cold whistle. Anka and I were walking back from the rehearsals. The rehearsals were intense.

I felt as if I was going to choke, any minute. My mind could not focus on one thing, it wandered about, like a moth, like a fly, briefly stopping on one point and taking off at another. It was as if all the houses, squatting like that in those different yards, were closing in on me, were right next to my nose, eyes, lips, face. The smell of the dirty water in the streets – the water, full of shit and all imaginable rubbish – felt as though it had become my saliva; the noise of the children, mothers calling, salesmen singing about their products, the music from radios and grams, crowded my head and seemed to become the pulse which I could feel heaving on the side of my head. My stomach felt hard, like a stone, it felt as if a pin was trapped somewhere in it. I wished I could get sick in the street. Maybe I would feel better. Or take a shit at least. I would maybe feel relieved. But nothing happened or was about to happen. Anka and I walked in silence. He was slightly shorter than me. He walked with his hands in his pockets. I knew, as we were walking, that he knew what I was thinking about. He and I had talked about Fix and where he was.

'Where's Nomsisi?' he asked at last.

'I guess at her place.'

'When last did you see her?'

'Maybe when? Last Friday.' We walked on. I saw the police van drive up, past us. The police were clinging to the sides of the van, as if they were flies buzzing around a rotten piece of meat. They were yelling as if they were children. Simultaneously, Anka and I looked at the van, turned our heads following it as it passed us.

'How is she?'

'I think fine.'

'I mean, how has she taken the brother's departure?'

'I don't know.'

'Have you asked her?'

'No.'

'Why not?'

'You know I am not able to talk to her.'

'But why don't you try?'

'Fuck it.'

'Why do you say that?'

God, I thought, won't he leave me alone? Why does he not ask me if she tried to ask how I felt about my brother? Fuck Nomsisi.

'Mmm? Why do you say that?' I looked at him. He was looking at me, straight in the eye. He began to slow down.

'Mm?'

'Anka, she and I don't go well.'

'But this is not about you two now, it is about Fix.'

'Look, I can't talk to Nomsisi. That is all.'

'Lily?'

'I have not talked to her about it.'

I thought about the first time Anka and I met. It was in Swaziland. We were at a work camp, building a school those days. Hard, uncertain, reckless, aimless. We drove into Mbabane in the morning. Anka was already there, kneeling, hammer in hand and a brick in the other. He had stopped knocking and was now watching us getting out of the car. I went to him, shook hands, then took the rounds with other people. In those days, the way boys from Johannesburg dressed and perhaps carried themselves, made them stick out. In a sense, I think, my having gone to greet him first was a kind of silent talk, a conspiracy, a wish to be clued about what was going on. There has always been a tendency about Johannesburg boys, to try and create a Johannesburg wherever they are, a thing which has, many times, alienated us from our people. I know that for some time after we had greeted one another, on arrival, we circled around each other. Greeting and going on.

The next time we met was in Johannesburg. And then, we just took off, in all sorts of directions, into all sorts of madness. We have been places together since then.

'Don't you think we should go to see her now?'

I really did not want to do that. I would hardly be able to say a word to her. In fact, I did not know where I wanted to go. I was not about to sit with Lily and Anka in the same room. Each one of them demanding something, each pulling this way and that like dogs playing with a blanket. They would tear me apart, I knew.

'God, I don't,' I said.

'What do you mean?'

'I know you are saying I should take up my responsibility, but . . . oh, God.'

'What?'

'I am fucking tired.' There was a brief silence.

'I think we should go there.' I stopped. We were at Fourth Avenue and Selborne. If we were going to Nomsisi, we had to walk one avenue down. If we were going home, we had to walk three avenues down then turn right.

One avenue down, we turned left. I wondered why I had not been able to say no. Just no. And then things like crossroads would not matter. Why? Anka was walking fast. I was almost following him. Why don't I say no. We antered the yard. We passed women and men and children sitting outside on benches. We greeted and went on. Anka knocked on the door.

'There is no one there,' an old lady yelled from somewhere in the dark yard. I sighed. I felt bad though, why could I not say no?

The traffic was thick on Selborne Street. The air was filled with cars and buses roaring up and down, taxis hooting madly for passengers. We walked in silence. I hoped Anka would not refuse. I realised now that I needed him, but somehow it seemed that he would say no.

'Why don't we pass by Aunt Miriam,' I said at last.

'Haai, haai, no, forget that.' I looked at him. I felt like slapping him across the face.

'I am going there,' I said.

'Haai, let's go home man,' he said.

'I am going there,' I said. I knew I was going there. Even Jesus Christ was not going to stop me now. After we turned at Seventh Avenue, I said I would find him at home, I told him to tell Lily that I stopped at Aunt Miriam's.

'How long are you going to stay there?'

'I do not know, how can I tell?'

'Er . . .' He looked at me. 'Okay, I will go to John. We may come and see you later.'

'Fine,' I said and went into the yard, into the house. There were two people seated on the sofa, a man and a woman. I greeted. I went into the kitchen.

'Aunt Miriam . . .'

'Tsi-boy, how have you been? Your friends were here, about an hour ago looking for you.'

'Which?'

'That silly one, what's his name?'

'Moipone,' a voice came from another room. It was Aunt Miriam's daughter, Kgoli.

'Kgoli,' I yelled back, 'show yourself here, stop shouting at uncle from the bedroom.'

'Uncle, uncle, you know you are lying ...' Aunt Miriam said. 'One day someone is going to shit right here on the floor.'

'Aunt Miriam, what kind of language is that?'

'Ja, people are full of shit. This one. What's his name, Boy-boy, yesterday he pretended to be drunk and walked straight into our bedroom, and fell next to Kgoli's bed, what kind of drunkenness is that? I am going to open someone's head with an axe one of these days!' she said, shining red eyes at me.

'Give me two beers,' I said and sat down in the kitchen.

'Castle or Lion?'

'Lion.'

'You know, people are full of shit, I tell you.'

'Ja,' I said. Kgoli came in from the other room. 'How's my personal niece?'

'Sweet,' she said.

'Ja, you do look sweet.' She giggled. 'Aunt Miriam, I want a second wife.'

'Second wife? You pay, that's all. All other things are your troubles.'

'Who wants to be a second wife?' Kgoli broke in.

'You don't want to be my wife?'

'You are married, so?'

'Would you otherwise be my wife?'

'No, you are the educated type, I don't like those, they end up on Robben Island.'

'Hee, Tsi-boy, where's your brother?' Aunt Miriam cut in.

'Still in jail,' I said, and hoped she would leave it there.

'Haai, you give the old lady unnecessary troubles,' Aunt Miriam said.

'Haa, Abuti-Fix is still in jail?' Kgoli asked.

'Ja,' I said.

'And if you don't watch, you are following.'

After all, there is nowhere to run to. Someone on the radio was singing 'My boy, Lollipop!' A few people had come in now and sat in the other room. Kgoli went to take the orders.

'So when is he going to court?'

'I don't know.'

'Do you think the case is serious?'

'I don't know.'

'What did he do?'

'I don't know.'

'How can't you know? You are his brother, and you are also a journalist.'

'I have no way of knowing, no one can ask, see, or talk to anybody about him. That is the law he is arrested under.' I thought about the talk between me and Onalenna during rehearsals. I wondered where Anka was. Fix, shit, what was happening to him. All the stories I read, all the tragic stories about political detainees falling from stairs, jumping out of the windows, committing suicide under strange circumstances, were unleashed, they flashed past me. I wondered where Fix was. Nomsisi, where was she?

'When did Moipone say he would come back?'

'I don't know,' Aunt Miriam said. 'Ask Kgoli.'

'He did not say,' Kgoli said, walking back to the room with bottles of beer in her hands.

'Can I crack if they come back while I am here, Aunt Miriam?'

'No, no play, it's Monday today, why do you want to crack?'

'Because it's Monday and I don't have money. Spent it all over the weekend.'

'No Tsi, no cracking. I am stocking tomorrow, and I need all the money I can get,' she said sounding final.

'Aunt Miriam . . .'

'No Tsi, no. No cracking. You guys are funny. Today you crack, tomorrow you are arrested, who loses? Me!'

'We always come back though.'

'No Tsi, no cracking.'

I could hear many voices coming from the other room, laughter, and people talking at the peaks of their voices. The music from the radio was drowned. Kgoli was going in and out of the kitchen with beer bottles and glasses. Aunt Miriam was cooking.

I went to take a pee. It was dark now. The stars were there, shining in their ancient distance. The moon was there, half, like the one they say the cow jumped over. It was a cool night. I do not know what happened, but it was while I was there, standing against the wall, that I made my decision. I must have been thinking about her. It took me wanting to take a pee, standing there, going through the joy of relieving myself against the wall. I must go to see Nomsisi. Anka is right. I must go to see her. I think the glasses of beer that I had been taking, were taking me away now, on their wings. I felt light, unaware of my footsteps, as I walked back to the house from where I could now hear Miles Davis's trumpet climbing, high, climbing high, high, cutting through distances, flying high, flying high, ah, what is it we do not know? To make ships and planes? We have built all that. To put rocks on rocks until they stretch to the sky? We have built that. What is it that we do not know? Despair? Fear? Crying? Laughing? Maybe we know too much of everything. Maybe. And maybe that is why, that is why we have never lived? So what? Miles Davis. Kinds of blue? The drums kept watch, a careful watch. Bass, there, behind, lonely, there as if all the time waiting to take action. Coltrane coming in with his battle, perpetual battle that must have at last killed him, at times going through walls, through barbed wire, sightless, uncaring, carrying his mission out, to seek to search, at times as if a dam had burst, and the angry water was rushing through everything, leaving nothing behind. So what?

I closed the door behind me. There was Aunt Miriam, cooking. Food smells came to my nostrils. I realised I had not eaten for a long time now. My one bottle was half-full. I poured myself some beer.

'Aunt Miriam. Give me another bottle.'

'Money first, sweetheart,' she said, extending her hand. I put a rand on it.

'That is my last,' I said.

'Well, you have no sense, you want to drink your last rand, so there, have your beer,' she said and gave me fifty cents change. The beer was taking me now. I must go see Nomsisi. Whatever it is.

I remember changing into a shadow, in the dark of the night. I remember the full blast of lights from a car coming and passing me. I knocked on the door. It opened. I went in. The room had a very soft, fresh smell about it. There were books on the table. Books on the shelves. That is what I saw when I came in. The bed. The wardrobe. The comfortable looking chair against the wall, opposite the door, against the window, with orange and yellow coloured curtains. A breeze blew, the curtains danced. I sat down.

'Tsi, how are you?'

'Fine, sister, fine,' I said, taking the comfortable chair. She was smiling. A smile, a familiar, friendly, searching smile. She closed the books on the table.

'Nomsisi, if you are busy, I can come another time.'

'I would say come another time if it were not you, but since you seldom come here, please relax. Shall I make you coffee, or would you like to continue from where you left off with your bottles?'

'Please, coffee.' I realised I needed my sobriety badly now. She put the kettle on the primus stove.

'How's Lily?'

'Fine. I have not been home since this morning though.'

'You been digging the streets?'

'Put it that way,' I said.

'Boy! Boy! Hehe?' she said laughing. 'As long as you know where home is, that is fine.'

Somehow, looking at Nomsisi walking around the room, I could see why she and Fix were such friends. We who looked from outside saw them, casual and ideal, something that has the happy-ever-after thread in it. Nomsisi is a short woman. Full. Beautiful legs. A beautiful person, dark, with huge eyes and well-kept hair. Somehow, she knew how to put clothes on her body. Easy. Right. Just right for her. She had strong arms. Neat clean hands. She spoke quickly, sometimes swallowing a lot of words. Gestured a lot. Everything she said was punctuated with 'gosh', 'hoo' and 'you know'. She put the coffee on the little table next to me.

'How's mama?'

'I saw her the other day,' I said, and realised I could not ask her the same questions, because I have never seen her mother.

'Gosh,' she said, 'I should be ashamed, I have not seen her since they took Fix.' She smiled. 'The day I go to see her, I will have to sit through the fire.' She laughed.

'What do you think is going to happen to Fix?' I asked.

'Anything,' she said. 'Gosh, how can you ask me a question like that? That is a foolish question. Do you expect them to fatten him?' Our eyes met.

'No,' I said, 'but what I mean is, or rather I wanted you to fill me in if you can.'

'How can I? You know I know as much as you.' I did not know whether she was angry with me, or whether she was stating facts and that was it. She sat down at the table and began to sip her coffee. Silence. I was feeling uncomfortable now. If the coffee was not so hot, I would swallow it and leave. But I stayed on.

'How's the Theatre going?'

'Fine,' I said.

'Where's Anka?'

'He is around. Actually, we came here earlier on to see you.'

'Oh, so it was you? Aunt May told me two guys were here, looking for me, but after she described you, I thought no, it could not have been the police. But I could not work out who it was.' She stood up and took a dry dish cloth and wiped the table. 'So it was you and Anka.'

'Ja, we had just come from the Theatre.'

'Onalenna, is she still with you?'

'Ja.'

'I liked your poetry programme, how we need to hear that! Who is the other guy in spectacles?'

'Tuki.'

'He is very good indeed, I thought. Onalenna too and the young boy, what is his name?'

'Jack.'

'Gosh, Jack, yes, Jack,' she laughed. 'The way Jack now and then looks at me, it is as if he will soon say, "Baby, I love you. I will buy you a helicopter!"' She burst out laughing. Her laughter was more like a scream, long, hysterical.

'I don't blame him,' I said.

'What do you mean?'

'I am sure many men would like to do that.'

'Shut up!' she said and laughed lightly. 'Jack is still a young boy.'

'So what?'

'So we cannot talk about him and think about men.'

'You can't, but he thinks of himself as a man.'

'He is a man there far away in the street, not here,' she said.

'But that's where you and he met, is it not?'

'You better drink your coffee, it seems that is the only good thing you can do this evening,' she said.

'Drinking coffee?'

'Ja.'

'I know other better things I can do.'

'Hold your mouth now, you will soon be saying big things,' she said, again with that light laugh.

'I can drink beer.'

'Gosh, you know, you and your beer, I wonder how Lily gets along with all this.'

'She does not mind.'

'You hope she does not, that is what you should say.'

'How are you doing at work?'

'Don't ask me that. I am sick and tired of it. If it were not for their car, I would resign this minute. But I need their car to do our work.'

I began to know now, I realised where Nomsisi was. I began to fear. 'Our work,' she had said. All the disjointed pictures came together. Pietermaritzburg. Durban. Cape Town. Pietersburg. All the time on the road. I began to know. I began to fear. I hoped my fears were wrong. Nomsisi now stuck out, vulnerable, as easy picking for the beaks of plummeting hawks. There was nothing I could do. I realised just how vulnerable she was. That is why when she was told someone had been looking for her, she had thought it was the police. There was something shameful in all this. We waited to be fetched. I looked at her, her beautiful face, her gaiety, her eyes. I saw her in a cell. I tried to make her comfortable there. Nothing fitted. I saw her soft, intelligent eyes, shining. Her strong facial features. Her strong bosom. I tried to picture her before the police, under lights, sweating, crying, screaming, lost. Would she beg? Nothing said anything. Nomsisi.

'I must go now,' I said.

'Okay, tell Lily I will come to see her soon,' she said. I felt tired. Weary. I sat there, looking somewhere above the door. Lost. The chair took my weight, all of my weight. I felt relaxed. I must have said again, 'I must go now,' for she said:

'Look, you don't have to go now, relax if you want to.' Something was warm in her voice. I had never thought of myself as Nomsisi's younger brother, but I now know what she thought of me.

'Where is your mother?'

She looked at me directly, surprised. Silent for a while.

'Why?'

'I want to know.'

'Gosh, in Orlando.'

'Your father?'

'He too. Why do you ask?'

'I have never met your parents, that is why.'

'Shame on you,' she said.

'I know.'

'Ja, the boy and girl are in Orlando with their last born.'

'Oh, ja? How old are they then?'

'Not too old.'

'Okay.'

'My mother is in her late fifties, my father about sixty-nine.'

'Brothers and sisters?'

'Brother. Two others died from some kind of illness on the farms. More coffee?'

'No, Nomsisi, I must go now.'

'Okay.'

'Ja.' I stood up.

'Are you going straight home?'

'Er . . . ' I had not thought, I realised, about where I was going. I had not thought about going home yet. Suddenly I wondered where I was going.

'I will see,' I said.

'What you mean, you will see?'

'I am not ready yet to go home.'

'So where are you going to?'

'I wonder.'

'What do you mean?' I really did not know what I meant. I wondered what I meant. I wondered why I was not going home. I knew that Lily was waiting for me. She did not even know where I was. What was wrong?

'I am going home.'

'Don't be funny,' she said, 'you must go home.' I was not being funny. Maybe I was being funny. I went to the door.

'Bye Nomsisi, I will see you.'

'You must go home now, don't do funny things,' I heard her say after I closed the door. God, I was not being funny. I really did not know where I was going. I wanted to go home. Something was not working well. I longed for those days when I longed to be home with Lily. What was wrong?

The night had become silent, darkness fighting the street light's glow. Lone cars roared past. I could hear my footsteps echoing in the ruins, fallen houses, dongas, dirty streets, as my shoes crushed against the soil. I was not really sober. But I was not drunk either.

I fear this feeling. It knocks me down. It puts the lights out of me. I do, I fear this strange feeling. I do not know, God, I do not know how many times it has grabbed me. Suddenly, not knowing where to go. It is strange, strange indeed; I fear this feeling. Lost. Big man I am. Lost. Lost, yet aware I had someone who loves, cares, wishes to be with me. Yet here I was, lost in the streets.

I went up the steps. I could hear the music coming. The voices. The laughter. Hands clapping. I opened the door. Smoke. Fumes. The smell of alcohol. Music. Voices and voices and voices. Laughter.

'Hey, Tsi!'

I knew who it was. Before I could say anything, someone held me tight, hugged me. Moipone.

'My broder, drink some beer,' he said. 'Hey, we look, look, look, look all over for you, we went home, found sis Lily, she say you no come home yet, where you be broder?'

'I was here, then I went to see Nomsisi,' I said, sitting down next to a girl. Then I saw Anka.

'You went to see Nomsisi?' Anka asked.

'Ja, I had to.'

'Good,' Anka said, and hugged me over the head tightly. I realised he must have been drinking a long time now. His voice told me. His walk. Oh, even his eyes.

'Man, what the sister she say?'

'Good,' I said.

'Okay, I hear you,' Anka said.

'Tsi! I thought you had gone home.' It was Aunt Miriam's voice.

'I came back.'

'You lie, you have never been home.'

'Ja, I went to see someone.'

'You, sies!' she said and pretended to spit. Everyone laughed. I felt like telling her to go to hell. But I could not. She was older than me.

'It's not what you think,' I said to her.

'What do I think, what?'

'Aunt Miriam,' I said, 'let me crack four.'

'Four, four? You crazy?'

'Man, don't worry about that, I have money,' Anka said.

'Oh, okay.'

'Not four, I can give you two.'

'Okay, Aunt Miriam, give me two.' I gave in. Moipone was kissing the girl next to me. She looked young. Shy. Obviously not used to going to shebeens. Anka was shaking his head, looking at Moipone. I introduced myself to her.

'Minki,' she said shyly.

'Minki, don't allow Moipone to bring you here,' I said to her.

'Ah, my broder, the child she love love me, what you talk?'

'That's not love,' Anka interrupted. 'Minki, Tsi is right, you should not allow this man to bring you here.'

Minki was smiling. She was smiling, shy, her eyes lighted with curiosity. She was smiling, I thought, as I watched her, like the devil, no, like a snake, no, like what? Minki was no devil. She was, yes, caught up in the ways of the devil. Not the devil of the bible. No, that one died long ago – he owed too much to live. She was smiling, with her eyes, with the wound that Alexandra leaves on young faces. She was smiling with that innocence, that unknowing, that thing, the wound, throbbing and bleeding. She was smiling with that wound of becoming a woman when you are still a girl, the wound of being a mother, sister, and almost a whore, when you are still wondering about things, completely unaware of the danger around you.

She was smiling, her little hand covering her mouth which knew all sorts of kisses. Kisses her mother and father new nothing about. She was smiling with her face, her young, beautiful face smiled amid smoke, fumes of alcohol, everything that we had used to hurt and destroy ourselves. She was smiling with her face, her eyes, her wounds, which she had not even become aware of; she was smiling, sitting there next to Moipone and me, crying and not aware of it. How could we sit and participate in all that?

I heard the man next to Anka laugh. Two other men were whispering to each other next to the bookcase, which was filled with encyclopaedias and huge books the size of bibles that I guessed had never been read before. Two others who sat next to the huge radiogram, which looked like an expensive coffin, were talking to a woman: wig, nail polish, false eye-lashes, painted face and all that shit. I looked at Minki. Her face was young. Her eyes curious. Moipone was fidgeting with her mouth. I was flying on wings, high up in the sky, and fearing to fall. The devil took me there. Lily kept flashing past me, but because I was flying, perhaps too fast for this world, I could not focus on her. I could not even focus on Anka. Minki's face kept dancing. Moipone's face was small. I was flying, flying. Tomorrow I will come back to earth. I will find Alexandra. I saw Anka take a sip from his glass. I could hear whispers. Moipone and Minki. I could hear music. Voices. I saw the many many brown bottles on the table, almost dancing, as if mocking me: you flew, flew, flew, when are you going to fall? Fly, fly, fly, when are you going to fall? I remembered Minki's smile. It was no longer a smile, it was a grin, right next to my eyes, a grin that was like the skeleton of a dove. No feathers, no flesh, just bones and eyes and beak. A grin, falling to become a smile, falling into my eyes.

I must have been asleep. I heard a voice. It seemed to jump around. Someone shook me. I looked. Everyone was on their feet and I saw Anka, Moipone and Minki. Aunt Miriam was talking at the peak of her voice. Someone had been fighting. I stood up. Moipone's shirt was torn. He had been fighting. I don't recall being with Moipone and not seeing him in a fight. Someone dragged me out and I followed. There was a cold breeze. There were stars. Dogs were barking in terrible unison. The silence was fighting for survival in the dark night.

When I opened my eyes, the dog was barking viciously. Then I heard voices. It was like my door was falling off its hinges. I felt my heart leap. Lily held me tight.

'Sleep, sleep,' she whispered in my ear. 'Sleep, sleep.' She held my chest. I heard her heart beating, as if its flesh was right against my shoulder. I heard voices. 'Tsi, Tsi Molope,' the voice said and went on about breaking down the door. I wanted to turn on the bed because my one side was tired. I held back because the bed would make noise. I felt sweat from Lily's arms. My head was pounding, pounding, pounding. I thought of Boykie. 'You can't be drunk and alert at the same time,' he had said. Why, why, why? Even before I completed the question I knew how ridiculous it was. Why can't they leave us alone, in peace? Shit, how could I ask a question like that? Moeskond! I thought of Nomsisi. Suddenly, I felt something wet on my shoulder. I thought God, Lily's heart is bleeding, the red flesh on my shoulder oozing blood. I was about to turn. She held me tight, not to turn. My hand went to my shoulder, my eyes on the hand. It was only sweat from Lily's breast. I remember shaking. Trembling. Anger. Fear. Despair. Combined. And then the door rattled. Shook. A loud bang, like thunder, continuous, hit the door. 'Hey, Tsi Molope, Tsi Molope, I will break this door down!' I thought fuck, fuck it, break it. I am not going to open it.

'Tsi is not here, and his wife is not here, we have not seen them for a long time now, maybe a week,' a voice said. I felt weary and feeble. Someone said something in Afrikaans. Then someone said something in Setswana.

I felt Lily lie back and sigh. And then there was deep silence. I turned to feel her breath brush past my neck. My head, God, my head was pounding and it was as if the pain would soon jump out through the eyes, just pop out and fall on the bed. A splitting headache. I felt Lily's warm hand touch my terrible muscle, which soon shot up as if it were a spring. It suddenly felt packed and about to burst. She held my head and kissed me full on the mouth. Dazed in her grip, lost in her strength, I gave in to her. I was groping with my hands when I felt her withdraw. In no time, she was in the distance. She went out of bed and I heard the sound of the primus stove. I lay there in bed, my muscle aching and throbbing. I could feel the heat at its tip.

'When are you going to pay the permit?' Lily said at last. She shot her eyes at me, looking at me, and at the same time, beyond me.

'Why do you run out of bed like that?'

'You fool!' She came over. For a minute I did not know where she was going. I was still dazed in her imaginary arms, her perfume still lingered somewhere next to me in bed. Suddenly I felt her nails dig into my arm, and then a slap on the face. That woke me up.

'What the fuck?' I said, jumping up.

'The fuck is you, you fool,' she said laughing childishly and victoriously. 'Sometimes you make me feel like I should bash your head,' she said.

Then she began to cry.

'I gave you the money to pay for the permit last week and you drank it, you fool, now here I am, scared because they are going to pick you up.'

'Lily.'

'Tsi, shuuut uuup!' Lily screamed. 'I am tired of your strange stupid life, Tsi, you hear what I am saying? I am tired of your stupid life. You think you are still a small boy. Why have you not paid the permit? Where were you last night? You know what time it was when you came here? Five in the morning! You hear that? I waited for you all night, where were you? Where were you Tsi? Why did you not tell me that you were not coming in? Why? Tsi, answer me!'

Everything became so heavy. Silence. Talk. The primus stove sound. Lily's footsteps as she moved around the house. Everything, all, was so heavy. There was nothing I could say to her now that would reach her. So I lay in bed and gave my life to her. Everything that I was was there with me in bed. My bad breath, probably smelling like shit, from beer last night or that morning; my pounding aching head; my fear, because my heart was still jumping; my recollection of the banging on the door; my helplessness, my despair, my anger; my limp muscle, which lay looped as if it were ashamed to have ever erected; I lay there and gave my life to Lily. I lay in silence, while she lashed with tongue, tears and terrible silence. Every time she wept, I thought something was going to snap, and snap forever. I lay there, while her voice joined in on the rhythmic pounding ache in my head. My eyes were blurred.

I turned on the bed. Lily was fully dressed. She was fidgeting with her handbag – she interrupted my thoughts.

'Are you not going to drink your tea?' she asked.

'I will,' I said. I had hardly closed my mouth when I felt her lips on me and then the door banged. Lily was gone. I lay in bed. The room seemed so empty. Suddenly I felt lost. I felt tears coming to my eyes. My head was pounding. I thought about the knock and the permit. A shit piece of paper, which was supposed to allow me to live in Alexandra. Permit. I had lived all my life in Alexandra. I need this piece of paper to permit me to live on. To live on this arsehole, my only, perhaps last world, or perhaps the only world I could claim to know. I needed a paper to allow me to live here. I had not paid for it for a long time and they had come to fetch me. 'Tsi, Tsi Molope, we will break the door down,' they had said.

I heard Lily thank the Auntie next door for saving us as she left. She sounded polite and thankful. And the Auntie had said, 'We live together, we must help each other.' And she had said in her polite way, 'That's true.' The Auntie had asked where I was. She said I was still asleep. She laughed. It suddenly dawned on me that it seemed as if I spent my life in that bed, lying, listening. But I always felt tired, weary, as if I would faint.

Where will I go from here? My mind could not focus on anything. Fix. I wondered where Boykie was now. It was terrible, so terrible to realise that I could count beyond my fingers, my fingers on both hands, my toes on both feet. I could count names of people and every time punctuate by saying, 'I wonder where they are now!' Am I growing older? Is it just this thing called tradegy? What is it? Fix. Pule. Boykie. I really wondered where they were. Somehow I had no choice but to twine my life with theirs. I would never be able to forget them. They were written with fire, engraved on my mind. Minki. The man who died after he was clubbed with a golf stick. Ndo. Lily. Nomsisi. Ausi-Pule.

Things were beginning to load me down now. I got out of bed. I sipped my cold tea and put on a record. I made up the bed. God, that knock this morning. I should try to raise some money. Pay their permit. I wondered how Lily was going to carry her day. Among all those distorted faces, faces of children who can't talk, some of whom can't walk. Sounds, sounds, so many sounds, unintelligible sounds from disabled children. The eyes of their mothers. Hope in hopelessness. Lily – shit, why did she choose to be a physiotherapist? In her way, I thought, she must already be crazy. I began to wonder how I could make her comfortable. She had said once, 'Have care, that is all I need.' Then I thought I knew what she meant by that, but days told me I did not. Care? Have care? What does that mean? I remember how, many times, we fought, so seriously fought and hurt each other, perhaps forever, because I could not come to saying to her, 'I love you.' I knew she needed me to say that. But I was not going to say so, because she needed me to say so. I said, 'I value you.' And she replied, 'You don't love me.' I said, 'That is not the point.' She asked, 'Then what is the point?' I did not know. I said so many things. I think what was happening was that I was thinking aloud. Oh, how we fought. She once asked, 'Look, are you tired of me? I am young, I can handle my life, there is no point in pretending. Tell me if you are tired, tell me. I want you to have peace, I don't want to make you miserable, are you tired?' I saw her cry.

What's all this shit? Heaven knows. What is going to happen to us? The men. The women. The children. What is going to happen to us? What shit is this? Does it not feel like mud, mud we have to wade through, mud we have to sink into? What are we going to do? Lily shrugged in resignation. No words were left. Everything seemed so futile. Energy. Strength. Care. Shit. Everything had become so futile. There was nothing I envied or liked about my father and mother. They seemed trapped in a painful terrible knowledge. I feared for the children. They still walked as if they were coming out of a vagina onto sheets. How unreal! What is going to happen? That hole up there can't know!

> The sunshine was laughing and laughing
> it held its silence
> it danced, in the street,
> dust, smell
> the deserted streets.

I walked up Seventh Avenue. My stomach was as hard as stone. There was a bad taste in my mouth. My shoulders were heavy. I could feel sleep weighing my eyes down as I walked. I was tired. But what is this shit, what is this thing called Alexandra? Seven streets. Twenty-two avenues. Houses. Tin houses. Brick houses. Torn Streets. Smell. Dongas. Dirty water in street. Dark city. The devil's kitchen. Township. Alex. What is this mess? Our home. Our country. Our world. Alexandra. Permits. Passes. Police. Security police. Permit police. CID. South African police. Pass police. Murder and Robbery squad. Paying water accounts. Toilet accounts. House permit. Resident permit. Tax. Rent. Bus fare. Taxi fare. What is Alexandra? Why do I ask? I have lived all my life here, why do I ask? Staring windows and doors. Some closed, some open. This all over the streets. Broken bottles. Bricks. Shit. Water. Children. Cars. Bicycles. Scooters. Mothers. Fathers. Old people. Donkeys. Horses. Cats. Dogs. Cattle. Sheep. Chickens. Cadillacs. Jaguars. Fifteen-roomed houses. One-roomed houses. What the hell is Alexandra? Nobody lives in Alex during the week, during the day. Old people. Children. Silence.

I found Anka and John having breakfast. They were silent. Eating. The curtains were still drawn and the bed undone. Books, towels, shirts, boots, underpants were lying around the floor. I lay on my back on the bed and wondered how long this was going to go on. This terrible futile life.

'Come and eat,' John said. I shook my head.

'You and Anka were drunk last night,' he continued with mockery in his voice. He looked at me and shook his head. 'This one came knocking at five in the morning. What are you guys doing?' Indeed, what is *he* doing, I thought. Dry-cleaning. Making money – and then? Pay permits. All the shit, and then? Buy a car and eat good food, and then? Futile shit all this. He laughed. He looked at me and laughed. 'My brothers,' he said, 'haai, for what are you really struggling, for what, though?' I would never be able to answer that question, even if it meant my life, I could not answer it. He laughed at my silence. Patted me on the chest. 'Haai, my brothers, why don't you just stay home and rest?'

'Fuck you,' I said.

'Come and eat,' Anka said.

'I can't,' I said.

'I know, but force yourself.'

I thought, God, how long am I going to move all the time, almost aimlessly? Silence.

I wondered where Fix was. That was another way out. Jail. The cooler as it is called. I could not imagine what was happening to him. There was so much silence.

'John, you have ten rands?'

'My brother, where do I get ten rands from?'

'I said, do you have ten rands?'

'No!' He laughed at my anger. 'What do you want to do?'

'I have to pay permit.'

'Did they come for you this morning?'

'Do you have ten rand?'

He began to search himself, seven, eight, nine, that was all he had. He gave it to me.

'Anka, one rand?'

'Ja.' Anka gave it to me. I stood up and went out. I could not, had no energy to explain anything.

'Hey, Tsi, what's up?'

'Will be back.'

'Where are you going?'

'You know.'

'They got you, they got you!' John stood at the door laughing. I wondered if he knew that that laugh of his could cost him his life. I walked away. I crossed Selborne Street, towards Ruth Street. Towards London Street. I saw many pregnant women walking into the clinic. School children. Elderly people. Police. I heard the machines running at the firms across the street. Kew township, that is what it is called, the industrial area, Kew township. Police. Men in overalls. Women in overalls. Familiar faces. Familiar sounds of machines, roaring, screaming, howling. People singing. Screaming. Yet, amid all that too, there was silence. I walked on and already, out of familiarity, I could pick out the people who were going where I was going.

Police. Police automobiles. The smell of the law. Guns. Grim faces. Dogs. This mingled with women, men in overalls, running to and fro, across the streets. Cars speeding by. I went through the gate and I found myself within the tall walls. I joined the queue. God, so many people. Sitting. Standing. Walking round. So many people. Within the walls it was terribly hot. I felt sweat hiss down my back. The noise. The monotonous voice, calling, calling name after name, and people answering. Women. Men. Old. Young. Answering, 'Yes sir, yes sir . . .' White police, with their straight fuck-you type of gait, going in and out of their offices, with (and some without) hats on. The sun visited its wrath on us within those walls. The many blank faces. Pained. Impatient. Old. Young. Faces. Faces all around. Laughter, and 'yes sir', police cars rolling in and out, unloading, women with children on their backs. Men, wiped out, broken. I sat there and waited. I had no more energy, no more strength, no more will; I just sat there and waited. They closed before we could reach the window. Lunch time. I held me tight, sat there, and waited. Once I leave this place, I know I will never come back here. At two they opened and the calling started again. I felt hungry. I was wet with sweat but I waited. I waited for my turn to come. I wonder where Boykie is? He had gone and left us, left Alex, he had not been able to wait. He had gone and I waited.

My turn came, I gave them their ten rand, they warned me not to owe so much, threatened to cancel my permit if I did, they gave me a slip and I left.

I no longer cared to see Anka and John. I walked down John Brandt Street, avoiding all the streets which held the promise of deviation and went home. I needed rest. I needed to wait for Lily to come back from Johannesburg, the big golden city. I needed her to come back and I was going to wait for her.

Home. The Auntie next door told me that someone had come looking for me. He was driving a car, he had said he works with me. Although I did not know what she was talking about, I said 'okay'. I opened the door, windows, drew the curtains, put Coltrane on and waited.

Boykie, I wondered where he is now. Fix. I had not seen my mother and father for a long time now. Ndo. I heard that sometimes when my mother was asked where we were, and if she was angry about something we had done, she would say, 'They have all gone to hell.' 'They have all gone to hell, their mother's head!' she would say. My father seemed never ever to know anything about us. He had long given up. He depended on what my mother said, and that for him was enough. My old man. He seemed easy. He seemed adamant. He seemed to know what he was doing. Sitting there reading the newspaper, and looking at us, above his strange, twisted glasses, in his silence. I began to suspect that my father felt threatened by our presence. He must now and then have wondered how he came to make such huge flesh. As we moved, in and out of the house, I could feel him watching, ready to bark. His silence now and then terrified me. I wondered how one could be so silent. When we came home, all of us, and were crowding our mother, talking and talking, sometimes fighting, he would move, go to his room and be there alone. His years had gone, my mother would say. He built a house for us. He fought, with his hands, mind, eyes, ears, feet, he fought to make a future for us. Which future? My mother never ever answered that question. She always walked away. I wondered what my father would say if once I dared to ask him what future he had built for us. I wonder what he would say. Fix's future? Ndo's future? My future?

We were brought here by two people who thought they loved each other. They brought us here. They met, wherever it is that they met and they said to each other they loved each other, and then they made us. What does all this mean? Memory fades. Glimpses. No fixed picture. Everything is blurred about what I was doing when I was young. If I tried to bring it out, lots of it would be fiction. Lots. Hopes. Disappointments. Everything in glimpses. Yet somehow it seems it is important to know where you come from, what happened; it seems important to link you to the present, so you can order the future, which is supposedly built for you. Fuck Coltrane. He was beating. Beating like the old woman of old, beating corn. Beating grass. Building a future. I want to know about you. Coltrane, beating, beating. Kneeling. Coiling. Curling. Searching, digging, digging and giving in, I want to know about you. Starting from scratch, as if he had had no journey whatsoever in his life; Coltrane, starting from the beginning, as if a newly-born baby, trying, finding, searching a future, searching the past that we all know so little about. Coltrane, beating, searching, slowing down, stalking, digging all the energy, using it, digging, digging, finding out, and beginning from the beginning. Shit. Coltrane, whose son was he? Kneeling and searching repeatedly, with the same energy, pleading, begging, I want to know about you. My father, who are you? Who the hell am I to hurl insults at you? My mother says you fought and fought with everything you had. You fought with your eyes, ears, feet, hands, and she should know how you fought. But I must say everytime I look at you I see a terrible, a brutal defeat. I want to know about you. Who are you? At least do you know? Your face is filled with defeat you refuse to accept. Your eyes, silence. Silence. Your gait, the way you talk, everything is filled with fear, defeat. Sometimes I wonder whether, when you die, when the flesh and soul snap, you will cry. I wonder. I would never be able to forget it, I know, I would never be able to forget it. You ask me if you will have grand-children. What for? Where is the future they will take in their hands? The wind cries and cries. The sky is empty. The sun just looks. Your face, stern, angry, filled with fear and defeat. What will I tell your grandchildren? That you cried when you were dying? In our time there was Coltrane. What will I say? I see Kippie move, with ease, ready to get insane, we look and say nothing. Shall I tell them that? That when Fix was gone we waited, we waited for him to come back? That you waited. That I waited. What will I say when they ask where is Boykie? What happened to Ndo?

Everything. As if that is what we came to witness here on earth: it never grows, but appears, is twisted, and then vanishes. I can see my father, sitting at the table, reading a newspaper. His small, round, brown spectacles clinging round his round fat face, like a frightened child, clinging to its mother, afraid to fall and hit the floor. Now and then he would remove them from his eyes, look at my mother and comment. About Sophiatown. The police had been there, guns, dogs, saracens, trucks, bulldozers, everything that spelled the defeat of all those people, who after they realised that Sophiatown was the only choice they had to build a home, raise children and come to when they were weary, set to build it with all their strength. The bulldozers had come, and wiped their homes off the face of the earth. I was small then. I used to sit next to the stove, on the floor, dreaming, looking at my mother as she was preparing food for us, listening to my father as he talked to her; I had feared, cried, and wondered with them all that was happening.

Many townships have gone down and many people have gone down with them. Sophiatown, Lady Selborne, and many others. All went, and with all of them all sorts of methods were used to destroy them. We even terminated Sharpeville. I remember how, every night, after Sharpeville, we used to sit, my brothers, my father, my mother, all of us reading what had happened in Sharpeville, and looking, wanting to know if we could recognise names from the long list of the dead and the injured. Every night we did that.

Now, I was thinking about my father. He is a short man. Muscular. He has a round face and a protruding forehead. Long ago, he used to walk fast, wake up early in the morning, work late into the night. Now something has happened to his movements. His back bends forward, he walks slowly, almost dragging his left leg. He still reads the newspaper, every morning, and every evening. But now, unlike long ago, he reads it all by himself, in the bedroom surrounded by silence. He asks little about what anyone else thinks about what the newspaper says about the world. He has become strangely quiet. He stared into space a lot. Talks in monosyllables.

Every time I see my father I think about the stories he used to tell us. About what happened to him as a boy. As a young man, when he began to work for white people, and when he realised he had to rely on himself. And about when he met my mother. And then Fix came. Then Ndo, me and my sister. He used to seem to enjoy relating to us his boyhood days. He would laugh and scream when he talked about his friends. Places they used to go and things they used to do. Then suddenly, as if the clouds had gathered and covered the sun, a gloom hung on his face, eyes, and even in the house. He spent a lot of time on his own. I began to wonder what he and my mother talked about when they were alone. I began to wonder whether I was the only seeing this. In a sense, I also began to feel pity for my mother. She talked a lot. Sometimes talked to herself. She too had a heavy step, as if her body was too big for her legs. We came and went.

> If you ask me who do I trust
> I will say it is the Lord
> I long for my Lord, my saviour
> home is where I am going.

Every morning when the breeze hit against the window pane, my mother would be standing there, slowly washing dishes, cups, spoons, and watching the people in the yard as they ran out of their houses to work. She would be singing. She sang a song, slowly, pausing for long moments, as if to feel or touch the words of the song. She sang in a thin voice, and now and then, as if the song was choking her, a thick sound would come from her throat. Somehow all of us, her children, even her husband, never interrupted her. If any of us talked to her, she would just look at us and continue to sing, or breathe to listen to her pause. That was the moment when everything in the house, we the children, our father, seemed to move, to climb, to go beyond, we seemed to be reaching out, in unison, searching for whatever it was that now and then snaps, to make a child a stranger to its mother, a wife a stranger to her husband, a husband a stranger to his wife. We searched. All of us, we searched. The footsteps. The sound of cups as they knocked against each other in the water. The coughing of my father. Something had snapped. Nothing was visible. No words meant anything.

'If you ask me who do I trust,' the song came, the voice taking it, dragging it, pushing and pulling, 'I will say it is the Lord, I long for my Lord, my saviour, home is where I am going.' But then, where is home? What is it that ever suggested to us that there was a home other than the one we had seen, lived in, which also defeated us? We, the children, perhaps a little bewildered by the realisation that we were about to lose, about to have to go it alone, about to have to experience a deep loneliness, a feeling of distrust for life, a realisation that death has, above all, power, triumph over life, we were witness to it all. These old people had, with all their strength, with all their lives, tried to build a future for us, but everything was against it. The eyes of the old people, their voices, their movement, even the way they chose their words to talk to us, or the way they would now and then hold our hands, had an end, an admonishment about it. Nothing seemed to be alive anymore. The peach orchard and vine, the flowers in the garden, the houses and the walls that surrounded the yard, looked old and broken down and seemed to say something about the triumph of death over life. 'If you ask me who do I trust . . .' the old lady sang with a sadness that made her face young, that made her eyes glow. I thirsted for the goodness, the kindness in life, I got snared while I was looking, I was thrown into the pitch dark, the pit of darkness, and I lost my strength . . . Yes, the old people had no more strength, there had not been any battles won, everyone of them was worn out and had decided to take the path that leads to the hole.

Suddenly, I heard the saxophone pitch down, go down, slow, drag as if to pull everything out of my guts, my chest, my head. I must have jumped from the bed, for I was now sitting up, when the voice came from the player – John Coltrane, Jimmy Garrison, McCoy Tyner, Roy Haynes . . . The sunrays on the walls seemed to shake, surprised by the silence the voice created when it took over from the music. There was a strange silence in the house now, as if something was going to snap.

Four

> Where, where does a river begin
> to make, to take its journey
> where does a river begin
> to take its journey to the sea?

I must have tried to clean the house. Maybe also to make fire. To put the pots on the stove and get them ready to make food. But now I was standing near the door. Many people had come and had passed me while I stood there. We had exchanged greetings and talked about the weekend. We had talked about the sun and the clouds and about people and things that concerned us. I stood there, half lost, hardly able to order anything from within me, so I could move and do something. I heard the footsteps approach. Fast. Light. Then they slowed down. Lily faced me while she made a loud noise with her shoes as she removed dust from them. She smiled at me.

'Why are you standing like that, as if you are lost?'

'I have been waiting for you.'

'How are you?' She looked me right in the eyes, examining me, examining my face and eyes. She came closer to me, and kissed me lightly on the mouth. Then she walked past me, into the house and I heard her sigh.

'How was your day?'

'Okay, like every day,' she said, sounding a little tired. She sat on the bed and began to take her shoes off. Then she went to the wardrobe, took out a pink housecoat and began to put it on. She did everything in a rush, as if she was hurrying to catch up with something.

'What did you do today?' She was obviously trying to break the silence that dominated the house.

'I went to pay the permit. I wonder what I did after that?'

'You did?'

'Ja, I got some money from John.'

'John gave you all ten rands?'

'Ja.' I turned to face her. She began to dust the table. And then she went out to draw water from the tap.

I had meant to get some water, but I had forgotten. She came back, put the bucket of water on the cupboard next to the tins of sugar, salt, pepper, etc. She began to peel potatoes and chop onions.

'You did not go to the office today?'

'No.'

'You do not seem to want to go there lately.'

'Well . . . ' I did not know what to say.

'Did you see the newspaper today?'

'No.'

'I have this morning's paper in my bag.' She dried her hands and then went to take out the newspaper. I turned the gram volume down, and put on Hugh Masekela's 'Americanization of the ooga booga'. The piano took off, lightly, softly, then the trumpet joined, then there were many many sounds, all of the clutching and grabbing at each other, producing order, almost obeying the trumpet. The headline in the township section read: 'MORE DETENTIONS: POLICE STATEMENT.' I heard the trumpet, as if taking a solo, in a rapid movement pitched high and low, followed by a guitar, crying, wailing, piercing. About ten people had been detained since Saturday. The police would not give names, but had said they had all been detained under security laws. Some big cop in the security police was not available for comment. However, another cop, also high ranking, had said that all those who had been detained, would soon be brought to court. Then names of those who had been detained three or four months previously were given, among them Fix's. The police are still investigating, the article concluded. I read the other things, about rapes, lists of deaths over the weekend, soccer, tennis, and began to read almost every advert.

'I wonder who are the others?'

'You know,' Lily said, 'I wonder where Nomsisi is!'

'I went to see her the other day.'

'You did?'

'Ja.'

'Sometimes you are such a nice man,' Lily said shining her beautiful eyes at me. She threw a potato peel at me, and laughed when it hit me right on the forehead.

'Why are you becoming so violent?'

'I am not violent,' she said smiling.

'You nearly peeled off my skin this morning,' I said.

'You deserve it, I wish I had taken all the flesh off. But I love you, you are such a mischievous boy at times. I wonder why I ever agreed that you marry me,' she said smiling. 'I should have married my musician boyfriend.'

'He would have played his flute all night, I am sure you would have loved that!'

'Of course, at least he would be home all the time.'

'You made a bad choice, that is your problem. Here you are now, stuck with me, a drunk, on and off work, crazy, night prowler. What are you going to do, Baby?'

'I love you like that. Why are you embarrassed?'

'Do you think crazy people have time to be embarrassed?'

'I saw you shy away.'

'No, I was getting a cue to craziness, that is all.'

'Don't say that, you will soon believe it,' she said, looking serious. I laughed. She stood there next to the cupboard, her back towards me, her legs tight, close together, her hands moving fast, as she peeled the vegetables. Her long legs were beautifully full in stockings. Her pink housecoat was tight around her body, curving, running along her tall frame. Her thick, well-kept hair and her bone ear-rings, which she got as a present from someone who had come back from Ghana. It was not desire, no! It was, it was ... What was it? A joy? Is it the beginning, the journey out of the old order, out of the things that you know, you did, you laughed about, cried about, into a pool of uncertainty, bewilderment, and realisation of things born, ordered for your toil? It was while I watched her move, her movements confident, strong, knowledgeable, weaving patterns of who she is, what she may be, or not be that I knew: because I had seen her smile and cry, had seen her sad and close to tears, I knew her, her voice, her laughter, I knew all the smells, all her deep wishes, and even within a fog, I could almost plot her future. While I sat there and watched her, within the silence that our presence, our togetherness created, I fell into a joy, a thing which expressed itself in excellence, in completeness, and because it felt almost too complete, I did not know what it was.

That brought a type of uncertainty to me. It was like preparing to make a journey. I could not only pack, watch time and get ready to move. I had to try and peep into the distance that time held before me, before us.

'How was Nomsisi?' Something seemed to shatter as I heard her voice.

'She was very sweet. She asked me how you were. She also said I should tell you she will come to see you soon.' It was as I said that, that I realised, I knew, I feared. Where, where does a river begin?

'You know, I do not think I will see Nomsisi again,' she said, her voice sounding strange. I realised that she said that because she knew something I did not know. It was at that instant that I knew that she and Nomsisi were indeed friends, sisters. They knew each other. She sat on the bed, then lay on her back. She sighed.

'Hey!' she said, at last struck, no doubt, inside her bosom by pain. 'Tsi, this is a horrible country!' I looked at her frame, sprawled out like that on the bed, helpless. Vulnerable. Hopeless.

'Why do you say that?'

'I think Nomsisi will be taken one day,' she said and sat up.

'Ja, but why do you say that?' I felt suddenly angry. She was silent for a while then . . .

Something slowed down now, something was hanging in, on, in the room. We together, locked like that, by time, place, blood, and a moment of life, by sweat, and by all that makes us think and wish we could know each other, love each other, care for and respect each other; if we were now, once more, to rise, to move closer to each other, in fear, desperation, uncertainty, moved by a sadness, helplessness, hopelessness, by a wish to know what it is we could do, we were capable of doing: so that, once and for all, we would be with those we love, those we have as our families, to begin a journey. Where, where does a river begin? We were born, and we had come to be witnesses of life, distorted by time and by place. Everything that we could claim immediately left bloodstains on our fingers. Here we go again . . . Fix. Pule. Moipone. Old man Zola. Where does the river begin, on its journey to the sea? Where does the river begin?

I heard the music. I did not see her move from the bed to the bookshelf where the record player was. Neither of us had heard Hugh stop with his trumpet. Nina's voice took off, as if running; like a gentle dangerous storm, took over the piano, which stalked along, slowly like a river. One more Sunday in Savannah. The cymbals stalked along. Bass, slowly certain, held hands with the voice, now the piano followed the voice . . . praise the Lord! I heard the dishes and spoons make their sounds. Lily's footsteps.

'Well, if what you are saying is true, what does it mean?'

'It is sad,' she said.

'What do you think we can do?'

'Tsi, you know there is nothing we can do.'

'I am quitting this reporting business,' I said at last. It seemed as I said that, that something fell off my shoulders.

'What do you mean?'

'I have no confidence as a reporter,' I said.

'Why?'

'Well, maybe I was not made to meet deadlines.'

'I think you have been doing pretty well. You need to have patience, that is all.'

'I hear you Baby, but now I know I can't be a reporter.'

'What are you going to do then?'

'I have to get an ordinary job, like being a van-boy, or something like that.'

'Well, if that is what you want, that is it.'

I had been a crime reporter. A social beat reporter. And, eventually, ended up anywhere, everywhere where I thought things were happening. Nothing was happening. Everything: a tumour! That was when I realised that South Africa was my home. For, in thinking about where to go, everything, all that I imagined, was strange to me. I had been to Lesotho, and throughout the year that I was there I was a stranger, a stranger forever. I did not know if I could take that any more.

Coming back from Lesotho, I felt grateful for what Alexandra's streets had taught me. Having had a chance to look at them from a distance, I had discovered that they had taught me a kind of animal agility, a kind of tiger alertness, cynicism, distrust, and a readiness to defend my life at all costs. Yet my awareness of the rules of the streets made me, to my surprise, an observer rather than a participant. In Lesotho, with its emphasis on communities, gentleness, there was a circular movement: where the beginning is humility and the search is a desire to be humble, in the process of making a life. It taught me the value of human life. Perhaps it was that realisation that showed me something else: that when man allows his heart to rot, we are capable of beginning to feed on the worms that rise, weave, create all sorts of patterns as they emerge from the rot. We can lick, and begin to enjoy their taste. I did – as a reporter.

When Lesotho was emerging as one of the African independent states, all South African citizens were to carry travelling documents issued by the South African government to enable them to travel into Lesotho. Fearing that by applying for the travelling document, I was exposing myself to the South African government as an undesirable – because, by studying in Lesotho, I was also making a statement about South African education – my parents decided to terminate my stay there. I had been away from the Alexandra streets for a year.

I woke up that morning, and even the way the sun was shining told me I was in a new place. At home, in the yard, houses seemed to crush into each other, people seemed to be riding on each other. There was no space, nowhere to move, all the time someone's breath was warm, close to your throat. Unlike Lesotho where people were always aware of each other's children, families, cattle, and would comment about the weather, the fields – people in Alexandra seemed not to see each other. They looked somewhere above, somewhere in the distance.

Layers and layers of walls were always between people, breaking the reach, erasing the touch. In Lesotho, I had been very close to the soil. I knew its smell, when it emerges with the rain water. I had tasted the smell every day on my tongue, from the food we ate. My life there was merged with the sun, the clouds, the sky, the rain, the soil, the plants. I had been humbled by the unison that existed between what my life depended on, the elements, and the realisation that indeed I had no choice about my life. When the time came to move, like a bursting light bulb all my hopes would explode and the darkness would take me away.

There was the church. There were the priests. Every day of the year and a half I was there, I had to go to mass. We prayed. We prayed for the rain, for the American and Cuban crisis. We prayed for our souls to be saved. And while I was there my memory haunted me. Glimpses, flashes of my streets days, flirted with me many times while I knelt to pray, while we made the pious voices in song, hoping to be redeemed and to be saved. I had seen too many boys and girls vomit their lives in the streets, and I wondered how I had survived. The priest said pray, pray that you may be saved, the lord loves you. I prayed. I sang. I fasted. Then, the same lord who loved me, who wanted to save me, threw me back into the Alexandra streets. He could not give me a travelling document.

It was in those days, my first few days back in Alexandra, that I met again with Boykie, who had been my classmate before I went to Lesotho, before the street claimed me. When we met, Boykie had a camera slung over his shoulder. What was it? Hope or daring? What was it that illuminated his eyes, which issued a spark from within their deep, deep holes, and sent it searching, catching everyone's eyes? It caught mine. Boykie and I began, he as a photographer and I to write.

> So, time, like a mad river, can take us away
> can erase our flesh?

The headlights of the car pierced the darkness and the empty space before us. Behind us, the darkness was a wall, a wall moving at high speed with the car, clinging to the rear window of the car, coating the sides, almost to our noses. It was a night without stars or moon, nothing seemed to breathe or was capable of breathing in the thick night, the thick darkness. Around us, I knew, were vast, empty patches, running for miles and miles into the horizon. There was a silence which seemed to scream in the thick night. The car, steady, but obviously moving very fast, swallowed up the formidable white lines which seemed to run steadily away from us yet disappeared beneath us, together with the black tar ahead which seemed to dare us to eat it all up. Boykie was whistling a song. His head rested on the side window, his eyes were fixed on the road and his hands relaxed on the steering wheel.

'That fucking Chief Lerato is full of shit,' Boykie said.

'Ja,' I said.

'I can't understand why someone would allow himself to be used like that. Okay, maybe allow himself to be used, but not at the expense of a whole people! No! But why can't he see that?' He banged his hands on the steering wheel. 'Why?'

'I think that is what happens when people begin to think only of themselves.'

'That's right. Beyond that, if they are ignorant and they don't want to believe that they are, and then suddenly they find themselves with ghost power in their hands, you can only expect chaos from a situation like that.'

'I still give Verwoerd a pat on the shoulder for his lovely package that he gave the Bantus, I do.'

'Well . . .' There was silence in the car. It was like rain hitting the earth outside, but it was the sound of the fast moving wheels as they rolled on the tar. For a moment I could not see what was ahead; the headlights of an on-coming car drowned our sight. I felt our car slow down. Then as if a huge storm was trying to take our car away into the sky, I felt it shake as the huge truck flew past us.

'Hey, your mother's leg!' Boykie said. 'Fuck it, what does that man think, that he moves alone on the road?'

'Shit, for a while I saw nothing ahead of us.'

'Ja, that is why I prefer to be the driver at night, you have bad sight.'

'I know.'

'You better get some specs boy,' Boykie said laughing.

'God, I can't imagine myself in those things, I have contempt for people who wear them.'

'Why?'

'You know, in the streets we used to regard boys in those things as siesies.'

'Crazy, really crazy.'

'Ja, I know, but that is my prejudice.'

'Baby, soon as you find out something is a prejudice, fuck it out of your system, f-u-c-k i-t o-u-t!' Boykie said, almost screaming.

'Well, you got to know how to fuck it out, it is not as easy as saying it.'

'Don't sound as if you are proud of that!'

'Hey, Boykie, you are misdirecting your anger, you should have aimed it at that chief, not me.'

'Hey, hehe?' he said and laughed.

'That man told you shit, he owns the Republic of Lebowa, that is all, no shit.'

'Shit, don't point that camera at me, don't point that camera at me!' Boykie imitated the chief's voice badly.

'And, you know, those bodyguards would have loved to plunge their spears into you, you know. You made me fucking sick arguing with them.'

'That is what your life is worth, I suppose, a photo of a Bantustan chief, shit!'

'Baby, that is taking things out of context. That fucking chief can go to hell, I would never even look at him, that is the limit, that is the fucking limit.'

Boykie concentrated on taking the curve. 'A monkey like that doing that to old people?'

'That is not the issue Baby, you cannot save those old women, no, you can't. They could even kill you to please that old chief, if you intervened. The issue is that you know how far all this shit about Bantustan has gone; we who profess to know whatever we think we are, what are we doing about it?'

'Right now, all I can do is take photos, that was what I did.'

'Are you going to be taking photos of people crawling or children dying in Dimbaza, Stinkwater, Limehill, all your life?'

'I said that is what I can do for now. If I see any other alternative, and I feel I can use it effectively, I will, without hesitation, use it. That is what I am saying.'

'Okay, I get you, but then, you still have a responsibility for your life, if you are looking in the future. So in a sense that photo is not worth your life.'

'Baby, don't talk shit, I said that is what I can do for now . . .'

'I hear that, I know that, but can't you get what I am saying?'

'Fuck what you are saying, that is what I can do for now. You either understand what I am saying or you don't and if you do, you don't go on the way you are.'

'Fuck that, what I am saying is that there are many other photos like that one, many, too many of them, and you can't die for one.'

'Okay, I hear you, but still I had to get that photo.'

'So long as you hear what I am saying, that is okay by me.'

'What did he say when you were talking to him in the office?'

'Sir, black students say you are irrelevant, you are a sell-out by accepting the Bantustan policy. Can you comment on that?' 'Ja, ja, you see they are small boys. Big thing is that they are disrespectful, we used to listen to our elders.' 'Yes sir, but do you want to say something about what they said?' 'No, no comment.'

'Shit, that is what he said?'

'Ja. He said he thought that the students were causing lots of confusion and that they were potential communists, and they should be put in jail.'

'His fucking balls must be put in jail.'

'No, but the thing to realise here is that that man will soon be wielding power over the students. Soon he will order Pretoria to put all their arses into jail.'

'I know that,' Boykie said sadly. 'Besides, I am against all the fucking press statements BSO is issuing all the time. Don't you see this is a repeat performance? All the black political parties did that in the past, and now, what have they achieved? The Bantustans? Why do we keep making the same mistakes, why?'

'But how do you as an organization communicate what you are doing, how do you communicate it to the people?

'We have to find other ways than the press. You see for now the Black Students' Organization is not even dealing with the people. No, the issue is still to get it straight to the settlers, to define what they have done, to draw the lines, and then make a move.'

'I do not understand that.'

'Baby, don't underestimate the damage the settlers have done to us. Don't! The reason why those people, the old ladies, are crawling is not that they are afraid of him, they are aware of the power behind him. You should not forget that those old ladies have a clear memory of what was done to them, when they were beaten into submission. You know yourself how now and then you have to consciously fight and fight and fight to keep your simple right to walk a Pretoria street, or any other street for that matter, you know that. You know that it is only in our memory that this is our land. We imagine that we have a home, we know that in reality, if there was a quick way that these settlers could wipe us out, they would, and if they did not need our labour they would. All these things live with us every minute of every day. The simple question that Lerato boy can ask you is, "What is the alternative to the Bantustan?" What are you going to say? Whatever you say, he has the past to back him that we will never succeed. The jails tell that story, death lists, even the graveyards can tell that story very well. What I am saying is that no matter what comes, or rather, who comes and professes to be with the people in fighting for our rights, they have to convince this whole nation that they have the power to do so. How do you do that? A few well-organized people have to challenge the power of the settlers, while the people watch, and if you convince the people that you know what you are doing, they in turn will lead the revolution. I am with the BSO right now, but I realise that that is only a stage, just a stage in our battle to reclaim a home for ourselves ... I do not know, but that is how I feel, that is the way I see it.' Boykie sighed. He had been talking very slowly, his eyes fixed on the darkness ahead of us, leaning back in his seat, one arm gesturing, the other holding the steering wheel. He gave me a packet of cigarettes to light one for him.

'You are no longer a heavy smoker,' I said.

'Ja, I have to quit smoking. That is a form of discipline.' Just after he'd said that, we saw flickering red lights. For a moment we glued our eyes ahead of us in silence. Then I could see that there were several cars, their roof-lights flickering into the darkness as if to set the dark sky above in flames. Boykie slowed the car down as we neared them.

'Baby, here is our fight, get yourself together, be alert,' he said. Now our car was almost crawling to a standstill. Two policemen were in the middle of the road. I felt my throat go dry. My chest was pounding. I recalled what Boykie had said: 'We have been beaten into submission.' The policemen waved us to a stop. Boykie swerved off the road, next to one of the cars whose red lights were still flying in the sky. One of the cops peeped through the window on my side. I opened the window. Another was walking towards Boykie's side. Boykie took his camera and flash and got out of the car. He walked past the policeman who was heading for him. My door went open, and I felt the policeman pull me by the shoulder. I could hear Boykie talking at the top of his voice, fast. I could not understand what he was saying, but I knew he was speaking in Afrikaans.

'Come out,' the cop said to me. He began to search me.

'What's all this?' I said.

'You will soon know what's all this, where's your pass?' I saw a flash illuminate the dark sky where Boykie and the other cop were. Voices were talking, loud and angry. First I heard Boykie's, then the other cop's. Suddenly the cop next to me grabbed me by the collar and pushed me against the car, with my back to him. It was just then that I saw someone, a black man or woman, lying on the ground. Suddenly Boykie was shouting. 'Just leave my camera alone, leave it alone, this is my property, not public property, and you should remember that you are nothing but a public servant, stop pushing me around!' I turned and faced the cop next to me. That is when something hit me. I tried to hold on, not to fall. Something crashed again, right into my face. I heard myself hitting the earth, and felt a dull heavy pain in my stomach.

When I opened my eyes, I felt light pierce into them, straight, as if to dig the back of my head. I heard voices. Shouting. I realised I was lying on the floor. It was cold. My back was like ice. The chill might have been pain. I heard Boykie shouting, 'What is the charge? What is the charge? You behave like you own this country, you are going to learn a lesson.' Someone laughed. And then I heard someone say in Sepedi, 'You are going to get killed boy, you are going to get killed, who do you think you are?' I struggled to my feet.

'Yes, how were your dreams?' The policeman came next to me, looking me straight in the eye. I saw that Boykie's left eye was swollen, his lips were huge as if they were sausages, his face was filled with blood. His camera, open, was lying on the counter, and the flash was broken. I realised we were in a police station.

'You take your fucking camera and vanish from here, and don't forget that other monkey!' the huge white policeman said, pointing at the camera and then at me. Boykie walked towards me, held my shoulders, and looked at me right in the eyes.

'Are you okay?' he asked. I nodded.

'You?'

'You can see. But I am fine,' he said and took his camera and broken flash. We walked out into the dark towards the car. The darkness was thick and right close to the eyes I could not see where I was walking. I kept seeing imaginary pits. It was so silent in that thick darkness. It was as if everything had come to a standstill.

'Be careful, someone is coming behind us,' Boykie said. Then I heard slow footsteps. I looked back: all I could see was a shadow. 'We may be shot, so watch, be alert,' Boykie said, walking fast. I followed him, still dizzy. I could fall down anytime and my head was aching. It was when I held it that I felt that my hair was muddy, wet, I touched my face. It was painfully, obviously swollen. I felt tears try to rush out. I wiped my eyes. We reached the car. Boykie opened for me. Then I saw the lights of another car flash straight on to us. Our car purred, Boykie engaged gear, the car moved slowly, and we were on the tar, with the other car right behind us.

'Ho, our people,' Boykie said, his voice appealing, sad, almost as if he was about to weep. I could not see his face clearly. But I could see that he was looking at the rear-view mirror.

'I wonder what those dogs are about to do,' I said.

'Don't worry about them, think about how you are going to defend yourself,' Boykie said sharply. 'You can't expect anything from them. They are up to shit as you know.' It was while I sat there, next to Boykie in that car, that I felt a deep need to survive, yet everything, the darkness, the vastness of the empty earth, empty sky, even the lights that kept a steady distance behind us, suggested nothing about life, or survival.

'What's the speed limit here?' Boykie said suddenly.

'Keep it at fifty,' I said.

'They are overtaking.' Before I could look back, the police car flew past us. For a moment, the darkness outside was broken by the police car's headlights, then all we could see ahead of us, moving rapidly, were the two red dots on the tail of the car.

'At times, the way black people take things easy, it would seem they are not aware of the danger they are facing,' I said.

'Ja, but that's because we are a defeated people,' Boykie said curtly. I realised now that all I needed was quietness. There was nothing we could say that could re-orient our minds. We had been beaten, defeated. I accepted that. Even so, there was still something in the air, in the dark, stalking, we could not say what the next minute held for us. We hoped, if anything, that the darkness would erase our presence, thus carry us to safety. Boykie increased speed. The car jumped forward, and pierced the darkness. Sound that was like that of rain kept our speed, travelling with us, in that moment of oblivion.

'They killed a man, those bastards!' Boykie said softly.

'Ja, what was going on there?'

'They must have beat the shit out of him. That is why I think we are not safe. Something is in the air.'

'God, everything happened so fast!' I had been trying to recall what had happened but all I could remember was the sound, the crash against my face, and the thud I made as I hit the ground.

'Those two cops really did you in,' Boykie said.

'Which two cops?'

'Right at the scene where they killed that man.'

'Were there two cops?'

'Ja, you were beaten by two cops.'

'Everything happened so fast! What happened to you?'

'You know, that was real funny. We had just been talking about dying for a photo, and there! It can happen any time.'

'Did you take the picture?'

'Ja, but they tore the film out of the camera.'

'I heard you scream about your property.' As I tried to laugh, I felt my lips hurt. 'And about public servants.'

'Ja, shit, that is what broke everything, they were not going to stand there and listen to me tell them who they are. I saw them come after that, my camera was out of my hand, and the flash off my shoulder in no time, and all I managed was an attempt to punch, that was all. Must have been four of them on me. They wrung the shit out of me. God, how I longed for my knife! We would not be here talking though, if I had had it with me. They would have shot us!' The silence took over again. No doubt, both Boykie and I were thinking about what would have happened if we had knives. I felt my whole back go cold, as if cold water was running down to the end of my spine. Flashes of all sorts of cruel pictures reeled past my mind, of us lying there, on the red soil, in the darkness, bleeding and bleeding, emptying our lives into the soil. The soil seeping and seeping until we were cold. What would have happened? The darkness, the moonless sky, the starless sky, the vastness of the empty patches running for miles and miles to the horizon, all were prepared to conspire against us, had presented themselves as conveniences, cloaking and encouraging the killers. I thought about how Africa once conspired and gave birth to a slave trade. And the sea too aided the insane adventurers. Everything, that time, had been against us. Those ships sailed for miles and miles and miles across the seas, to far and strange lands. Canned inside their guts was a terrible pain, a brutal pain, the worst results the human heart can produce.

When I looked ahead of us, I saw that there were police waving us to stop.

'Oh my God!' Boykie said in Setswana. The horror clung to me, erased my speech. We were lost in the night and the drama of our time was this time set again. It was not just another story to be written and submitted at some deadline. It was us who were the issue of the drama, of the vicious hatred white people have managed to have against black people. The car slowed down. It came to a standstill. I locked my door. Boykie locked his and opened the window slightly. Two policemen walked towards our car. How different a man is when he is exposed to power! I had seen their walk in the movies before.

'Where is your driver's licence?' the policeman asked. I realised he was a traffic cop, not a regular cop. Boykie, after searching himself, gave it to him. He lit a torch and looked at it.

'This is not you on the photo,' the cop said, looking and shining a torch on Boykie's face. Boykie stared at him. 'Yes,' he said, 'there is something smelling badly for me here. What's wrong with your face?'

'We were assaulted,' Boykie said calmly.

'Who assaulted you?'

'We were assaulted by cops.'

'Why did you lock your door? Open it!' he said, pulling at the door.

'Why?' Boykie asked.

'Don't ask me questions, open the door!'

'I am not opening the door. I told you that we have just been assaulted by cops, how do we know you don't intend doing that?'

'I will charge you for interfering with the ends of justice,' the cop said.

'Well, I am not interfering with the ends of justice, I am defending myself,' Boykie said.

'We will break the door if you do not open, what are you hiding in the car?'

'I have nothing to hide in the car. I told you we have been assaulted,' Boykie said loudly.

'Who are you talking to like that?'

'Hey, drive straight to the police station,' the other traffic man said, banging on the window. 'And remember, if you try anything we will not hesitate to shoot,' he concluded, and they walked back to their car. Boykie swung the car back to the road and they followed us.

'What the hell do we do when things are like this?' Boykie said. He said that with a controlled voice. It was a voice saturated with memories, a voice brimful of and spilling with despair, it was a voice determined to live, determined to die if need be, if indeed the cycle would be broken, once and for all. Again, the lights of the car behind us glowed on our heads, casting shadows before us, pushing the darkness ahead of us, only slowly as in a controlled death, a death meant to teach the victim all that is intrinsic in pain, in suspense, in uncertainty.

'We must have asked that question many, many times in past centuries,' Boykie said, answering himself with a sigh.

'What question?'

'What do we do when things are like this?'

Well, we drove straight back to the police station although that was the last place we wanted to go to. We did. We were hardly out of the car when we were taken by our scruffs, pulled and pushed, almost not walking the earth any more. Once more . . .

'Where is your pass?' A mixture of deodorant smells and paper, tobacco, old furniture, turned into a single smell, which characterises all the places whose functions are proclaimed by notices, where warnings burden walls, counters and filing cabinets, where the sweat, tears, vomit and blood of many many people, who came and went, who never made it out of the doors, leave their spirits hanging in the air, which can never ever be cleaned. All these seemed to sing, seemed to whisper, seemed to warn us about where we were, and said something about our fate. The fluorescent lights seemed dim, and in rhythm with the voices they seemed determined to penetrate, destroy, and hung over our head so delicately, it was our lives hanging on them. There was going to be a display of power. All the eyes, the movements, the faces, the silence in the room, even the way those lights issued their light, everything was about power. Now I was standing astride, my head bent over the counter, my neck held firmly by a hand which felt as huge as the treacherous heavens. I was struggling to breathe, to see, to say something about my discomfort, and I could hear a loud voice, which I knew so well, tearing the silence, tearing the faint fluorescent lights, tearing through the huge anger that dangled over us. It hid its power and pierced straight into the heart, painfully, slowly and deliberately. I felt hands touch my legs and rise up to my thighs, almost between my buttocks. I tried to lift my head, but my forehead was banged against the wooden counter, so hard it was like the bone in it was melting, giving in to the anger that now filled the room. The huge hand, with vicious, flexibility and an unnerving agility, got hold of my balls. I felt the grip tighten, hold, squeeze and pull. I could still hear the shouting, or was it a scream, I could hear feet shuffling, struggling, and bodies banging against the furniture in the police station. Lights went out of me. Thin stars took over. I tried to stand up, to lift my head once more, and again, with a terrible force, it crashed against the counter.

I felt my face become wet, my knees shake, tremble, and now it was my body, trembling, trembling like the sky shaken by thunder. Then, at first, it felt like a relief, right inside the penis, piercing and I knew I had to hold, hold with all my might. I held on. It was like everything, all the muscles in my body, the shoulders, the stomach, the muscles which close the eyes, even the way my mouth was tight, all seemed to be a power, urging, urging me to release and now I knew that I was holding with all my strength, I was holding the scream from escaping my lips. I felt my wet hands tighten on the wooden counter, they held so tight they began to hurt. My feet, trembling, wet, seemed to want to assure me that they were still on the ground. Everything now was hurting, was like a huge terror, unleashed, wanting my penis to let go. The scream, stuck somewhere inside my mouth, seemed to have mighty strength all of which fell on the lips, pushing, pushing, wanting them to let go. It was the penis and the mouth. Then the arsehole too joined, the muscles around it seeming to dance, mocking me, daring me, wanting to know if I had any control over them, and the air, that terrible-smelling air, kept escaping in tiny bits. I thought of my grandmother, there was no way that I could call her name, and not lose, fall, lie down in shame, there was no way. I thought of how she would hold my hand, call my name and tell me that I should know that on this earth, I have a journey to make, and the journey has to be made with and among other people, and that I was the only one who would know which people I could make the journey with. And what that means, she would say, is that if on my journey, I met people who could not sing, or who did not take with them their guitars, their drums, and their songs, who, when they tried to sing, their voices became hoarse, mine too would be hoarse, we would never make the journey. I thought of her saying to me, 'Child, you must know, in the darkness of your past, where you come from, and in the faint future where you are going, that you were issued by loins which bathed in the fire that made the lightning, that dared the clouds to join and curl into the blood of man, that you were like the plants, so merged with the soil, and water, and wind, and the sun and the moon, that your past is so scattered, nothing could hold it, that you have a future to build.' She would say, 'You choose how you do it, we are going, we are on our way. We tried to show you everything, we loved you, took your hand and walked with you. One day you will have to remember that you are alone, among other people, and that you have a journey to make.'

A voice snatched my grandmother's face and voice away from me, from the darkness that the pain had put me into. I felt the hand around my neck, wet, shaking in anger, dig its nails into the flesh. I felt as though the bag of my balls was going to be torn off. I felt the air in my arse escaping, I heard its sound, desperate, I tried to hold, I saw the light, and it was then that everything happened: first, something warm ran down my shoes, then my legs had this cold feeling running down them, into my shoes. And then my trousers too were cold, my penis felt as if it was shrinking into oblivion, as the huge hand let go. Tears came into my eyes, and ran down my cheeks, pouring as if forever. The air from the arsehole seemed to sing in laughter, then I felt as if the whole sky had fallen on the back of my neck, something snapped.

'You fucking farting . . .' the voice said, and broke into a terrible laughter. That was when I began to weep, and scream, and I fell down, tired, wet all over my body, ashamed. I wept on the floor, feeling shadows hovering over me, footsteps, coming and going away. I lay on the cold floor, tears running away from me, feeling my urine all over me, the smell of my arsehole. I remember saying 'Grandmother, grandmother,' calling and calling and getting no reply.

'I am through with this job,' Boykie said. Up to now we had been locked into a terrible silence. We had not seen or talked to each other for the past seven days. I had not see Boykie when I rose from the floor. I realised where I was and knew that the only thing I had was my journey, and that, if I did not believe that I came from a huge past of lightning, of the soil, of the sun, of the moon, that I was once loved, that I was once held by the hand. For seven days I lay in the cell, alone, eating, drinking and dreaming. I lay in my cell preferring to be there and nowhere else.

Now we were driving again, along the same road that a night had not allowed us to travel on and finish. We were now driving along this road, bathed in the bright sun, the warm sun of our country. The vastness, the emptiness, the horizons, the blue, blue sky, everything seemed to want to know, 'What have you learnt? What have you learnt, children?'

'I am through with this job,' Boykie had said, breaking a long peaceful silence.

'I am through with this job,' I said. It was then that I felt like weeping again. There was silence now in the car. The hills in the distance, the grass, the trees, the vast open space seemed to keep calling, calling, calling, 'Child, what have you learnt?' When I tried to know what I had learnt I knew I could never say what I had learnt. Did I believe that those hills, that grass, the sun, the sunshine, the horizon, were witness to my past, my future? A loud silence took over.

I realised that I had never really sat down to think about my grandmother. I had refused to accept her death. I had been there. I had buried her. I had hardly wept or thought or stopped to wonder about the way she had gone. I had been very cynical about her death. She had died, I had to help to bury her. That was all. I had helped to carry her shining coffin. I had held her daughter's hand, my mother, when she was staggering, weeping and trying to throw soil into the holes. I held her hand then, and took her through the many people who stood there, singing, staring, and I put her on the ground, on the grass, and left her there. I took the spade, and shovelled the soil into the hole. I heard the soil crash on the coffin with amazing loudness, and then the loudness became thick thuds, as soil hit against soil, the soil rising, above the hole, erasing everything about my grandmother. Then I put many, many wreaths on the heap of soil, putting stones on them, so the wind would not take them away. I remember lifting my head up from the grave, and wondering why everybody was still hanging around, singing and staring; why didn't they go? Then I saw my mother, sitting there, heaving like a sick, tired cow. I went to her and held her hand, I tried to lift her up, she shook her head, weeping and weeping like a child. I remember letting her hand go with a carelessness born of terrible anger. She had pulled me to her, close to her mouth and whispered, 'Let the priest say the benediction first.' I looked at her, thinking what the hell, what power does the priest have to give back my dead grandmother in a benediction? I moved away from her and stood next to Ndo, who then was singing a hymn with his thick voice. Fix was there, next to my sister, whose tears seemed not to stop. He held her arm, she had her head on his shoulder. I saw them walk, after benediction, I saw them, Fix and my sister, walk hand in hand, slowly, towards the many, many cars which stood in the open field, shining their colours to the sky. The Ndo came to walk next to me, saying something about, 'God, granny is gone.' How I wanted to tell him to fuck off and shut up! My father held my mother by the hand, she seemed not to be able to walk. I felt like saying, what the hell, walk straight! Then there were sounds of cars, purring the shitty-smelling fumes in the air.

We moved, and we were back in the streets, Alexandra, fucked up, filled with its Sunday afternoon people, who seemed to be walking aimlessly, looking at the passing cars as if we were caged monkeys. The crowds at home. The washing of hands at the gate and the people talking and laughing. When the night fell I remember taking off the clean white shirt, borrowed suit and tie. It was like I had to tear them off my body as quickly as I could. Then Moipone and I walked away from the crowds that still seemed to linger on, away into the street to the shebeen, and I began to drink. I fought with someone that night. I remember his blood, spurting, raining little drizzles on my face. I remember Moipone's laughter, and the anger of the boy, the man, or whatever, whom I hit and beat mercilessly, and who was coming at me like an ox, and I was calculating his moves and hitting him hard. Every time I hit I knew he was hurting badly. He dropped down on the floor, I kicked and kicked, and Moipone began to pull away.

I must have slept. When the car came to a standstill, I woke up trembling. Boykie yawned, stretched, and opened his door.

'Let's get something to drink,' he said. He went out to the cafe. I saw all the white faces. I feared them. I felt myself tremble. I looked at Boykie walk, with fast footsteps, bent motion, sure and aggressive movement, disappearing through the door, among white faces. After some time, he came back holding two paper cups and a parcel with 'Cakes' written on the outside. He came to my side and said: 'Baby, it's your turn now, take the wheel.'

He smiled his gentle yet cynical smile. I thought about his, 'I am through with this job now.' Shit. I moved over to the wheel, pleased that I was going to drive, for when I drive I never talk. He knew that. The white man's machine was agreeable. It purred, and moved gently back to the tar. It was as if we were sailing on top of the sunshine. He was whistling a song which I recognised but could not place. Now and then he whistled and hummed it. I looked at him, peaceful, with a face that never betrayed his age. His darting eyes and slightly twisted lips, which seemed to warn you about his cynicism. I have always pitied anyone who, meeting him, opened up and became vulnerable, for he seemed to delight in tearing, hitting, lashing with his tongue. I had seen so many people get into a fight with him, desperately try to hold themselves together, lose and get lashed mercilessly as they pitted themselves against his sharp painful tongue, and then become victims forever. From then on, he would trample on them mercilessly, as if to say: if they did not know what he knew, all they were worth was his wrath.

He always did that with me. Every time I became absent-minded, he would lash and lash. If I was not like him, always alert, I was going to be thrown away, forever. He would say to Fix, 'I have always wondered how this one survives the fights he seems to get into so easily, everywhere he goes. He will get killed one day. Maybe he deserves just that. He can't afford to be alive if he is going to walk around asleep and fighting.' He and Fix, almost every time they met, fought so viciously with their tongues: he saying Fix was sharp and clumsy, Fix saying, 'I was taught to love and to respect and be polite. I cannot disregard that because whites are doing what they are doing. I have to find a way of using their gift.'

'Gift? Gift? Boykie would say, 'Shit like that you call gift?'

'You are calling your past shit,' Fix would say.

'My past has left me in shit, that is why!' Boykie would say. When I told him that Fix had been picked up, he said coolly: 'That will teach him a lesson.' After that, every time I wanted to talk to him about that, he would say: 'Many black people are in jail. Fix is just one of them,' and then go on to talk about something else.

He was now sipping his Coca-Cola, eating his cake, completely relaxed on the seat of the car, whistling now and then, and humming his song. Yes, it was a Nina Simone song, 'Assignment'. I placed it at last!

As I sat behind the wheel, occasionally using my muscles, I could feel some of them hurting. I could feel the smell of the cell on me, of the dirty blankets, of the shit that was in the bucket. I saw how my trousers were creased, dirty, and smelling of sweat, shit, urine, the lot. I felt like laughing aloud, but I held on. I listened to Boykie humming his song. The car was still in very good condition. I overtook many cars, and left them far behind us. We were piercing the light, the car eating the shadows and the tar, and there we were, weaving along the road. We joined the freeway now. The car seemed to breathe in, to take strength, and it leaped forward, with a gentle roar, smooth, challenging the road ahead of it. The scenery changed now. There were buildings along the road, below the road. Now and then we passed men, working and watering the beautiful gardens along the road. We went for miles and miles, coated in the sweet scent of flowers, shimmering their colours to the bright, bright sunshine, the flowers and the sunshine dancing in song and rhythm to the sky, in reds, blues, greens, yellows, making a pleasantly-woven mat lining the road. And the evergreen trees rushed past backwards, as buildings danced up and down above and below them.

At last we hit Pretoria. Many black faces and white faces, like ants, knowing nothing about laziness, or hate, or joy, but engaged in building forever. Cars, many cars, turning, hooting, screeching, traffic lights changing their colours.

We went past Central Prison. The car took in breath, sighed, and climbed on to the freeway. They named the freeway after one of their fathers, Ben Schoeman Highway. Many cars, weaving in and out of each other, sped on and on along the road, within the bright sunshine, heading for wherever they were heading. Boykie was now snoring. He lay, sprawled on the car seat, relaxed, eyes closed, peaceful. I felt very gentle and caring about him. I wondered if I had done my best, given the bad situation we had found ourselves in. I wondered what was in Boykie's head as he lay there, harmless, like that. What next? I felt determined to head on, go on with the reporting job. It hurt. That was okay. It had no future. What had any future? Something told me, I did not have to worry about Boykie. He was okay. He was going to be okay. He had to be okay. He was snoring now, with his mouth open, and saliva going down his chin.

What had they done to him that night? I recalled hearing him shouting, talking at the top of his voice, but I could not remember what he had said. How could I have heard him? I remembered how I stood at the counter, how I tried to stop the hand from reaching my balls, how, when it got hold of them, pulled and squeezed, I knew what was going on, and I knew there was nothing I could do to help or protect myself. Strange, as all this went through my mind, I felt a smile, a sweet smile, take over my lips. I was going to relate this to Lily in detail. I laughed. Boykie shook himself awake, looked ahead, a little lost at first, then yawned and stretched.

'Nobody is alert when they are asleep,' I said, teasing him.

'Ja, Baby, and the hands will get your balls if you sleep,' he said.

'So, did they get hold of your balls?'

'They nearly sent whatever it is that is contained in them, spurting across that room,' he said laughing.

'Shit, why do they do that?'

'Tsi, fuck you, don't ask such stupid questions,' he said.

'Well . . .'

'Well, if you go on like that, they will kill you man, understand the name of the game, it is called, "them and us". No shit, the rules are fuck them up, kill, destroy, ride on their backs, rape their women, get hold of the men's balls, pull and tear; anyone disobeying this is unpatriotic, is against the traditional way of life in South Africa, and will be punished. You see what they did to

Fischer? Even when he had cancer in the brain, they would not let go of his life. It was a lesson for those white boys who disregard the white rules. You remember what they did to John Harris? They hanged him. Any white person who does not keep the rules of the game will be punished, and that will be a lesson for the others who want to get out of step. The rules are there. They were set by white people, and black people don't understand them, so now and then they catch you and pull your balls.' Boykie laughed and clapped his hands and added, 'You understand the rules or you don't, that is all.' Alexandra began to show ahead of us now. The smoke, hovering in the sky, above the rusted tin roof-tops, seemed to proclaim our world doomed, doomed forever. It seemed that smoke was the mark, so everyone would know where to go, to catch and get hold of balls, and to rape. That seemed really funny! I slowed the car down, indicated to the left, and turned. Many people, in the streets, walking, standing and talking at the corners of streets, children running, playing in the streets.

'Take me home, boy, and tomorrow, if you still want to keep the man's job, report early at work, tell them I will see them when I am rested, right now take me home.' Boykie's determination, his voice issuing orders like that, made me feel mocked, made me feel ashamed, alone and angry. I dropped him at his gate. He said nothing, just took out his bag and left. I drove down Selborne Street, terrified by my aloneness, among the many many people, some of whom waved at me, and I merely nodded, feeling betrayed.

Now I could not bear to relate what had happened to anyone. It was my secret. Suddenly a strange, heavy sadness set into my heart, or wherever it is that these things happen. It was as if the car would go out of control.

I took a shower at the gym, then drove to my home, to my parents, for a meal. My mother was there, so was my father. They were sitting at the table and my sister was in the other room. After I had greeted my parents, and sat down, they asked where I had been because Lily had come looking for me several times. 'Why does she look for me, does she not know I work?'

'Go to hell, you always think you live alone in this world, other people are concerned about you,' my mother said angrily.

'Well, I will go to hell. Next time, tell them not to come asking after me. Tell them I am in hell, that is all,' I said.

'Who you talking to like that, heh? Rubbish, a thing without a sense or manners, all you know is run after girls, and run in the street like a dog. I wish they kill you there, what do you want all the time at night in the street? Sies!' She spat or seemed to spit on the floor.

'Don't worry about what happens to me,' I said.

'Tsietsi, Tsietsi, if you think there are two bulls in this house, you better choose to go through that door,' my father said. He was looking at me through his broken spectacles.

'I came home to see you all,' I said.

'I said the door is there, if you think you are a bull. That is all. No word from you.'

'We sit here worrying about you and now you come talking as if you are farting,' my mother said. I nearly laughed. But instead, I stood up and went to the other room where Mary, my sister, was. When I stood staring at her from the door, and she saw me, she giggled.

'You got some hot beans,' she said.

'How are you?'

'Okay,' she said, still giggling.

'What's funny?'

'Nothing,' she said.

'Okay then, stop that laughing.' She hugged me and kissed me on the chin. But she was still giggling, so I began to laugh lightly too.

'Where were you?'

'Around,' I said.

'We have been looking for you. Ndo went to your place several times, and did not find you. I went to see you, you were not there. Where have you been? And Lily was looking for you too.'

'I was in hell,' I said. She laughed.

'And I met Anka, he asked where you were.'

'Okay, now, talk about something else, unless you are considering making more hot beans for me.'

'Do you want tea?'

'God, I would love that,' I said. Mary went out of the room and I sat on the bed, looking at what she was reading, something about true love and romance. Her room smelt of perfume, was neat, filled with strange fucked up books, about how to make love and enjoy it, and true love confessions. She came back with a tray and put it on the table. I looked at her, and I thought, shit, you may as well have it, you bitch!

'Why are you reading all that shit?'

'What?' She turned to face where I was pointing.

'All that.'

'That is not shit.'

'Do you think there is anyone who can teach you how to make love?'

'Ah,' she could only say.

'Why don't you read better things?'

'What's better things?'

'Better books.'

'Which?'

'Why don't you come up to my house and pick up a few books that you can read?'

'You have not been there.'

'Ah, Mary, come on now.'

'You have not been there, you are always all over the show,' she said and passed me the tea.

'Would you read them if I brought them?'

She shrugged and went to look out of the window. While she stood there, with her back towards me, I saw her body, full. I could see the shape of her breasts, protruding forward. She was no longer the little girl we used to tease

60

and occasionally thrash. I recalled how once she tried to make a pee standing up, and the urine ran down her legs, and her mother, angry, looked ashamed, slapped her and pushed and pulled her to the house screaming at her. How we laughed at her and teased her for days, that she could not pee like we did. Now that seemed so long, long ago; when she would be crying, running to our mother to tell her what we had said, and mother would run after us, with a stick in her hand. Mary was no longer that little girl now. She wanted to know about true romance and true confessions and how to make love. But she always seemed to be in her room, all the time. Always sweet, wanting to make tea for us whenever we came home. Somehow, I felt there was something very unreal about her. I feared for her, the day she found what the street had for her. The streets in which her mother would not be, with her biting tongue, to tell her that she would be climbed, make to take journeys into the centre of the sea, and be left there, to be mocked while she was fighting the current. On the other hand, she seemed to sense it, and as a result, she kept in the house, in her room reading her stupid books and washing several times a day, and singing with the radio.

I had tried to take her out on several occasions but every time I tried to do it, mother came between us, with her church tongue, getting spirits about me taking her child to the dogs, cursing her, and not wanting to have her child join me in my miserable ways. Mary wept, and I realised then how much pain and conflict I caused. And every time we walked around with her, she would be right next to me, like a frightened dog, not wanting to stray because other dogs were barking and wanted to bite it. I at last gave that up, but now and then snatched her to a movie, in those days when we still went to the movies, or to a jazz festival. But she was always right next to my skin.

'What are you doing in there?' my mother shouted.

'I am choking Mary to death,' I replied. Mary came rushing at me, slapping my back and wanting to hold my mouth.

'Abuti-Tsietsi, ah, shhhh,' she kept saying. The old lady was quiet. I knew she was angry.

'I know you can do it, your mother's head,' she said.

'That does not sound like a mother of prayer,' I said.

'Ah, shut up!' Mary said, shocked.

'Your mother is crazy,' I said.

'Ah, yooooo,' she said and left the room. I lay on my back thinking, feeling rested, choking in the perfume of the room, and wondering about the rubbish books that kept dancing their titles at me: Romance, Confessions, Love, Loving, If you know what love is . . . About me . . . Then I heard the dishes and cutlery being put on the table. It was when I lifted my head and looked outside that I realised that it was getting dark. The sun had gone now, the shadows were growing.

I was looking at my father's face, as he dug into his plate, opened his mouth, and chewed, thoughtfully, now and then saying something to my mother. I thought about the scene at the police station, the scene on the counter, how I screamed, how I fell, how I lay on the ground, weeping like a child. I wondered, I wondered how my father would have handled that scene! Would he scream? Would he weep? What would he do when he shook his body out of its slumber and found himself lying there on the floor, in shame? Yes, it could happen, it could happen to him, like it happened to me. It could happen to him. Suddenly, he looked very old, weary, and feeble as I looked at him and the thought crossed my mind. I thought of the many times he had driven along the same road, the same road where we saw a man, lying on his back, in the dark, in the middle of nowhere, surrounded by red and blue flickering lights.My father had driven many, many times along that road. He had driven many times, even before I was born, along that same empty, dangerous road, where the red, blue lights flicker in the dark. In the vast empty fields, that run for miles and miles into the dark horizon, with my mother, all by themselves, alone, in that darkness. Now, as he sat there, chewing slowly, tasting his food and looking away, staring into space, he suddenly became a stranger to me. I could not place him on that terrible and bloody road, or in that terrible and smelly room, where hands stalk for balls or even, in the dark, dark streets of Alexandra, where women are raped, men killed, shot, stabbed, run over by cars. I could not place him anywhere in the city, where the rule is signs about blacks going to the back; where white women are dirty-tongued, find delight in humiliating black men of any age, where looks can take away any black man's life. My father was a stranger to me, his son, as he sat there chewing. How did he make his journey? I began to understand why he never wanted me to talk to him about the streets, or the city, or the police stations. I began to understand why he had forbidden that in his house. I wished he could die, and rest.

I began to understand what kept him so quiet. I began to understand why he seemed to be frightened by us, Fix, Ndo and myself. I began to understand why he was so close to his daughter, so far away from his wife, and I realised what his eyes were saying, with their ever-weary, bloodshot look. I began to understand why his shoulders were so bent, why his movement, as if carrying an unbearable load, seemed to creak, I began to understand. But then, that was just the beginning, it was just an understanding, I trembled to know, I had my own journey to make. There was nothing I could talk to my father about, if I could not talk to him about what had happened to me in the past seven days. There was no way I could talk to him and not hurt him, or kill him. I had no courage to hurt or kill him. He sat there, as if the fork he lifted to his mouth was too heavy for him, for his abnormally huge arms, which seemed to be making inconvenient excursions.

Yes, I could understand how it came about that every time he talked about Kaunda, Nyerere, Nkrumah, he became irrational, he became like a small boy, talking about heroes in a movie he had seen. I understood now, as he sat there, that he could not afford to see any fault with his heroes, he had to believe that they loved him and were going to build Africa for him, that they were almost like God. Every time one of them made a statement in the press about South Africa, he seemed to memorise it word for word, and he would talk about the article to everyone he met, and then shoot them with the lines they had said. He had to believe that one day, his heroes, his supermen, were going to fly into South Africa and seize it out of the terrible grip that now held it. He never listened when we talked about them and always had buts; then he would shout about what they were capable of doing. They were the ones who would punish the white man, why did I not see it like that? Education had fucked my mind up, he would say. His heroes were old men like him, who knew the law, who had respect, who were not like me, reading what white people said and believing it, and then walking the streets at night, hardly having time for God, cursing him for creating day and night instead of a long, endless day. 'You ashame us, you young people,' my father would say.

'Abuti-Tsi, when are you bringing my shoes?' Mary said. There was silence while I tried to think what shoes she was talking about.

'You will never see those shoes. Why do you want to break your heart over nothing?' my mother said, looking at her daughter.

'Ah, shoes? Where did you see a man working who calls himself a writer? How can he buy shoes? He is always in these funny trousers of his,' my father said wrathfully.

'You will get your shoes, Mary,' I said, ignoring all the words that were meant for me, but directed at her.

'Stop making a fool of my child,' my mother said.

'Why do you say that? You sound as if I was not your child.'

'I am ashamed of you,' she said, standing up and walking to the sink.

'Ashamed or not ashamed, you are stuck with a son like me. You are Ma-Tsi, there is nothing you can do about that.'

'Hey, I said there can't be two bulls in here, and you know what to do if you feel like a bull,' my father said.

'Why are you all so angry with me?'

'Abuti-Tsi, be quiet you too,' Mary pleaded with me.

'He better,' the old man said.

'What have I done?' I asked.

'Nothing, that is the trouble,' my mother said. 'You go on as if you are the only person alive, everyone must worry about you and you think about yourself and that is all.'

'But what has that to do with Mary's shoes?'

'Don't talk to me about that, I said leave that alone. We dont want those shoes. I can buy her shoes, don't bring stolen things in my house. If you are a pagan be a pagan in the street where you live not here in this house, and you must leave that poor child Lily alone. I don't know what she sees in you, a dirty, foul-mouthed rat, that has nothing; that sleeps in stinking blankets. You leave that child alone, that is all. Don't make that poor child miserable.' She was breathing heavily. I knew, I knew it was time for me to go. That is if I needed to sleep.

I began to swallow the food quickly, pushing it into my mouth.

'Sies, you bring up these children and then they think they know better than you do. Look at Ndo, always drunk, beating his wife, sies, you make people laugh at us . . .'

'It's like they have never ever been taught any law, no law for living,' my father said, switching to English at the end.

'These are dogs, how can they know any law?'

'And when you see that Ndo, tell him to bring back my wheel spanner. He came here and took my car and lost my spanner, tell him I want it back,' the old man said, banging on the table.

'He has not brought that back yet?'

'No, the fool,' the old man said. I stood up and put the plate on the sink.

'I have to go,' I said. There was silence. 'I will bring your shoes,' I said to Mary and closed the door behind me. In the dark cool, with the silver shining moon, I walked to the car, and thanked the white people that I had their car that day. It was indeed in demand. It felt like the only agreeable thing in the world as it bobbed and weaved on the many bumps on the road, purring quietly beneath my control, taking me wherever I was going now. The needle showed almost empty. I would never make eighteen miles unless I got money somewhere to put in more petrol. Yes indeed, I was a dog, no money, nothing.

She stood in the door smiling, looking straight into my eyes. 'What do you want?' she said.

'Tshidi, please, now don't be funny. Let me in.'

'What do you want?' she said again.

'You, Baby,' I said.

'What do you want with me?' She began to smile, her gentle beautiful smile, her innocent smile. She stood at the door, leaning against the frame, her head resting on her hand, and the other hand lay softly on her bosom. Her eyes were fixed straight into mine, almost not blinking, but her face was pleasant, on the verge of a smile. I moved closer to her, and our noses almost touched. She did not move.

'Tshidi, please let me come in. I will collapse if you refuse me entry. Shit, how can I take a battering all the time?'

'Frankly, I don't want you to come in,' she said, this time not smiling. In fact, her face was expressionless and as a result had something sad, something vulnerable about it.

'What's the matter Tshidi?' I held her shoulder. She moved back, away from the door, then turned away, leaving the door open, walking towards the table which was in the centre of the room. At the door, I wondered what it was that I was seeing. Her eyes were unwinking, hiding the troubles of her heart; she wished to be left alone, yet she feared to be all by herself.

I went in and closed the door behind me. No decision had been made in my mind yet. All I knew was, I wanted to sit down, and then she would dictate. There was silence in the house. The child on the bed was snoring softly. He was a heap of blankets, looked very warm, peaceful and so innocent. Tshidi stood by the window, her back towards the curtains. Her arms were folded, her head bent down, and her legs were apart. Her shadow fell on the table from the light that was just above her head. She seemed about to say the words which would describe what was in her heart. She was not tall, she was slender. Knowing that she carried her height with pride and dignity, striding, almost walk-running, with absolute confidence in every step she made, made watching her, obviously torn by conflicts, break my heart. I did not know what to say to her, so I sat there, feeling a little uneasy, a little cheap, feeling as if I had talked myself into playing the role of a trickster.

Why have I not made up my mind about my relationship with Tshidi? Why have I kept on this hit and run tactic for so long? I had a future with Lily. Tshidi, as long as she allowed me to continue coming, sitting with her, talking, drinking tea, and ending up in all the kinds of position our feelings dictated, encouraged herself to be doomed. I knew that I was responsible if Tshidi was doomed. There was no way I could shed that responsibility but leave her alone. And that was tough.

'Tshidi, I do not know what to do,' I said at last. She looked up for a while, then looked down and sighed painfully. The silence in the room was unbearable. I could smell the mixture of tomatoes and onions and meat. Everything in the house was shining as if it was a mirror. There was a neatness about the house: if one did not know Tshidi's casual approach to life, one would even have been afraid to walk in. But something about her always allowed people to feel at ease, and many times that was what made her a target for abuse. I often wondered to what extent I misused that very susceptibility of hers.

'Do you want tea?'

'Please,' I said. She moved from the orange and red curtains towards the stove, and filled the kettle with water.

'Have you eaten?'

'Yes, I have,' I said.

'Where have you been?'

'Can I talk about that later?'

'Where's Lily?' She looked me straight in the eyes.

'I have not seen her for about a week now,' I said. Silence.

'How have you been?'

'Well . . .' She shrugged, leaning against the wall, next to the stove.

'Well what?' I tried to push her out of her tired state.

'Tsi, leave me alone.' she said. It was her tired state, more than anything else, that seemed to carve out all her beauty. When she was tired or sad her huge eyes, forbidding to be lied to, forbidding to be pitied, rendered her vulnerable, exposed her helplessness, thus betraying her state of mind. I was immediately roused into moving towards her, which was a way of avoiding the real issues. Tshidi needed something to hold on to, something to assure her that, even if she was alone, facing the storm, she should not fear, because storms are for us.

'Okay, I will leave you alone, if that is what you want,' I said. And, as soon as I said it, I knew how much I needed her, how much I needed to be close to her, how much of her warmth, her understanding I needed. Yet I sat on the chair, thinking how she and I could take a journey, toy with the storm, and, as it had happened so many times before, before the storm was over, when it was ready to uproot trees she and I would be tearing at each other.

She put the tea before me on the table. I held her hand just when she was about to go back to the stove, to her lone position. At first I felt her resist my pull. Then, as if feeling hopeless or helpless, I felt her muscles sag, and her perfume, sweet, as if somewhere in the distance there was a garden of roses, reached me. I pulled her towards me. She was staring at me. Suddenly I saw that her eyes were wet.

'What's on your mind, Tshidi?' Her wet stare, the glow of her eyes, the silence, erased all the words that could have been on my tongue. I felt her breasts against my chest, hot; I felt every part of her body trembling, held tight in the heat of her flesh. For a moment her tears were hot on my cheeks, then they were cold.

Five

Something shook me. Then, with my eyes still closed, but without shaking, I lay there, my head buried in the pillow. I listened. Again something shook me, gently, then I felt warm flesh next to me, the smell of clean sheets, and the smell of perfume.

'Tebogo will soon wake up,' Tshidi whispered. That is when I knew where I was. I immediately shook up and got into my trousers.

'Are you going to work today?'

'Ja, I will be around your area about one,' Tshidi said, yawning.

'Okay, why don't you phone me around eleven if you are near a phone, then we can arrange to meet?'

'Okay, same extension?'

'Ja. Okay, I will see you then.' I turned the door handle gently, opened it slowly and slipped out. The world was already up. Crowds and crowds of footsteps, all of them in a hurry, all manacled by time, by the cruel and real time of moments, when machines demand attention because something called gold demands to be crushed and sifted and sold. Women and men had already filled the early morning with their haste, to get to buses in time, to trains in time, to taxis in time. And this haste was to satisfy those who have decided that they own everything, the stones in the gut of the land, the land itself, and everything above the land, including the women, men and children, controlling everything right down to decisions about where blacks will make a shit.

It was while I drove slowly up John Brandt Street, weaving through crowds of people, avoiding bumps, dodging a cow or a donkey or a horse being chased from a rubbish bin by dogs, that I tried to think about Tshidi, about her and me, about what the future really had for us. And these thoughts now and then intermingled with what Alexandra is about. What Alexandra and South Africa are about.

It was a pleasant morning. Because of the warm bright sun falling on the leaves of trees, making them appear like dappled little mirrors, millions of them, and because of the trees, looking asleep, and the many, many shadows of people rushing past, and perhaps because of the journey Tshidi and I had taken, I felt at ease, alert, I felt as if I was stalking everything. I thought about the floor of shame and the eyes that had pierced me, pushing me into accepting that I belong to shame, by pulling my balls, almost tearing them out. That took me face to face with the past night I had spent with Tshidi, when, for whatever reason, I failed to have an erection. Through the night, she had to shake me and ask me why I was screaming. When Tshidi began to realise how hollow a man I was, her first reaction was to retreat, take a look at my face, in silence, and demand that I be a man. But I could not. Instead, I went through vast spaces that we had driven through, the darkness, the fluorescent lights, the wooden counter, the faces, the eyes, the pain, and the wet floor. My mind, no matter how much I tried to resist, raced through all that journey, and again I was right on the floor, with shame, with Tshidi's eyes, this time, searching me, demanding and bewildered. And, in a sense, it must have happened to Tshidi too; she must have wondered if she was a woman at all when we both knew what was happening, because I could have lain there with her, having no penis, having no balls. When I realised what was happening, I wondered why I had come to Tshidi. Shame pushed me into being brutal with myself. I felt I deserved to be ashamed, I deserved to be told that I was not a man. I felt I did not deserve Tshidi's beauty, kindness, understanding. I would not have been surprised at all if she had pushed me off the bed, to the floor, and if she had chased me out of the house. I waited for her to do it. We lay there silent, distant from each other, both of us asking who we were.

'Are you okay?' Tshidi had asked me. Lost and torn apart, my mind erased speech from me. There was this darkness of the room, this heavy silence, and the giggling night outside, pounding, pounding, pounding on me, wanting me to lie on the floor in shame. Something in the way Tshidi looked at me and the way she asked me, 'Are you okay?' – whatever it was, it made me see her, recognise her, identify the little girl in her. I was a small boy now, bewildered by my biology. She was a little girl, unknowing, knowing, yet unable to connect the two, so the terror that now brutalised us in bed could be overcome. Tshidi and I have known each other a long, long time. In a sense, there was no way we could lie to each other; our eyes told the truth when our tongues lied. We knew the look of us when we feared, when we were about to cry. There was no way we could hide that from each other.

The streets, in those days, had claimed me. As we lay in bed, Tshidi's eyes and face and voice reminded me of the first day when she and I met. I was in the streets, and she was no doubt on her parents' errands. I was with Casino, Lekeleke, Jeeps, Margo, Sdi at some corner of some street, when she came by. She did not know that she was a marked person. I knew she had heard of us; no one had not heard of us. I knew that when she saw me, she did not see me; she heard the stories about us, about our knives, our bricks. In tears, shaking, holding my hand to stop it from hitting her, she told me she loved me, she told me she would not love anyone else, she told me that to see her I would have to whistle at her parents' door, and she would surely come out. Tshidi was a young girl then. She was emerging out of being a little girl into being a woman. Her breasts said so, her thighs, her legs, her voice, all of which, when she was frightened, brought out in her something of a trapped animal. She used her nails, her teeth, her voice like animals did. She shook like an animal beneath me, making strange sounds, scratching me, biting me, kicking, her eyes wild with fear, like those of animals. I was a small boy becoming a young man, she was a small girl becoming a young woman. Alexandra had arranged our meeting. I met her, with the rumours about my friends around me, and a knife in my pocket; she met me, with nothing else but her knowledge of cleaning the house and washing her panties, when she was still learning to wash her body, when she had just gained knowledge about her periods. All she said once to me while we lay in bed, and I kissed her, was: 'I mens, we can't sleep together.' She smiled and pinched me on the cheek. When I came back from Lesotho, Tshidi had a walking baby boy.

One day I had gone with Casino to see Tshidi. When we reached her home, after I whistled, she came out. She took me by surprise. She hugged me and sobbing said, 'Please leave the gang, look what has happened.' It took time to get what she meant. Then I pulled her aside, away from Casino, into the dark, and we began to talk. She had been to the hospital after school and Lekeleke was dead, she said. Two or three days before we had been in a fight and Lekeleke had been stabbed. We took him to the clinic, then he was moved to the hospital; we had been to see him. The day we went to see Tshidi we had decided that we would visit Lekeleke at night, not during the day. So, we did not know that he had died. I did not believe what Tshidi was saying. I took off, left her there in the dark. On the way I told Casino what Tshidi had told me. Indeed, when we reached the hospital, the eyes of the other patients who were used to seeing us when we came to see Lekeleke, told us what had hapened and his bed was empty.

It was when I looked at the empty bed that the reality of what had happened struck me The way the other patients looked at us, almost not looking at us, for many knew who we were, and what we could do, made me realise that something had been taken away from us. What was it? Lekeleke? The need to know that we belonged to other people? Dead? What was it? But we could not look at each other, me and Casino. We stood there, staring at the empty bed, silent, lost and alone, no one saying anything to us.

The funeral came. Tshidi was there. All of the boys were there. I could not believe that Lekeleke was in the box which we carried from the house to the hearse, to the graveyard and finally into the hole. I kept thinking I would hear him laugh and say, 'Shit, this soil will choke me, don't put so much soil on me.' However, after some time there was no hole, but a heap of soil, and Lekeleke never said a word. He was indeed dead. My mother told me that I was next to follow. She would be glad to bury me, and my father agreed with her. Fix told me I was to leave the gang. Ndo hardly talked to me.

It must have been Fix who told my parents to take me to Lesotho. By then, the Alexandra streets had become a terrible torment. All the things which were familiar to me reminded me of death, and I could smell blood every time I passed the places where I had been with Lekeleke. That was how I went to Lesotho.

I saw what looked like the back of Boykie's floral dashiki in the rear-view mirror. As the car purred and slowly moved out of the gate into the street, Boykie vanished. On the road, getting out of Alexandra, heading for the bridge which would put me into Louis Botha Avenue, the song Boykie and I had listened to came on strong – Nina, singing 'Poppies'. It seemed to me there was no way, no way of breaking the cycle. It seemed that the tragic series of events linking the time when I was a boy to when I was a man was going to go on and on forever. The memory of boys laughing in the dark streets, their laughter ringing with a youthfulness which seemed to have many, many promises in it ... sometimes the screams which broke the silence in the dark, and set millions of dogs barking ... the running, running footsteps in the dark, and then the revelation in the dawn, a corpse. So many, many times has this happened. You look into the eyes of the boys, the girls, as they walk the streets, innocent, searching, bright-eyed and full of joy. Then without warning, one day you meet them, the glitter snatched so violently away, their faces and eyes shut up in an eternal, sobbing darkness.

Boykie had said, when I talked to him about Tshidi, 'Leave her alone.' But my head had kept screaming, screaming and ringing with the same question, why? Why? Why? And when I asked Boykie why, all he said, or seemed to say was, 'Because you have no business fucking around with her!' Well, for me that was no reason. If, when I said I thought I loved Tshidi that seemed a feeble explanation for fucking around with her, well, it was not like that to me.

Along Louis Botha Avenue, the traffic was thin; now and then I was the only one on the road. It was pleasant driving at that time of the day. The neon lights, the signs, the colours, all the words, all the tricks that go with advertising night or day, kept leaping into my mind. SHOES. CHICKEN. FLORIST. MUSIC. EGGS EXTRA LARGE. Words, colours kept flashing as if they were shouting, demanding attention. KENTUCKY FRIED CHICKEN. COME IN AND SEE. COLGATE. And the mind that I have, turned to these verbal signals, kept grabbing the words, pushing them down in there wherever it is that words stick. The sun was sailing westward, but still in the centre of the sky. The leaves of trees kept up their cultural dance, on and on; Louis Botha Avenue, with its flowers on the islands, went weaving uphill, downhill, to the centre of the city. I followed it, at a slow pace, at ease, thoughtful about Tshidi, about what was waiting for me at work – having been away for so long, a week, and having to explain. I stopped at the entrance to the basement garage. The light was red. Green, I drove in. The basement was busy, its peristaltic movement curling and uncurling. Cars, in all sizes and makes, all shapes and colours, wove in and out of it. I pressed button five.

I could hear the typewriters clatter. I could hear someone laughing, other people laughing. Back at it. Give it hell, that was the understood motto in here. Give the time hell. He was seated behind his desk, his bald head bowed. I went past his desk, and stood at the notice board. Messages. I grabbed all Boykie's and put them in my pocket. I took out mine, then walked over to my desk. Papers, everything scattered around. The messages kept saying, in all sorts of handwriting, phone so and so, so and so phoned. Then I came across one, Tshidi's. She had phoned and had only said I should be told she had phoned. I began to clear the desk. I felt like talking to no one. I was happy that no one had noticed me yet, but I knew my comfort would not last. When I had cleared the desk, I waited. Fucking shit. Boykie should have come here himself, talked for himself and not passed the buck to me. But there I was!

'Hey, is that Tsi?' a voice said. It was Ted, of all people. Ted! He came over. 'Shit, where have you been?' Our eyes met.'Where have you been?' He came closer. 'Where have you been?' He held my shoulder. 'Where have you been? We can't pay you for not working!'

'Kaffir boy, shut your fucking mouth,' I said. He laughed. His eyes kept leaping to Mervin, the white Chief Editor, who now was looking at me, silent. Ted looked like a dog appealing, wanting to hear its master give it orders to bark. I felt Mervin's eyes glued on me. I could see him, out of the corner of my eye, scratching his bald head. I knew what he was doing, he knew what I was doing. We both waited, like cocks about to leap at each other. A game, just a game, but a serious game, a game of centuries. I thought about Boykie. I could see him resting, lying on the sofa, reading a magazine, drinking coffee, and listening to music. I could see him. And here I was, about to get into a fight for him.

'My man, what is it?' Mervin asked.

'Shit,' I said.

'Give it to us then,' he said.

'I am coming.' I said.

'Give him the door,' Ted said. 'We have been waiting for that car too long now.' He said it laughing, and something about his eyes told me he was fighting, not wanting to feel a fool. All Mervin did was wave him away with his arm, telling him to shut up. I went on clearing my desk. When I looked at Mervin, he was looking at the newspaper before him which was spread over his typewriter.

'Take the shit,' I said. 'Boykie has asked me to give you this letter.' Our eyes met. 'If you want, I can tell you what's up about me. If you want you can read the letter first, it will give you an idea of what I am going to talk about.'

'What do you mean?'

'Are you saying you will read it now or later?'

'I said what do you mean?' Mervin said, looking cool, collected like the boss he was.

'Here's the shit then. We were assaulted by cops, kept in a police station for a week. I spent yesterday getting myself together and this morning I am reporting for work.'

'Where was this?'

'Near Hammanskraal,' I said. He tore open the envelope and stared at the paper. Then he folded it and looked at me, wiped his face, covered it, sighed, then looked up at me again.

'What does Boykie mean?'

'That is surely between you and him,' I said.

'No, I mean, what's all this?'

'What?'

He began to read the letter. 'Sir, your brothers have, like they have always done before, wronged me and my people. I do not see my way clear, Boss, to make any explanation about what happened. I feel *I am owed* an explanation. So Mervin, or Boss if you want, I am staying at home, where I belong, forever.' Mervin looked at me in silence.

'What does this mean?

'Mervin, like I said, I can only talk for myself.'

'No, what I mean is, what happened?'

'We stopped after we saw police cars surrounding a black man who was lying on the ground. We were told to move, we did not, the assault started.'

'Right,' Mervin said, and stood up. 'We have to have all the details. Anne will do the story, and we are going to have a brief meeting just now, to see what steps we can take against the cops.'

'No sir,' I said. 'The story yes, but I am having no case against no one.'

'We will talk in the conference. Anne!' He picked up the phone, dialled and began to talk. Anne stood next to me.

'Haai Tsi,' she said.

'Yes Madam.'

'Madam!' she said. 'I am younger than you, why call me Madam?' She laughed.

'Anne, how are you?' I said.

'Fine Tsi,' she said, her face a little red. 'I have not seen you for a long time now, where have you been?'

'The boss called you about that,' I said. 'Wait a little, have patience, Ma'am.'

'Yes sir,' she said, and bowed a little.

'What are you and your brothers and sisters doing to my brother this time?'

'He is fine,' she said smiling.

'I said what are you doing to him?'

'Nothing, he is still painting, hating us, but he is okay, I think he is a nice guy.'

'Is he still fucking the whole shoot of you?'

'I am not answering that question,' Anne said.

'You have never answered any questions, so I am not surprised at all,' I said.

'Not stupid questions,' Anne said.

'Tell Yao that I will see him tonight, and that he should have something to drink when I come there,' I said.

'I will sir,' Anne said.

'I hope he has not started painting white cunts and breasts.'

'No, he is still painting what you know.'

'He better be.'

'Give it hell!' Mervin said when he dropped the receiver and faced Anne and me.

'We are here to do so, sir,' Anne said.

'Anne — Tsi and Boykie were assaulted by cops, can you find out what happened and give South Africa a story?'

'Oh my God!' Anne said, turning to face me with her red face and brown eyes.

'All I can say Anne, is that we were assaulted by cops, kept in a police station for a week, while we were on duty as reporters, and that I am not making any case. I do not recognise the police, the courts, the law which is made by white people in this country. Our time will come, that is your story if you can use it. May I start working, sir?' I said to Mervin.

'Will you co-operate, Tsi?'

'Yes, if my conditions for the story are met.'

'Talk to Anne, and when you are through, I have a timetable for you.' He stood up to leave.

Anne and I sat opposite each other at her desk. She took out her writing pad, biting the end of the pen she held with her left hand. She looked straight into my face, not blinking, staring straight like that. Anne's brown eyes had nothing pleasant for me to remember. How the world has hung on brown eyes, ready all the time it seems to tumble and break forever under the weight of the mystery in the brown eyes. Yet I was certain that they were judging me. There was something pleasant about Anne, that I had always acknowledged. There was even something kind about her. I could, if I dared, rely on her; I could if I dared almost place my life in her hands; in fact, that had happened many times, when we went out to get stories together. But I relied on her only if the situation demanded a white face for an okay; she relied on me only if the times asked, in ever so many brutal ways, 'Are you black?'

'Shall I bring you some coffee?' Anne asked.

'Yes, do that.'

'Sugar, milk?'

'Everything, and a cigarette if you can find one for me.' She stood up, sighing, and I saw the muscles in her arms tighten as she held the arm of the chair and put the weight of her body on them. What am I going to tell Anne? I had nothing to tell her indeed. And, I think, as we sat there, both of us knew what was going on. Anne knew that I did not believe in what was about to happen. She knew that I had contempt for her, for her symbolic self, for her having been born into that world whose dreams were my nightmares, whose nightmares challenged my life, luring it to death. I knew she knew this. We had talked about it, in those days when my eyes were blurred to the flame that now and then came closer and closer to my wings as I grew up. I had gotten lost from the streets, from the desk and classroom, from myself, and, South Africa being what it is, my little black self had nowhere else to go, but the coffin or the cell.

I saw Anne come back. She had a paper cup in each hand, a cigarette hanging from her thin red lips. Her face frowned from the curling smoke getting into her eyes.

'Well, there we are,' she said, putting the cups on the desk. She sat herself down, leaning back on her chair. She handed me the paper cup.

Six

The story was in some corner, on page two. That was all right. It was all right because my grandfather had paid with his blood and that of his posterity, to enable other men to make newspapers. 'Two black reporters,' the story began, and I could not help but laugh to think that people, young boys and young girls, were paying huge prices so that I could be called 'black' first. 'Two black reporters,' the story went on, 'who work for a Johannesburg newspaper, were allegedly assaulted by policemen . . .'

I was standing in the middle of the street one morning, reading this story. I had not been able to sleep the night before. So first thing, when at last I saw the day trying to penetrate the curtains, I got out of bed and into the street, to buy the newspaper from the boy at the corner. He was there, in his oversize trousers, already confronting the world of workers, and whoever else was on the street, whatever their business at that hour of the day. He told me he had seen a picture of me in the newspaper. I told him I forgot to bring some money with me; I would give it to him on my way to work. 'Sweet, Bra-Tsi,' said Nkutu, the boy at the corner. Discovering myself like that in the middle of the road, amid a million footsteps, hasty footsteps, and wondering what was coming my way, this time from the gods of wrath who seized the land of my father, I began to envy those who had never read, who had never dared to be ambitious about anything, those people walking so fast, laughing, producing millions of almost directionless footsteps, these people who like my grandfather, mindless, were born in South Africa, black, children of pagans, heathens, children who, cursed because they dared to see their fathers naked, were to be punished forever, and forever were to draw water, chop wood, and be servants to cruel masters.

I envied them, for, in their movement, in their faces, in their laughter something was there, the graffiti written in the dust on the paved streets.

The graffiti were legible, but all of us, the masters and the servants alike, did not want to know anything about them. So they were not legible. Those of the cursed who tried to decipher them ended on some island near Cape Town, where the law of the white people was made. The island had been used before, for criminals and victims of leprosy. There were many, many of them there, and many were still headed there, but a lot more refused to look at the graffiti. The price was too high.

That morning's sun was now rising, golden, spreading rays of all colours over the rusted roof-tops of houses which stood in style, brick upon brick, put together hastily, house upon house, put there carelessly, meant to house as many cursed people as possible. The sun spread its rays over all this, erasing the morning and writing about the day that was coming.

It took time to be able to get out of the house. I played Coltrane. Lee Morgan. Eric Dolphy. I played Nina. Miriam Makeba. But something was not about to hold together. Something wanted to fall apart. Dazed, trying to feed myself, to wash myself, to feed the soul, or whatever this thing is called, I wished there was a way, just a way for that day to pass without me having to face it, without me having to walk into that room, among those typewriters, among people who were informed about my shame. Eyes and eyes, in all their colours and meanings, kept darting at me. 'What happened? Why? What did you do? Oh we are sorry!!' Eyes and eyes did not let me let go and sail with Coltrane, or Miriam or Dolphy; they held on and wanted me to go through that other journey again.

The queue, as usual, was long. The buses coming from town, going back, were never enough, and the queue-marshalls shouted and cursed, hurling their whips violently against mothers and fathers, against young men and young women, brutally being what they were. They were employed to keep the long, long lines in order, to make sure no one got into the bus before their turn. The queue-marshalls walked like John Wayne. People risked themselves, slipped in at the slightest opportunity, were caught, and knew the price. Some people bribed the queue-marshalls, so they never stood in the line. Bus after bus came in, bus load after bus load went out, until in the late morning the queues began to get shorter and shorter.

By now, when my bus roared out into Louis Botha, I had been told, 'We saw your picture in the newspapers, what happened?' 'You know we are at war,' I replied, and the answer sounded strange as it left my lips. But I kept saying it, and in no uncertain terms I made it clear I wanted to be left alone. The bus was packed. Some people were standing, holding on to the straps as if for their lives. People talked about soccer, about the police raids that morning, about their children, about their difficulty in keeping them in school, about the work that was waiting for them, about white bosses they liked and disliked, about Kurt Waldheim, Nyerere, Vorster, Kaunda, about who had been murdered that week, who had been arrested, about men and women and sex, about everything under the sun. And the bus roared, stopped at the traffic lights, pulled out and sped on, roaring like a cow tired of grazing. People got on and off, women and men, all sorts of expressions on their faces.

By the time I reached the door and walked into the lobby, I was sick of answering the question, 'What happened?' Or, 'Hey, es bad!' The lift man, white with a smile on his face, looked at me. No doubt he saw victory in what the article had said. We put each other in our places all the time. His job, as a white South African, was to remind me that I was a kaffir, and I had taken it upon myself to remind him he was a settler. This morning, while smiling and then looking me straight in the eyes, he said, 'Boy, this writing of yours will put you into real trouble one day!' I did not look at him, I kept my eyes on the newspaper, smiling. A colleague, white, who was with us in the lift, perhaps thinking I was speechless, as kaffirs should be, said to the other white man, 'What are you talking about?'

'I am not talking to you,' the lift man said. They went on, like fire and grass in rage and destruction, talking about me, about what one should say about or to me. I stood there, watching the lift numbers change, and barely heard what they were saying. At last, the number five showed. I walked out of the lift, leaving heated voices in there.

There was a notice on the door. 'Asahi Pentax, spotmatic camera on sale, a bargain.' I went straight to my desk, and dialled the number.

'Hullo, dark room,' the voice on the other side said.

'Yes, I'm on the fifth floor, I am interested in the camera.'

'Why dont you come up and let's talk?'

'Okay, I'm on my way . . .'

'What really happened?' a voice said over me. It was Tuki. His face, beneath his stetson hat pulled over his eyes, made him look like a detective. He was a short man, with a face tapering to the chin, eyes set in, always sparkling, as if they were looking for something that is to be found instantly.

'We were assaulted by cops, they did not want us to see what they were doing,' I said.

'Hammanskraal?'

'Ja. You know that place?'

'Ja. So how is Boykie?'

'He is okay, I have not seen him for the past two days now.'

'Is he still coming back?'

'No, he is through with this place.'

'Oh, ja?'

'Yes. Look, I am on my way to the eighth floor, I have to see what this camera they are selling is about. A camera, a Pentax.'

'Oh yes, I saw the notice this morning on the door.'

'Are you going out?'

'Yes, on a job.'

'Can I take some of your time? You know more about the camera than I do. I would like to buy it if it is not too expensive.'

'I will come with you.' He picked up his gadget bag, slung it over his shoulder. We walked out. The doors opened and we entered the lift. The lift man was there. He looked at us as if we were strangers.

'So what is Boykie up to now?' Tuki asked.

'I don't really know. I don't think he knows either, he only knows that he does not want anything to do with this place anymore.'

'That is a pity, because he has a feel for camera and news.'

'Yes, that is true.'

Tuki was looking at the lift man.

'Tuki, forget that fool,' I said.

'It is dangerous to educate a kaffir,' the lift man said.

'Oh, is that what's going through your head? There will be thousands of us educated soon, and you won't be here, Mr Koek,' Tuki said laughing.

'We will see to it that you are all dead before it comes to that,' the lift man said, almost spitting on the floor. The numbers kept changing. Seven . . . eight. I was the first out of the lift, while Tuki talked to the lift man. The lift door closed and Tuki came out laughing, his eyes darting mischievously.

'Haai, that is an insane racist,' he said.

'Well . . .' I really had nothing to say.

'You know, the other day, when was it? Thursday? Ja ja, Thursday, Bella and Koek grabbed at each other. Bella caught Koek's neck, gave him two blows with her head and knee, you should have seen that!' He was laughing.

'Who is Bella?'

'Bella, the sister who takes orders from the floors to the kitchen.'

'Oh, yes, I know her as Morongwa, not Bella.'

'Right, oh ja, not her slave name, heh?'

'It's not about slave names, it's about proper meaningful names. Anyway what happened?'

'The night watchman stopped the fight. I took good pictures of that.'

'You were taking pictures while they were fighting?'

'Ja.'

'Oh, ja?'

'Yes, I am putting them in for tomorrow, township edition.'

'That is my conflict. I have never known whether I am a die-hard reporter or a die-hard fighter.'

'What do you mean?' We went into the dark room.

'I mean, I feel there is something about being there taking pictures while a fight, a clearly unbalanced fight goes on.'

'Unbalanced, what do you mean?'

'Morongwa could be locked up, purely because she is black, fighting a white person – and you know the price of that.'

'Well, I have a clear stand on that. I am a black photographer, and that is how I fight.'

'What if she was killed?'

'I have recorded it.'

'What do the records help? Who believes them?'

'Records are not to be believed, but used, that is how I look at it.'

'Used? By whom? How can you use a thing if you do not value it?'

'You are looking at things in the short term. I am looking in the long term, that is my only hope. Otherwise, I would never be a photographer in this country.'

The darkroom, with its many pictures of famous people, famous events, notorious events, and reels and reels of films hanging from stands and in tall filing cabinets, had fascinated me right from when I started working on the paper. Sometimes the films became spider webs in an old deserted room; at times they seemed to breathe; they could make dead people come alive, and sometimes there were ghosts in that darkness. Pinto the darkroom man was standing there behind the counter, with his usual cynical smile, looking at one as if asking, 'What do you want, why don't you walk out?'

'Yes, my friend, can I help you today?' he said.

'I hope so, Pinto, how much do you sell the camera for?'

'Two hundred rand,' he said in his Portuguese accent.

'Can we see the camera? I want Tuki to look at it.'

'Yes, yes, my friend.' He pulled the camera out of a desk and handed it to Tuki.

'This lens only?'

'Yes.'

'Who used it?' Tuki held the camera with his left hand, almost at arm's length, looking at it like a dog sniffing a bone.

'I did. I am buying a Nikkon now.'

'Anything wrong with it?'

'No, my friend, no, nothing wrong.'

'Can we use it for a few days and then bring you word?'

'Sure, sure, but leave a deposit.'

'Let me give you fifty now. I will give you more tomorrow, how's that?'

'I trust you my friend, give me the money.'

'Tuki, how much to do you have? I have forty with me.'

'I will give you ten.' Tuki clicked the shutter, focussed, clicked and looked at the camera again.

'Here, Pinto, okay, if all goes well you get all the money, right?'

'Okay, friend, remove the notice from your door. I don't want people troubling me again.'

We walked out and Tuki was still looking at the camera as if he had never seen anything like it before. He walked slowly, turning the camera in his hand, and now and then feeling his bag, full of all sorts of things, cameras, lenses, ties, shoes, almost everything. One man who worked with him on jobs called it the 'miracle bag'. It always came in handy, because of its miscellaneous contents.

'Tuki, why don't you take the camera and use it for a while?'

'It looks like a good camera.'

'Ja, but take it with you and use it say for a week, then you can tell me.'

'That is a problem, I don't like using other people's cameras.'

'Now don't fuck me around, a week, that is all.'

'What if it gets lost?'

'We hope it does not. If it does, and I accept the story of how it got lost – fine, I will pay and that is it.'

'Besides, you may need it when I have it loaded.'

'Fuck you Tuki, go use that camera.' He slung it over his other shoulder. He was smiling, looking at me as if he was searching for a clue to something.

'You want to become a photographer?'

'Well, don't put it like that. I need a camera, that is all.'

'Ja?' he said, with his silly smile. 'That is good,' he went on, and looked at the numbers. The lift was on the first floor, coming up.

'There comes your man,' he said.

'So, what eventually happened with Morongwa?'

'Koek was bleeding. Morongwa was angry and talking in seTswana. The night watchman was talking in Afrikaans and pulling her away.'

'Shit, where is she now?'

'I don't know.'

'She may be fired for all I know.'

'No, I don't think so. Anne is doing the story.'

'Anne? Oh, ja? She has lots of work lately, heh?'

'Ja, she did yours, right?'

'Ja, she did.'

'She's being hospitable to the kaffirs, keeping them at their jobs, and seeing that justice is done.' He gave me a pat on the shoulder.

'Don't pat me for shit like that.' The lift came, the doors opened and we went in. The lift man was there, as if frozen on his chair; his hand on the lever seemed never to have left it. He glared at us and spat on the floor. Tuki laughed.

'It's revealing the way they assign Anne . . .' I had just said, when the lift man interrupted.

'Julle maak geraas,' he said.

'Drive your lift,' Tuki was saying.

'Just leave that man alone,' I pleaded with him.

'We arrested baie van julle nou die dag, môre is dit julle, komoniste,' he said.

'I was saying Anne's assignments are interesting. Why do you think she has been put in the role she is playing?'

'Who knows? Only Merv knows.'

'Boykie would have said that is a futile question, the thing to know is what we are doing.'

'I will miss Boykie,' Tuki said, 'and it will be tough for you.'

'Ons gaan julle skiet, die hele lot van julle . . .'

I got off on the fourth floor and went into the cafeteria. There was no one there. I sat at the table and ordered tea. From the window opposite the building I was in, I could see many, just so many cranes, lowering their beaks, lifting them up; and men, black, many black men with crash helmets in many, many colours, walking up against the horizon; white men, black men at work, building the golden city. There were many, many buildings rising to the sky; many, many cranes which seemed to be picking them up, and lifting them to the sun; many men, black and white, looking like ants, walking at that terrible height, moving to and fro, on their different errands. Far in the distance, I could see the many, many yellow mountains which characterise the golden city, mountains of sand, dug from within the belly of the earth, in search of the precious rock.

Seven

The hot and furious days of my time as a journalist and would-be photographer had gone. I had the scars to show, nothing more. The streets, perhaps because the scars were so visible, still demanded a photo from me, or cued me for my part after someone had been murdered. I responded, but this time without a pen and note book, and without the camera. I witnessed. I left the white paper blank. I refused to return the stare of the typewriter keyboard. The terrible township images, which forever kept staring at me in the dark of the darkroom, became just that, a dark room, blank. What I could not leave in the newsroom, my memory, I took with me, and was going to make sure that it never haunted me. I was glad to walk into a shebeen. But something else: Lily, the streets, the children — since I was an adult, all of this, the breath, blood and ash of life in silence, kept staring and staring. I walked into the theatre. That act soon saw me out, by the back door.

I had been naked. In the brightest of days, in the most open space, I had — first, unwilling, then willing because of what was pushing me — dared to be naked. I flushed it out, raw nakedness, as clean and bright as the sun and as pure as filth. I produced my nakedness and put it there, on the floor. Perhaps that is why I could not stay in the theatre. None of us, then, was ready to go naked. We taunted each other. There was no one brave enough to dare others to be naked, or, be naked to dare others. We just about did it, but never got there. Nobody noticed me walk out the back door. Perhaps all of them were still charmed by discovering their dresses and panties still on, their underpants clinging to their buttocks. It seems there is always something terrible which happens when suddenly people discover the value of something they had, because they had taken it for granted.

I walked out the back door, leaving the sounds and the sights behind me.

Wherever I had been, before, I had seen something similar to what I was becoming. I did not believe it, there was no way that I could, until one day I saw it in my father's face. He became silent. I heard the silence in me. When I sat in a shebeen, or kept talking to Lily, I heard the silence. It was tangible, it had colour, it had smell, it was familiar; there was no way I could not recognise it, it had been with me while I was still learning how to hold my cock and pee. It was here now with me. I took it with me, home, and it kept us company with a bottle of whiskey which Lily brought for us. And then I began to become aware that between the melody, harmony and rhythm of the music that now and then filled my house, from Hugh, Dollar, Nina, Letta, Miriam, Kippie, Cyril Magubane, Coltrane, Miles . . . between their melody, harmony and rhythm, when the pants are down, the silence is there. This is not an easy find. It is heavy. I could no longer listen to the music that had taught me so much!

Out there in the streets something with a loud bang, called soul, screamed and popped and dragged our children along. It overspilled out of house windows and doors; it leaped over stadium walls; peeped through bars at shops, got off out of fast-moving taxis and buses — soul, it followed us everywhere. The children, responding to this soul music, discovered their cocks and cunts and buttocks and thighs and stomachs and navels as they spiralled and twisted and jerked and pointed to the sky and looked at the earth, and cried and laughed — bewildering the old; the old had nothing to do, they could do nothing; soul did it, the old remained silent. The children, with unkempt hair, and the girls in hot pants which forever want to expose but never do — these our children crowded the streets, walking aimlessly.

The same streets, which now took our children — and souled them, so to say — still claimed corpses. Alexandra, at this time, having succumbed to Verwoerd's Group Areas Act, was a wide, vast space of ruins and dongas, semi-broken houses, empty patches, tall weeds in the middle of anywhere. There was nothing clearer to signify defeat than what Alexandra had become in those days. And soul music banged and banged our children, it banged and banged everywhere. The cops still came and went, dragging their catch along with them.

Since I had nothing to do, I stayed at home. I watched Lily, every morning, every day, go out of the house to Johannesburg and come back. Each of her eyes, each of her stares, each of her footsteps as she left the house, was like a nail, a nail being nailed into my skull. Nobody tailors a role, we wear them as we find them; sometimes they fit, sometimes they don't. If they don't, it is like walking in a crowded street, naked, among strangers whose eyes search yours, and ask you about the missing clothes. I stayed home or visited my parents every time I felt strong enough to defy God. And that was often. I was the only son my parents had. I do not know if sons look like me. Things have become so relative these days. However, I believed I was my mother's and father's son. And God was not going to stand between *that!* All of us, in conversations whipped up by the glimmer in my mother's eyes, had come to accept that Fix's name was a way of refreshing an unhealing wound. We had all speculated about what could be happening to him wherever he was, and tried guessing when, if ever, he would come back. The only hopeful news about Fix we read in the eyes and faces of the Special Branch, who now and then came to ask for a pair of trousers, or for Fix's middle name, or mine, or Ndo's or my father's, or to say: 'Your son got mixed up with communists; punishment for that is severe.' That meant that Fix was still alive.

Day-by-day praying by my father and mother, and by me whenever I was there and did not want to quarrel with my parents, did not change the confidence with which the Special Branch knocked at the door, walked into our house and stared at us. Nor did this praying say anything about whether Fix got strength from it, which strength he certainly needed if we could go by the talk of his guardians. All I know and can say is that we waited, while time mercilessly sped by, or mockingly tortoised by, and all of us got older: Fix, my father, my mother, myself, while we waited to hear what Vorster had decided to do with my brother. Vorster had a gun and the South African Air Force, that I knew. And so, we waited.

Ndo had been a lucky fly. He had hopped away from this web to another, where his buzzing for freedom made him believe that he would get away any time. We prayed for him too. We prayed that while he walked the streets at night drunk, knives should slide over him and not tear his body. We prayed that his wife's heart would turn to steel and cease to be flesh for, if it remained flesh, she would soon be weary. I do not know what my father thought when my mother also prayed for Pusi, her daughter, and Oupa her grandson. We prayed and prayed gallons and gallons of beseeching words.

In between praying and going to the shebeen, after which I went to Lily, somehow I kept pace with the fury of my town. It was a Saturday night. Aunt Miriam, with the coldness of shebeen queens, told me that Lucky had killed Moipone the night before. She told me this above the melody of 'The Crusaders Pass the Plate'. In the same breath someone, over a glass of beer, asked me if I had heard about the boys in Durban. Word had come from that end that universities, black universities, were going on strike. Lily confirmed the news about Moipone and the word from Durban, when I came home.

This word from Aunt Miriam's house turned, as days went by and years came and went, to a clenched fist, thrust into the sky by infants, boys and girls, adults, and articulated itself as 'Power'. We did not know then what distance that fist and that word would cover. When the Christmas cards came from Vorster, banning and banishing the students, the girls and boys, and soon the adults as well, they were too late. The word black, which until then was synonymous with devil, was prefixed with 'I am ...' and suffixed with 'I am on my own'. Nina Simone, above the soul music, was to sing 'To be young, gifted and black' and the white man had become the devil. The flood had come, had happened; the infants of that year bore their real names. Children asked their parents what they thought about being on their own. Adults, in their silent far seeing, kept their familiar silence. We all expected a loud bang, having become accustomed to loud and thunderous bangs in our country. It was strange to walk the streets in those days.

It is not easy to know how these things happen. My mother and father had changed in many ways. My mother now talked a lot about Fix, who had become a long-term prisoner. At first, when she went to the trial, she wanted to know where on earth Fix had met those people with whom he appeared in court; and then, after they had talked, one by one, and they had been taken away, she began, now and then, to sing the songs she had heard in court, sung by her children; they, my father and mother, began to go to what were later to become freedom funerals. Pusi's stomach had deflated, and I teased her by singing 'Mary had a little lamb'. By that time my father's fury had chased her out of the house. She was now nicknamed Mary. Mary, fat overnight somehow, had learnt to smile or stare with a certainty that made you leave her alone by the time she left, with her bundle in her arms.

I could never forget how she looked. It took me a long time to search for and find her. I found her in a hole somewhere in the middle of Johannesburg. She was wearing a pink cap and a pink dress and had Oupa by the arm.

When Mary, Oupa and I met, the long, long time in which we had not seen each other, the life we had put away from each other, had erased whatever it was which had made us familiar. There was the noise of the traffic, the red, green and amber traffic lights, the millions of eyes, ears, mouths, in buses and taxis and cars, flying past us, who now were in a hurry to meet and part. Mary told Oupa, in a quiet way, that I was his uncle. She said this, her eyes gentle, moving from Oupa to me and back. Then with that disarming smile, asked me:

'Is he not a big man?'

'Yes, he is,' I said, and groped for the little man's hand, which he brought to me as if uncertain what it was supposed to do. I held the soft, lame little hand in mine, shook it, looking at the little amused, staring eyes.

'Hullo Oupa, how are you?' I managed to say.

'I am fine,' he said and held his mother's dress, hiding.

'When are you coming home?' I was looking into Mary's eyes.

'When they feel they need me,' she said.

'I think mother needs you.'

'She is not on her own,' Mary said.

'If they send word that you should come, would you?'

'Oh yes, not to stay though. I work now.'

'Where?'

'In Lower Houghton,' she said.

'What?'

'Kitchen.'

'You happy?'

'I am all right.'

'When will you come to see Lily and me?'

'You tell me.'

'Soon as you are ready. When?'

'You will see me pitch up there,' she said.

'I love you Mary, you hear?' Soon as I said that, I suddenly became aware of cars, buses, lights, mad motor-bikes, the tall buildings, their million windows, the sound of a train. Mary looked at me, calm, bright eyes, gentle face.

'Okay,' she said. I had never said that to my sister in my life. I was dead scared to hear she was working in kitchens, and I heard myself say, I love you. I meant it. I knew there was nothing I could do for Mary and Oupa — there was nothing I could do for them!

'Lily and I love you Mary, we love you,' I said. 'Tell Oupa that we love him too.' We looked at each other, and I saw her smile.

'I must go now,' she said, 'I will come and see you.'

'Okay, all right.' I walked down the road. It was when I got home that I realised I did not even know where I would find Mary. Lily found it unbelievable that I had met my sister in the middle of nowhere, and did not bother to find out where I would find her again. It had happened though. That was Lily's way of quietly dragging me and pushing me into things. She made me find myself once, face to face with my father, talking about Mary.

It was a Sunday afternoon. I found my father seated at table, having a late lunch, all by himself. He had on his dark striped Sunday suit, a snow white shirt, tie and all. He held his knife and fork as if they were motor-bike bars. He was seated opposite the huge kitchen window, chewing slowly, looking out through the window and chewing and chewing.

'Yes, my man,' he said when I sat down, 'where are you from?'

'I am from home.'

'Well, and how is Lily?'

'She is fine. She said I should greet you,' I said.

'Yes, yes. when is she coming to see us?'

'She has been talking about doing so, but she has not come yet as you realise.'

'Yes, you must tell her to come here and see me. I have not see that child of mine in a long long time,' he said.

'How is Mama?'

'She is all right, she is at church.'

'I see. How are you feeling?'

'I am old now, I feel very old, otherwise I am okay. Now and then the knees ache, the back, but then that is old age.' He sat back, still holding the knife and fork, chewing.

'I came across Mary the other day,' I said.

He looked at me, silent, started to be busy with his food, began to chew, then looked at me again.

'You came across Mary?'

'Yes.'

'I see.'

'I asked her if she would come back here.'

'You asked her that?'

'Yes . . . she said if you will let her she would but she cannot stay.'

'She said that?'

'Yes.'

'I see.'

'She will come to see us soon, Lily and me. I thought I should come and ask you if she could come to see you.'

'Where is the child?'

'In Lower Houghton.'

'What are they doing there?'

'She is working.'

'What?'

'Kitchens.'

'So the child is working kitchens also?'

'We can say that.'

'But Mary had her chance to go to school. How come she does not give the child the chance to go to school?'

'Maybe he goes to school. I don't know.'

'You mean you did not ask?'

'I did not.'

'Mary is working kitchens?'

'Yes.'

'What she means is that if we do not say come, she won't?'

'No, she seeks your permission to come.'

'No, this is not a matter of seeking permission. Mary wronged us, and on this I differ with your mother, but I feel she wronged us, now she must right that first.'

'How can she?'

'How can she, you ask?'

'I mean how can she go about that?'

'If you wrong someone you ask for forgiveness, didn't we teach you that?'

'You did.'

'We taught her that too.'

'Yes.'

'So how do you ask what you ask?'

'I just wanted to know if I understood what you said.'

He stood up and walked towards the sink. He took out a dishcloth and wiped his hands. He began to pick his teeth, standing by the sink, looking out into the day. I had to turn to face him.

'I will give her the message when she comes.'

'I will tell your mother what you have just told me,' he said and moved back to his chair.

'Have you eaten?' he asked, after sitting down.

'Yes, I have.'

'Have you had tea?'

'I will make it,' I said.

'Tell me, just tell me this, what are you doing now?'

'I don't really know.'

'How come you don't know?

'I am trying to find something to do.' I sat down at last, face to face with my father.

'Lily is working for you?'

'That is a hard way of putting it.'

'No, I don't want you to feel guilty, a man must not feel guilty, but a man must know what he is doing. That is all I want to know, do you know what you are doing?'

'I am looking for something to do.'

'Do you think you will find something?'

'I do not know.'

'You have been out of work a long time now, you realise that?'

'I do.'

'I know very well that things are tough, I know that white people are doing us bad, I know all that, but we must not go down the drain because of that!'

'I agree with you, dad.'

'How does Lily take this?'

84

'Lily wants to know whether I know what I am doing.'

'She is right.'

'I am looking for a thing to do, something I believe in and will work on.'

'We are all looking for that, we all are, but we are not going about it the way you are. The way you are doing it can make those who live with you feel you are a burden, you realise that?'

'I do.'

'Are you doing something about it then?'

'Yes.'

'Okay then, okay,' he said and sighed.

Lily was lying on the bed when I got home. I lay next to her. I told her what the old man had said.

'Onalenna and Nolizwe were here looking for you. They asked whether you are still coming to the theatre,' Lily said, as if I had said nothing to her.

'How are they?'

'They said they are fine,' she said. 'It looks like Anka has left the country, that is what they say.'

'How do they know that?'

'He told Tuki.'

'Really?'

'What did you say to the old man then?'

'I told him I am looking for something to do.'

'Nolizwe says there is a correspondence school in town where they are looking for a extension worker.'

'Extension worker, what is that?'

'Why don't you go and find out?'

'Okay, maybe I should do that.'

'I brought you a bottle, it is in the bag,' Lily said, pointing at the bag on the table. It was a bottle of whisky. Lily and I sat at table while I had my whisky.

'Lily, do you know that it is impossible for me to stay home and not work?'

'All I am aware of, to be frank with you, is that you are always quitting, quitting for nowhere,' Lily said. 'I am . . .'

'I have to understand one thing, I think: why all of us are in a trap. Once I understand that, I will perhaps be able to stick and not quit.'

'I was going to say that I am aware that some of the jobs you took exposed you to the wrath of South Africa, but Tsi, I do not see why you are quitting reporting and going for the bottle. In that case, I think it has something to do with reporting.'

'I will go to see the McLean's people tomorrow, I promise.'

Eight

A year at McLean's College, heading a research unit which was aimed at compiling syllabuses for high school drop-outs, and investigating ways of effectively introducing the correspondence school to the blacks in South Africa, took me again on the rounds and into the areas where I had been as a reporter. I recommended that Anne join the unit, and she and I worked as a team. Anne, with lots of initiative, and a mind as sharp as a razor blade, threw herself into the work. We turned the 'Whys' which our research unit brought in from the field work into 'Hows', and that brought us into head-on collision with the Institute for Christian National Education, an offshoot of the Broederbond.

Dr McLean, the American who was the founder of the correspondence school and my boss, with his casual manner and radical utterances, stood firm behind our unit. The unit grew in numbers. Soon the ideas coming out of it bore fruit in study centres for high school pupils and adults.

The five members of our unit, hard-working and dedicated, turned an otherwise impossible job into a thing to enjoy. We all felt challenged and also began to believe that at last we had something constructive to do. Visiting these centres we saw young boys and girls who otherwise would have been in the streets, exposed to Afro-American literature, Afro-Caribbean literature, African writers. We were watching what we believed to be the crumbling of the walls of ignorance. Dr McLean and I had many meetings together. At these meetings we gauged the progress of the unit, discussed the problems facing it, toyed with and tested suggestions, and talked about large sums of money. McLean talked a lot about self-reliance, self-awareness, 'fucking apartheid' and the 'stupid boers'. At McLean's we all had tea together, officials and cleaners, and during these times we talked about almost everything under the sun, black people and white people.

I don't know why it happened. But Lily and I moved out of Alexandra to Dube. In Dube we had a three-bedroomed house, and plenty of space in the house. We had two cars. And we were expecting a third member of the family. Over two years had passed since I became head of the unit. During these years I had criss-crossed the length and breadth of South Africa. The McLean's arm was stretching out, reaching out, breaking through language, urban, rural barriers – the tutorials from the college, the mobile tutorial units, and several newspaper spreads, all these were a result of 'The Unit'. The unit was growing, in numbers, in influence. The salary scales at McLean's were attracting all sorts of people.

One morning I came into the office, found a message on the desk with a phone number, and returned the call. I was taken by surprise.

'Yes, Captain Botha speaking,' the voice said on the other side.

'My name is Tsi . . .'

'Oh yes, how are you this morning?'

'I am fine, and you?'

'Okay. Look man, you and I have to meet to talk about something, do you have time this morning?'

'To meet and talk about what?'

'Look, if you don't mind, I can come and see you at your office. What is the best time for you?'

'To see me about what?'

'Something is worrying me about your college. I would like to talk to you.'

'Let me check my diary . . .'

'Okay.'

'My only free time will be now, for about an hour, how is that with you?'

'Okay, I will be there in about five minutes.'

I ran into Anne's office.

'Anne!'

'Yes Tsi, what is the matter?'

'The Security Branch is visiting me in about five minutes, can you contact Tuki and keep him on stand by. Tell him what I told you, and tell him to keep checking.'

'Okay, but what the hell is this?'

'I don't know.' I could feel that I was shaking. 'Captain Botha, whoever he is, says there is something he does not like about the college.'

'Fuck him, what does he mean by that?'

'Anne, I do not know.' I walked out of her office, and was about to sit down when there was a knock at my door.

Three white men, immaculately dressed, stood at the door with expressionless faces. When our eyes met, one of them smiled. Anne walked past them into my office.

'Mr Molope, how are you this morning?'

'I am fine thanks. I do not know your name . . .'

'I am Warrant Officer Nel from the Security Branch.'

'I was expecting Captain Botha.'

'Yes, I know. I and my colleagues are from John Vorster Square. Something urgent arose which needed Captain Botha's immediate attention, so he asked us to come and see you.'

'I see . . .'

'Can you excuse us, lady?' Nel said abruptly, facing Anne.

'What is this?' Anne said.

'None of your business lady, if you don't mind. Can you excuse us?'

'What do you mean . . .'

'Anne, do excuse us please,' I said. Anne, red, her eyes shining, walked out.

The three men from John Vorster Square looked at her, then at me, and Nel moved his mouth in what was intended to be a smile.

'Shall I ask for coffee for you gentlemen?'

'No,' Nel said. 'Actually, we have been asked to accompany you back to John Vorster Square.' The two silent gentlemen accompanying him stood by the door, looking this way and that with curiosity.

'What do you mean by that, Officer Nel?'

'Just that.'

'Am I under arrest?'

'No, no! There is a matter Captain Botha wants to discuss with you.'

'I will have to call my lawyer before I accompany you . . .'

'No, you do not need to do that.' The two gentlemen with Nel came towards me, walking round the desk. Without saying anything, one of them touched me lightly on the shoulder.

'You will be back here in forty minutes or so,' Nel said, not even looking at his colleagues. We filed out of the office.

'Anne . . . !' I called out as we were at the door, 'I have to accompany these men to John Vorster Square. They say I will be back in forty minutes, okay?'

We joined the traffic. Nel was a good driver, who obviously enjoyed driving. I know one when I see one. We were silent in the car. I was thinking about all the people I had met since I started working at McLean's, people who I knew Nel would be interested in. Anka. I remembered what he had said when we met in Swaziland. I thought about the meeting I had with one of the student leaders. We had agreed about what it meant to be in McLean's. We were then finding out how the college could be used, if it could be used at all. The mindless crowds in the streets, criss-crossing, and the roaring cars made me long for my freedom. I felt caged.

Nel lit a cigarette and offered his silent colleague one; then me. I preferred my own blend to his strong one, so I lit mine. Nel's friend, with me in the back seat, kept staring at me. 'We work hard for the Republic, hey, no sleep . . .' Nel said to the one next to him.

'The bloody communists don't sleep either, they are like mosquitoes,' the one in the back seat said.

'Look at what they are doing in Rhodesia, just look at that,' Nel said.

'How about Mozambique and Angola, the black communists killing all those people, their own people, so that Russia must take over. I can't understand that,' Nel's friend in the front seat said.

'And the bloody liberals, they put so many of the Bantu into trouble!' the one next to me said, puffing at his cigarette.

'What do you think, Mr Molope?' Nel asked me.

'I don't know what you are talking about,' I said.

'Really!' Nel laughed. 'You work as the public relations officer of a well-known institution and you don't know these things?' He struggled to get a look at me in the rear-view mirror. 'Come on, Mr Molope,' I said nothing.

'Don't you do PRO work for McLean's?'

'I work for the college yes, but it is not PRO. I am doing extension work.'

'What is the difference?'

'I organise research, and I implement.'

'That is PRO work.'

'I don't regard it as that.'

'I don't know the difference,' he said. 'Anyway, that is not the issue. The issue is that we are all aware of what is going on around us, especially all of us who are in learned positions.'

I was not going to say anything about that. He swerved the car into the basement of John Vorster Square. We filed into a lift. At the ninth floor, the lift stopped automatically.

'Okay Jan,' Nel said to the man sitting behind the bullet-proof partition. The lift to the other floors of the building was operated from there. The man pressed a button, the lift doors shut and we were moving again. It stopped at the tenth floor, and we got out. The other two disappeared. Nel and I were walking along a long passage with many doors on either side, doors which, it seemed to me, you would have to enter by crawling.

'Wait here,' Nel said. I was standing between two doors. He went into an office.

'Molope, come over here,' he said when he reappeared. He ushered me into an office. I met a man, tall, bearded, wearing a chocolate safari suit. A handsome man with green eyes and a mocking smile. He had just stood up behind his desk when I entered his office.

'Thank you, Nel,' the man said. 'Molope, you are in a bad place. How did you work your way here? I am sure you have heard of the tenth floor of John Vorster Square?' He stood there, hands in his pockets, looking at me. 'That is the famous window,' he said and pointed to the window behind him. I looked at it. All I could see were trains and many railway tracks, and people working. I felt uneasy standing there in that office. I was used to being asked to take a chair whenever I went into an office. He walked back to his desk and sat down. 'Have you heard of the famous window?'

'What famous window?'

'You have not heard of Timol?'

'I have read about Timol, yes.'

'Didn't you read that he went flying out of a window?'

'I heard that he fell from the tenth floor here.'

'Yes, this is the place, this is the window he flew out of, this very window. He could not take it any more, so we gave him the choice. Talk or the window. You read what happened, hey?'

'I did read about Timol, yes.'

'How did you get yourself here?'

'I don't understand what you mean by that.'

'I mean, what are you doing here?'

'You called me, or rather, I am to see a Captain Botha.'

'Oh yes, yes, I am sorry, I have not introduced myself yet. I am Captain Botha. Welcome, Mr Molope.' He stood up from behind the desk and extended his hand. We shook hands.

'When last did you see Fix?' he asked.

'I visited him a year ago.'

'Where?'

'On Robben Island.'

'He is in for a long, long time – heh?'

'Yes,' I said.

'You want to follow him?' Our eyes met. He stared at me. He smiled. 'We locked him up and threw the key away,' he said, still staring at me and smiling.

'Captain Botha, I am lost. Did you call me to tell me all these things or is there something else?' My legs were now tired.

'You are not lost, no Mr Molope, you are not lost. You have come to a place where many come brave and leave a little shaken,' he said. He leaned back in his chair. 'Tell me, what do you think of Separate Development?' He took me by surprise.

'I, er . . . nobody likes it,' I managed to say.

'Nobody likes it? What do you mean? Mangope likes it, Mphephu likes it, Phatudi likes it, and the people in those different countries like it. What do you mean?'

'The people there were put there, they have no choice.'

'Who put them there?'

'The Nationalist Government.'

'You are talking about my Government. The people chose their leaders, didn't they? I will tell you what I don't understand, Mr Molope; I don't understand why you want to turn the whole of South Africa into a McLean's College. Why do you want to do that?'

'No, that is not what we want to do.'

'You and Anne and the rest of you. You remember Woodstock? Why on earth do you want to turn South Africa into a music festival?'

'I don't understand that.'

'You want white people and black people to sleep together, and smoke dagga, everyone sleeping with anyone. Why?'

'That is not what we do at McLean's.'

'Anne sleeps with two blacks, we know that. Joe and Robert, is that not so?'

'I don't know.'

'You don't know. Maybe you know this; that the liberals put all you Bantu into trouble, and then take a plane to London or Tel-Aviv. You remain here in big trouble. You are in trouble, Molope.'

'But what are you talking about?'

'I am talking about McLean's. You are not a teacher, you are a journalist, and an actor. What is your business at McLean's?'

'I was trained as an extension worker.'

'Do you know that people who do the things you do go to jail for a long, long time?'

'What things?'

'You stand there and ask me what things? I am not working for McLean's, you must tell me what you do there.'

'I do research into how we can rehabilitate high school drop-outs, how we can interest them to study and improve their lives.'

'High school drop-outs, what is that? You know, we know all about that college: it is communist-inspired.'

'I don't know anything about that.'

'I am telling you, then.'

'I hear you.'

'You will regret having ignored my warning. It will be too late because you will be rotting in jail. You will join Fix, and your mother and father will have no one to bury them, you realise that?'

'But I don't understand what you are talking about.'

'I am saying watch out.'

'Are you threatening me?'

'I am a lawman, I don't do things like that.'

'Are you saying I must not work at McLean's? You don't like my working at McLean's?'

'Stop talking nonsense. What were you going to do in Swaziland?'

'I went there to consult with other educators.'

'Anka is not an educator. He is an actor like you.'

'I've known Anka for a long time, he is my friend.'

'Your communist friend, right? What did you talk about with him?'

'About what I do, about people we know, and . . .'

'About the Movement. Did you not talk about the Movement?'

'No.'

'That is funny, how come he did not tell you about what he is doing?'

'He did tell me.'

'What did he say?'

'He is resuming his studies.'

'Studies in what?'

'Civil engineering.'

'Where?'

'He is still looking for a place.'

'You think you are smart. I told you, heed my warning,' he said.

'I know that Anka is a member of the Movement. All I can say to you is that we know everything. You people think we are fools. Go on the way you are going, and we will see . . .' He paused. 'You want to sit down?'

'Yes.'

'Have a chair.' He pulled a chair for me, walked towards the door and called a name. A black man walked in.

'Sergeant, you know this man?'

'Yes,' the man said, smiling. 'Molope from Alexandra. No no, he is in Dube. Do you still work at McLean's?'

'Yes I do,' I said. I had never seen this man in my life. 'Who are you?' I asked him.

'Sergeant Mokgothi,' he said.

'Okay Sergeant,' Captain Botha said. The man left.

'Let's go Mr Molope, I will see you. Er, Koos . . .' He peeped in at an office door. 'Here is your man,' he said.

A boyish-looking man came out smiling, and extended his hand to me.

'Haai Molope, how are you? I am Lieutenant Visser,' he said. Botha had vanished. Visser escorted me out of the building.

Back at the office, Anne told me that Tuki had kept contact throughout. The report was on the front page of a Johannesburg newspaper:

'Mr Tsietsi Molope, an extension worker at McLean's Tutorial College, a correspondence institution based in Johannesburg, said that he was picked up by three security policemen from John Vorster Square.

One of the policemen identified himself as Warrant Officer Nel. Mr Molope was taken to John Vorster Square, where he was questioned by a Captain Botha. The police spokesman at John Vorster Square said he had no knowledge of Tsietsi Molope, and that Captain Botha and Officer Nel were not available for comment.

Mr Molope said that Captain Botha questioned him for four hours. He said that Botha asked him about his job at McLean's, and about some of his friends who have left the country. He was also told that he was associating with communists.

"I would like to make it clear that I am not a communist," Mr Molope said during an interview with him at his office. "I am working for McLean's College because I am concerned about the plight of so many children who are out of school. Education is a socialising agency; in South Africa, black children are subjected to an education which is instrumental in imparting the dominant ideology of apartheid or separate development, a system which the black people in general abhor," he continued.

"History is taught, in both white and black schools, to distort the reality of South Africa; enforced segregation in schools entrenches the segregation system as a whole."

Mr Molope said that he had travelled extensively in South Africa, and had come to the conclusion that McLean's College is not the answer to the problems of pupils in the country. The root cause of these problems was the system created by the Government. It is evident in South Africa that there are different kinds of education for the different races. There is abundant evidence that no black child is encouraged, in any way, to attend school. In fact, the contrary is true. He said that his research unit at the College had shown that education for blacks had deteriorated since the introduction of Bantu Education in 1955. Only discrimination could explain why R41 per year is spent on educating a black child while a white child receives R621 per year. Drop-outs among black children, at secondary and university level, increase every year.

"There is an alternative to the present educational system for blacks," Mr Molope suggested. "The alternative system would be based on the dynamic relation between consciousness and reality, and would respect the principle that knowledge must be supplemented by action. I do not underestimate the work that has to be done to re-establish an educational system which will teach the black child that he is a citizen of South Africa, and that he bears responsibility for this country."'

The following morning, when I arrived at the office, Mr McLean called me in.

'I am sorry about what happened yesterday,' he said.

'Well, what can we do?' I said.

'These fucking boers,' he said, 'they are ruining the country. And it is such a beautiful country!'

'I have lots of work this morning, if you don't mind. Do excuse me,' I said.

'Tell me Tsi, what do you think we can to to make the changes you're after?'

'Frankly, McLean's is not the answer,' I said.

'But surely we can do something!'

'I have to work. Why don't we arrange to discuss this some time?'

'Do arrange a discussion in the unit. Tell me when.'

'Okay.'

'Don't you think you were rather hard on the College?'

'Hard?'

'Yes.'

'No.'

'You discredited the College.'

'I spoke the truth.'

'You've got to see that we don't pay you to say things like that.'

'I thought I got paid to investigate the truth about the education of black children and that is the truth that I spoke.'

'This college is paying you.'

'I know.'

'We have nothing to do with politics. We are educators,' McLean said.

'May I go?'

'I think you must arrange for a meeting with Anne for tomorrow.'

'Okay.' I walked out of the office.

Lily and I, at my request, visited my parents that night. I told her what had happened. We drove through the deserted Johannesburg streets, silent. We reached Alexandra when my parents were preparing to go to bed.

'Lily, my darling,' my father said, 'that was a nice suit you bought me.' He held her by the hand.

'I am glad you like it,' Lily said, embarrassed.

'How are you all?' my mother asked, coming from the bedroom.

'Fine,' I said, 'how is the old lady?'

'Sweet,' she said. 'Can I make you tea?'

'I will make it,' I said. Lily was talking to my father, and my mother joined them.

McLean's work had taken me away from them for a long time. Now as I looked at them, I realised how old they were. Lily was laughing, and my mother was looking at my father, who was supporting his head, bent, looking into Lily's eyes. Suddenly, looking at them seated there, I realised how now I was taking over from my father. It was a funny feeling. It was frightening.

'Mary's boy is a big man,' my mother said. 'They were here last Sunday and they will be coming to stay in Alexandra. I don't like the house they live in, over there in Lower Houghton.'

'Oh, how is Mary?' Lily asked.

'She is fine. Oupa really looks after her.'

'How is Oupa?' I asked.

'He is doing well at school now. He says he wants to be a pilot.'

'A pilot? What does he know about being a pilot?'

'He gets these ideas from Mary's employer.'

'I see.'

'My man, what's this in the paper about you?' my father asked.

'Well, there we are,' I answered.

'Yes, yes,' my mother said, 'these boers are mad.'

'They are frightened,' my father added.

'We went to see Fix last month,' my mother told me. 'He asked a lot about what you are doing.'

'How is Fix?'

'I hate that place, I hate it,' my father said.

'God is with them,' said my mother. 'That is not a nice place, but they are in high spirits. They make you feel ignorant being outside. They are in high spirits, hopeful . . .'

'Now I know what it means,' my father said, taking up her story. 'When people's minds are made up, nothing can stop them. I never used to know that the way I know it now. It is as if you are reliving your life . . .'

'I don't envy anyone who tries to control people's minds,' my mother said.

A silence fell among us.

Part II

Nine

John was standing by the window, sipping coffee. He could hear the voices of women and children; he could hear someone laughing, and someone else singing a hymn. He had just come back from his rounds, collecting clothes for dry cleaning. He still had the white dust-coat on, and could feel the weight of coins in his left pocket, pulling his shoulder down. Many times, after that dreadful day when Nolizwe died, he would stand like this, and then he would be fighting, fighting so hard, using any trick of the mind he could think of to forget the sound of the FN rifle. He had heard it so often on that day. Also, he wanted to forget the sound of running, mad footsteps running. The smell of smoke. The sight of fire. The panic-driven, roaring cars. The screaming, screaming as if the skies were ablaze with screams, and the certain presence of death.

Death was present that day and in those days, in the street. Many people got to terms with it. John knew this, and had come to terms with it himself one day, as he was standing near the window he stood near now, watching smoke curl out of a chimney from the roof-top of a house opposite his. He had allowed his mind to run through what had happened on that day, and got it clear for the first time.

They were standing at the gate. The policemen, maybe ten or twelve of them, spread across the street, FNs held in the shooting position, were walking slowly towards the men, young and old, dogs, chickens. Without warning a car, driving madly towards the cops appeared. The cops scattered, the car passed them, and then there was a sound like several peals of thunder. The car zig-zagged, crashed into a pole, overturned and in no time was aflame. Something exploded. There were stones being thrown; gunshots rang repeatedly. There were running footsteps all over. John remembered that then he held Nolizwe's arm. She was moving away from the gate to the car. She was saying something and pointing towards the shooting cops. When in that confusion he eventually heard what she was saying, she was already out of his hold. There was no one else in the street now, but four cops who were squatting, who were taking aim. John ran for cover. Nolizwe ran towards the cops.

'You've killed my brother, you dogs!' Nolizwe kept saying, pointing at the overturned car and running towards it. Her voice was swallowed by the voice of thunder. Her gait became distorted, she slowed, twisting this and that way from the impact of the bullets which were piercing her body; she spread her arms, and then she stood very, very awkwardly in the middle of the street, alone, face to face with the killers, and like a sack, she went down head first, face into the earth, and was still.

John had watched all this from the verandah, behind a pillar. He saw the cops stand up, walk-run to their cars, and then there was dead silence. The flames from the car were reaching the sky. Several people lay like bags of coal or potatoes in the middle of the road. 'Move, everyone move back, go home, or you will be shot!' The voice from the cop car came sailing above the flames, the smoke and the dead. John stood still behind the pillar, shaking.

He had gone home that day. The radio, from that day on, had told him about many, many such scenes in his country, in those days when some of his countrymen had gone mad. He had listened to the Prime Minister say that people who thought there was a crisis in South Africa were out of their minds. John wept that day. He understood that Nolizwe was among many, was only one of the many, many people who were dying because there was no crisis in his country.

John remembered very little about the funeral. His father, after all had been done, after the dead had been cried for and buried, told him that he handled that matter like a small boy. When someone you love dies, you bury them, you don't leave them to be eaten by dogs. That is what he said to him. It was after his father left that John had gone to the window, and watched the smoke.

Nolizwe was a slender girl. She was twenty-five when she died. She had just come back from college, where she was studying law. She and John were then staying together and were going to get married one day. John had a room in Alexandra. Nolizwe, who came from the Transkei, loved and feared Alex. She had always said that she did not know why she loved it, when John asked her; perhaps, she would say, it is because I love you. She had seen many people killed in the streets here, that is why she feared it. John and Nolizwe had met, long before, at college when John was doing fine arts.

He had been expelled from there when there was a strike. There were always strikes at the black colleges, during which many were expelled and the college shut. Sometimes the cops were called in and they came with dogs and guns. Like many others, John was later detained. John and Nolizwe had talked about what had happened when he was detained. He never thought that he would be able to say, in one sitting, what had happened in those eleven months when he was in solitary confinement, in the hands of mad men. When he told her about how, when he was inside, the police took him to a window and told him to jump or to tell them the names and addresses of the people he was working with, she had said that he must know that a time was coming when we would rather die than give the names; when we would rather fall from the top floors of buildings to save the lives that must take the lives of these mad men. They never talked about it again.

Nolizwe had held his hand and kissed him full on the mouth. Then she went to bed. He stayed up that night, trying to read and to think, and also to atone. He had felt alone and ashamed of himself. And now he was driving around Alexandra, in a Kombi, collecting clothes. Many times he saw the pillar where he stood when Nolizwe fell and died. And many times, he looked into the eyes of people who knew him and who used to know Nolizwe. He did not feel guilt. He read the newspapers. He listened to the radio. He talked about the days of upsurge and power. He missed Nolizwe. Now, as he stood by the window, sipping coffee, he wondered what she would say if he told her that it was not all right that she was dead, that he missed her. He was missing her, and wanting her to know that he was feeling helpless. He was feeling helpless because his heart, which knew calamity, had frozen to steel. He was helpless because he knew now that he was a deadly man. She would laugh at him, he thought, and smiled.

She would laugh at him and say, how can you be helpless when you are deadly? And he would say, I won't get into that. That is too intellectual, believe me. She would say no, I can't believe you if you don't know what you mean. She would talk and talk and talk, but he would be as silent as she was in death. The one thing he wanted her to know was that he did not only possess a heart of steel because they had killed her, but mainly because their love, like all love in this country where there was 'no crisis', would otherwise rot and be vulgar. She would then look at him with her big, questioning eyes and say, John, what do you mean? He would laugh at her and say Noli, I mean that I feel helpless because I cannot go to anyone now and tell them, I am ready to fight, teach me how, so we can end the horror of our country. She would hug him now.

Nolizwe. He wondered now what she would say, how she would talk about what was going on. The many weeks after the 'power' days were strange weeks indeed. Alexandra had changed. There were no more beerhalls; they had been burnt down. There were many, many wrecked and burnt cars. Some shops had gone in the flames. Even the school John had attended had gone. Alexandra had been a stage for a battle. Many people had gone. Now there was this silence which pretended that things were normal. Children were not going to school. Older people were going to work as before. The buses had begun to go up and down Selborne Street again. In the power days they had stopped; many had become the property of the street; some had been rammed into stores, some into dongas, some had been fuel for the flames lighting the dark streets. Some, even after the days of power, were still glaring evidence of what rocks and bricks can do – they can smash steel! The most enduring evidence of the 'power' days was glass like that which once had glittered, sometimes adorned withmany coloured neon lights, at the Indian shops, and now glittered among the stones, rubble and debris which forever belonged to the Alexandra streets.

Glass is strange. It wails when it is hit; rings as if forever; and when it is on the ground, scattered and piled, it still winks as if to warn of impending danger. John still missed Nolizwe. Sometimes, the way he longed for her, ached. He wondered what she would say, how she would say it, how she would react to these many weeks after Power, after blood had been spilled, and many had died, and had been buried, and there was this silence. A silence during which suddenly, people asked if it were so easy to pay such a high price, what really was there still to lose? Well, Noli was gone. He was alone. The days of Power had passed. Some people had cleaned up the blood, on the stoeps and floors; some cleaned their guns. A relationship had been established; time was to nurture it.

John moved his face away from the window. His eyes were a little wet when they met the face of the clock. The vivid recollection of a bundle of clothes, red, so red, a white petticoat, a leg, without a shoe, bent awkwardly, had struck him. It was five. He put the cup on the table, took the key, locked his door and left.

Alexandra had gone back to normal. The fruitman at the corner, having saved his life during the Power days, was back. And the newspaper boy too. The hordes of workers were again out, walking to their burnt-down factories, or, having been fired for staying home during the Power days, were now going to look for another job. The shebeen queens and kings were again selling beers and all sorts of liquor. Now and then you saw people in mourning clothes. The cops, too, were there with their guns and tear-gas contraptions, to keep the peace and make things normal. No one was saying a word about what everyone knew, but for all sorts of reasons, different groups reacted differently to this knowledge. There were the people of the Alexandras, silent, walking differently, and then there were the cops, who knew how they were looked on and walked and talked as such. They could not act any other way, a button had been pressed and they were responding.

Seeing all this around him, John sometimes thought he would go mad; and then, he would decide that he personalised these public issues too much – how could he not, he would ask himself. Yet if anything was needed now, it was clear vision. As day after day, sometimes night after night, he collected clothes, talked to people, listened to them, he watched, and became more and more restless. Every day he criss-crossed Alexandra. He was at First Avenue now, and soon at Twenty-second; or now in Vasco da Gama Street and soon, right over in London Street. All the time he talked to women, men, young and old, and not a single hour passed when he did not have to sit down and talk about the days of Power and the school children. And as he emerged from the houses, from the yards, the street was there all the time, no matter where he was in Alexandra, to remind him that there had been days of Power and the time of the school children.

At night, when he went back to his room, he sometimes found Vuki waiting for him. They talked about the days of Power. Sometimes Vuki came with Dikeledi, and sometimes Onalenna, Nolizwe's great friend, would come; they would listen to music, talk, then part. Vuki also talked about theatre. Onalenna seemed to hold Vuki in high esteem for this, John always thought. She and Vuki were now engaged in a production which they said would be staged soon. It would run for a few days in Alexandra and then they might take it to Soweto for a few runs, then shelve it for a while.

For some reason or other, John stood strictly on the periphery of things. He liked Vuki a lot, and knew that Vuki liked him too. He did not know how to act with Dikeledi. Sometimes he felt shy, without knowing why. Sometimes he felt he should listen to her, at which point he felt hostile towards her. He could not explain this either. They were never at ease with each other.

He got on very well with Onalenna. But she, now and then, from the way she looked at him, seemed to ask: what are you going to do now that she is gone? She seemed uncertain when, now and then, he smiled at her, as if she was thinking about him and Nolizwe. He knew that despite her own strength, she had a very simple and idealistic view of his and Nolizwe's relationship. This always amused him and he thought that if it were not for this tragedy which explained their silent lips, he would one day tease her. He had seen her once during a performance of 'We looked for each other in the day and the night', and had realised suddenly, that in what he had always reckoned to be frivolous thought and action, there was much more. Some immense strength and knowledge was hidden in those very evasive and shy eyes.

It was at the Alexandra Creche and Welfare Centre that he saw her. That Sunday afternoon the Takalane Players, Vuki's group, was performing for Church women. The hall was packed with red, blue, green and black blouses, hats and skirts of mothers who believed in God. It was very quiet in the hall. John came in just when Vuki had dragged something back behind the stage curtains, and come back cleaning his hands. Onalenna walked forward from the back stage. She was walking slowly, with long strides, and then she spread her arms out to the sides, coughed lightly, and said:

My people the streets are clean now
We can walk them and talk to each other
Everything has been removed.

(She had stopped. Now, again slowly, she walked towards the front stage.)

They took the guns away
They took the killers away
Maybe, maybe, just maybe they won't come back.

(She smiled. It was a strange, sad smile, and her eyes were shining.)

Remember, they did it in Sharpeville long long ago
And in Cato Manor
In Sekhukhuniland and in Pondoland
In Bulhoek
Every time, after they do it,
We clean the streets.

(She gestured behind her, where Vuki was sweeping.)

We remove the blood, it's not nice to walk on
We remove the bodies
It would be terrible to see dogs eat them

And then we hope
Hope for what?
That they won't come again
That they know we don't like what they are doing?
    No
I know we know much more than that
We are people
Who have struggled a long long time
Now we have to use the lessons of our struggle!

John had sat through the play. When it ended, he walked out, into the faint sunlight, alone, and walked slowly back to his room. But he had told himself that he would never ever forget how Onalenna looked. For him, she had ceased to be the laughing, polite girl, Nolizwe's friend.

He knew now that when she was there on stage every word, every step and gesture, was real, so actual for her.

Yaonne, one of Onalenna's close friends, and John had known each other a long time before. That is how Onalenna met Nolizwe. Yao, in these terrible days, was in America somewhere, gathering fame as a painter. He and Onalenna were still in touch. Once, a long time before, Yao had written to John saying, 'I don't want to join this mess.' John never wrote back, so they lost direct contact. However, John kept in touch with Yao through Onalenna. In this way he got to know Onalenna a little better.

He knew that they, Yao and Onalenna, were going to have trouble, the distance between them accentuating the different knowledge each had acquired since they parted. He knew from Onalenna that his friend was in great danger. Yao was in trouble with himself, and since he knew nothing about being calm, and being objective, he would blame it all on the heads of those that loved him. He was dangerous in that way. Onalenna understood what Yao needed, but now the distance, the ocean with its terrible vastness, snatched the chance of helping him from her. So, since there was nothing she could do, she was going to wait. John made it clear to Onalenna that he thought she should. If Yao was in trouble she must find out more and more about how he was doing in his work, and get him to talk about that in his letters.

When Nolizwe was killed, John received a letter from Yao. He had read, and reread the letter many times. And then, after much thought, he had given it to Onalenna to read. He felt it would strengthen her. Onalenna, after reading the letter, had said nothing, and they had never talked about it after that, but John had taken it from her, put it on the table, and when he realised that she was not going to say anything, had waited impatiently for her to leave so he could read it again.

Dear John,

Fana, Nolizwe is my sister. You are my brother, So, you understand that what I was told happened to my young girl, sister, woman of fresh flesh and spirit did not hit me lightly. I am far away from home. That is terrible enough. I hear that my country has gone up in flames. That is horror, because

I cannot even move from here to there, and do what you may ask. Perhaps to be a witness is my immediate answer and now, knowing that the flames took someone I love, I must add that perhaps to die is part of the answer also. Many other people have died. This distance, and perhaps the callousness that this place is teaching me, have made me able to receive the news of the dead as a great number, that is all. I have kept newspaper cuttings of reports of what happened, how our country went up in flames. I hope to be able to record all this on canvas. I need strength and courage in case I fail. Nothing is easy now, in fact, everything is deadly difficult.

Nolizwe is dead. Was shot in the middle of the street. It was a like a movie when I saw it. I saw it on T.V. I wondered where the hell you were, and, at the same time, I said no, no, please, no, John must not appear at this hour, it would be the final blow if he did. You did not appear.

I wonder where you were. I wonder where you are. I wish I were close to you now to say to you, be strong, be strong, these times need us to be strong, that is all. Be strong my little brother, be strong, these are our times, and they have nothing nice to do to us. Keep intact until we meet again, let me hear from you.

Tell Onalenna that I do not need to get fights from her. I need to be helped, because I've fought and now I'm on the ground. She must not kick me when I'm in this state, she must not spit into my face. Sorry to give you my burden, when I should be helping you carry yours. Love and strength, Your brother.

John never replied to the letter. He merely said to Onalenna, tell Yao I received the letter. Tell him to be strong too. That is how they both ended the news of the letter. And, in time, all these silences created more complex silences. One day they would have to talk about Nolizwe; now they never did. One day they would have to talk about Yao; now they never did. One day they would have to talk about the days of Power and the school children. Now they never did. If anyone dared to talk John made it clear that that had nothing to do with him. Pushed, he either exclaimed or shrugged, that was all. Dikeledi disliked this, John's attitude. She interpreted it as self-pity. She always asked Vuki if John thought the other people, who had also lost their loved ones, did not feel pain too. Why, they went on with everyday business. Besides, it was not healthy to be so quiet. Vuki had said, maybe you should say that to him. But Dikeledi had never said it to him, though she was capable of saying it. It was not that John was not talking about these things that bothered Dikeledi. It was the way he made it clear to every one of them that whatever they were doing, he must be excluded. This they did not take well. It was as if it were a comment, a negative comment on their activities, as if John treated whatever they were doing with contempt. It was as if he was saying he was superior to them. He had an idea of what they were doing. He said nothing to them as to what he thought of their actions. They asked him. The most he said was, do what you want to do. If they asked him to join in, he merely said, 'No,' shaking his head from side to side. That was all.

'Well, I don't owe you an explanation,' John said, with a very quiet voice, not angry, not fighting, but clear.

'I know that, and it is not an explanation I want from you. I am merely saying that you have changed,' Dikeledi said.

'Have I?'

'Yes, and you know it yourself.'

Silence.

'Maybe you want to collect your clothes and be left alone, but I am saying that I have no qualms about expecting more from you,' said Dikeledi, breaking the silence.

Silence. John was looking straight into her eyes. Every now and then she looked away. He sat there, on the chair, with folded arms, not moving, hardly blinking, accepting the confrontation and meeting it for what it was in his own way. He knew that he respected Dikeledi. He found her strong, fearless and a woman of morals. She was beautiful. She knew how to wear simple clothes which fitted her well. She was a hard worker. He could shower her with praises. He liked her. True, at times he felt uneasy with her: he had not yet worked out why it was so.

'I think you are indulging in self-pity,' she said at last. It was as if she had said nothing. John recognised this for what it was. It was meant to hurt him, and he thought it very petty, so ignored it.

'I have to go now,' he said, stretching.

Silence.

He stood up to go. She looked at him. He stood there, leaning against the bookcase, at ease, expressionless, as if they had hardly said a word to each other. She was hurt. She had opened up to him, and it was as if nothing had happened. But she knew she had to let him go.

'I will see you,' she said. He walked past her, opened the door, and closed it behind him. She went into her bedroom. He drove slowly along Selborne Street under faint street lights, a semi-dark and deserted street. He wondered whether he should drive up Twelfth Avenue to see Vuki or go straight home. He wanted to go somewhere where he would not have to spend lots of energy. He wanted to be easy. He was in a loving and understanding mood. He went past Twelfth Avenue. At Fifth, he turned right. Onalenna was there, in her back room, reading. She was happy to see him, pleasantly surprised that he had stopped by.

'Haai,' he said, in his quiet manner.

'John! How are you?'

'Okay,' He shrugged. She laughed at the indifference with which he said it.

'Guess what I am reading?'

'What?'

She took the book from the table and showed him. He took it from her. Looked at it, read the title.

'Where did you get it from?'

'That's an irrelevant question,' she said.

'I see,' he said, and looked around the room for a place to sit down.

It was a neat, warm, homely room. A long room, with a table, chairs and small cupboard at one end, a bookcase in the middle, a coffee table, two sofas and a single bed which also served as a sofa on the other side of the bookcase.

Onalenna was obviously a neat, meticulous girl.

'Tea?' she asked.

'Yes, yes please,' he said.

'Have you been collecting clothes?'

'No, not really, I am a little tired.'

'So, where are you from then?'

'Dikeledi.' He sat on the sofa, at last. He stretched out, sprawling all over. Nolizwe always told him that, the way he sat down, it seemed he intended never to stand up again.

'How is she?'

'I don't know, maybe fine.'

'I have been reading here all day,' she said.

'You seem to have interesting books here,' he replied.

'Yes,' she said, 'they keep me good company.'

'I don't know if there are good books to read any more,' he said.

'You know that you are being funny when you say that,' she said.

'Okay,' he laughed lightly, 'that is true.' She brought the two cups and they sat down to drink tea.

'What's Yao up to?'

'Yao is in a terrible state, I keep trying to say he must know that he has charge of his life, he will destroy it or build it, then back comes a mad letter, completely crazy.' Her eyes were shining.

'He has charge of his life?'

'Yes.' She was not looking at him. He was staring at her.

'What do you mean by that?'

'That he can take care of himself or be reckless with his life.' She was still paging through her book, with one hand, while the other held the cup of tea.

'So you think that Yao woke up one morning and said well, from now on I am going to write mad letters to Oni?'

'I do not think Yao could do a thing like that.' She looked at him, and saw his stare, cold, full of contempt.

'Do you know why he writes mad letters?'

'John, I am out of touch with Yao, I do not know him. I can't recognise him in the letters that he writes to me.'

'I think if you can help him, you must, if you think you have the energy, and the care. It looks like Yao is in some kind of trouble spiritually, it looks like . . .'

'He is.'

'Help if you can.'

'I will try to phone him tomorrow, just to assess what is going on.'

'Where will you phone him from?'

'I will talk to Dikeledi.' She stretched on the sofa, yawning.

'Are you good friends with Dikeledi?

'Ja, why?' Oni was hiding a smile.

'I told you that I just came from her place?'

'Ja.'

'What's with her?'

'How do you mean?'

'Yes, indeed, what do I mean anyway . . .'

'I think it is important that you realise that she respects and likes you. I think that is important, but she expresses it in all sorts of strange ways as I can gather from what you say about her, and what she says about you.' She was silent for a while, fidgeting with her fingers and nails. Then she looked up at him. 'I do not think that it is correct for either of you to push or pull anything. Both of you are mad enough to be able to break loose and go mad.'

'I see what you mean.'

'She is a good woman.'

'Well . . .'

'Nolizwe liked her a lot.'

'So I am to like her too?'

'No, that is not . . .'

'I was going to say Nolizwe used to think she was the toughest, brightest woman on earth, and I used to tell her: in her earth, not everyone's earth!'

'She had a tough mother, too.'

'Has no one heard about her father?'

'No, she has not said anything to me about that yet.'

'Oni tell me, what do you think is going to happen in this country eventually?'

'I think the right question would be, if you don't mind my correcting you, what can we do to change what is going on?'

Silence.

'Because otherwise, if you put it the way you put it, it means all we can do is react.'

'Well, Oni, I am putting it like that because you and I now know a lot about the holocaust, the most one-sided one.'

'So you are expecting another one to come and take you too?'

'Me too . . .'

'The first took Nolizwe.'

Silence. He stared at her. He thought she was a very beautiful girl. Her eyes said so. She was an intelligent and sensitive girl, even her fingers said it. He got up from the sofa and walked towards the door. He put his back towards it, put his hands in his pockets, relaxed, put all his weight on the door.

'That is not a nice thing to say,' he said eventually.

'I did not mean it like that,' she said, and stood up from the sofa. 'You know I would not mean it like that, John.'

'What do you mean then?'

'I am saying that that lesson must at least teach us how to defend ourselves,' she said, breathless.

'Dikeledi thinks I am drowning in self-pity,' he said. Ono had never seen

John in this state. He was not blinking. He stared straight. His eyes pierced through, shining, twinkling, and he had this easy, very easy smile as he said: 'I do not care who says what about this, but I know I loved Nolizwe. I loved her with all my heart and I don't think she died the right way, and it is not because I loved her that I think so, it is because I do not think that any child should die like that. But since they do, we shall start from there . . . I am hurt that Nolizwe died. I am horrified that she died the way she died, but I realise that something else has to happen. When I realise how many people died in Soweto, Langa, Guguletu, Witbank, Kagiso, Atteridgeville and many, many other places in these past days, then in a sense I feel helpless. But then, also I don't, for I know things cannot go on this way forever. Then I ask myself, what do I mean by that? Do you realise that as we talk now you and I are not safe?'

'We may not be safe, but that does not mean that we may not learn how to be safe.'

'By hiding behind a pillar? . . . I don't want to be safe in that way.'

'Did you see our play?'

'Yes, I did. I thought you were great.' He smiled, stretching his hands out.

'We are trying to say that if they come back with guns, it should not be as if they have not been to us with guns before. They must know that we learnt our lessons, and that we mean to change the system they carry guns for.'

'How did you get those old ladies to come to the play?'

'We talked to the priest. And then we talked to the ladies, and then they came.'

'Do you think that people understand what you are saying in that play?'

'There is nothing as intelligent as human beings,' Oni said quietly, and then lay back on the sofa. John began to fidget with his shirt button, looking down. He thought, you bitch, I don't know what to think of you, of all you say. John wanted to go home now. He wanted the silence of the Kombi. The silence of the deserted street.

'I agree with you,' he said finally, and walked back to the sofa. 'There was nothing intelligent, though, in the actions of the past months, no matter which way you look at it, the way people were shot or the way they died, there was nothing intelligent in all that. I agree with you, though.'

'Do you want more tea?'

'Yes, give me another cup.'

John, sipping his tea, now sitting on the sofa again, in that sitting-forever posture of his, was thinking that indeed, he could not agree more with Oni. Indeed, there was nothing as intelligent as a human being. It was as soon as this intelligence manifested itself that you discovered how stupid human beings could be. 'We are so intelligent, so intelligent we chose to live here, in this hole,' he said, smiling; it was a very sad smile. John was lost. He agreed that human beings were intelligent, but nowhere around him, around those he thought he loved, was there a sign, just a sign that said anything about anyone being intelligent. He was now completely relaxed on the sofa, he eyes moving slowly up and down Oni, wondering what really Oni thought of Yao, and what

Yao thought of Oni. Noli would have said, they don't know how much they need each other, that is why they will indulge themselves in petty pride and frivolous action. How foolish, how foolish people are, that is what Noli would say. She would say that most broken marriages were so for no reason than that. People, the men and the women, indulged themselves in such petty things, that by the time they were through with each other, licking wounds all round, it was only then that they realised that they had come to know the other person, had come to love each other. They had spent so much energy exploring and finding out about themselves, about the other person, and they would never be able to do that again with any other person. He and Noli had argued a lot about this, and many times when they quarrelled Nolizwe, in her rage, would ask: 'You do still love me, don't you?'

'What do you think?'

'No, say yes I do, or no I don't, face it!'

'Do you?'

'John, you are being petty, I do love you, and if you love me shall we drop this foolishness,' she would say, and she would talk about something else, or walk out, or do something else until she had been able to forget their quarrel and to approach it with calmness. They were silent now. Oni, folded and curled on the sofa, stared at the dancing candle flame. It was blue, pink, red and yellow, dancing, dancing, eating the wax slowly. She wondered where Yao was, what he would be doing wherever he would be. It seemed like a long, long time, so long ago, since that time when they were together. It was obvious that he, Yao, was trying very hard indeed to deal with the Power days. He said so many things. Oni smiled.

'John, shall I read you something?'

'Yes,' John said, sitting up, 'sure.'

Oni left her sofa, and went to the bookcase. She took out a file, paged through it, then went back to the sofa after she had extracted a letter from the file.

'This is from Yao. I will just read parts of it . . .'

'Yes, otherwise I would be bored,' John said, and they both laughed.

'I . . . I saw it all on TV,' she read, 'children dying, mothers, fathers, I saw it, fire, blood, and these two in their own way look alike. So they died. Many times I wondered whether I would also see you stagger, give the death dance, and fall dead. I love you, even though I sound so reckless with your life. I wonder what I would have done. Sit here in America and say they killed my baby, or paint your face, hit at by bullets, or would I have taken a plane and come over, die like you did? Which do you think would have had wisdom?' She lifted her head, like a bird that had been drinking, looked at him, was satisfied, looked back at the letter again and read some more. 'There has been lots of action here around that damn issue. They call it Soweto here. Sometimes, when I am sitting around and talking about the Soweto issue, with both the black and the white yankees, I feel like saying okay now, you bloody shits, did you know that as I am sitting here and talking, I think that you are directly responsible for the deaths in this, *your* Soweto? I wonder what they

106

would say? Also, I wonder what that means politically . . . does it mean anything? You must know these things baby, you taught me about all this, remember . . . I was painting so I should not go mad, and you came with your story, I changed, began to paint to either record or express the truth about my people . . . big deal hey? . . .' She stopped.

'What's mad about that?'

'It's mixed up.'

'Do you understand what he is saying?'

'Ja, I do. I wonder if he does.'

'I have to go now.' He stretched, yawned, took the keys from the table, and began to walk towards the door. He grabbed the door handle, and turning to face her, said in a strange voice. 'How can you love someone you hold in contempt?'

'What do you mean?'

'Anyway, that is not my business, you all go on and love each other. I will see you.' He closed the door behind him and left. The night was dark now. The streets empty. The lights faint and twinkling. He drove slowly, back to Eighth Avenue, to his house. John knew that he was living alone. He knew that he did not know any more what he would talk about. He did not believe in all these things that people were saying. Something was wrong. What? He parked the Kombi. He took out his door keys, unlocked the door and sat down, wishing that his mind could go blank. He thought about Nolizwe. He thought about Oni. He thought about Yao. About Dikeledi. He wondered what in this silent night, dark, empty, was happening to Dikeledi's father. South Africa is a strange country. The people of this country are locked in a tight embrace which is going to destroy them. The white people. The black people. The gold. The diamonds. The guns. The bombs. South Africa, such a beautiful country. The bright sun, the warm days and nights, the rainy days, the mountains, trees, rivers, such a unique country. John felt illiterate, naive and stupid, thinking all these things. What had all these to do with a reality which was death? He began to make up the bed, undressed, and got into it. No, this must never happen again, he must never go back to Oni's house, it was dangerous. It was obvious that both of them were lonely. Both of them needed soothing and to be comforted; it was dangerous for them. He wondered where, here on earth, would he meet and talk to another girl, and begin to form a relationship which would push him back to life. He felt tears coming; Nolizwe, God, Nolizwe. He must never go back to Oni's house. That would hurt Yao. He must never, ever be responsible for regrets and hurts which possibly could last for a lifetime. He must never put himself in that situation again. He was not even going to talk about it. No reason could pierce this. He was going to handle it the way he knew, the way he thought best for them all. He must go to see Vuki soon. John lay there, and felt his whole body scream. It was screaming, and screaming, and he called, in a whisper, Nolizwe's name. He lay flat on his stomach. His eyes closed. His hands spread, and his legs clenched together till the tightness of his buttocks began to ache. Death had taken his companion. He wondered if Nolizwe had gone to heaven, or to hell. He wondered if she lay there dead and torn in the street, whether that was it. There was nothing any more called Nolizwe, anywhere, not in the empty sky nor anywhere else. What a waste, he thought.

He wondered where Themba, Jully and Tuki were now. He had known them a long, long time ago. They had been to the funeral, Jully and Themba together. Tuki with Dikeledi and Vuki. He liked them. They all came from the same place, from the same time. He had not seen them in a long, long time now. In all this, Nolizwe was missing. She was not there. The violence of this country.

With gold and diamonds, with lakes and mountains, the most civilized country in Africa, the most powerful, the last of the potence . . . the violence of this country had within a very short space of time shrivelled this young girl's life, in the most cruel, most crude way, and ended it. He missed her. He thought about her. He fitted her in spaces where he thought she should be in life, since he believed that in death Nolizwe had turned to nothing, she was no more, she was not even in the empty sky, or even in the fire of hell, she ended there, in the middle of the street, with her nose in the earth, as she fell. He remembered how Jully looked when, after the funeral, Themba stood there looking at him and said, 'Power to you, John.' He had never heard it being said like that before. With strength, with confidence, even if they killed her that won't stop us. Jully, silent, her eyes shining, had smiled at him.

John had been struck by them. They had not only come from the same place and from the same time, they had also come from the same space, or to put it correctly, from no space at all. It was this that made John wonder about them. Alexandra is a very small place. It is big in terms of space. It is small in terms of numbers the space is made to carry. Here, everybody knows almost everybody. It had taken Nolizwe's life being snuffed out like that for John to know that indeed, they had been in the public eye. Many people, old and young, many many people, some staring, some searching, some crying, some laughing, some, God, all of these things, had come to him, had said something about Nolizwe and about him. They had been in the public eye.

When the Power days were over, there was silence. The law said it had cracked down on unlawfulness and disorder, and had been able to suppress it. The newspapers and radio spoke of hundreds. It was now impossible to count, but hundreds of school children had been killed. Everything had died down now. Things had gone back to normal. The police, with their guns and dogs, still came, to keep things normal. The people woke up and went to work. They saw the police and they never talked to them, except when it was necessary to say yes, I will move, or no, I am not walking around, I am going to work. The situation was normal. The children refused to go to school, even urged their parents not to go to work.

The newspapers and the radio seized on a theme. The big industrialists, the people and companies who owned hordes and hordes of people, who owned the land, what was above the ground and below it, who owned everything and anything which produced, who made this country, South Africa, a topic

108

in all the capital cities of the world, these people and companies now welcomed what the newspapers were throwing around as a theme, a solution, that white and black can share lifts, can sit in some places together, in toilets, or restaurants, or even buses and park benches. South Africa, fearful, vacillating, attempted these solutions; in sports, that white and black could swim together; that they could play ball together; or tennis; or dance together. The big civilized party was on. Somebody called Kissinger visited the sunny land. Things, it was said, were normal. The dead had been buried, those in mourning were to be consoled. The guns were kept ready. The jail doors kept swinging, and swinging.

Tuki had been all over South Africa in those days. And he had been back to Alexandra in time to attend the many, many funerals. When John went to see them, he was told that they no longer lived in the same place. Nobody had seen them. Oni did not know where they were. Dikeledi did not know where they were. Jully said Themba was all right. She would tell him that John was looking for him, but she did not know when she would see him. Their son, Fidel, always asked about Themba.

This morning, when John started on his rounds, he stopped at Fourteenth Avenue, collected his clothing. Mary was there, and Oupa. John knew Oupa, he also knew that Oupa was trying his hand at painting or sculpting, and was an aspiring writer. Yao had told him so. Oupa, it seemed, also wrote poetry or something like that. When John arrived this morning Oupa was sitting outside, on the stoep, sipping coffee. He smiled when he saw John.

'How is business, you are still at it, heh?'

'Well, how are you?'

'All right.'

'I have not seen you in a long, long time.'

'Yes, I was out of town for a while.'

'Are you still working with Vuki?'

'Yes, on and off.'

'Where is Mary?'

'She is in the house.'

John sat next to Oupa. He kept swinging the keys to the Kombi around his fingers. Oupa offered him tea. They sat there drinking.

At nineteen, Oupa had managed to see his country. He was a bright boy, with a strange ringing laughter, a bright smile, a typical boy from the corner, moulded and nurtured by Alexandra. It was a miracle that he had not died in the donga, or was not doing time in jail, or was not paralysed from some knife wound or gun shot. It was a miracle that Oupa did the things which he was doing now, which he did with all his heart. He was writing poetry. And, now and then, he took to the brush. He thought of himself more as a writer except that English, which he learnt at school, gave him problems — but he took it as a challenge. He read, asked questions, kept the company of those who had been to higher institutions of learning. We could say, terrible as that might be, that there was hope for Oupa. When Yao was still here they put in lots of time together and when Tuki was still here, they put in lots of time together. Now, when he saw Tuki, Tuki was in a hurry, always in a hurry and Oupa understood why. John occasionally treated Oupa as his younger brother. He liked Oupa because he was respectful. Oupa was taking care of himself in many ways.

The sun was pleasant on their skin. It was warm. There was a cool breeze blowing. Since it was during the day and it was Alexandra, most people were gone to work, yards were deserted, it was quiet. Now and then you could hear a dog barking. Now and then you could hear a car roar away into the distance. Oupa and John felt quite relaxed; and, since they had not seen each other for such a long time, and since each held the other in respect, it was pleasant for them to be there together. They both felt very relaxed, and close to one another. Oupa wanted to know how John was doing in his dry-cleaning.

'I manage to eat, that is all,' he said.

'Long ago I would have thought that is important, you know what I mean?'

'I think so.'

'It was very foolish to think so.'

'Well, there had been too much foolishness around.'

'Why did you call your dry cleaning thing "One Day Service Dry Cleaners?"'

'People always wanted their clothes back as fast as possible, so I was saying I will bring them back fast,' John said smiling.

'Did you?' Oupa was laughing now.

'You, as my customer, know I did not,' John said, nudging him.

'But the trick does work, though.'

'It is not my fault really, you know I don't own this thing, I am working for someone else. He gave me this Kombi. I have to work and pay him back. He runs the show really, since I owe him, and I will always owe him. The roads are bad. I have to keep the car on the road all the time, to be able to pay him my monthly repairs, and all the other things. It drains every penny I make, so he does me favours, and I have to know that, so I owe him all my time.'

'What would happen if you did not pay?'

'He would take me to jail.'

'You know this is very funny. Why is it that the employers, the police, all of them work together against the ordinary man?'

'It's a network.'

'You remember how the police protected the factories, shops, cars, everything that belongs to the big guns, during the Power days?'

'Ja. Many people were killed because they got too close to the property of the big guns.'

'You know, really, I never saw anything like it, those Power days! Those days! I have never seen anything like that.'

'Lots of people were killed.'

'Yes, but also, for the first time, we were one; school children, father, mother, teacher, shopkeeper, rich and poor, we stood as one and fought, and helped each other. For the first time, you know.'

'You know what still surprises me is that even the boys joined in. It was safe to walk the streets then, no one got killed by the boys in the street, no one was robbed; the police were the most dangerous people out there in the streets, you know that?'

'The man was unmasked for what he is, he can tell no one a lie any more.'

'He killed many people; God, so many children.'

'You know, I just came back from Cape Town. I talked to a few people there. You know what, John, South Africa will never be the same again, you know why? People have realised, have discovered who they are, and what they can do.'

'What were you going to do in Cape Town?' ·

'Work.' Oupa stared at John. Somehow John knew he was not to ask further questions.

'Ja.' John picked up his cup and sipped, staring at the sky.

'It is not only in Cape Town or Johannesburg and in other parts of the country that people have discovered that they have some power.'

'I know what you mean, I have been thinking that. I had never realised before how guns can be so helpless.'

'People were shot, but it does not end there.'

'No, it does not; we all are resting now.'

'I heard about Nolizwe. I am sorry John.' This took John by surprise.

'I could not attend the funeral. I was in Pietersburg then. I went to some funerals there too.'

'There were many funerals in our country,' John said, and strange as it was, this seemed to soothe him.

'Ja.' Silence fell on them. Oupa started to write something on the stoep, then did something to his shoe. Remembered the cups, took his, and stood up.

'Do you want more tea?'

'Well, okay.' John shrugged as if to say it did not make any difference. Oupa took the cups and vanished into the house. John could hear him talking to his mother Mary. Oupa called his mother by her name.

Mary had always struck John, even when he himself was still young, as a strangely quiet woman. She seemed never to talk. She went about her business, keeping a distance, saying nothing, but never hostile, though something clearly told you to leave her alone. There are people like that. People who it seems have so much strength, they can go on their own, isolated, taking the storm and surviving it. John knew that Mary, one day long ago, when Oupa was on the way, had been chased out of her father's house. She was told never to put a foot in that house again. John knew this, maybe Alexandra knew this. Mary vanished for a long, long time, and now here she was. Silent. She now has a house, two rooms, lives with her son; it seems they are the only two in the world. Oupa had given her lots of trouble. John knew this, many people knew this. Mary still smiled, she talked in a very soft voice, such a soft voice, her eyes shining, smiling, even when Oupa, loud, fighting, reckless, like all children are, uttered so much foolishness to her. Mary remained quiet, smiled, talked. Somehow, you knew she knew Oupa was listening.

Oupa emerged from the house carrying the two cups like huge eggs which were to be guarded with one's life. He put the cups down on the hot stoep. He sat down next to John.

'Mary thinks I spend too much time in the street. She says she is happy you are here to keep me in.' Oupa smiled.

'I could never keep him in, Mary,' John said.

'I know,' came the quiet voice.

'Mary, be nice, I stay home when I have to,' Oupa said.

'Which is once a month,' Mary said, 'and that is too little. How can I say I have a son?'

'You do have me,' Oupa said conclusively.

John's thoughts had drifted away. The day was going. He had not covered all the things he meant to cover when he woke up that morning. He still had to go to town. He had not collected many clothes.

'Have you heard from Yao?'

'No, I have not written to him. But Oni tells me he seems to be a little disturbed.'

'He wrote me about the upheavals.'

'That seems to have troubled Yao a lot.'

'It must, he is far away.'

'What else did he say?'

'He does not like America. Not at all.'

'Yes, so Oni told me.'

'He even says that it is wrong to think the way we do about Afro-Americans.'

'What way?'

'He says they are totally different people from us.'

'They are Americans.'

'Ja.'

'I have to go now,' John said and gulped down his tea.

'Where are you going to?'

'I am still doing my rounds.'

'Have you seen Vuki lately?'

'Yes, I see him often.'

'You saw their play?'

'Yes, yes, I fear for them.'

'Ja.'

'It's good, though.'

'Ja, it is.'

'Are you still working with them?'

'Not really, not in the sense that I am in their play any more.'

John stood up and stretched, yawning loudly. Oupa took the cups inside. He came back and walked down the steps. John followed him. They both walked towards the gate.

'I will come to see you soon,' Oupa said.

'Okay, anytime.' John got into the Kombi, started it, and began to drive down the road.

Ten

David Horwitz had long greyish hair, green darting eyes, a neat beard and, although there was nothing fantastic about his clothes, he dressed meticulously. He was clever, confident and very polite, almost shy. Whenever Dikeledi listened to him talking, she smiled. She thought that David's tongue was big in his mouth, and words seemed to struggle out as his thick voice and tongue made them. David's eyes, when Dikeledi smiled, darted about seeking a place to settle on, but without finding it. Dikeledi was aware of this, but unconsciously she would stare at him, deep into the green darting eyes, listening to his voice build up. David would turn pink, and begin to look as if he wanted to run away. What surprised Dikeledi was that although David seemed to be having a tough time, not a single morning passed without his coming into her office, unnecessarily she thought, and when he was there, he seemed not to know what to do with his hands which now and then brushed his long legs, drummed the desk top, or fidgeted with the papers on her table.

This afternoon, just before knock-off time, David walked into her office, pulled on his cigarette, puffed a cloud of smoke up to the ceiling, then coughed. All the time Dikeledi was looking at him, her face expressionless.

'I have a story to do in Pretoria, would a lift help you?'

'Sure,' Dikeledi said, giggling unnecessarily.

'Okay, I'll call you in a minute.' He walked out immediately. Dikeledi looked up at the ceiling thoughtfully and she smiled. She stood up, cleared the desk and put on her coat. She sat down to look through her diary.

Although she was paging through the diary slowly, she did not see what was written in there; she was thinking, thinking about David, Pretoria, lift to Alexandra — since when? She smiled mischievously. Her beautiful, childlike face, her dark staring eyes, wore a watchful expression.

Her phone rang.

'Black reporters, Dikele . . . ja, oh, yes, yes! . . . okay.' She hung up. She took her bag and looked at herself in the mirror that hung behind her. Satisfied, she took the keys from the table and walked out. She got into the lift, pressed B3.

'Hi.' He turned pink as he opened the door for her. She closed the door.

'How is Susan and the kids?'

'Er . . . ja. Fine. Sorry,' he said as the gear ground. 'Er, she's fine, did I tell you that she has left her job?'

'Oh, no, you did not tell me.' She was staring at him.

'Yes she had. She feels she would like to have time to look after the kids. We have, well, a little problem. Our ser . . . I mean, our er, the woman who works for us — Sue says her conscience can't allow her to keep her . . .'

113

'Why?'

'Because, well, you see the problem here is how different are we from other whites who have servants, who have swimming-pools, two cars, a garden boy, you know what I mean?'

'Ja.'

'What do you think?' He cleared his throat. 'You see, it is a bloody conflict because, you see, if we don't employ her, someone will or she will starve. I don't know, but what's your opinion?'

'I have no opinion about that. I have no woman working for me.'

There was a strange silence in the car.

'Ja, I see what you mean,' he said after some time. 'The kids are also very fond of her. When we told them that Doreen might have to go home forever, Mark protested. He would hear nothing of that. He said he would go with her.' He tried to smile. Dikeledi looked at him. She caught him, he was not looking at her, at her face, he was looking at her lap. She stared at him, and she knew, she knew what he was thinking. She looked out through the window, feeling anger rise in her chest. The car stopped at the light. Another car pulled up next to theirs. Her eyes met the blue ones hissing out from the other car's window. A second car pulled up on David's side. A woman looked at him, past him at Dikeledi, and then back to the huge man next to her. Another pair of eyes joined the interrogation. The light turned green.

Dikeledi looked straight ahead. David had turned pink. He sighed, shook his head and leaned back in his seat. Maybe it would be best to move to England. He would have to move first, then the kids and his wife would follow. They would leave behind them all the bloody problems. Servants. Nasty neighbours. Guilt of being white. Shit, the lot. But before they left, he would like to go to the Cape, to Cape Town where he grew up. In that beautiful city, so peaceful, so natural, they would stay maybe three weeks. Then, then, he would fly out to London. Maybe Germany. France. Which? In London he would not find difficulty adjusting, but he wondered if the children would adjust. Sue, what would she do? Teach, but she always complains when she is teaching; or maybe study, get her MA once and for all.

He looked at Dikeledi.

'Er . . . D, where would you like me to drop you? I mean, will I have any trouble if I go into Alexandra?'

'No, don't take me into Alexandra. I will show you where to drop me, and I'll walk down.'

'Okay, if you say so,' he sighed. 'Are they still raiding for permits?'

'Who are "they"?'

'I mean the police,' he smiled.

'Don't you think the best knowledge is first-hand?'

'Ja, I see what you mean.'

'Drive over the bridge, then turn left.'

'Okido.'

Hordes of people were pouring into Alexandra, some in groups, others in twos, threes, fours, and the steel river was roaring under the bridge. Packed buses sped in, slowing dangerously as they turned the long corner.

'Turn right here.'

'Okido.'

As the car slowed down, Dikeledi recognised many, many people hastening home. She felt a little sad, she did not know why. She just wanted to be silent, to look at all those people, to think: it was peaceful that way. She took her bag from her lap. She stretched, and fidgeted with her skirt.

'I'm okay here Dave, thanks, I will see you tomorrow.'

The car stopped. David was looking out through the window at the many, many people walking like that. He turned to look at Dikeledi. 'It's a pleasure, D, good-bye.' He engaged gear, and the car moved. He looked in the rear-view mirror but could not see her. She was one of those many, many people.

Dikeledi walked down slowly, lazily, her bag dangling over her shoulder. She felt tired, but a little happier now that she knew she was near home, near her mother and sister, Mpho. She stopped at the corner of Sixth Avenue and Selborne Street, unzipped her bag and took out money. She bought bananas and apples and oranges from the woman vendor. A bus stopped and people flowed out like water. There was a *World* poster at the corner. 'Pantie slitter shot' it read, in huge red letters.

Dikeledi walked into Seventh Avenue. She greeted the old man who sat on the stoep, his spectacles almost falling down his nose.

'Where are you, my child?'

'I'm here, may I hear from you?'

'I am awake my child, getting older and older every day.'

'It's time.' She walked on, then turned into a gate. The dog, Bobby, wagged its tail, ran towards her. She did not take notice of it.

'Mpho, how can you have the radio on so loud?'

'Ausi Dikeledi, greet me first, don't complain first.'

'I'm sorry,' she laughed. 'But how could you hear me if the radio was so loud?'

'Nicely, you know what? Ntate-Jake's wife says Mama gave her luck with her dream.'

'What dream?'

'Mama told her that she had dreamt bees. Ntate-Jake's wife bet a beautiful woman for twenty cents and won.'

'Yes, she gave me fifty cents,' their mother interrupted.

'You took it, Mama?'

'Yes, how can I refuse a gift?'

'But she needs it more,' Dikeledi protested.

'You can never refuse a gift,' their mother maintained.

'Mpho, there's fruit in that paper.'

'My sister, many thanks.' She unwrapped the paper.

'Hey, that is my child, bring that here,' their mother said to Mpho. 'Bring, bring here.'

'She's my sister too,' Mpho protested.

'So what?'

'Nothing.'

'Hey, you two!' Dikeledi was taking off her coat.

'Mpho, make tea, make tea now, come on!'

'Mama wants to hide the fruit in the wardrobe, and eat them alone when I am at school. Ja, I know. You know Ausi Dikeledi, I had three sweets from that packet which you brought on Saturday. I never smelt them again.'

'Hoo, I forgot them, where did I put them?' She stood up and vanished into the bedroom. She came back, carrying an O K Bazaars paper bag.

'Come and choose, my child, and then make tea,' she said, holding the paper bag out towards Mpho.

'How's work today, Mama?' Dikeledi asked, coming out of her bedroom, dressed in a loose frock.

'Fine, fine, nothing new.' She peered into the paper bag and chose a chocolate. 'You came early today.'

'I got a lift from a white man we work with.'

'I see.'

'Ausi Dikeledi, I met Aboeti Vuki. He says I must tell you not to forget about Sunday.'

'Where did you meet him?'

'When I came back from school.'

'I said where?'

'Er, er at Fourth.'

'I must not forget about Sunday?'

'Ja. I don't know, I did not ask anything.'

'O ja, I nearly forgot, they have a performance on Sunday, let me check my diary.'

Dikeledi sat back on the sofa, spreading her legs, almost stretching. 'Shall I go with you?'

'When, Sunday?'

'Ja.'

'Okay. Mpho, make tea, stop swinging on that cupboard!'

'Sorry.'

'And er, Dikeledi, your father needs an overall.'

'Who says?'

'They were here today.'

'An overall?'

'Mmmmm.'

'What are they doing with an overall?'

'Do we know?' their mother said in resignation. She lifted her hands to her head and locked her fingers over her floral doek as if there was a huge load on her head. Silence fell in the house while the primus stove roared monotonously.

'When were they here?' Dikeledi asked after some time.

'Just after I came back from work,' their mother said. Silence fell again. Grace, their mother, was a tall, not slender woman in her late fifties. Even at her age, she had big sensuous eyes, bright white and deep black. They stared

116

as if not staring, and very few people could take their stare. Her mouth was big and her pretty nose lay there gently, like a miracle. She had strong, almost manly hands. Her legs were long and beautiful: she stood and walked erect. When she was young her bust had been her pride. Dikeledi was her duplicate, still in the bloom of her youth. When Grace spoke, she would lean forward, her hands caught between her thighs, her upper abdomen erect, her bust shooting out, her eyes staring straight. Her voice would float with command, the words rolling out.

She was the director of the Alexandra Welfare Centre, and the creche. Her husband had been the principal of Alexandra High, until trouble came. They had had three children. Morolong, their son, was the eldest, then came Dikeledi and Mpho. Mpho had her mother's features, but she took after her father more. She was not going to be tall, but she was dark and pretty, and she had his curious mind. Her mother thought that her father had spoiled her a bit, and now and then she took Mpho in a firm grip. Mpho always took it well.

She gave her mother tea, then gave some to her sister. She sat down on the mat, almost leaning her head against her mother's knee. Her mother dug her nails into her head.

'Have you seen how muddy your neck is?'

'Ah, Mama, I washed it this morning, I did, with soap.'

'Dikeledi, just look at this, can you say this has been washed?'

'Ah but Mama, I washed it this morning.'

'I will have to wash you every morning from tomorrow.'

'No, how can you wash me?'

'Don't go on like you are fifteen, you are still a baby.'

'I am not a baby.'

'Here, pour me some more tea.'

'Mama, say please,' Mpho protested.

'Please my child, give Mama some more tea.'

'Good, Mama,' she said smiling.

'I will get Papa's overall at month's end, is that okay Mama?' said Dikeledi, coming back from her world.

'I told them I would take it there on Monday.'

'Do you have money?'

'Ja, I think so.'

'I will pay you back month-end.'

'You don't have to!'

'No, I want to buy it, with my own money.'

'Well, if you insist.'

'Ausi Dikeledi, you are cooking today, neh?'

'What? I'm too tired, I am not cooking, I am not in the mood.'

'Haaa, but it's your turn today.'

'Hey, shut up, I am not cooking, you think I'm your equal at times, neh?' Dikeledi shot out in a sudden burst of anger. 'I have been working the whole day, now you want me to cook.'

'But . . .'

'Hey, just shut up and do your work, stop answering back,' Dikeledi cut in.

'Mpho my child, just be a nice one and cook,' her mother pleaded, knowing Dikeledi.

'Ah, but why must Ausi Dikeledi cheek me then?'

'What do you think? What do you think? You think I should not talk to you?' Dikeledi stood up and went into her bedroom. She threw herself on the bed, buried her head in the pillow.

She was feeling very tired. Not only tired. There was a lonely pain that struck her in the centre of her heart. David. She turned over, and lay on her back, her legs crossed. What's he up to? She knew, but she allowed herself to be uncertain. There seemed to be some kind of huge wall, dark and thick, which protected her. She would never allow David to come near her. She would never. And it came to her mind how that day, long ago, when she was from school, from Botswana, it had nearly happened. She was seated in a train, in her compartment, looking out through the window. There was a knock on the door, she had opened, and he had come in, smiling, his eyes flashing. Zeke, her class mate. He sat next to her, uncomfortably close to her, and for a long time he was talking. She did not hear what he was saying, but she heard his thick voice, rolling over the rattling train wheels, and the scenery, dry and sandy, rushed past backwards. The small, thorny shrubs rushed past, backwards, and the voice rolled on and on, and the rattle went on and on. And then, suddenly, he had held her hand. His was warm and shaking; she did not know what to do. She nearly screamed with fright, but then she did not. Something told her that she would appear stupid. She waited, feeling his hand moving over hers. He was saying, I love you Dikeledi, won't you answer me? She looked at him; his eyes ran about, then almost looked at her face. She looked at him, and he began to stammer. She looked at him, and he leaned back, looked up at the ceiling, talking softly. She looked out through the window: the same shrubs, sand, lean cattle, lean sheep, lean goats, grazing dry, almost brown grass. His hand was no longer on her hand, it was on her lap. She looked at him. He was looking up, but she could feel him watching her, she could feel him closing up, and she did not know what to do. His hand was moving. She looked at him. He did not look at her. His hand was tightening up. She felt something, something, in her breast, no, in her thighs, no . . . she began to shiver, she felt hot, her face was hot, and there was this thing throbbing, somewhere. In her breast? Where? She leaned over his shoulder; she felt his hot face. She looked at him; he kissed her full on the mouth, clutched her tight. There was a knock on the door. She had jumped up, pushed him away from her. One look at her had told him he would never get her again.

Dikeledi sighed. She turned over on the bed and felt tears in her eyes, her chest heaving. She wiped her face and got off the bed. She felt light, as if some load had been removed from her chest. She stood before the mirror. Her huge eyes were red as liver; her nose was broad and flat; her lips grey; she could see the veins on the side of her head throbbing as if they would burst. She took out some tissues from the box on the dressing table and wiped her nose, eyes and mouth. She moved from the dressing table, to the wardrobe, to the bed, with no aim.

There was a knock on the door. Mpho peeped through the open door and called her sister's name.

'Ja?'

'Food is ready.'

'Bring mine this side.'

Mpho stood for a long time, slightly away from the door. Then she walked away. She held her mother's hand.

'Mama, do you think I wronged Ausi Dikeledi?'

'Why?'

'She does not want to come and eat with us.'

'What did she say?'

'She says I must take her food to her bedroom.'

'Take it there. She wants to be alone. That does not mean you wronged her.'

Mpho took the plate from the table, and walked towards Dikeledi's room. When she heard her sister's small footsteps approaching, Dikeledi opened the wardrobe door as if to search for something. Mpho knocked and waited.

'Come in.'

She walked in. She was sorry she could not see her sister's face.

'Here's your food, Ausi Dikeledi.'

'Thaa,' Dikeledi said, without facing her sister. Mpho walked out disappointed. Dikeledi changed into her nightdress. She peeped out through the door.

'Goodnight, Mama, goodnight Mpho,' she said and closed the door. She lay on the bed, on her back, looking at the ceiling, thinking she must buy a bookcase, she must renew her room. Her thoughts floated, like a thick cloud wandering in the sky, curling and curling, round and round. Her eyes closed.

Grace, from the time when Dikeledi was a small girl, had treated her daughter with care. Her care curled round Dikeledi, protecting her first woman child. The male child, Morolong, was weaving his way through school while Dikeledi stayed home. She was very fond of Morolong, who in many ways resembled his father. He was a tall, broad-shouldered boy, not handsome. He always had something going on, he alone knowing it. Morolong was a lone male, unsure of his step, shy. When he was small, his mother had a difficult time guiding him along; he seemed not to care about anything. His room was always littered with lots of things; trousers on the floor, socks, papers; and when Grace reprimanded him his big red eyes would torch around, his lips swollen, his hands in his pockets. He would stand there as if nothing was happening to him. This always infuriated her. She would bang around, shout, scream and almost grab her boy by the scruff, throwing him back to his room, letting loose violent words which poured on Morolong's head while he wept silently.

Morolong had had to persevere through school. It was almost taken for granted that he would have to repeat every class. Dikeledi was hot on his heels, and when the dust rose it really did blur Morolong's vision. Before he knew what was happening, Dikeledi was just a class behind. Her childlike mind had made her tell her elder brother that if he dare fail, they would be in the same class. Morolong had nightmares about this and then, one morning when everyone expected him to emerge from his room clad in school uniform, he emerged wearing his long blue Sunday trousers, his hands deep in his pockets, his eyes gracing the floor.

That was the last time he ever thought about school. His parents and teachers had done all they could to lure him, to pull him, to push him back to the classroom, but Morolong stuck to the street, tight as a bug sucking blood. And the street was not very friendly to him. He found it fast and tricky, and soon discovered it could be deadly, but he stuck on. He was always silent; his friends always mocked him; but he stuck. Soon he was throwing dice, throwing the penny, and the flesh of his stomach got used to the blade that stuck there, hidden, covered by the clothes. Although Grace had never seen him in the street doing things, she knew, somehow she knew, and that knowledge was a breeze over some memory which flamed high into her heart.

One day when he came home, he announced that he was going to work. Soon after it came out that he was a caddie. Soon after his mother lay on the bed, thinking about her burden. And when they got into bed, her husband Mike told her that the boy must leave his house. They lay there that night, talking in whispers. She was pleading. He was determined to carry out the law of the house. It was when the cock crowed that she knew there was nothing she could do for her male child. Her husband fell asleep while she listened to her throbbing head, and her eyes seemed to have taken over the beat from the heart. She could not weep; somehow her age would not allow it. She lay there very still, until the silver light showed above the fairlight pane. She woke with a start, looked at him and knew there was indeed nothing she could do for her son. When her husband woke, he slipped out the blankets and into his trousers, and left the bedroom to get the early morning paper. She had laid her head on the pillow a bit, eyes closed. When the news was broken to Morolong, he looked at his father with hardly a word, and his father's words followed him as he passed through the door without looking back. He had walked twelve miles, now and then forgetting where he was going. He had ignored the pain in his thighs, the pain in his stomach, and the sweat rolled from his head, down his neck. He had crossed many steel rivers, meeting the white faces which walked straight and unwavering until he was tired of giving way, but he walked on and on. He had plunged into the hordes and hordes of small and big boys at the course, and become one of them, silent, his red eyes shining.

Dikeledi had wept bitterly when her brother left, begging her father. He had merely said, go to school, and she did. For many days, the head of the house was gripped by a deep, sullen mood. He came back home, read the evening paper, ate, and went to bed. In bed, he merely lay on his back, dug a comfortable space for himself by shifting to and fro, then closed his eyes and soon the whisper in and out of his nostrils began. Michael Ramono, that is him, Grace's husband.

He was very, very fond of Mpho, more cautious with Dikeledi because, he thought, she was her mother's daughter. He called Mpho 'my darling' with amazing softness, looking at her with those glaring eyes, buried in that stern, serious face.

There was also the way he stalked his wife, with deep care, slow, always as if he was unsure of what he wanted to do but always accurate, so much so that when they were still young, all that time ago, she would respond to all this mystery with anxious, excited giggles, landing in his arms which, when they got hold of her, exerted something between a tight grip and an embrace.

They were young then. He was older than her. She was a young, extraordinarily intelligent girl who never accepted second position to anybody; she was always up there, in front. Michael Ramono, a silent, stern young boy, hardworking, always with a book under the armpit if walking, and always reading if seated, was the senior prefect at their school. He had no close friend; everyone who spoke to him made it brief, and was in great trouble with the sword his eyes wielded.

It was one morning, on his way to school, when he saw a young girl, well-built, walking fast, but with ease, ahead of him. He knew from her uniform that they were at the same school. For a long time he walked behind her, keeping a little distance between them, watching her tall figure weaving its way with grace. After some time he caught up with her. She looked at him with those huge eyes, and she smiled, her eyes bright, embarrassed. She recognised him immediately; but to him she was just one of those girls at school.

'Lady Macbeth or Lady of Shalot?' he said as their eyes met. She giggled, holding her mouth.

'I do not know!' she said, still giggling.

'Or Juliet?' He smiled, as if reluctantly.

'Grace,' she said simply, and laughed.

'Lady Grace heh?'

'No, just Grace.'

'I see, Grace who?'

'Grace Thlase.'

'I'm Michael Ramono.'

'Glad to know you.'

'Same here.' They were silent for some time, and she felt her steps faltering a little as she walked near him. But he looked ahead of him, as if he was walking alone.

'What form are you?' He took a quick glance at her. 'Are you Mr Mokgatle's class?'

'Ja, and I did not do his homework. I am frightened.'

'Maths?'

'Yes, I had lots of homework yesterday.'

'There's always time to do work.'

'Ja, but I'm lazy.'

'You mean you are lazy to pass?'

'Perhaps,' she laughed.

'Ja, that's all it can mean.'

'But I have lots of difficulty with Maths.'

'Work hard at it: it will yield.' He was looking ahead, as if he was talking to himself. She was looking at him, seeking his eyes, his face. When he looked at her, and found her eyes shining into his, he glued his on her face, and she laughed. They got into the school gate, and he waved at her as he turned to his class. She waved back, laughing. That day they had criss-crossed each other's paths, he nodding his head, she smiling back. He watched her from a distance without being aware of it. She just thought of him as one of the boys at school; only, most often, she did not know how to react to him, whether to say hullo first when they met, whether to walk with him when she saw him, or to wait until he made a move, made a sign that they were friends. He kept that uncertain distance, sometimes walking with her, sometimes walking past her, after merely nodding at her. By now he was aware of her school record, and he was also aware of the company she kept; but he had seen no boy yet, and he was watching this very carefully. Once, he had seen her hug a boy, playfully, and that nearly upset his strenuous routine of work. He arrived home that day, and could not get near a book, nor was able to listen when his parents talked. But he had struggled, got hold of himself, and managed to read a long article in the newspaper, which was about Jan Smuts. After that, he had waited for his parents to go to bed so that he could make up his bed on the floor in the kitchen and sleep. He had made up his mind that his studies were not going to be disturbed by girls. The best was to keep them at arm's length.

Michael's father was a traditional doctor who had gone to Pretoria for a certificate when the white people made the call, which was also a threat. He conducted his business in his two rooms in Sophiatown. He also had a rondavel in Ga-Molepo, a small village outside Pietersburg town, where he now and then went to get herbs and to meet other traditional doctors. Michael grew up close to his mother, at a distance from his father who, he felt, belonged to his clients more than to his family. His relationship with his father was amicable, but he was kept in the dark about the bones, herbs and beads he saw neatly fastened round his father's arms, which were also loaded with golden rings and bangles.

One morning when Michael woke up, he immediately missed his father. When he asked his mother where the old man was, she merely said, he is still in bed, not feeling well.

This had worried Michael all day at school, and the first thing he did when he came back from school, was to ask where his father was. Only to be met by a man whom he knew from long ago, in Ga-Molepo. He only knew this man as Ntate-Ramphela, his father's close friend, and also a traditional doctor. This man had broken the news to Michael by saying, your father is in hot blankets. Michael knew what that meant, but dared not speculate on what it could result in. Ntate-Ramphela was washing his hands in water as red as blood, and if it were not for the smell of the herb, Michael would have believed it was his father's blood.

When the sun set, Michael's heart raced as he heard Ntate-Ramphela's thick voice booming from his father's room. 'Haaayaaa, gone are the people, down the mountain, below the darkness, the witches will dance, the people will weep; gone is the husband of the widows and the father of the orphans! Haaayaaa, hulululu, aahaa, arrive home Ramono, arrive and give us your knowledge, arrive and take your throne, let the wise and old meet you at the gate of the kraal, let them give you water to drink and bread to eat, you have walked the mountains and the wilderness and the jungle, arrive Lion, roar no more, lie and rest.' Ntate-Ramphela's face was filled with sweat as his voice fell from the sky above to the earth below; his eyes were red, and the folds in his face cleared as he looked at Ma-Ramono, who sat on the floor, her head bowed. He held Michael's arm tightly, and looked him in the eye. 'Your father has left us, my son,' he said.

'I hear,' Michael said, and sighed. Then he saw his father, eyes closed, lying on the floor wrapped in cow's hide. It was as if his father was sleeping. He was to look at this face a long time while they drove to Pietersburg where the Lion, Ramono, rested forever.

That was the day when Michael's future became uncertain. He was now to wade into the dark, his eyes seeing only as far as his next footstep, his hands groping in the deep darkness, the thick darkness, which slipped between his fingers as he sought a grip on something called a future. His future blinked in his mother's legs, folded beneath her body as she sat on the floor, day in day out, seemingly watching or waiting for something to happen. Ma-Ramono's last days were spent in that gruesome, lonely waiting, watching, waking up, sitting in the sun. And her only son, others having been reclaimed by the ancestors, watched the old, wood-hard hands fidget in the breast and pull out an old goat-hide, from which emerged the things that now and then procured a book, a chance to continue his studies, a chance to sleep soundly. Although Michael never asked if the contents of the pouch would see them through, many nights he lay with his eyes open, uncertainty throbbing in his head, and the horror of what might happen if, one day, his mother's fingers emerged from the pouch empty. His eyes bored into the darkness which seemed to envelop him.

But those fingers always emerged till that day when his weary, aged uncle came, and left with one of Ma-Ramono's neighbours. When they came back, Michael was called. He sat facing his uncle whose pain-struck face, for a moment when announcing it, glowed with delight. 'Michael, my nephew, you are a man today. You fought like a man and now your mother will have a daughter, your father where he is will shine his face on you, for indeed you have never disgraced him.'

Michael wept silently while his heart turned back and he took a look over his shoulder at what his past was and had meant. He was a man now, and would not cry; a man never cries, he just bows his head, so he can forget what weighs down his heart; he looks up and seeks the light.

A few weeks later Grace arrived, no longer her mother's daughter, having shed her people's name as a chicken sheds its feathers when it grows older. She stalked his mother's house and invaded her husband's room. Ma-Ramono was proud of her daughter, who stood up like a woman. She was brought tea in bed, before her daughter went to work; she now had someone to make sure that her snuff tin was always full; and she could now look other women in the eyes, for she also had something to boast about. She never touched the pots and plates, never swept the earth before the stoep; she always received a doek and a khiba; and other women commented that she was looking bright.

Michael had bought a bed, a bookcase, a wardrobe; and there were now lined curtains hanging from the windows while the sun shone, warm and bright, into the house. Michael had no time to think, for when he came back from teaching, his wife was there with news of the day; there were requests to chop wood, to fix the cupboard. Somehow, he could not sit still in his transformed house; he felt uncomfortable, restless and fidgety. Grace was unaware of all this. Then suddenly she sensed that somehow her husband seemed to be on edge, wanting something. She was always asking if she could help, but always he said no thanks. There was uneasiness in the bed they shared: when he wanted to read, she wanted to talk. To him it appeared that what she really wanted was attention.

So now and then one slept with a sore heart; one feeling ignored, another feeling invaded. Sometimes Grace wept, and Michael did not know what to do. And at times Michael was silent, almost sullen, and Grace searched his face with her eyes. But Michael only wished that she would understand that all he wanted was to lie and look at the ceiling, and think.

One day their mother died peacefully while sleeping. Michael arranged that she should be buried in Sophiatown. By then, Grace had announced that she was expecting a baby. Something had told Michael that his mother's departure was not to be wept for, that she must be laid down to rest, needing that most. Yet now and then this feeling gnawed at him; he asked himself if he really could be this cold towards his mother's departure. He kept this struggle within him, for himself; seeking answers by imagining his mother's face, whether it would be smiling when it appeared to him, or sad, or angry. But nothing assured him; the old woman's face appeared in all forms at all times, and he was not sure whether he was seeing her image, or pretending that he saw it.

One day when Grace said, 'Mama has rested,' Michael felt offended, but he did not know why. Grace observed his sullen response, and launched into a lengthy explanation of why she had said that. But he merely nodded, looking uninterested. When he saw her looking so disturbed, he had hugged and kissed her silently, fearing for the baby in the stomach: it may be disturbed, he thought. She had held him firm in her shaking arms, and he felt her huge stomach push into him, shooting a tremor through his blood. He felt like a man, to be able to swell her stomach like that; and he thought she looked beautiful, with her huge eyes searching like that.

Grace was happy. Something had happened to her husband for now, every day when he came back, he kissed her full on the mouth, almost as if their mouths were becoming one. He was careful; his hands were always ready to touch her, caress her, tighten around her; his tough hand, breaking inside her, exploding, and making her knees melt. She would cling to him.

When the time was near, she went home to her mother. Michael came to see her every night. One day when he came, he told her that he had bought a property in Alexandra. She laughed, enjoying the long-held secret, and she told him, with a strange excitement in her eyes, that the baby was kicking in her stomach. He placed his hand there and looked at her; she was smiling. He said her stomach was tough. She burst into laughter.

The news came to him at school: they had a baby boy. Michael wrote to his wife, 'The boy's name will be Morolong, a brilliant African political leader.' This took Grace by surprise. A political leader? Anyway. She told her mother the news. Grace's mother knew Morolong personally, and she was proud that her grandson was named after that man. Grace became aware of Morolong who, it seemed, was too young to be saying what he was saying. But people listened to him, and the newspapers seemed to take him seriously. Her husband talked about him as if he was a new discovery. Then Morolong was defeated; Sophiatown was going to be pulled out, roots and all, like an unwanted tree.

Alexandra stood high up to the sky then, a tree still going to grow, filled with many buds, promising good fruit. Michael was vice-principal at Alexandra High School, Grace a social worker. They arrived in Alexandra, moving into a six-roomed house. They were, almost, the owners of the property. There were thirteen tenants in the yard who paid Ramono rent. He, in turn, paid into the bag held by a white hand, a bag which was as insatiable as a stomach.

The big house stood near the gate, like a castle, and the other thirteen single-rooms stood in an L-shape, as if to guard the big house. Ramono was a tough landlord. He did not allow bachelors to rent his rooms because they had filthy ways. The married couples brought their family problems to him, and he would call the other tenants to come and help him solve whatever problems there were. Those who understood him got on well with him, but now and then he had to chase others away: their children swore, or they were always fighting. But whatever he did, he consulted his other tenants: and whatever decision was taken was a collective decision. Grace's part was played out in the background and in the bedroom. She only heard what the men had decided from her husband. Every woman in the yard had her turn to clean the toilets, to sweep the yard, and women in the yard went to Ma-Morolong for advice. They brought their children to her if, while they were playing, they hurt themselves. When the children were ill, Ma-Morolong advised them to take the children to where she worked to see a doctor. If the older children played truant from school they were brought to Ramono who took strong exception to this, and was hard on parents who did not force their children to attend school.

People came in and out of Ramono's home — Indians, coloureds, whites. And people in the yard along Seventh Avenue, all over Alexandra, respected Ramono. He knew it, and lived up to it. When his principal was pensioned, Ramono became principal. In his inauguration speech, he sounded the trumpet. He spoke about the importance of education. He told the students that Africa needed them. He likened an African to a lone person walking in the desert. The African alone was the one who was going to find his way out of the dry sands to the oasis. The only way to do that was through education.

By now Ramono, because of things he said and the numbers of people who came to his house, had become used to being looked at when he walked the Alexandra streets. He had become used to being greeted by people he did not know, and he knew that he was liked — and hated. His face, and his words, were now and then in newspapers. He was now often on the road, less often at home with his wife, or marvelling at their little daughter whom he had named Dikeledi, because he had come to believe that Africans were weeping every day. He loved his children. He loved his wife. He missed them a lot. But, every day now seemed to draw him away from his house, as he began to know and understand his country. He spent many nights reading, writing, planning. He spent many days and nights travelling, dreaming. Romano spent days and nights dreaming about being near the oasis. His wife knew this, but not the details, and she made it a point not to stand in his way. She was always ready to help, to pack his suitcases and to unpack them, and to know only his destination. She, in turn, was dreaming about him and about his oasis. At times her heart slipped out of sleep into a terrible nightmare. Fear and love waged a terrible war against each other in her bosom. But all he said when she told him was, Africa needs me. Not that he himself did not fear but he believed Africa needed him. He gave all he could to respond to Africa's need. He lost his principalship. Weeks passed without his being at home and, when he was home, whites, Indians and coloureds came. His wife became clearer about the oasis from what the newspapers said. She was as the earth to a tree: this sometimes made him weep.

When Morolong left school and was chased out of the house, Ramono turned his back on him. Shortly after this Ramono suffered a stroke. He was at home, recovering. He watched his daughter Dikeledi climb the ladder, carefully, slowly, and he marvelled. Mpho was walking around the house, groping, crying, and sitting on her father's lap. Ma-Morolong was winning bread for the house, almost single-handed.

It took some years for Ramono to realise one of the truths about working towards the oasis: that one may reach it, or one may never see it. White laws had reared him and, like chicken now walking the ground, now in the air held by the claws of a hawk, Ramono had vanished.

The last time Morolong has seen his uncle was when the whirlwind spiralled

126

into the sky, sucking up bits of grass and dust and his uncle's fury as he shouted and screamed at his wife.

His uncle was standing there, his eyes slightly closed because of the dust that rose, one hand holding his now battered hat, which looked as dry as cardboard and as colourless. All the children of the house sat in the sun, eleven in number. They seemed to be like women awaiting a black maria to fetch a corpse they were guarding, only they were very small and one was crying, the small one, as children do when they are hungry. Meanwhile the chickens pecked and chased each other, and made love there in the dry, red, vast ground; the groaning of the pigs and the mooing of the cows mingled with the angry screaming of his uncle.

Apart from that one memory, Morolong had only heard from his mother, or maybe his sister, what his uncle was like. Lots of things had happened to Morolong since, and these could be seen in his face, silent, and his way of looking away into the distance.

Someone was asking why he pushed if he was not getting out. 'I'm sorry, sorry, but I'm not sure where to get off . . .' he said with a very timid voice.

'Where are you going to?'

'I don't, er, er, I wonder if you can help, I'm going to my uncle . . .' A crowd of people laughed.

'Your uncle and you are well known, heh? Just like that, and we must know who your uncle is?' someone said, laughing. 'Who's your uncle?' Women were giggling.

When the bus stopped, Morolong walked out in disgust. He hated that man. He walked blindly. Then he recognised a shop which was almost demolished. He walked up the footpath. And the old, old picture unreeled itself. Indeed, this was the right stop. The place lay around him, a vast space spreading all the way to the horizon. It looked like a head with dots of hair on it. Everything was dry, red and dead. The sun was very hot. Isolated houses, standing like people with bowed heads, spread into the distance.

He saw the house. The whirlwind and his uncle came to his mind. There is no peace in this world. The house looked pathetic, worse than it had been. The doors were shut, the trees brown, there was no sign of life. As he neared the house, a lean dog started to bark viciously, approaching him. He stopped walking as the dog went for his trousers, and felt cold sweat running down his spine. A small boy appeared and stood there, looking on. 'Hey, you fool, stop this dog!' he shouted, and the dog got its teeth into his trousers, barely missing his flesh. The boy, reluctantly, called the dog. The dog released his trouser-leg but when he started to move, it came rushing back at him. The small boy threw a stone, feebly, at the dog, called it by its name, and it went to him, wagging its tail obediently.

'Who are you?' the boy asked.

'You won't know me. Where are the older people?'

'No one here. The old man has gone to that house there, the old woman's gone to do washing in Pretoria.'

'Who are you?'

'Piet.'

'Who's child are you?'

'Ausi Rebecca.'

'I'm your uncle.'

'Who?'

'From Alexandra.'

Just then, Morolong heard a voice he had heard somewhere before. He looked up at the gate and saw him. His hands were flying to and fro like a piece of cloth blown by wind as he shouted, calling names, stopping to point at something. The children came out, running towards him, answering Ntate! Ntate! They answered in turn, as their names were called, and they dashed to and fro on their errands.

He had grown old before his time. Mucus ran down from his flat, huge nose, and there were wrinkles thick like worms all over his face, a face that looked like a corpse's.

'Who's this?' he said angrily.

'Morolong.'

'What? Morolong? You swine, you people in Johannesburg, what do you know? Nothing. We here have cattle and pigs, all you know is how to kill each other. The hell with you.' Morolong did not know what to say.

'Where's your mother? She's a fool, she thinks she knows everything. I'm not interested. She's like the boers; now they want to take my land. Where's the money? Buy me a scale.' Morolong bowed his head, and looked at the red earth . . .

He saw the red earth, cracked, cracks running wild like many rivers, ending beneath the green-grey grass. Morolong's eyes rose from the earth. There was the path, the path to the gate, lined on both sides by long and dry mealie stalks. The path was broad where he was standing, but narrowed as it reached the gate. The gate was two stone pillars, almost falling down to the red earth. There was no fence. His uncle's voice was rumbling over him, pouring like dam water set loose. They were standing there, beneath a semi-dark sky, its bare silence now and then torn by a mooing cow or a bleating goat; the emptiness now and then relieved by the passage of a flock of birds sailing gently to the other side of the sky, where it met the earth.

' . . . Like these girls, they give birth like bitches, packs and packs of children running around in the house, every month a mouth to feed. And they vanish, they go back to Johannesburg to drink and get men, to Pretoria, to all over the show. What do they want? What do they want? Tell me!' When this silence fell, Morolong raised his eyes to his uncle who was wiping his nose with his hand, his shadow like a body staggering in the dark. He could not see his uncle's face, it was just a round thing with a shadow shaped like a hat on it. And the huge coat seemed to hang from a long thin shadow, which was blown by the wind, and was swaying to and fro like a piece of dangling cloth.

Morolong's uncle, Russia, was a tall man, thin, with a face and eyes that had seen just too much. His eyes were bloodshot, his thick lips, always parted and grey, revealed snuff-stained teeth. Russia had seven daughters. All except

Rebone were gone into the white areas to look after the houses, children, dogs and errands of white people. Some were in Johannesburg, others in Pretoria. Rebone had come back from Johannesburg to Walmanstadt because she was five months pregnant. It was her third pregnancy by the same man, or rather, the same boyfriend, Tito, who was still in Johannesburg living in a hostel for single men, working as a wheelbarrow boy for a building contractor. Russia and Rebone got on well, and Tito was Russia's favourite man. Russia's weary-looking wife, Rebecca, worked in Pretoria as a washerwoman, wifed her husband, and mothered her eleven grandchildren. Rebecca's favourite child, Morwesi, the eldest daughter, seldom came home from Johannesburg, and as a result Rebecca's bleeding heart poured its wrath on Rebone's head. Rebecca was a short stumpy woman, with a bent back, strong arms, and hands like steel. She was capable of long silent spells, but once she started talking, she almost never stopped. Her husband walked away when she started talking, and talked a lot when she was silent, demanding that she answer him.

Rebecca, whether silent or talking, always had something to do with her hands. She wiped a child's nose, stirred a pot, squashed the bugs on her frock, tasted some food for salt, reprimanded the children and Rebone, and whispered something about Russia and her misfortunes. Russia belonged to the vast, dry yard outside; in the house, he demanded food and snuff, and fell asleep on the chair until he went to bed.

Morolong was now finding his niche in the house. He was very shy, perhaps also feeling guilty about sharing the meagre, hard-earned food of the house, but he never said anything. He ate, drank, and sat in the sun, or listened to his uncle's sad stories, and buried his terrified heart deep in his chest.

Early one morning, he heard the small, old-looking, four-year-old boy waking up. He too woke up. They both went to the kraal where there were four very lean cows, lean because of the drought, everybody believed.

'Can you milk?'

'No.'

'Why? Why can't you?' The boy laughed.

'I don't know, maybe because there are no cattle in Alexandra.'

'So you don't drink milk in Alexandra?'

'We do.'

'Where do you get the milk?'

'From the dairy . . . ' Morolong said, and as soon as he said it, he felt sad. He knew he was not going back to Alexandra, but he also knew that he was not going to make it here in Walmanstadt.

Eleven

Mr Ramono and twenty-five other people had been on trial for a while now. When the trial started, the newspapers had given it prominence. It was on the first page of the main Johannesburg newspaper. Now, only one other paper still carried it as major news. Every day in Pretoria when the twenty-five people walked into the dock, they were accompanied by armed police and dogs. There was tight security. Every day, when the twenty-five came in, walking up the stairs, a freedom song broke loose, climbing the stairs slowly, heavily, through the two huge doors of the Pretoria Synagogue. In there, it rose, above the floor, above the many, many benches, above the Judges' bench, to the ceiling, and out of the building to the sky. Every day at this time when the twenty-five came in, crowds and crowds of black faces, white faces, crowded the streets before going to work to see the men and women, singing, fists clenches and raised high, go up the stairs slowly, into the court. It was said that these were the people of the Movement. They had been on trial now for a long time indeed: one year gone, and another half gone.

Everyone who went to the trial talked about it afterwards. It was said that those men and those women were strong, were fearless. It was said that South Africa had become a strange place indeed since the sixties, when there were many, many such trials. Not that there were fewer now, there were many, many others going on around the country, in which even young children were charged with burning schools, burning beer stoves, cars, trains, houses; defendants in one trial had allegedly killed a white woman. There were many trials in South Africa in those days. However, for some reason or other, this one of the twenty-five people attracted everyone's attention.

In those days there was not a single major city in South Africa where there was not a political trial. The police, the magistrates, the judges, the attorney-generals and ministers in parliament were all, all of them, very, very busy. They were arresting people. They were sentencing them. They were telling lies in newspapers. They were very, very busy indeed. In most of the cases it was children who were in court. In these trials the police, the magistrates, the judges, the attorney-generals and the ministers talked a lot about how this or that store was burnt, how this or that school was burnt, how this or that child was caught while trying to flee the country, how this or that child was caught throwing stones at the police, how this or that child led others to do this or that. But the main attention was focussed on Pretoria Synagogue. The Synagogue's public gallery was always packed, by black and white alike.

At first, when the trial started, Dikeledi, Mpho and their mother Grace went there every day. Then they took turns. Now, it was mainly Dikeledi who went to court. She sat there every day, from one session to the next. Now and then she and her father looked at each other and exchanged smiles. Often the security police stopped her, either when she came into or when she went out of the Synagogue. She knew they were trying to scare her, so she never gave thought to what they said to her. Occasionally Dikeledi helped to cover the trial for her newspaper. But most times she preferred to listen. She knew that this was a very serious trial, not only because it was a political one, but because of the charges laid against the accused. In May of that year, it was clear that the trial was coming to an end. One day in that month, Mr Ramono stood up to speak. The court was silent. It was packed. There was something sad yet also tough in the air.

David Horwitz stared straight ahead. The car entered the Ben Schoeman Highway, travelling towards Johannesburg. In the car were Susan, Dikeledi and Mpho. Grace had left with her sister and other family friends. There were many cars on the highway. David held the steering wheel tightly in his hands. He knew that his face was red. He did not look at Susan, who looked out of the window. Dikeledi and Mpho, in the back, held each other's hands. David, driving rather fast, twisted in and out of the traffic, going from one lane to the other with ease, yet he was fighting. Susan knew this. Dikeledi suspected this. It was quiet in the car, quiet and terrible. There was a great roar of cars on the highway. The cars, with their many, many colours, dappled the road, curling and twisting with it. David, a good driver, held the car under his firm control.

It was sunset. The empty, vast fields running along the highway, spread with the gold of the setting sun, looked very quiet, very peaceful. Dikeledi was looking at this running yellow space, which rolled on and on along with them, never seeming to tire. From the tip, where the sky and the fields touched, right up to somewhere high in the sky, it was red, red like spilled blood. Dikeledi thought it was beautiful.

'Please give me a mint,' Mpho said, looking straight into Dikeledi's eyes. Mpho, young, quiet, had learnt that in situations where she found herself with Dikeledi, it was safe to take a cue from her as to how to behave. She looked at her now, searching her elder sister's face and eyes. It was not a blank expression she found, everything was under control. Mpho sat back, took the mint from Dikeledi's hand and putting it into her mouth, looked out of the window. The silence had been broken.

'Shall we drop you at home, D?'

'Yes, it will be helpful,' Dikeledi said. 'You still have your permit?'

'Yes, I do. I don't care really,' David said.

'Oh, this country, good God, I am tired,' Susan said, and sighed painfully.

'If you don't have the permit, I don't think you should come in, for your-selves and for our sake,' Dikeledi said strongly.

'I do have a permit, but Susan does not have one,' David said.

'Oh fuck it, I don't care, I really don't,' Susan said with all her strength.

'How did things ever go so far?' David said. 'I have never heard it being said like that. How did things ever go so far?'

'What's that?' Susan asked, still angry.

'Did you not hear Mr Ramono say that?'

'I don't want any part of this madness, no, I don't, I don't want to be white, I don't want it, oh my god, I don't want it . . .' Susan began to sob.

'Sue, Sue, please now, Sue,' David kept saying.

'Oh, I am sorry, I am sorry, I am so mixed up,' Susan said.

Dikeledi and Mpho were silent in the back seat.

'Fifteen years is a long, long time,' David said. Dikeledi felt tears coming to her eyes. She was going to fight them, no, she was going to fight them, no, she was not going to cry. What her father had said in court did not invite people to cry, no, she was not going to cry. She knew so well what was needed, she knew it so well. What mattered now was to master the art of it. Dikeledi knew and believed this, and she knew, she told herself, that this could not be brought about by crying. She did not cry. Soon as she thought the way she thought, she realised that her mind went blank.

It seemed as if she had never known anything. She wondered how this system could be destroyed, what system would replace it. Her father had said it in court. When he said it, everything seemed so logical, so understandable, but now it seemed her mind was being clouded. She felt very sad. She felt sad because she knew, she understood so well that South Africa had shut out all other choices. There was no way now that any other thing could be done with the present way of life, with this South Africa, with the South African way of life; there was nothing else that could be done to save it; there was only one way left – people had to fight. She understood now that there was no such thing as people being born free. She understood that there was no such thing as freedom being asked for, that freedom must be fetched, must be won, must be fought for. Her father had said it in court, and she agreed.

The car flew on. David and Susan kept exchanging notes about the speech, about the meaning of the sentences, about how there was no way that South Africa could be changed. Although they did not address Dikeledi directly, in a sense they did. They were trying to tell her that they did not in any way feel that they were associated with the present regime. Knowing Dikeledi, they also understood that she would need a much more fully explained and thought-out argument than what they were giving each other now; so they kept talking. They were now thinking aloud, all their thoughts were scattered.

'Oh, God, Dave, I don't know, I really don't, I think we have to get out of here, as soon as we can. I said that straight after the Soweto days. You keep postponing! I think we have to go.'

'Ja, but where to?'

'You don't know, but we have to move, that is all. Can't you see, I am going to go mad.'

Susan was getting loud now. David knew; he had heard this, he had seen this before; he hoped she was not going to scream like she did in bed. She sat, silent, her head leaning against the window, her face now pale, empty of blood, her cheekbones standing out. She was silent. She felt very tired, very sick, as if she would throw up. She kept very still. Holding the vomit. Holding the tears. Holding the scream. Her eyes shot out.

'Sue, please relax,' David said. She nodded; he touched her lightly on the hand. He, too, felt any time tears would flow; they did, but they were droplets. He wanted to go home now, straight home, to rest, to be with Sue, to be with his children, to go far away from this, mad, cruel, sad world. As he thought all this, he also realised there was no way of running away. They could never run away from it.

'Dikeledi, do many people know about the trial in Alexandra?' It was a tough question. Dikeledi thought it a tough question: not because it had no answer. If she said yes, it would have been an understatement. Most people knew and followed the case. It was a tough question because somehow she knew that deep inside him, David wished she would say no. It was a question which had reared its head many times, in many different ways. It was a question of Freedom.

'Does it matter really, Dave?'

There was a silence, then: 'How do you mean?'

'Just that, does it matter?'

'Ja, I think it matters.'

'I don't know, I do not know, Dave.' She looked down.

He was trying to catch her face in the mirror. He had lately, more so since the Power days, or maybe since the trial, come to realise that there was some-thing that Dikeledi was hiding. She seemed always to want to hide her face.

'What don't you know?'

'Look, you know I am ducking this question, why don't you let it go?'

'I see, I see, but why would you do that?'

'Dave, cut the shit out, will you?'

'Dave, this girl's father has just been sentenced to fifteen years, and here you are asking her, do her people know this!' Sue was about to scream. Dave held her hand.

'I see, I see,' he said. 'Sorry, Dikeledi.' He was again trying to catch her in the mirror. Dikeledi said nothing. She was trying to relax. To sit back and be quiet. To take care of her younger sister. The car had devoured many kilometers. They took the first exit out. Dikeledi was thinking that it was very strange indeed, the way she and David related to each other. She was coming out of the Black Consciousness days. Then, there had been lots of rock-throwing from the Davids, and even from the John Vorsters. In those days, when whites talked about blacks being racists, and how the world was going to go crazy because of this, and urged that someone must do something about it, that the Black Consciousness boys must be stopped – in those days, a new, a brand-new black woman and man had been created. Dikeledi in those days had believed that something was going to happen. She had talked this over with her father, who had told her, 'This is a long, long struggle; it has long been here, we used to talk about the same things which you are talking about.' Then Dikeledi would feel frustrated. It was so long ago. Now, there was a sense of loss, a sense of defeat; there were no more fists and shouts of Power. It seemed quiet.

'I think we will be all right at the bridge,' Dikeledi said to David.

'Really?'

'Yes, please,' Dikeledi said. She was fixing her dress.

'Are you sure?' Susan asked.

'Oh please, come on now, I said we will be all right.' David swerved the car, down the bridge. The car stopped. Dikeledi and Mpho got out of the car, and joined the many, many black people coming from the industrial sites into Alexandra. There were crowds and crowds of people, all of them in a hurry to go home, to meet and be with their husbands, wives, sisters, brothers, to be with friends, to make Alexandra what it is, a deadly township, with terribly mean streets, a very close-knit township, where almost everyone is related to everyone else, related through the skin. At the Pan African Store, many people who had come in on the buses from the golden city surged out, spread across the streets, scattering and going their way. Dikeledi and Mpho, hand in hand, were in a hurry to go home. They were in a hurry to be with their mother. The sun had set.

'When papa comes back, I will be thirty-one,' Mpho said. Her voice was shaking, it seemed some terrible truth had just hit her; a truth that had nothing to do with her safety; a truth which said nothing to her about being a child of God, or even a child born of man. She held tight to her sister's hand; she was fighting, fighting hard, saying to herself that if her sister, Dikeledi, had not wept yet, maybe she had no business weeping either. But she felt the pain, deep, too deep to be ignored.

'Dikeledi, I am, I am sa-a-d,' she managed to say, and then she broke down. She began to weep. Dikeledi, silent, suddenly feeling strong and angry, held her sister's hand, pulled her gently towards her, and buried her head on her bosom. She caressed her neck; she could feel that Mpho was struggling, fighting, trying very hard to be strong. Dikeledi could feel her breasts getting wet. Mpho was heaving, battling. The shadows of darkness were there, floating in the sky. Then Dikeledi and Mpho began to walk. They held each other's hands tightly. They were walking quickly. There were other people in the street, walking along, going their way. For Dikeledi and Mpho, at times these people were not there. They were going down Selborne Street, and Selborne Street was very busy now, buses, taxis, crowds of people, going up and down. They went past Third Avenue.

'We have to take care of ourselves now, now that Papa is gone,' Dikeledi said to Mpho.

'He will be seventy-eight when he comes back,' Mpho said.

'Yes,' Dikeledi said. 'We also have to look after Mama now, she is old and she is tired. This must have caused her a lot of pain. We must look after her.'

'Will she be home when we get there?'

'She must be, by now.' Dikeledi tried to look at her watch, but she could not see. They turned at Seventh Avenue. They were in a hurry to get home.

'Have they taken papa to Robben Island now?'

'They will, maybe in a day or two.'

'Did papa do the things they say he did?'

'Papa is a revolutionary. When they are caught, that is what happens,' Dikeledi said. She had never thought of her father as revolutionary. Even as she said it, it took her by surprise. She even wondered now, what exactly is revolutionary? They turned into the yard. Yes, their mother had arrived. There were other people in the house. Mpho and Dikeledi greeted them and went into their rooms. Dikeledi had seen her mother's face. It had taken her by surprise.

She looked very, very tired. But she was talking, and her face was filled with a wonderful smile, though it was tired. Dikeledi changed into an Afro-dress, put on light slippers and went into the sitting room. She went to the kitchen and there Oupa was seated, reading a newspaper.

'Oupa! How are you?'

'Fine sister, how are you?'

'Okay, where have you been?'

'Around,' he said and smiled. 'I have been reading the papers.'

'Ja, they got long sentences indeed,' Dikeledi said. She tried hard to keep the emotion out of her voice. Oupa was staring at her, straight into her eyes.

'The old man spoke well,' Oupa said. 'His spirits are high!'

'Ja.'

'Every one of us must make a cutting of this speech and read and study it. It has lots for us.'

'It was strange listening to my father say things like that, under those circumstances.' She held her bosom as if she was getting cold. 'You know what I mean. I sat there listening, knowing that we may never see that man, my father, who is saying all those things which I agree with, we may never see him again, and he is my father.' She began to wring her hands, looking searchingly at Oupa's face, wondering if he understood her, if he knew how she felt.

'I know what you mean. It was too close,' he said, smiling.

'Maybe that is it,' she said, her big eyes dilating.

'When that happens, when it is all spelled out, then it seems so strange.'

'Ja.' Dikeledi started to make tea. They had not said anything to each other, she and her mother. Mpho was sitting close to her mother, her head on her bosom. It was strange indeed. People who had come to console the family, suddenly had nothing to do. When they came in, there was Grace, all smiles, warm, welcoming, shaking their hands, and asking them to make themselves comfortable. At first, people did not know how to handle this. Grace, calm, obviously strong, said: 'Yes, it will take us time to get used to the idea that he is not here. He is not dead but he is not available to us. It will be some time before we get used to that. We loved him, we will miss him. But he is not the only one. There are many others who have gone like he has. He believes in what he did, that gives us strength. Our country needs to be healed. It will be our children, our husbands, our loved ones who will have to die or go to jail to save us all, it will have to be us.' Some people took this away with them and twisted it around in their heads; some made sense out of it, some thought it to be madness, some just did not know what to do with the information. However, all of them agreed Grace deserved respect. Many knew her from her work as director of the Creche and Welfare Centre, others knew her as the mother of Dikeledi who was a good reporter, but all of them agreed that there was something about her – the way she carried herself, the way she smiled – that demanded respect. They were aware that she knew what she was doing and saying, and that it must be right. Grace had a way of striking a balance between gentle and being terribly tough. She knew how to say no, and not humiliate and make you part of the decision that says no. She was a beautiful woman, tall, strong-looking, appealing, yet acted as if she was completely unaware of all this. It was through this that people came closer and got her warmth. You always knew you could go to her.

That night, many people came and went. Grace received them all with dignity and love. They talked about the boers, about the country, about the jails, about trials, about the Power days.

They left, each one knowing that he or she had to help the other. They knew this: how was this to be done, how? But all, all of them were ready. After all, Mr Ramono had been taken to jail for them, for the nation, and Mr Ramono was to be respected. His family too was to be respected and helped where it was possible.

Then Grace and Dikeledi and Mpho were left alone. For a long time they sat there without a word to one other. The house felt empty after so many people. There were many empty and dirty teacups on the table. The chairs were shifted this way and that. Grace lay spread out on the sofa, barefoot, her hand on her head, her eyes to the ceiling. Dikeledi, next to her, was looking down. Mpho had almost fallen asleep.

'Your father was very strong indeed,' Grace said to Dikeledi.

'Yes,' said Dikeledi.

'The boers have hit us hard indeed,' Grace said with a great sigh. Now it was as if she had not only to accept but to deal with what all this meant. Her Michael, her Mike, had been taken away from her, had been taken away from her, had been taken away from her. For fifteen years. The father of her children, Dikeledi, Mpho and Morolong, her husband, a father, brother, man of the house, her bed companion, her everything, her what else, was now gone. She knew now that she was going to cry. She knew now that there was an enormous vacuum in her life and that for the next fifteen years she was going to have to live differently from the past that she had lived with her Mike. The three women of the house sitting side by side, silent, had their thoughts running this and that way, thinking about the man who had played all sorts of roles in their lives. For Dikeledi, indeed, the adviser was gone. Mpho was going to miss the 'My darling' which made her think of Papa affectionately as a mischievous man. Now and then she wondered privately, what happened in bed when her father said this to her mother. Even now, when she thought about this she could still smile a bit with tears on her cheeks.

'This is a strange country,' Grace said, still almost talking to herself, dealing with her thoughts, yet also aware of her children, aware of their heavy thoughts, the terrible pain that was holding them, burdening them, pushing and pulling them this and that way. She could feel how, under the weight of this pain, her children were dragging, fighting, holding, wanting to be hopeful, wanting to say so they could believe it because it was true – that even then everything would be all right. She could feel Mpho heaving, slowly, in broken rhythms, fighting, and Dikeledi quiet, so silent as though she was not even next to her. She knew she was the one who would hold their hands, hold them and tell them that it was bad, very bad, but they were to live on.

'I wonder where my son is?' Grace heard herself say. She had not even thought of saying this, but she heard her voice say it. Dikeledi and Mpho knew all about Morolong. Many times they had thought about him, wondered where he was, why he did not come back home, what he was doing wherever he was. But since they had parted in the way that they did, and since Michael made it obvious that he really did not care or want to know where his son was, all the women had thought about him privately but said nothing. For Grace, most times, it was almost conspiratorial. Many times, without telling Michael, she had tried to find out where Morolong was. She had heard that he was with Russia. And she had kept in contact with him there. Then he left.

She had traced him back to Alexandra. She knew, sometimes through some of the people who came to her for help, that Morolong had slipped, had fallen, was down below the bottom of Alexandra. She had attempted to save him. Once he had come to her office, and after they had talked, she had asked him to wait until she was less busy. Morolong had left without telling her. She had come to know some of the girls who loved and looked after and housed her son, but then Morolong was here now and gone tomorrow. Now the only contact she had with him was through seeing his two sons, by one mother, and his little girl, by another. No one knew where he was. At first secretly, then openly, before and after Michael was arrested, she had started to look for her boy; in jails, morgues, hospitals, at all the garbage places of South Africa. In this she used the welfare system that employed her, which was created for this purpose, since it was often, so often, that mothers came, wives came, husbands came to her offices, wanting to be helped to trace their loved ones.

She thought of him and about his father. Both had been snatched from her, from them.

'We must look for him, he is my son,' she said. 'He is your brother,' she added, and began to stroke Mpho's hand. Mpho was not deep in sleep. She hugged her and then facing Dikeledi said, 'Just so we know whether he is alive or dead or just where he is. He can live his life the way he wants to live it, that is all right.' Her gentle touch on Dikeledi's arm turned into a grip. She shook her daughter a little. Dikeledi nodded.

'He is our blood after all, and we can't just throw it away like that.' She took a deep, deep breath. 'God knows,' she said as she was breathing out.

'Tomorrow papers will have what Papa said in court,' Dikeledi said. 'I think we should have it.'

'Yes, yes, I am very proud of your father,' Grace said.

'I could not recognise him, standing there and saying the things he was saying,' Dikeledi said.

'Oh, that is him, that was the Michael I know,' Grace said. 'I am proud of him.'

'Did he and the other people really do all those things?' As soon as she said it Dikeledi realised that she was asking a stupid question.

'Well, mmmm, I always knew that your father belonged to the Movement. That is all I can say.'

'It's a stupid question I am asking,' Dikeledi said, 'I think . . .'

'It is not stupid. We are in that moment where nothing is left unquestioned.'

'But God, we lived with someone, and we never knew what he was doing?'

'Your father is a strong man,' Grace replied. She stood up now, she felt very tired. She felt weary. Now it was her time to be alone. She walked slowly from the table to the sink, then to her bedroom. Dikeledi took Mpho by the hand. It was one in the morning.

'I have to go to bed,' Grace said, peeping through the door, her voice soft now.

'Goodnight Mama,' Dikeledi said, feeling her strength run out, feeling that she was going to cry now she had seen her mother's face. But she held on, and went into her room. Grace lay on the bed and wept. Dikeledi and Mpho fell asleep in a light embrace. Dikeledi did not even bother to go to work. Grace went but only for half the day. Mpho was sitting outside on the stoep, unwashed, miserable, her head buried between her thighs. Someone touched her. She looked up.

'Haai.' The voice was now soft, the owner saw the tears on her face. Oupa understood why she was crying.

'Haai,' Mpho said shyly and looked away, then stood up to go into the house. When she stood up she saw John who stood leaning against the pillar. Oupa followed Mpho into the house, John followed Oupa.

'Haai, Dikeledi,' Oupa said, looking at Dikeledi who was seated on the sofa, cutting her nails. She smiled when she saw Oupa. She was very glad to see John.

'Where do you get this one?' she said giggling and pointing at John. He smiled, and as she came towards him he held her hand lightly and winked.

'One, where have you been?' Oupa said, looking at John. John merely shrugged, and got himself a comfortable place to sit. Nudging Dikeledi, and indicating the door Mpho had gone through, Oupa said: 'Why don't you take care of her?'

'What, why?'

'She was crying when we walked in.'

Dikeledi went to look for Mpho in the bedroom. John and Oupa were left to themselves for a while, and sensing that matters might be too heavy where Dikeledi and Mpho were, Oupa suggested that they leave, and maybe come back later.

'Tell her then,' John said.

'No, let's just go, we will be back,' Oupa insisted. Oupa walked out of the door, but John hesitated.

'Oupa, Oupa, I am coming, please be patient,' Dikeledi's voice came from the other room.

'No, let's wait,' John said.

'Was that her?'

'Ja, she says she is coming.' They went back to their chairs, sat down and waited. When Dikeledi came back, she was looking strange. She was strange because she was smiling a bright smile, yet it did not work.

As soon as she sat down and looked at Oupa, she began to weep. Oupa held her around the waist, and gently stroked her head. John was trying to look away from her.

'Gosh,' she said, wiped her face and her eyes, pulled her dress straight and sighed. She sat up. Oupa moved to sit on the other chair. John was looking straight into Dikeledi's eyes.

'Be all right now, okay?' Oupa said, smiling still. 'I expect you to cry, really.'

'Okay, I will be all right,' she said.

'We thought we should pass by to see you and say haai, John and I,' Oupa said.

'Actually, Oupa asked me to come along,' John said, wanting to set the record straight.

'Otherwise you would not have come?' Dikeledi asked, looking at John.

'I don't know, I really don't.'

'It's nice of you Oupa, to come and to bring him along.'

'Fine, all right, I did the right thing. How is Mpho now?'

'She will be all right. You know, she and Papa were very close, so this hits her hard,' Dikeledi said.

'Ja.'

'Were you in court yesterday?' John asked.

'Yes, yes, we were all there.'

'Must have been heavy for you,' John said.

'Sad, but after a while you felt you had to be strong. You had to stand by the mood, the atmosphere which was created in there. Once I looked at my mother, while Papa was talking, and she was so beautiful, all bright, I felt ashamed to be wanting to cry. Gosh, I don't know, I really don't know.'

'Fifteen years is a long, long time,' John said.

'Yes,' Dikeledi said, 'yes, it is a long time.'

'Where is Grace?' Oupa asked.

'She said she was going to work half-day, and then she will come back to rest.'

'I like her spirit,' Oupa said, smiling.

'Ja, I don't know how I would react if I were in her position, it must be real hard for her,' said her daughter.

'Ja,' John said.

'But she's taking it well, that's important,' Oupa added.

'Yes, I guess that is important,' she replied.

'The boers are fighting us, as simple as that. We have to pitch up a battle, fight back, that is all. All this that is happening now, happened to many other people. It happened in Guinea Bissau, Algeria, Angola, Mozambique,

Vietnam, Cuba, you know: the people there pitted their strength against the mighty, the strong. During the Power days, you saw what they did. You see what they are doing now to bontate Ramono. We too have to fight and win our country back.' Both John and Dikeledi looked anxiously at Oupa but said nothing. They were alarmed by the enthusiasm that suddenly lit up his face as he said this.

They wondered whether he knew what he was saying. They had heard this so many times. They had been in the firing line during the Power days. They wondered again what they should have done in those days. Here was Oupa now. Here he was, young, bright-eyed and big-tongued talking about pitting their strength against that of the boers. What strength?

'People must organise themselves, rally themselves as fighters, discipline themselves, and fight,' Oupa said. John looked at him. John had always suspected that there was something that Oupa was doing, but he could not pinpoint it. Now he looked at him and his eyes asked, what are you saying?

'People are ready! What do you mean, people are not ready? People are ready! Aren't you?'

He looked at Dikeledi.

'Even if we were, there are too many informers. The boers have their thing tight. That is what took my father and them into jail. Otherwise how would the boers know?'

'That is true, and that is no minor problem. But it is not an impossible problem to tackle, and it will be tackled one day.'

'Where do you start?'

'I ask you, where do we start?' Oupa said. John and Dikeledi looked at each other again. They had, both of them, got the message. And Oupa had intended it to be so. He wanted them to know that he was not just talking. He wanted them to know that he was doing something about what other people were talking about. But he did not say so outright. Now all of them in the room knew.

'When one man falls, another must pick up the gun,' Oupa said.

Dikeledi thought that all these things which Oupa was saying were not new. She had heard them before. She began to fear for him, because she could feel how determined he was in whatever it was he was doing. She looked at him.

'Do you belong to any Movement?'

'I am doing something, and maybe you can think about joining me. We need you.'

'How do you know that we are not spies?'

'If you are, stop now – that is all I can say.' Oupa said, and smiled.

'Do you guys want tea or something?'

'Tea,' John said.

'Yes,' Oupa said. Dikeledi went into the kitchen to make tea.

John looked at Oupa straight in the eye without winking and said: 'This is your life, you know that?'

'I know,' Oupa said, quietly. John looked away, through the window, into the distance and the half-circle of the blue sky, the silver light out there, and the rusted roof-top, and the bit of tree, the leaves that kept shaking and shaking, and the big windows staring as if they were huge eyes. None of these things could give him the answer he needed.

He looked back at Oupa. He was a young man indeed. Besides, John knew that he liked him. He liked Oupa and Oupa had won his respect, had made him careful when he talked to him. Now here he was, Oupa. What the hell was this he was saying? Oupa was silent. He knew that what he had said had kept both John and Dikeledi thinking. Oupa knew that both Dikeledi and John were very serious people. He respected them. He had, many times, tried to approach them, but had failed. He had discussed this with Mandla, who had warned him to take time, to be careful, not to be sentimental.

Mandla had now and then watched them, and others. He had met David Horwitz, after he had seen Dikeledi with him on several occasions. He had been to where Dikeledi worked. He had once asked John for a lift. They had driven to town, and on the way they had talked, almost about everything, and Mandla had wanted to come back, to meet John again, but he did not say so to him. Then once, when Oupa mentioned them to him again, he had said, talk to them, make them understand that they can be part of the revolutionary process. Mandla had then decided to keep away, to watch from a distance. He had told Oupa that now he had talked to them, Oupa must report to him every day about what they said when they talked.

Oupa did not look away when John looked at him. 'Well, the African people are going to win this war, about that there is no question. But it has to start somewhere, and perhaps you and I are the initial milestones.'

He sighed, and sat back. John was tapping his shoe softly on the floor. Dikeledi brought the tea to them. John thought he would rather talk to Oupa about all this later, when they were alone. Dikeledi sat down. Once, not so long ago, she had known hope. She had talked to men and women who, it seemed then, knew exactly what was going on in their country. Young men and women who were full of the fight, who were going to die if need be.

In those days she had been on the beat, all over the country, and she had met these young men and women, some working out in the country as doctors, some as teachers, some literally building their future with their hands. Now and then, at their conferences and meetings, she had heard them talk. At first she was afraid of them. It was not easy to talk to such clear-minded people. You had to know which side you stood on, and the sides were clearly drawn. You were either on the side of the Black people or you were not.

At first, she found it hard to define. That was when she changed her name. Her byline was no longer Rose Ramono but Dikeledi Ramono. Then she had fought, with her career at stake during inner conferences at the newsroom, for the right to talk about blacks, not 'non-whites', in her articles. One bright day she had won. Then some of the people who were fighting in hospitals, in classrooms, in those empty, dry, country schools, at conferences, had shown her that they respected her.

They had shown her that she was one of them. She had talked to her father about this. While he encouraged her, he also made it clear, somehow, that he regarded what was going on as something which still had to be cooked, looked into. Whenever they talked, he was careful. He questioned her. Made it known when he thought something was wrong, or when he disagreed. 'I want you to understand that colour here must not be the issue. Once we get to understand that, then we can talk on, but I am afraid that you have put too much emphasis on the colour question,' Ramono used to say to her. They talked for hours about this. Dikeledi then talked to the other people. Most knew about Ramono. Some came to see him. Most times they disagreed. Most other times they agreed. They liked each other and respected each other. Ramono always said that he thought they were very bright boys indeed, the material to bring liberation to South Africa. They have to learn, yes, they have to learn, he would add sadly.

Most of these people were gone now. Some were in jail. Some dead, killed inside jail or killed while walking the streets. Some were in exile. Some had gone mad. Some had become traitors. Some were just silent. Now here was Oupa talking calmly and confidently about the certainty of victory. When some of those people had gone, the Power days had come. No one who had seen those days would ever forget them.

'I feel very tired,' Dikeledi said.

'Yes, I think we must go after this,' John said.

'You did not mean it like that.' She looked at John.

'Yes, I have to go to work,' he said.

'Ja, we had come to say that you must have strength, your father is a hero. He did not steal. He did not kill anyone. He is not a criminal. So why is he in jail? In fact, all those killers and thieves might be released tomorrow, not him! Why? His ideas are what they fear.

'Why? He talks about the liberation of the African people. He wants to destroy oppression, to destroy exploitation, he wants to set us free, to build a new country.' There was silence when Oupa had finished. John swallowed his tea. Dikeledi looked at Oupa and then began to laugh.

'It's funny,' she said, still trying to suppress laughter, 'but I am not laughing at what you are saying, Oupa. You are so young. I don't mean that, I mean I have heard all that before, I have, I really have, and I believed in it. I have since seen so much disaster, so much. My father's gone to jail for fifteen years. There you are saying all these things. What do I say?'

'There is no one who can promise anything. You can promise us your unshaking participation, and then you can begin to know that one day, one day, we must win. That is the inspiration. It is going to be hard, but we must win,' Oupa said.

'Oupa, I have heard that so many times, I said so to you.'

'Well, you will never stop hearing it until we win. It is our certain victory which will rescue you from these sounds.'

'You are so funny, talking like that,' Dikeledi said.

'I wish I were not, I really do,' Oupa said.

Dikeledi brought back the filled cups. She sat next to John.

'What's new with you, John?'

'Well, nothing really,' he said.

'Oupa, do you know that John spent eleven months in solitary confinement?'

'Yes, I do,' Oupa said.

'Do you really think you would like to take him back there?'

'Why would I like that?'

'No, please, please don't drag me in like that,' John cut in.

'But John,' Dikeledi said.

'No, don't,' John said.

'I am asking Oupa why he thinks we should believe what he is saying.'

'Okay, don't believe it, then.'

'I don't think it is even a thing which we have to believe or not believe; the issues are much bigger than that. We all believe that we must be free. We all believe that we must work towards that, that it is necessarily a voluntary act. And then, we also know that many other people tried this out before us; so we are saying to Oupa, how do we know we are going to be saved? And I don't think that Oupa can guarantee us that. He cannot. It is a matter in which we must realise that we are risking ourselves, and voluntarily take the risk. I agree with Oupa that perhaps the hope we have is that eventually what we stand for must win. So I ask, what do we stand for?'

'We stand for the destruction of oppression and exploitation,' Oupa said.

'Who is we?'

'The Movement,' Oupa said. It was as if some thunder had hit the room. John looked at Oupa. Dikeledi looked at Oupa. Ramono had said that he was with the Movement and that he believed that the programme of the Movement was going to save South Africa.

'Did you and my father work together?'

'I knew of him, and I am sure he knew of me, but I did not work with him directly.'

Dikeledi did not know what to do. She did not know whether if she screamed, it would be out of joy or misery.

'What I have just said must end here,' Oupa said eventually. 'No one, just no one outside the three of us must be told.'

They looked at him.

'I am asking you a favour, knowing that you cannot refuse to offer me it, since really you are on my side.'

'I won't say a thing about it. Now I must go, really I must,' John said, and stood up.

'But, Oupa, what does one say?'

'Nothing, be quiet, wait. You know a lot now, protect it, that is all,' Oupa said and stood up too.

Oupa and John went out, into the Kombi. It was no longer early morning. The streets were deserted. Soon it would be noon.

'Where are you going?' Oupa asked.

'I have to start working.'

'Can you drop me at the bus stop?'

'Yes, oh yes,' John said. They turned up Selborne Street. They were silent in the Kombi. In their new and sudden realisation, they had become total strangers to each other. It was a relief for Oupa to realise that John was willing. John had realised that now there was no way they could retreat from whatever proposal Oupa might bring to them. No, he could still back out. He could promise never to say a thing about it, and that would be that. John had created a way for himself. Yet, he also knew that he was going to listen to Oupa. He drew up at the bus stop.

'I will see you,' he said to Oupa as he was getting out.

'I will stop by when I come back from town,' Oupa said.

The bus came. He chose the back seat at the window. There were few people in the bus. Opposite where he sat was a group of old ladies. Oupa thought about his mother. Mary had worked all her life as a domestic servant and now as a washerwoman. She worked in Lower Houghton when she was young, and during the time when Oupa was born. She worked in Hillbrow. In Orange Grove. In Highlands North. In Sandton. In Rosebank. Oupa knew the places where his mother had worked. He even knew some of the people she had worked for. He hated many of them. The bus stopped at Highlands North. One old lady got off.

Oupa could see the street down which, when he first went to school, he had often walked. He had been told then that he must hide himself he should not go to school publicly, because the neighbours might tell the cops about his presence there. He knew how to do it. He did it well. But he was relieved when his mother told him that they were going to move to Alexandra for good.

God, what was Mandla going to say? Somehow, Oupa knew that he had nothing to fear, that he could trust John and Dikeledi. Somehow he knew this. He knew that since he had asked them not to talk about his association with the Movement they would not talk about it. Both of them knew exactly what he meant by that. But he still wondered how Mandla would respond. He had learnt to be so careful, so extra careful when dealing with anyone. He had come to know that mistakes could be disastrous; so much so that now he felt weighed down, burdened by this news that he had. He must reach Mandla and talk to him about Dikeledi and John. He must talk to Mandla, and then know what step to take next. He felt a sense of achievement today. He knew that one day he, John and Dikeledi would have much in common.

He wondered what news Mandla had for him. There were cars in the street. The bus was swallowing many people now. A girl, maybe Mpho's age, sat next to Oupa. Oupa felt her touch him with her arm as she sat down. She looked like an animal the way she seemed to be scared, or shy or something. She sat there, staring straight ahead. She had hardly looked at Oupa. Oupa looked out of the window. He saw cops with their captives out there. He turned to face the girl. He said to her, 'People áre going to jail out there.'

144

She looked, or stole a look, and quickly looked ahead murmuring something.

'Where do you come from?' Oupa asked her, and realised that she was a pretty girl indeed.

'From down there,' she said, indicating with her thumb, pointing behind them. Oupa realised that she must be scared . . . She must have been told not to talk to anyone. He decided to leave her alone. Someone was talking about how women are devils, how they must never be trusted. He was talking at the top of his voice. Someone asked him if he included his mother in the kingdom of devils. She was a devil to my father, and to the rest of the world, perhaps not to me, the old man said. The whole bus laughed. Someone asked if he still slept with women. I do, he said. But soon as the fruit is eaten, I disappear. Why do you want their fruit? Oupa realised that the girl next to him was suppressing laughter. It is nice – he wiped his mouth – it is nice. They know that they have something nice, that is why they become devils. Oupa stood up, it was at Harrow Road. He got off the bus. It must be around lunchtime, he thought. The traffic was thick. He could see the double-storey house where he was going to. He crossed the empty space into the yard, passed the huge house and went to the back. He knocked on the door. A woman came out. Mary's son, she said. How are you?

'I am fine.'

'Mandla is somewhere behind there,' the old lady said. Mandla was sitting in the sun, reading. Mandla and Oupa smiled at each other. Oupa sat next to him.

'How are you, comrade?'

'I am fine,' Oupa said.

'Yes? And you look it.' Mandla, short, heavy, with strong-looking arms, was always ready to smile. He had a handsome face, a round, bespectacled face which now took to being serious, now was about to laugh, now looked uncertain, now searching, now ugly when people talked. He was quick to ask questions, or to ask that something that was said which he did not understand should be explained. Mandla was a very reasonable man. He asked for very little from people, but was ready, always ready to give. Oupa took the book he was reading. It was a red book. In white was written 'Lenin', and in black 'What Is To Be Done?' Oupa wondered if Oni had finished reading the one he had given her.

'So, comrade, what have you been doing?'

'I talked to John and to Dikeledi this morning.'

'Yes, I saw that the old man and our other comrades got fifteen years. How is Dikeledi? Did you see their mother?'

'No.'

'How is the family taking it?'

'They seem mixed up at this point, obviously. It is a disaster, but I think the old lady is taking it well. I listened to her yesterday, talking to people who had come to her. She was clear on the political issue. She saw it in perspective, and said so to all the people.'

'What did the people say?'

'They varied really, but I think what is important is that, as you know, they will respond to this as a community. People understand what the comrades were doing, and they support them.'

'Were you able to see the other families?'

'No.'

'I do not think you should, you may be exposing yourself unnecessarily.'

'I thought so. I thought I should check that with you.'

'Yes, comrade, I think you should leave it. I also think that for a while you should stop coming here. I will give you the details of your work before you leave. What did you say about John?'

'He is okay.'

'I will arrange to meet him as soon as I think it necessary. I will tell you when I am ready. Now do you know this man, Mpando?'

'Yes, I know him.' Oupa had not learnt yet to call Mandla comrade, so he never spoke his name or addressed him directly.

'You see, during the Power days, and even now, this man stood like a huge formidable, all powerful statue against the people. The felt defenceless before this man. The people must know that they have an arm which is ready to defend them. Also, those who are not sure, who still want to help the enemy, must know that they will be dealt with; we are extending the arm that was created by the students, and also strengthening it. In two or three days, I will take this man. Talk to John and to Dikeledi about it. Nothing about how we are taking steps against him, but push them to get their own opinion, before and after.'

'I understand,' Oupa said.

'Let's see now comrade, I really need your opinion on this. I have all sorts of information relating to the movements of this man Mpando. I have done thorough work on him. I think that we can eliminate him without much difficulty.

'Now, we would like to do this on condition that it is a mobilisation tactic, an extended arm of the young comrades who, when some of them were fighting and falling, took action against traitors. We want the people to know that they have their own defence, that they can defend themselves against their enemy. We also want people to know that their arm of defence is extended by the Movement. What do you think, comrade?'

'I do not know. But are we focusing only on Soweto and Alexandra? I mean, this man Mpando is known for what he is here, by the people of Johannesburg, and that is all.'

'Well, all areas have their Mpandos. We are dealing with ours here. You can say we are setting a precedent for dealing with the Mpandos of all areas. This Mpando is a very big man in Johannesburg. The enemy will not take his elimination lightly; they will say all sorts of things about him. And, comrade, this will be a trend. There are other comrades all over South Africa who know that the Mpandos must go, and that they are going to go.'

It was eight o'clock on Friday night. The streets were deserted. Occasionally a group of people, coming out of the bus, spread through Selborne Street. It was not a dark night.

A stream of buses, taxis and private cars was moving down Selborne Street. A maroon Valiant was among them. It was delayed by a long queue of vehicles at Eleventh Avenue, where the buses were off-loading people. The driver kept craning his neck to see if he could overtake. When the chance presented itself, he swerved expertly out of the long queue at high speed and overtook the stationary buses.

He turned into Twelfth Avenue and swerved into a yard where there were many other cars parked. The four occupants of the Valiant locked their doors as they moved out into the semi-dark night.

All four of them were neatly dressed, in suits and ties. As they walked to the house they could hear Miriam Makeba's voice, 'Lelizwe lino Moya' from the powerful speakers. One of them began to whistle the tune. The music came out from a brightly-lit house where many people were gathered, drinking. The four neatly-dressed men went up the steps into the house.

In the house there were many people, seated in groups, talking. Once the four came in, people began to nudge each other, pointing at them. Joyce, the owner of the shebeen, met them at the door and asked them to follow her into an inner room, divided from the others by bamboo curtains. 'Joy, how are you?' said the man in a brown suit.

'I'm fine Captain, how are you?' Joyce was smiling.

'I'm all right. I suppose we need the same thing,' he said.

'Regal?'

'Yes.' He leaned back in his chair, pulling his jacket down to hide the revolver at his side. Joyce brought the glasses and the bottle of Shevas Regal.

'We have T-bone, would you like that?'

'Yes, plenty of it,' the man in the brown suit said. The others were talking to each other in low voices. Joyce disappeared to the kitchen and came back with four pieces of T-bone.

The bamboo curtains rattled as Joyce passed into the other room, where many people were. She looked around, and when her eyes met Mandla's she winked. Mandla winked back. He took his glass of beer, and sipped. Joyce went back to the four men. She sat at table with them.

'Do you need some?' the man in a grey suit said, lifting the bottle and looking at Joyce.

'No, I have been doing fine, let me fetch my glass.' She went into the kitchen and came back with a glass full of red wine.

'It's been a long day,' Joyce said.

'Yes,' the man in the brown suit said. He was a tall, broad-shouldered man. He sat sprawled in the chair, leaning to one side, showing signs of being tired. He had a broad face, huge arms, and seemed never to stop staring at people when he spoke to them. He had a bald patch, which made his shining forehead seem huge. He had a bright white shirt on, and a brown striped tie. He kept pulling at his jacket.

'I never know when is day and when is night, all I know is I am all the time on duty,' he said.

'Well, that is what it means to be a cop, is it not?'

'Yes,' he said smiling. 'One of these days, I want to pull out back to Northern Natal, and start a poultry farm business there.'

'Really?'

'Yes, you see, I am getting old, my job needs young men.'

'That is true,' Joyce said.

'If I go back, I will run poultry. That has been my wish. I don't know how it came that I got the job I am doing now.'

'But you are a hard-working cop.'

'Well . . .'

'You are. You are a captain already.'

'That goes with hard work I agree, but one makes enemies in the process.'

'I think people fear you.'

'That is no good for my work. People should love me, then I can do lots of good.'

'It is just that people don't understand your type of job, but one day they will,' Joyce said.

'I have to go for a pee,' Mpando said.

Joyce stood up and went into the other room, to Mandla.

'He is going out to pee,' she whispered, and met Mpando at the door. She blocked his way.

'Are you leaving?'

'No, I am going outside. I am coming back,' he said.

'You are such a tall man,' she said, still standing in his way.

'Am I?'

'Look,' she said, showing his height with her hand. Mandla had slipped out. Joyce embraced Mpando, holding him tight against her.

'I will soon pee on myself, let me go,' Mpando said.

Mpando saw the man walking towards the door, towards him.

'Haai,' he said, 'you coming to drink?'

'Yes,' Mandla said, approaching the steps.

'Don't overdo it, it is not healthy.'

'I know.'

'These steps are going to break someone's neck one day,' Mpando said, and turned at the corner towards the toilets.

When Mandla was sure that he was a little distance away, he followed him. He saw Mpando fidgeting with his zip. He waited. Mpando was dead still, head bowed, legs astride. Mandla walked towards him. Mpando turned, and that is when the shot rang. The bullet hit him on the side of the head. Another rang, hit straight into his heart.

Mpando staggered back, his hands flying outwards, his head sagging, and hit the ground. Mandla jumped the fence and slowly walked into a nearby house, where he changed into other clothes. The Shevas Regal bottle fell and shattered on the floor as Mpando's three colleagues simultaneously and with great speed flew to the bamboo curtains, guns drawn.

'Everyone against the wall!' the one in the grey suit shouted to the customers in the shebeen. People, men and women, rushed like cattle to the wall. 'Come on, quick move, against the wall, hold it, hold the wall! Come on hold it, open your legs, open your legs!'

The man in the navy-blue suit, taking cover against a nearby car, gun cocked, was listening intently for movement, for any sound. His colleague in the sky-blue suit, following instinct, experience, and his sharp ear, pressed against the wall, moving swiftly, was heading towards the toilets from where he was sure the shots had come.

Navy-blue opened the Valiant car door and radioed for reinforcements.

'Joe, Joe!' Sky-blue was calling, 'this side!' He held his magnum tight in both hands, pointing towards the toilets. Without leaving cover Joe propelled his long legs at great speed to where his colleague now was, at the toilets.

'Peter!'

'Joe, Mpando has been shot!' Peter said, his eyes flashing this and that way in the dark.

Joe flew past him, over the fence, against the wall, and stood still, listening. Plain-clothes police, both black and white, flooded the yard and the surrounding streets, blocking all the accesses to Twelfth Avenue. The area was flooded with torchlight.

Joe stood next to the body of Mpando. He had fallen into the urine which had flooded the primitive sanitary system of Alexandra. His brain had spilled and was mixed with the shit and urine. Joe, looking at all this, tasting the Shevas Regal on his tongue, felt bilious.

The people in the shebeen were being searched. Already several had been arrested for pass offences, and some for carrying dangerous weapons. Grey suit joined Joe at the toilets.

'Joe!'

'Someone has killed Mpando,' Joe said, and, as he said so, his stomach turned over. 'Oh my God, Ndlovu,' he said after the first bout of vomit.

Ndlovu held him, looking at the dead Mpando. In the confusion, no one had thought about the radiogram. The powerful speakers filled the night with Gladys Knights: 'Midnight Train'.

Twelve

One of the main newspapers in Johannesburg ran a column called 'Window On The Township'. This column had passed through many hands. Black journalists, some quite able, some lukewarm and some just outright tikey rubbish, had through time given the column all sorts of characteristics. The last journalist who had handled it was supposed to have been on the socialite beat. Whatever that was, he had managed to turn the column into one of those that is looked at and quickly passed over.

Now, for the past three weeks, people had been looking for the column. In the trains, in buses, in taxis, as soon as people picked up the newspaper they went straight for the middle page, looking for the face of the pretty girl. Dikeledi, staring, her eyes shining, her smile, now looked out at all those people who wanted to read the column. The news in this column was Mpando. For three weeks, Dikeledi had managed to get all sorts of people in Soweto, Alexandra, and the Reef talking about the death of the Top Cop who was shot in Alex. The first article had been an interview with the head of some Police Division in Pretoria. The cop, at first difficult, and then guarded, had talked about where Mpando was born, how he had built himself up from a constable to a captain in plain-clothes, how this man had solved many crimes involving car thefts, murder, arson, rape and many other crimes. He said that the act of killing this man was ghastly, irrational and criminal. The police were going to do everything in their power to bring the people who did it to court. And he had added that all the law-abiding people on the Reef would certainly feel that the cops had done their duty if they brought them to court. Dikeledi had used this.

She asked, first, the top business people in Soweto. Colonel-Major van der Walt in Pretoria says people on the Reef will certainly feel . . . What do *you* say?

The first person, who did not want his name mentioned, said: 'While it is true that people can't just be killed like that, like it happened with Mpando, the police themselves must now begin to change their attitude. They are feared. No black person sees a cop and thinks that he will protect him. The police must remember that it was not long ago that there were the Power days. The cop's image, to say the least, left a lot to be desired, and Mpando is known to have shot many people.' An article was quoted from some Johannesburg newspaper in which Mpando had been photographed with an FN rifle, during the Power days. The caption had read, 'Mpando: how do you tell a stone thrower from a schoolchild?'

One day the column said that an unidentified person had called the offices of the newspaper to say that the Movement took full responsibility for Mpando's death. Letters came to the columnist; she quoted them.

It was lunchtime. Dikeledi picked up her bag and David, meeting her at the door, invited her to lunch at his house. They walked out to the lift. There they were met by two people in suits, who wanted to talk to Dikeledi. They asked her to accompany them to the police station, John Vorster Square. They identified themselves as Sgt Visser and Warrant Officer Van Wyk from the Security Police.

'What for?'

'We have to talk to you.'

'Is she under arrest?'

'No, no,' Van Wyk said.

'Can I talk to my lawyer first, then?'

'You don't need to,' Visser said. They began to show Dikeledi that they were getting impatient with her. They walked into the lift. Down it went. At B floor, Dikeledi asked David to phone her mother, and tell her that the cops had taken her. Her voice was shaking. Her pretty eyes darted around, helplessly, shining. Her face felt dry. She saw her hands shaking as she tried to hold her bag. It was strange, strange indeed, to drive away in that long black Valiant, alone with the two sons of God. Dikeledi did not feel safe at all in the company of these gentlemen. She thought of John. She thought of Oupa. She thought of her father. She wondered! The Valiant, smooth, obviously a well-looked-after car, swerved and danced through the traffic with ease. No one said a thing to anybody. Once Van Wyk coughed, that was all. Dikeledi felt her stomach harden. Her mouth was dry.

Back at the office Dikeledi wondered some more, as she read the letters which kept telling her that people wanted to know more about the Mpando affair. The next day the column said that Dikeledi had been called in by the cops. They had told her that they did not want her to pursue the Mpando affair further, that otherwise she would be put in jail for the rest of her life. Dikeledi wrote that since she did not want to go to jail for the rest of her life, she would stop writing about the matter. She thought of Van Wyk and Visser. Both of them, at their office, after questioning her, had asked her what she thought about the Mpando affair. She had said she had not thought about it. Pushed, she had said she abhorred any kind of violence. Did she think killing Mpando was a criminal act? As a journalist she preferred to wait until the people who did it had been arrested and brought to court. She had confidence that the cops would do this, and her stand would be dictated by the court's judgement. She would even declare this in the column. Both Visser and Van Wyk had looked straight into her eyes as she gave this little speech. Both had thought, you bitch, you dirty fucking bitch, one day we will catch up with you. All she said was written down. Then she was taken back to her office. It was long after lunch. David had come back. Had waited for her. When she came back, he had asked if they could go for supper. Dikeledi told him she would rather be with her family.

This morning she sat at her desk, reading the letters. She put them in a file, for the sub-editor. Just then her phone rang.

'Hi, who is this?'

'Oni.'

'Haai, how are you?'

'Fine, look, I am in town. I thought maybe when you knock off this evening we should go back together, how is that?'

'All right, where do we meet?'

'I will come and collect you.'

'Fine.' The line went dead.

It was four-thirty when Oni and Dikeledi met. They walked together, in silence, towards the Alexandra bus stop in Noord Street. When they met, Dikeledi looked into Oni's eyes, smiled and said. 'You!' and shook her head still smiling. Oni had merely smiled back, and said nothing. Now, they were much closer; yet now they seemed to have nothing to talk about, since it seemed that their past had now been erased. But they were about to discover that they had the world to talk about, since what now bound them together involved their lives or deaths. Indeed, they had the world to talk about. They walked quietly. All Johannesburg was on the streets.

Everybody heard the explosion. Oni and Dikeledi walked faster. They walked, hurrying to get back to Alexandra now. Knowing that the Golden City, a few minutes from now, would be filled with all types of South African cops. The number one enemy of black people. For a second, it was as if Johannesburg, for the first time since it was created, stood still; just for a second. Then it got into action. Everywhere, it seemed, there were sirens. Oni and Dikeledi took a taxi, trying to rush out of the city. Their taxi stopped more than ten times in a nine-mile drive. They were taken out of the taxi. The packed vehicle was searched, passes asked from passengers, names taken, and then they were told to drive on. All the roads leading to the townships were sealed, tight. Oni and Dikeledi made it home. There were cops all over Alexandra. Some houses were searched. There were many arrests made for passes, knives, guns, and other minor offences. The real owners of Alexandra had now moved in, had taken the township over at gunpoint. The people were used to this. They shook a bit as this massive power moved towards them, otherwise they went on drinking, singing, and listening to music. They went on watching, as if not watching, showing their children what was going on in all sorts of ways: shouting at them to come in early, didn't they see, the cops were out there?

Without saying a word to each other about it, both Dikeledi and Oni knew that now they were going to have to be serious with each other. It was a moment of great shock for both. It was a moment of great surprise and joy.

Oni, joyful and pleasant, kept her eyes stuck on Dikeledi. Dikeledi felt welcomed in a way she could not describe. She felt she knew nothing, and at the same time she felt that now she was going to have to learn a whole lot of new things. And, in her way, she was curious, wanting to know how Oni, in all this time that they had known each other, could have withheld such important information from her. She wondered how she could have had such discipline. When they got to Oni's room, and had settled and were drinking tea, Oni immediately said that Oupa had told her all about Dikeledi's recruitment. She was happy that now they were not going to relate to each other as friends that only met and talked; that now they were comrades.

'We have to start a study group here,' Oni said. 'We have to try and gather all the girls, and start a women's group too. I will welcome any of your suggestions.' She went into the other section of the room, and brought back a book which she gave to Dikeledi. 'The two of us can begin to study together, while we watch and work out which of the other girls can come into the group. Maybe you can read that book first, and then we can try to discuss it, and from it create our own ideas for working. No one must see it in your hands – that can lead to all sorts of trouble, as you know. Please be careful.'

Dikeledi was silent, watching, unbelieving. She tried to think back to the old past, which really was just yesterday, when she did not know that Oni belonged to the Movement. Oupa had made it clear to her that she was going o work under Oni for a while. He had done it in his own sweet way, in the way that he knew how. He had made her feel that while he understood that he was younger than her, and also that there might be other things between her and Oni, now all that was to be overlooked; all that was going to be pushed back and new priorities created. Dikeledi had been willing.

The night grew older. The night sounds came, and the radio, now for the hundredth time, beeped and then gave the news. Terrorists had planted a bomb in a parking lot in the centre of Johannesburg. Many cars were damaged, but no one injured. The police said that the bomb was manufactured in a communist country. They were working full out to catch those responsible. Anyone who could give information leading to the arrest must phone such and such a number, source to be treated as confidential.

Oni switched the radio off.

'Did I tell you that Yao wrote to me?'

'No, what is he saying?'

'Oh, Yao . . . ' Oni pulled herself up and went to her bookcase. She found the letter and gave it to Dikeledi, who sat back and began to read it. Oni sat on the carpet, her back against the sofa. She stretched, and began to drift away in thought while Dikeledi became absorbed in the letter.

Dikeledi was overwhelmed by everything at this point of her life. She felt strange, knowing that now she belonged to a force which was slowly, very slowly but very systematically, like water flowing from a dam, approaching every corner of the country. In the past few days, having heard that Alexandra had killed its Mpando, Cape Town had done it, Durban had done it, Port Elizabeth had done it; and somewhere near Pietersburg some terrible chief had ceased to flog and sell his people; from the Natal and Transkei countryside came similar reports. The Movement was like the wind.

It was strange to know that she was one with this wind. She wondered how she would integrate into it, be part of it and it part of her. It was obvious that the power which had for so many years, with such strength and brute force, beaten down her people into state of such meekness, ignorance, fear and poverty, had lost the initiative now. And it was because of this that she also wondered a lot about herself. She wondered who indeed she was. She wondered whether she really could, whichever way it had to be done, gain the calmness, the discipline she had observed in Oni and Oupa. For her it was a miracle how they managed to be who they were. She wondered a lot about herself; would she be able to cope, could they teach her how to be like them. How was it done, she wished she could know, that she could be sure it would be all right, that she would be all right, that she would qualify to be a member. At this point, there was only silence. She was alone, with herself. Oni was lost in her own thoughts. Dikeledi remembered that she was reading Yao's letter.

'Gosh,' she said at last, and sat up.

'What's the matter?'

'No, I was just absent-minded, let me try and read the letter now,' Dikeledi said.

'Isn't he funny?' Oni said.

'Yao, Yao, he says such strange things. Listen to this: "American life is a big party. What makes it a party is that everyone here is dead drunk. How can you do anything when you are drunk?"'

'No read on, read on Dikeledi, that man is funny indeed.'

Oni was thinking that the parcel Oupa had given her was a powerful parcel indeed. Twenty cars damaged beyond repair.

Nearby windows shattered. It was proving difficult to get all this under control. All this what? She began to shake a bit. If they caught up with her, if they did, surely she would never come out alive. They would kill her, as they had killed others. She wondered where Oupa was. She felt alone now. She wished she could talk to someone about all this. But she could not.

'Listen: "The old man Ramono, I hear, stood in court like the priest we have never heard of, who says nothing about God or Jesus, but a lot about us; I hear all the country heard him. What is Dikeledi saying, is she not proud to have been brought to earth by such a man? A new type of priest? Kiss her for me, tell her we expect things from her!"'

'You know that Yao has to be there for two or three years yet.'

'I am sure you miss him.'

Oni laughed, throwing her head back as if something, some pain had hit her. 'Oh, how I miss that mad man.'

'Yao, he is a real mad man. He was so funny.'

'But you know I think he is suffering in America. I don't think he likes it there, I really don't think so. Yao can be humorous about a whole lot of things, just enjoying humour, but this isn't the kind of humour he likes. He sounds bitter, he is like someone crying. I feel so for him. I wish he could realise that he really can quit, and come back home. I have tried to say this to him, but he thinks he will have failed in life if he abandons what he is doing now. The price we pay for rubbish!'

'Gosh, I know. Yes, now and then he strikes a funny note, real painful.'

'But he keeps in close contact with what is happening here.'

'He does.'

'I must tell him to stop writing such dangerous letters.'

'About Ramono.'

Dikeledi looked at her friend, and laughed.

'You are right,' she said. Dikeledi wanted to ask Oni if Yao knew that she was in the Movement, but after a while thought she should not. It was too early. She was unsure of herself.

'He does not know that I am in the Movement,' Oni said. Dikeledi looked at her.

'If he knew, maybe he would abandon what he is doing.'

'He would not. He would stick to it to the end, then come running.'

'He is deep in this thing, heh?'

'Neck deep, I come second to that.' Dikeledi laughed. 'I mean it,' Oni said.

Dikeledi put the letter down. She stretched and yawned. For a while there was silence. Oni had started to listen to the sounds outside. Dikeledi

154

wondered whether she must go now. She wanted to go home, to read the booklet that Oni had given her. She thought maybe it was not right that she take it home. Already she had exposed herself, she thought. Already the cops had called her in. She thought God, how close they were, if only they knew what she knew. She began to wonder whether being in the Movement, it was all right for her to be in the newspapers too. She would talk about this with Oni or Oupa. She wondered where John was.

'Have you see John lately?'

'No, I have not. He seems to be keeping Vuki's company a lot lately.'

'You mean he seems to be in your theatre?'

'Not really. John thinks such things are funny, he thinks that they don't have anything to do with reality.' There was a knock on the door. Oni looked at the watch. It was exactly twelve midnight.

Oupa walked in, with his calm young face; short, thin, with shy-looking, yet very curious eyes. He smiled at Dikeledi and then at Oni. He sighed, and sat on the sofa.

'John dropped me here. He is picking us up at about half-past. How is it?'

'Okay,' Oni said yawning.

'I am fine,' Dikeledi said.

'Tea or something? I am also starving.'

'Tea yes, maybe also bread,' Oni said and went to the kitchen section of her room.

John came back at half-past. He picked up Dikeledi and Oupa and left. Oni remained behind, dreaming, going through nightmares. She missed Yao immensely. She wished he was here today, even if he did not know about all this, just so he was here, to hold her, and so that they could talk to each other, even if it were about how hot it was this summer. She sat up that night. She wrote Yao a letter, telling him about the weather, how now and then it rained and how now and then it was very hot. It was funny to receive letters from him complaining about severe cold and snow and gloves and overcoats, while she was wearing very thin dresses. It was a long letter. She knew that Yao was going to be angry with her, wondering why she did not give him reports about what was happening in Alexandra, in South Africa. He would be so angry with her. She must find a way of sending a letter to him that would tell him to stop expecting news like that from her. She signed her letter. Then – *P.S. Since we are not the only ones reading the letters, as you know, I cannot say anything else, not that there is anything. Why ask for trouble unnecessarily?* She folded the letter, put it in an envelope and addressed it to Yao. She would mail it in the morning, if she had the time. She crawled into her bed, and in no time she was asleep.

When she woke up in the morning, she just stayed put in bed. She did not want to read as usual. She did not want to get out of bed and make tea for herself. She lay there, now turning, now trying to lie still, trying not to hear the cars stopping outside. She did not even want to hear what the old lady next door was saying. But sounds reached her. And the light from outside and even the breeze got in. And the children with their noises, noises imitating adults, reached her.

She could feel the flesh between her thighs. She could feel their warmth. She could feel where they met or ended. She could even feel right deep beyond them. There was a heavy, a brutally heavy feeling there, wet, throbbing. If only Yao had listened, she would have had their baby now. Yao had wanted to be there, to be with her and their baby. He could not bear the thought of her being with their baby without him. He did not think she was incapable of looking after it. No. He knew she would look after it and bring it up in such a way that he too would love it. But he wanted to share with her every moment, every minute of that experience. She had pleaded with him. He had asked her please to stop, because that caused much pain. She had been tempted more than once, in that time, to go ahead without his knowledge and allow the baby to come. She could have done it. But she did not. Sometimes she regretted it. Sometimes she thought well, that was right. He would never have forgiven her for that, if she had dared to do it.

She reached out for the radio knob. The police were certain that they would make an arrest soon. They were pleading with the public to watch, to keep their eyes and ears open, to help the police. If anyone saw a person with a parcel, they should stop them, or call the police immediately. In public places, people who look suspicious should be reported immediately. The public must cooperate. The police, who were working around the clock to make the public safe, depended a lot on the cooperation of the public. The police had no way of knowing when and where these terrorists would strike again, but the cooperation of the public was the first step towards ensuring the security of all. So the radio said. Oni switched it off. She covered her head with blankets. She lay on her back and spread her legs to relax. Somehow, she fell asleep again.

It was already afternoon when she woke. She had missed the one o'clock news. She got out of the blankets, stretched, and began her daily exercises.

She washed herself. She made tea and enjoyed it in the silence of her room. She put on her floral Afro-dress and walked out into the sun. In the yard, everyone was up. She greeted the old lady next door, who told her that she had heard that the Movement had exploded cars in town. Why is the Movement doing this? Yesterday, there were too many police all over in Alexandra; it was like the Power days again. She was certain that many other people had been shot again, why was the Movement provoking the law? Oni said she would get the newspaper and soon she would be able to talk and know what had happened. The old lady, standing by the coal box washing clothes, did not look up. But she spoke on and on, as if she was talking to herself. Oni began to move. Yes, read the newspaper and tell us, the old lady said. The cops have gone mad, and you don't provoke mad people. They will come back with their guns and hippos and smoke and everyone is going to be miserable again. Why don't people realise that you can take so much pain and no more . . . By this time, Oni was walking away, hardly listening.

The streets looked deserted, except for Hofmeyr Street. There was a police landrover, with police in camouflage dress and FNs. They had stopped a group of boys. Oni walked towards them. As she passed them, a black police-man whistled at her, praising her figure. She looked at him and smiled. She went on her way. At Second Avenue she saw another cop car, the notorious Blue Granada. As usual, guns were peeping out of its windows. She passed that too. There were four white cops in it, in plain clothes. They were eating lunch or something. She went towards the Pretoria main road. There, at a Chinese shop, she bought a packet of fish and chips, some tomatoes, milk and canned beef. She wondered if she should buy a newspaper. There were so many police. She might stick out as odd, the educated type. She decided to buy it, and walked back into the street. The Blue Granada was still there. They were still eating and talking. She passed them. She went back into Hofmeyr Street, down it, walking slowly. People were out in the streets. Obviously there had been police action. At Fifth Avenue she turned left, back to her room ... The front page had a picture of the car park. Another page had the face of an old white man, the owner of the shop next to the park, who said his window had shattered when the explosion happened. It was a fright-ening sound. He had not thought he would see the next day after hearing that sound, the man said. Somewhere at the bottom there was a report that a railway line used mainly by goods trains had been sabotaged the night before. However, things were back to normal. Oni went up to the old lady and showed her the paper. She exclaimed that the way the thing exploded was dangerous. So many cars wrecked! Why is the Movement doing this?

Oni shrugged her shoulders. Whispering, the old lady said: you know, it is right to do away with people like Mpando. She whispered into Oni's ear, and told her not to talk too much about that. She should hold that within her cheeks, very few people are to be trusted, the old lady said. Then she asked where Yao was and what he was doing. Oni told her about the letter, and that Yao did not like America. The old lady said no, young people don't know, they must know that there is nowhere like home. He must stick at it, learn, and the time would come for him to come back; then everyone would be proud of him. He would have learnt many things from white people, which he would teach to other black people. Yao was a clever and good man. Oni said how she missed him. Hold on, hold on, the old lady said, wait for him, he will come back, and everything will be so nice, so nice, it will be as if he had never left. She gave her a mischievous smile. Oni smiled back, and hugged her. The old lady held Oni's hand and pulled her towards her. 'You know,' she said, still whispering not wanting the sun or the sky to hear what she was going to say, 'you know you girls of now, sies, man sies.' She showed a disgust in her face, frowning, looking almost as if she was going to spit any minute. 'Sies, you know, I come from the valleys of the North, from Pietersburg, from within the mountains, you know. If my husband was still alive, he would tell you. I was a bright girl, the pride of my village, and you know why? Because when my husband left for the mines — you know, those days, trucks used to come, they were red trucks driven by hard-looking white men — when these trucks came, all of the young men of the village were gone. We remained behind, mothers, sisters, girlfriends, sweethearts, crying and crying, feeling that we might never see them again, or that they would be gone too long, or just feeling very sad that these men were somehow being taken away against their will.

'We knew that when they came back, most of them would be very different people. They would talk strange things. You would trust a snake under your bed sooner than them sitting at table. When the truck came to fetch my young man, he had just come back from the mountain. He was looking strong, had this hard, shining look in his eyes. When they took him, I went to him and told him, you look after yourself now. I am waiting for you, I am going to wait for you, don't shame us. After that, I had to live up to my words. It was hard. You know what? I realised that if you give in easily to your desires, there are very few things that you don't give in to. How can you not? You have never fought, within yourself, and sized up your strength, you don't know who you are. I watch these girls of today. Always, all the time, they are ready to pull their bloomers down. They could do it every five minutes, sies. If your man comes back funny, you know he does not deserve you. He will know that too, leave him.' She laughed, she stood back and looked at Oni. She looked at her legs. Her eyes moved up Oni's body. 'You must be able to tell Yao when he comes back, when he touches your behind with love, that it has waited for him, touch it with care.' She laughed mischievously. 'Let me not go too far my child,' she said, and went back to her basin of clothes. Oni leaned against the wall. The sun baked her to the marrow. She thought she could feel her blood, or all the fluids of her life, melting and running all over her body.

'I hear you,' she said, 'Ma-Maria.'

'It's like that, my child,' the old lady said. 'These days, our lives are made up of flinching. Sometimes the flinching is almost like a gasp, when you see things that people do to themselves, to others. You know, I am not a Christian, but I heard that somewhere in the Bible they say these are signs that the world is coming to an end by fire, when every woman becomes a whore, when a son kills his mother. Those are parables, my child. None of us, no, not one of us is going to stand for the pain that these things cause us, and it is bound to change. If God isn't bringing any fire, we are going to make the fire.'

Her face had changed. Inside her eyes, which earlier on were watery with laughter, mischief and joy, her grey, almost jelly-like eyes had become hard now, dry, unwinking, piercing. Her face was stern, the smile had vanished in no time. Oni watched all this. She wondered, who is this old lady? They had known each other a long long time indeed. She had on many, many occasions given her snatches of her life, of who she was, and if Oni could sit down, she would almost be able to piece it all together and bring it to the present, to where she was standing now, her old, wrinkled hands wringing out old cotton petticoats. She could bring it to this time, and she was certain this was a strong lady. She had been abused, pulled and pushed, beaten by this her time, yet here she was, still a fighter.

For record, for history, for memory, Oni thought, I am going to dare and ask her. Oni for a very long time now had wished to ask her, had wanted to know, but she had not been able to ask it in the right way, the respectful way. She did not want to offend her. However, somehow she had always thought that the answer to a certain question was important. It was important for her in that she was young, she knew nothing really, and the times were crazy, she was crazy, everyone was crazy, but she did not want to die crazy, or give in to being crazy, she wanted to fight, fight to the last. Ma-Maria, in her silences, her singing or humming, in the night and in the morning, was a fighter. She had fought a long, long time now. How long, how long can one fight on, relentlessly and if needs be forever?

'Ma-Maria,' Oni said, not looking the old woman in the eye, 'tell me, how old are you?'

Ma-Maria looked at Oni. She looked down. She continued to wash her old cotton petticoats in her old hands. 'You are a silly girl,' she said without smiling. She looked at her. 'I was born five years after Sekhukhuni swallowed the sweet potato and died.' She smiled. 'No really, I don't know,' she said, and a flush of sadness engulfed her face. 'I don't know,' she said. 'Had I gone to school, I would be able to calculate. I don't know, but I remember, when I was a girl, there were many troubles in the land, white people were fighting each other, and we were fighting each other, some whites came to us to help them fight others, there was lots of trouble in those days, and I think I was this high then.' She held her hand at the height of her knee. 'But why do you ask me my age?' Her face was stern again as she looked at Oni.

'I want to know, because then I think I would have hope,' Oni said. Ma-Maria looked at her. Her face was expressionless. Oni knew that now Ma-Maria must be thinking about her daughters, Maria, Lydia and Stephina. All of them had now been swept away, and swept away forever, by Alexandra.

'Hope?' she said, staring at her old petticoats. 'Hope,' she said again, and smiled. She took her petticoats to the washing-line. She was walking slowly. Indeed, she was a very old woman. Oni waited. When she came back, Oni said, 'I hope you don't think I am being disrespectful, Ma-Maria, but I mean it, I had to ask you that question.'

'Well, you know if you weren't being disrespectful.' She took the petticoat to the washing-line. It was then, just then, as the old lady walked away towards the line in that slow, jerking gait, that something struck Oni.

Women seem to be waiting, waiting, all the time waiting, for the men to come back, and then waiting after the men have died, to follow them. She looked away now, into the sky, into the huge silver sun. Then she looked down to the earth, brown, hot, stony. The men have paid their price for that. The women have paid their price too. All that trouble was unnecessary. It was the result of oppression. Oni looked at Ma-Maria coming back from the line, walking her walk, then looked away. No, there was a lot to learn from Ma-Maria. These are the people who have kept the faith, who have made certain that the struggle is forever assured of its victory, when those who carry it forward follow the correct line. Oni also knew that if she was going to live to the age of this old, tired, but forever fighting lady, she would live in a different country. Already, the two of them were totally different, yet terribly the same. The old lady took the basin in both her hands and spilled out the water. The earth, coming in contact with water, began to smell. Oni watched the bubbles bursting and breaking.

'I have to see some of my friends this side, so we can eat snuff,' the old lady said to Oni. Oni nodded and took her newspaper, folded it slowly, and put it under her armpit. She said bye-bye to Ma-Maria and walked away back to her room.

Oni had been sitting on the sofa a long, long time now. Indeed, she had criss-crossed the world a few times in her mind. She sat, one leg on the cushion of the sofa, the other on the arm of the chair, her legs spread wide apart, her dress folded to her stomach. She sat there in that way, her head resting on her right hand, the other arm dangling on the side of the sofa. She felt very tired. She thought how it was never good for people to be idle. People and labour are one.

She looked at herself, sitting like that. She thought about the days, so many, so long ago. She remembered her days at the church school in Swaziland, surrounded by nuns. If she was caught sitting like that, she would pay with almost all her soul. She closed her legs. She buried her head on her lap. It was three-thirty. She could feel that she was a little dizzy with hunger. She did not even have the strength to begin to make food for herself. She would wait till four, then she would ask Oupa to take her some place where she could have something to eat. Somehow she wanted to get out of the house. The bed was unmade. She had not even cleaned the room. Everything in it made her feel tired.

When Oupa arrived, Oni was waiting for him at the door. She had her door key, her bag, ready to move.

'It's just four, what's this?'

'I know, I am starving, can we get something to eat?'

'Sure, where?'

'I don't know, anywhere as we move on.'

'Okay, er, Dikeledi managed to get us David's car, but he wants it back after eight.'

'That is all right, not so?'

'Ja, I think so.' They got into the car. Oupa slid the gear and they were off.

'There are roadblocks everywhere. I have been stopped more than twice, driving from Parktown,' Oupa said.

'Well,' Oni said. She was not really concerned by that. She wanted to eat; she was starving. They stopped at a cafe. Oupa rushed in and came back with a brown parcel. They went down Corlett Drive. It was just as they were going to drive onto the highway that they were stopped.

'Yes, where are you going to?'

'I am going to Soweto.'

'Where you stay?'

'Alexandra.'

'Where is your pass?'

'Here.' Oupa gave it to him. He was a young boy, perhaps Oupa's age, but the way he was talking he was older, superior. He was in the usual camouflage dress. A woman came and asked Oni to come out of the car to the tent. Oupa was almost dragged out. 'Where is your driver's licence?'

'Here.'

The policeman grabbed it from him. 'Here, here, here, can't you talk?'

Oupa almost ignored him, but then thought, what the fuck! 'I can,' he said.

'You can – so why don't you talk and stop your here, here, here? Heh?'

Oupa looked him straight in the eyes. He thought about how Malcolm used to talk about the green-eyed devil. This boy made his green eyes dance, like those of a snake. They were amused, they were contemptuous, they were angry. Oupa looked down. The boy grabbed him.

Oupa thought, good God, why don't you leave me alone. Okay, I am going to give you what you want. He began to cow down. The young green-eyed, camouflaged man was now dragging him, pulling him away, into some empty space. Oupa allowed himself to be led. As they stopped he thought, okay take it, you need it, it's your dose forever. He said: 'Baas, what's wrong now, what have I done baas?'

'Shut up, shut up,' the baas said. He was angry. He started to search Oupa from the top, through the cock, to the toe. He ordered that the car be searched thoroughly.

'Whose car is this?'

'My baas at work.'

'What is she doing here?' The man pointed at Oni.

'She is my girlfriend. We are going where she is staying.'

'Does the baas not need the car? Did you steal it?'

'No.'

He took down the number plates and gave them to someone to check out over the radio.

'Hoe is sy?' he said to the policewoman, nodding towards Oni.

'Goed,' she said.

'Hey, ry, ry, you wasting our time,' he said at last. Oupa got into the car and they moved off.

'You know,' Oni said, 'I was thinking that it is wrong, absolutely wrong, that we should allow these people to fetch us, like they did bontate Ramono, fetch us, take us to jail, and do what they want to do to us. If they come to fetch me, I must fight them, they should have to take my dead body away. Why not fight the battle once and for all?'

'You are angry, Oni. Calm down,' Oupa said. They were on the highway now. There were many cars, in all colours, carrying all shades of South Africans in them. Oni sat back. Yes, she was angry and she must never let herself be led into that trap.

'Thanks, Oupa,' she sighed. She looked at all those cars. And in the far distance there was the tall building, still pretending to dance in harmony with the setting sun. God, that white woman deliberately went straight for her sex, held it in her hand. When Oni looked at her, there was no expression, nothing, on her face. She could have been fast asleep, unaware of her actions. Except that she was not. She was looking for what she was looking, and if she had found it, the whole South African police force would have been out, out to get Oni.

Oni sighed again. When she touched her, Oni had looked at her; when her fingers moved, around and inside, Oni had looked away, winced, stood dead still. She really did not know that anything could be put into that, she did not know that.

'Soon as we cross the city, be prepared for another roadblock. In fact, any time now, here on the highway. It is wrong, completely wrong, to let these people take you by surprise.'

'I know,' Oni said. Oupa was completely relaxed, looking straight ahead of him. He was enjoying his driving, playing around with his thoughts, amusing himself. Oni was watching him. She thought really, Oupa, who the hell gave birth to you! Such a calm man, reliable, so young. Oni, sitting there, next to this young man, thought with fire inside her, with the rage of a tigress, that if they dared to touch this man, if they dared, she would make them pay. There were too many, just too many bright boys, the only ones the nation had, who had gone, who were erased just like that, by the madness of this country. If they dared to touch Oupa, nobody, nobody would stop her rage.

'Sometimes I think this is a really beautiful country,' Oupa said. He did not look at Oni when she looked at him. He sighed. He tilted his head, the way he did when it seemed he was about to cry, or was fighting hard not to cry.

'Well, this is a nice, beautiful country, no doubt about that,' Oni said.

'Yes, I know what you mean.' He sighed again. 'You know, when I drive from Cape Town to Durban, and watch the sea, the mountains, the sky, the theatres, good God, I always think that indeed, this is a beautiful country. I hear that some old white sailor who came here long ago called it the fairest cape in all the world. I don't know about the others, I know that that one is very beautiful.'

'This is a beautiful country, Oupa,' Oni said again, and looked out of the window.

'I know, but tell me, what makes the country beautiful?'

'Well, you cannot say that the Cape you are talking about is not nice. But the people who run this country are selfish, dogs in the manger, making everyone miserable to satisfy their avarice and greed. Only the landscape is beautiful.'

He looked at her, and laughed. 'Okay sweetheart, I know,' he said. 'Sweetheart yourself,' Oni said. They left the highway. They could see Soweto now. The sameness of the place. Huge and so vast, spreading and spreading, in its sameness. Smoke stood guard above Soweto, hanging there, as if to listen, floating above there, as if trapped. They saw him in the middle of the road.

He stood there, holding the FN legs apart, standing straight up. The son of South Africa. Oupa slowed down, swerved, and parked behind another car.

'Yes, how are you?' He opened Oupa's door.

'Fine baas, how are you?'

'Tired, working all day and night,' he said. 'Whose car is this?'

'For my baas, at work.'

'Where you going now?' He tested the key, by switching the car off and starting it again.

'I am taking my girlfriend home.'

He looked at Oni. Oni met the hazel eyes. 'Can you get out of the car please?' he said. Oni smiled a little and got out, obviously being polite. Three others came, and they began to search the car. A woman fetched Oni to the tent.

'I wonder how many more,' Oni said as they entered Soweto. There were many people. Coming from the train stations, women, men, old and young, crowding their streets, and smoke and terror, walking home. You could hear the sound of the train, stopping, pulling out, the rattle of its wheels. Oupa and Oni drove past the shops in Phefeni towards Dube, past Dube towards Mofolo.

Oupa was back on the highway. He was thinking that indeed, Vorster or no Vorster, crisis or no crisis, the South African terror, the holocaust machine, had been unmasked now. Throughout the whole of South Africa, he was sure you could not drive for more than a hundred kilometres in any direction without meeting a roadblock. Now was the time to hit, to hit where it hurt, to hit with everything you had. This was the time, Oupa felt. He remembered that once, when he had said this to Mandla, Mandla had said, 'Comrade, we are hitting, but our blows must build the struggle. We must be very systematic, knowing that this is going to be long, mastering the art of attack and retreat. I agree with you, there are times to hit hard. There are also, comrade, times to retreat; we are fighting a very strong enemy.'

Oupa would do nothing without a direction from what they called 'The Centre of Directives', 'TCD' they said for short. But he maintained, this was the time to hit. This was the time to spread them, in their camouflage uniforms, throughout the country, and begin to snipe at them. Oupa became aware that he had clenched his teeth, that his hands were now tight on the steering wheel. It was six o'clock. He swerved the car off the highway, got into Commissioner Street and passed John Vorster Square. He got out of the car near Park Station and went to Platform Thirteen. Tuki was wearing a blue overall. Themba was in jeans and boots. Both of them had old-looking hats on. They greeted each other.

'No tickets, or anything else to show you have just come back, right? Vorster's boys out there are hot. They're everywhere.'

'Nothing,' Tuki said.

'How's it?'

'Fine, but man, as you say, the Vorster boys are out there, all over, we have just brought a lot of them in the train.'

'When did you arrive?'

'Past two days,' Themba said,

'Saw anyone I know?'
'Yes, Anka, he sends his regards to Tsi.'
'Oh, Anka!' Oupa said.

Thirteen

Themba and Granny were walking down John Brandt Street in silence. Out of instinct Fidel clutched his mother, his arms around her neck, his legs tight around her waist. Now and then he moved the balls of his eyes, watching, listening, amazed by the silence among them. He had no speech to ask questions. The warmth which separated him from his mother was very comforting, seeping through his stomach, and his mother's movements rocked him, made him keep rhythm with the pace set by his silent, sullen father.

Themba was aware of all the sounds around them. His eyes were on the ground, moving along with the two elongated shadows that danced before them. At intervals his mind drifted to Tuki and to Oupa and to the unknown; to a darkness which loomed, engulfing everything, challenging him, wanting to know about his skills and his knowledge. As they walked their footsteps, their silence, the noises around them, all somehow belonged to the past. And the past was symbolised by his not being able to say a word to Granny or to Fidel. The present was now merged with the future which loomed heavily over him. Mixed with that burden was the deep pain and sadness of his recognition that the only relation he and Granny had now was to prove how expertly they could scratch each other's eyeballs out. They had done that ever since Themba had come back. And now their blindness had, like a dark cloud, settled in Fidel's eyes, leaving him silent.

What worried Granny was how come she had not been able to grab her life and, like the cripples in the scriptures when hurled against the power of Jesus Christ, stand up and walk forever. Walk away from Themba. She knew, as well as she knew the sight reflected in the mirror when she stood before it, that her acceptance of Georgy's proposal had been nothing but a way of punishing Themba. If she still had the right to punish him, what did that mean? She looked at Themba, whose grim silent face asked her if she could stand up and go, forever, throwing away the crutches. She suspected that the reason why she had looked at him now was because they had arrived at their departure point. They had just walked past Fifteenth Avenue.

The Alexandra bus terminus had opened its floodgates. Suddenly there were thousands of footsteps. Dust rose to the sky. Within it swirled the roar of buses, the footsteps, and the many, many inaudible voices. The sun hung on the horizon, spreading the multi-coloured vastness of the sky like the sound of trumpets.

They stopped at Sixteenth Avenue, in the middle of the street. Their scratched eyeballs met. 'We don't deserve each other,' Granny said. Themba saw a very beautiful, gentle, vulnerable, strong, upright woman before him. What else could he see? This was his interpretation of the words which now hit him, clutched him, shook him in the middle of the street.

'What will happen to Fidel?' That was not what he wanted to say.

'What do you think?' Granny shook Fidel to make him more comfortable on her back. They stared at each other in silence, a silence as big as their pain. 'I have to go,' Granny said.

'Okay,' Themba said, but he did not move. Granny turned and walked away, she hoped forever.

Tuki was lying on the sofa, looking at pictures. Quietly Themba walked in, taking off his jacket and putting it on the chair. He sat down and sighed like the sky. Tuki looked at him. How come it was impossible for people to see themselves as others saw them? The largeness of the question hurled him into despair.

'This thing between you and Granny must stop,' Tuki said. He stood up and went into the kitchen. Themba thought any time now, any time, he was going to weep and weep forever. He grit his teeth and stared at the wall. Every muscle in him was taut, ready to snap. He felt like a dam whose walls are on the point of giving in to pressure, like the flood that would launch itself like mad running footsteps and trample everything before it. His mind went back to the time when he had first seen Granny and Fidel after his return. He had walked out when Georgy walked in. He had gone back to find out what he already knew, how things stood between Granny and Georgy. There had been something else that he wanted to know.

He knew Georgy. Georgy owned the streets of Alexandra. He owned them against the will of the policemen who eventually, in the eyes of everyone in Alexandra, had the worst of it against him. Tall, black like the night, thin, meticulous, soft-spoken, Georgy walked the street like a cat conscious of threatening noises around it. Then there was his smile, deep and warm, and of course his name, Georgy, which no longer was just a name you could spell like that, because that was not what it meant. Yet such things together with what everyone gathered from Hollywood films, and all the original intentions and unintended consequences which had made Alexandra, and a hundred and one gruesome murders, such things meant Georgy.

It was not going to be easy for Themba to get used to what had happened. He had been ready to explain. He knew that what he had done might have enraged anyone. He had left and not told Granny that he was leaving. And while he was gone Granny had met Georgy, and now she had brought Georgy home to meet him. They had met. 'Georgy and Granny are in love,' Themba said at last. It was a way of trying to accept the meaning of that and its consequences.

'Georgy Valiant?'

'Yes.'

'Georgy?' Tuki repeated.

'I found myself in the same house with Georgy yesterday, and I left him with Granny.' He looked down. 'I went back today. It is obvious that there is nothing I can do. I am concerned about Fidel, though.'

'She is concerned about Fidel too, remember that when you say it.' Tuki was leaning against the door frame, still holding the photographic magazine.

'But Fidel with Georgy?'

'Georgy is nothing in this, you know that too well.'

There was a knock. 'Gentlemen, how are you are all?' Oupa said, and looked around for a place to sit down.

'Oupa, how are you?'' Tuki said.

'Fine.' He looked at Themba. 'How is Fidel?'

'We were just talking about that. He is okay.'

'I am in a hurry. Are you expecting anyone?'

'No,' Tuki said.

'Themba, you have to go and see Dikeledi. Tuki and I have to leave — we may be back tomorrow morning or so.' He seemed unable to sit down. Tuki threw the magazine on the sofa and went to find his jacket.

'Themba, I was in the darkroom before you came. Can you take those pictures out and dry them if you have time?'

'Okay.'

'I will see you,' Oupa said.

'Okay,' Themba answered.

'Themba, don't allow this to drag you down. Keep a distance and think. I know you will think straight, but keep your distance.'

'Okay.' Themba stood up and saw them out.

The darkness of the darkroom and its silence, as picture after picture popped out on the white paper, corresponded to another darkness and silence as Themba tried to resolve his pain over Granny. He clung to Fidel. But somehow he knew that that was not the reason. Could it be that he was unable to accept that he had been told to walk out of the door? It was dark when he left the house.

Oupa and Tuki arrived in Lower Houghton from Soweto late at night. Mandla heard the footsteps and waited. He looked at his watch. It was fifteen minutes after midnight. He opened the door and Oupa walked in. They shook hands. Oupa went past him. Tuki followed Oupa and as he saw the smiling Mandla, he nodded.

'You are Tuki?'

'Yes, how are you?'

'Fine, Comrade. I am Mandla.'

'Glad to meet you.'

'I heard that you and Themba had a good time while you were away?'

'We worked hard.'

'Did you meet the people you know?'

'Yes, Boykie and Anka.'

'Yes, yes, you would know both, yes. How are they?'

'Fine.'

'Comrade, what is new?' Mancla turned and faced Oupa who was sitting on the bed. The room was very small. Mandla had always asked himself, really, what had the people who built servant-quarters been thinking of when they built them? Such rooms were cold or hot, depending on the change of the weather. They had no electricity. They were hidden behind everything on earth that would serve the purpose.

'Nothing new,' Oupa said.

'I see everyone is still talking about Mpando.'

'Yes.'

'They have tried to make it a criminal event, to strip it of its political significance, but they are failing.'

'People know who their enemies are.'

'Yes. Comrade Tuki and I have work to do – thanks for bringing him. When are we meeting in Noord street?'

'You will receive a confirmation of the date. Provisionally it is the twenty-fourth of next month.'

Dikeledi saw the dark clouds in Themba's face. She had given his troubles a lot of thought. She had known Themba a long time. In the past they had laughed together, talked, and never played with fire. But now she knew, without Themba knowing that she knew, that he was going through a bad time with Granny. She did not know whether that was her business or not.

'Themba, how are you?'

'Fine.'

'You look tired.'

'I am all right.'

'We have a long way to go,' she said, almost giving up. 'We have to use the Volkswagen. I will drive if you like.'

'Okay.' They were silent.

'I know that you are going through a bad time,' she said at last. 'If you think I can help, please let me.'

'Thanks.'

'What do you make of it?' Mandla asked.

'A lot of work has been done on this,' Tuki said, putting the file down. 'I . . .'

'You knew of the blue Granada, though?'

'I have seen it around. I did not know that it carried such big people.'

'Yes, as you see from the file, Major Viljoen is with the Flying Squad, Colonel van Niekerk with the Murder and Robbery Squad. Major Van der Merwe and Colonel Van der Linde are chief interrogators at Compol.' Mandla got up from the bed. 'They are big people indeed.' He began to pace the room. 'They came to the fore during the Power days, and spread terror among the people. Their mission, it seems, has been to identify ringleaders. They pick them out in a crowd and shoot to kill.'

'Yes. In Soweto and in Alexandra the blue Granada is well known.'

'We have information that they are going to be at Willy's funeral,' Mandla said. 'This information comes from a reliable source within their ranks.' He stopped in the middle of the room and looked at Tuki. 'You read the suggestion?'

'Yes. I agree that this is something to be followed up.'

'I think that is the shop,' Dikeledi said and slowed down.

Walmanstadt is a small village, about thirty miles out of Pretoria. Whenever Dikeledi saw it from a distance, its houses of mud, of brick, of zinc, she wondered why it was still called a village. Something about it resembled Alexandra. But there were many cattle, pigs, goats, and sheep, and the people of Walmanstadt, except for the young, seemed to depend wholly on the soil for food. Life here revolved around the cattle, the pigs, the goats and the soil. It also depended on what the young of the village brought back from the cities where they worked.

When the young came home what they asked about was how the battle against the removal of Walmanstadt was going on. Their interest was three years old. For three years the people of Walmanstadt, through courts and lawyers they did not trust, had battled with the government to remain there. They had come to this area, cleaned the bush, and turned it into a home. Now they ploughed the soil and they ate from it. They had fought as a community to build it, and even if it did not compare with the farms of boers in the surrounding area, they were proud of it. They were not moving from there. So they battled. They had now been through the courts, and after a silence of months on the government's side, they were waiting for the trucks carrying policemen, guns and dogs. They knew. What they did not know was when the trucks would come.

At the shop Dikeledi turned right, into an untarred dusty road. She swerved in through a gate which she could hardly see and drove straight towards the dark shadow ahead, knowing that it was Russia's house. Themba was silent in the passenger seat. The car stopped at the house. Russia came out of the house to meet them. Dikeledi was surprised that he was not in bed. She switched the lights off.

'Park the car under the vine,' Russia said.

'I was wondering if we would have to wake you up,' Dikeledi said.

'Wake me up? Why, I knew you were coming,' Russia said.

'But that did not mean you had to stay awake and wait for us.'

'I did. Park the car. Is this the man?'

'Yes.'

'I think people are waiting for him. Let me take him there right away. Coffee is boiling on the fire. Have some, I will be back soon.'

Dunlop Restaurant is a restaurant as Alexandra understands that word. Bus drivers count their days' takings here. Soccerites come here, talking at the tops of their voices, heaping praises on their teams. Socialites, sitting stiff in their chairs, whisper to each other and regard the other customers with dismay. The owner of this place and his wife are the only cooks and waiters.

They cook porridge and chops, custard and jelly. Sometimes there is mealie-rice, sometimes just bread. You don't say what you want, you ask what there is. On this day it was porridge and T-bone steak. A special.

Tuki was enjoying his T-bone. He was not going to eat all the pap. He sat by the window, listening to the conversation between two soccerites. Now and then he looked out through the window. It must be about twelve. Soon the yard would be full of people. It was a cold day. He wore black trousers and a jacket over a polo-neck jersey, ready for the funeral. Waiting is a strange business. His mind kept asking, what if something goes wrong. He knew what he would do if that happened. But then nothing must go wrong. There was no reason for anything to go wrong. He thought about Jully. When he had seen her she had asked nothing. She was calm, but something told him he should not say anything to her. Not until she asked. They might never see each other again. Well, he had told Mandla that if anything went wrong Jully must be looked after.

The Beetle arrived and parked opposite the window. Tuki recognised Mandla and Oni, who was driving. Mandla looked at the window and showed him the fist. Tuki nodded. Oni got out of the car and walked down the street. Just then, a Granada pulled in. It cut off Tuki's view of the Beetle. Mandla walked into Dunlop and sat at a table opposite Tuki's. Their eyes met, and simultaneously they looked away. One of the blue Granada passengers walked into Dunlop. He went straight to the kitchen, carrying his FN with him. Tuki was watching him. Mandla was watching the door. He saw the Hippo pass. And another one. The tall, heavily-built man came back from the kitchen. He wore his camouflage hat, khaki shirt and grey trousers. Besides his rifle, he had a gun in an armpit holster. He went out into the sun.

Oni came in, looked around, and went out. Shortly afterwards, Mandla followed. Then Tuki. Mandla saw the Beetle drive away. He walked on, crossed the street, saw the passengers in the blue Granada. They were relaxed. Down the street, two Hippos stood. The cops were searching someone. He went into Eleventh Avenue. He saw Dikeledi at a distance, but she did not know who he was. He walked towards her, passed her. She was talking to someone. There were lots of people now. The whole of Alexandra had come, most of the people in black. Mandla joined the crowd and saw Tuki in there too. They both saw the Beetle. Hippos were arriving with their passengers in camouflage, their FN's peeping out like the noses of curious animals. Somewhere in the crowd, a little girl wearing school uniform started a song. The cloudy sky through which the sun was breaking received the song. Mandla looked around. The crowd spread and stretched, flowing, flooding the yards along the street. Everything was black, black clothes and black faces.

> Go well, go well, young fighter
> We will always remember you, Willy
> Go well, go well, young fighter
> We will always remember you.

So the song went, in a rumble, held and led by a young voice which seemed to be carried by the momentum of older voices. Mandla looked at Tuki, then at Oni. He moved away, sensing danger. As he was walking away he caught Oupa's eye in the crowd. He walked out of Third Avenue, into Selborne. He looked back once and saw that Tuki saw him. He went into a yard. Tuki walked back into Dunlop. The Beetle started, and as it moved two camouflage uniforms came directly towards it and waved it to stop. Oni braked and sat still in the car as they came towards her. One opened her door, the other went to the passenger side.

'Come out.' She got out of the car. The one on her side took her bag, and started searching it. She wished they were not doing this here where everyone, that whole body of the crowd, was watching.

'Where are you going to?'

'I am going home.'

'Where are you from?'

'I am from the clinic.'

'Whose car is this?'

'It is my husband's.'

'Where is your licence?'

'In the bag.'

'Are you attending the funeral?' He nodded with his head towards the crowd.

'No.'

'Why are you not going?'

'I do not like going to funerals like these.'

He turned towards his colleague. 'Okay.'

'Okay.' Oni got into the car.

'Hey, where are the petrol bombs?' It was a joke, for Oni saw the smile on his face.

'I don't know,' Oni said, in all seriousness.

'You people are full of lies, go away.' He started towards his Hippo. Oni drove off. She saw Tuki vanish into Dunlop. The blue Granada with its four occupants was still there. The crowd was into another song.

> Vorster, Vorster is a dog.
> Vorster you own guns, we own history
> Vorster, Vorster is a dog.

Someone was screaming his voice hoarse about owners of cars having to park them correctly, in a line at the side of the road. The song was taking the skies. This crowd, this Alexandra which had been burying its children for such a long time now, was getting uneasy. They had been shut in from both sides by Hippos.

Tuki saw the blue Granada move. He tried to take a look at the crowd, but his view was blurred. He saw the Hippos move. Just then the hearse crawled out of Third Avenue into Selborne. Then it was car after car after car. Hippos too. The crowd was in another song.

> This is a heavy load
> This is a heavy load,
> It needs strong men and women
> This is a heavy load.

The procession went on and on. Tuki was siting next to the window, watching. He began to feel strange in his black clothes. He must change. The people, the men and women of Alexandra, on foot, in cars, singing, took Willy away. Tuki was disappointed that he was not part of them, that he could not go. He must change. He looked around the restaurant. There were two other people, sitting face to face talking about golf. He pulled off his polo-neck jersey and was left in a blue round-neck skipper. He folded the jersey into a roll, took a newspaper from the counter and wrapped it in it, then went back to the table and ordered coffee.

'Why are you not at the funeral?'

'I don't want to get shot.'

'I see,' the owner of the restaurant said, looking straight at Tuki as he put his coffee before him. Tuki looked away, making it clear that he did not want to pursue the subject.

'Well, yes, people are getting shot lately. I was going to close the restaurant in respect, but they asked me to keep open because some people will come here to rest. I'd have loved to have taken that young man half way. I knew him, I know his parents very well.' The man was cleaning the tables. Tuki was watching him, listening to him, but he was not going to say a word. The man walked away.

Mandla peeped in at the door and immediately backed out again. He was now walking down Selborne. Tuki came out, saw Mandla, and then the Kombi with its big red letters: One Day Service Dry Cleaners. The street was empty, as if swept clear by the flood of people going to the funeral. Mandla was walking quickly. He got into the Kombi. Tuki followed him in. Around them were clean clothes in plastics, and guns were wearing them. The Kombi picked up speed. Mandla and Tuki were now wearing white dustcoats and caps that announced: One Day Service Dry Cleaners. When the Kombi stopped they got out with suits over their shoulders, ready for delivery. John watched them as they walked away. He looked around once, and then drove off. He thought, God, it was the last time he would see Alexandra.

The blue Granada was parked at the side of the street, one door open. Inside, four men sipped at cool drinks. Major Van der Linde was talking over the radio.

One street away, Oni had seen Mandla and Tuki coming. By the time they were close to the Granada, she had started her car and turned into the street where the policemen were parked. Major Van Wyk saw the Beetle, and had just decided that this time he was stopping it.

Tuki and Mandla opened fire. The windscreen shattered, then the rear and side windows. Oni hurled the two grenades, and the sky thundered. They dived into the Beetle and accelerated away. Not far from there they switched cars out of Alexandra, driving more slowly now.

The news hit the funeral crowd. The blue car had been attacked, its occupants killed. The camouflage uniforms were streaming from the Hippos, advancing on the mourners, blocking exits, firing teargas. Oupa tried to pull out. He went through yards, over fences, and nearly got away. He was walking down Thirteenth Avenue when he heard a car stop behind him. The cop, rifle at the ready, yelled at him to stand still. Oupa stood still, raised his hands. He felt himself shaking as he had never shaken before. It was as the search began that he knew, God, he was not going to make it. One cop stood behind him with a rifle while the other searched him. That morning Oupa had been reading a booklet Mandla had given him. And at home, without thinking, he had put it in his shirt pocket. It was as the policeman touched it, that Oupa remembered what it was. He thought no, they are not taking me. He knew that if he ran they would shoot him. He hoped they would shoot to kill. As the man was trying to take it from his pocket Oupa hit out with his fists and tried to get away. Instead of shooting, the other cop hit Oupa on the leg with the rifle butt. He fell. They handcuffed him and took him to the car.

The other cop was talking over the radio while paging through the book. Suddenly he said: 'The Movement?' He took a quick look at Oupa, and then showed the other man the book. The car sped off. From Wynberg Police Station, Oupa was taken to John Vorster Square, from John Vorster Square to Pretoria Central Prison.

He could not think straight. Things had happened to him so fast. They had happened so fast all his life. He blamed himself for having allowed them to arrest him the way they did. It was unforgiveable that they had caught him because he had become careless. Oupa was merciless with himself for this. Many times he tried to think about other things, trying to tell himself that even where he was now he still had immense responsibility, that many other things pivoted on how he was going to handle this new situation. He still needed strength, he needed all the strength he could find. But his mind kept going back to that moment when he was at home, leaving the bedroom, sitting down to read, hearing someone coming, putting the booklet in his shirt pocket, going to the door, meeting as expected his mother coming in, talking to her . . . Why did he not remember the booklet, not even at the funeral when they shot teargas, when he was running, going over fences? Why, why, why? It was such a thin booklet, made to be hidden easily. That was why he could not feel it as he was running, or during the funeral. Carrying that booklet, on such a day! How, how, how could he have left the book in his shirt pocket?

It was deep in the night. He was badly smashed. He was alone in the cell. His leg was aching. His face was swollen. The police who had arrested him had done a thorough job on him. They regretted it when they realised that Oupa was to be handed over to the Security Police, after discovering the booklet. But the older one, who was driving, said they would explain that Oupa had tried to resist. The station commander at Wynberg Police Station had not even asked what had happened to Oupa's face when he saw the phrase 'the Movement' on the third page or so. He had telephoned immediately, and Oupa was whisked over to John Vorster. They had banged him some more there. They asked him if he was a member of 'the Movement'. Oupa said no. They wanted to know where he had got the booklet from. He said he had received it by mail. He did not know who had sent it to him. They worked him over. Oupa maintained his story. Without warning they hand-cuffed him, and he could see that they were in a hurry. They drove away. He thought they were taking him to Alexandra, to search his house. The car flew past Alexandra. He knew then that they were going to Pretoria.

He had been here now over three hours. He stood up painfully and began to walk around. He touched the water bucket. He touched the shit bucket. The blankets, the mat. For no reason at all, he began to hope. They might just make a mistake and let him out. God, they might just do that. That would be a terrible mistake for them. They just might. But then he thought about the blue Granada. He knew that by now the Security Police must know that he had tried to fight, and that he had tried to run. Maybe that is why they brought him to Pretoria.

He thought, Oupa, you are in now. What was he to do? It was just then that he heard the key at his door. It opened, they took him out. No one said anything.

'Where are we going to?' Silence. He was walking in front, two security cops and a warder behind. The warder told him where to turn, unlocked a series of gates. They followed him through passages, down stairs, through more gates, until they came to the reception centre. He was handcuffed. One of the security policemen held him by the shoulder of his jacket. Pretoria was asleep. It was silent, as if a storm had hit the town and taken everyone along with it. Oupa could hear their footsteps. He knew that he had not seen them before. They reached the car. There was a driver behind the wheel. The other two got in the back with him. The car drove off. No one said a word to anyone.

'Where are you taking me to?' Silence. The car crawled on, smooth, waiting at the red lights. It was not in a hurry. A train hooted in the distance. After a five-minute drive they entered a yard and parked. There were many other cars, some with SAP registration, some without. They all got out of the car, turned left, turned right, went up the stairs. Oupa saw written on the door, Police Museum. One cop opened the door, and let his colleague and Oupa pass him. As the door closed Oupa felt something hit him on the head. He made it into the Museum, Compol Building. As he was staggering, trying to gain balance, the man who had hit him behind the head, held him by the scruff, pinned him against the wall, and smashed his head against it. He pushed him further into the place and then, as if he had suddenly gone mad, he let loose a torrent of kicks and punches. Then he grabbed Oupa and gave him a hip throw. He kicked him in the head, then the stomach. He lifted Oupa and lift-dragged him into the other room, pinning him against the wall, hit him in the balls with a sickening blow. As a hand tightened around his throat, Oupa's knees gave in and he hit the cement floor like a sack.

Oupa came round and felt something heavy hitting him. He lifted himself, tried to sit up, and then something hit him again. It was wet. He staggered up, and the blanket caught him in the face, sending him back to the floor. It was lights out again. One of them held him by the scruff, pulled him to his feet, stood him against the wall.

'Who is Tuki? Who is Tuki?' the man was shouting at the top of his voice, shaking Oupa, bumping him against the wall. 'You are going to tell us who is Tuki, who is Themba, who is Onalenna, where are they now? What are they doing? Who is Tuki?'

'I don't know who is Tuki.'

'Strip, you dog, strip, come on strip!' The man turned Oupa to face the wall, holding him by the ears and pulling them. He kept shouting, at the top of his voice, 'Strip, strip!' Using both hands, he slapped Oupa on the ears. 'Strip, come on strip! Oupa undid his belt, got out of his trousers, shirt, vest, shoes, until he was naked. For the first time Oupa began to cry. 'We have your mother here. We will keep her until you tell us who Tuki is, who Themba is, who Onalenna is; we have Granny and Jully here, so you better know that we know a lot. But you are going to tell us who they are in your own words. And let me warn you, don't waste our time.'

'Kill this fucking black dog,' another man said, and caught Oupa with a kick on the spine. He dragged him across the room, stretched his arms out. They handcuffed him and attached the cuffs to bars which were standing upright from the floor. Oupa began to pee.

'Don't pee on that floor, don't pee on that floor!' one of them shouted. Oupa held his pee.

'Who is Tuki?'

'He is my friend.'

'Where is he?'

'I don't know where he is.'

'Who is Onalenna?'

'She is my friend.'

'Where is she?'

'I don't know where she is.'

'Who is Themba?'

'He is my friend.'

'Where is he?'

'I don't know where he is.'

'Do you know that there is no one who knows where these people are?'

'I don't know.'

'When last did you see them?'

'Long ago.'

'I told you not to waste our time, you dog.' They closed ranks around him. Oupa looked at them and thought, God, I am in it now. Here I am. Two stood behind him. Two stood at his sides. The one who was questioning him stood in front of him. Oupa saw him look at those behind him.

He grimaced, but nothing happened. He heard shuffling sounds from both sides, and looked from one side to the other. The man in front of him hit him full in the solar plexus. Someone kicked him full on his naked arse. Those on the sides held the rings of the cuffs and tightened them. It was blow after blow.

'When last did you see them?'

'I don't know.'

'I am doing it,' the man in front of him said, looking at his colleagues. He went away and came back with the equipment. Oupa felt something cover his head, it was wet. He felt something being tightened around his sex. He felt something being tightened around his waist. And then nothing happened. He waited. Grimacing in the dark of his covered head, eyes, ears. He felt cold water running down his chest, from the wet sack around his head. There was a dead silence. He began to scream. Nothing happened. His scream was choked by the wet canvas, which was being tightened around his neck. He tried to scream. Nothing happened. They were standing there, looking at him, watching him. Oupa tried to bend his knees, trying to go down on the floor. The cuffs held him and ate into his wrist. He peed. It was dead silent in the room now. He tried hard as he could to scream. Nothing happened. Nobody heard him scream. Then something happened. It was as if his whole body had snapped, was hit by something huge, he felt his sex shoot out, and again he tried to scream. Then he passed out.

When he came to he saw them, still standing around him. They said nothing to him.

'I am telling the truth. I don't know where they are,' he said.

'We want to know who killed Mpando.'

Oupa began to weep.

'Your family is talking. We have them all here. We know who you are. You are going to tell it to us, all of it.'

Something covered Oupa's head again. His cock shot out again. 'Are you a member of the Movement?'

Oupa was lying on his back. He did not know where his head was or his toes. Everything clung to him like a huge pain. He was trying to sit up. His hands were weary, they did not let him, his head whirled and whirled and whirled . . .

The feel of liquid. The smell of urine. The feel of mucus and tears on his cheeks and nose and mouth and face. The smell of blood. The weak limbs. The sight of people standing over him without jackets, their ties loose, their shirts unbuttoned, their shirt sleeves folded back. All these crowded Oupa. He thought, I must stand up. He threw all his weight on the weak hands, pushed and pushed, and then the weight was on his legs. He staggered back, summoned all his muscles to support him, asking them to support him for the last time. 'Yes, I am a member of the Movement,' he said.

The silence here is stubborn. The mountains and hills and the trees, even the sky, persist and persist and are stubborn. Their sizes and heights are sizes and heights of silence. The way cattle stare at you. The way sheep keep eating and eating, in the silence of the grass and the trees, in the silence of the sunlight and the sky, in the silence of the wind. The silence is stubborn here. It does not matter whether the birds sing or horses neigh. The silence; it seemed to cover everything. It seems to cloak, it wants to protect, like a womb, like a mother. It spreads itself, it covers, it spreads and spreads. In a way that it alone knows, it is there . . .

This, Themba thought, is what makes Walmanstadt different from Alexandra. In the month that he had been here, time, the silence, the trees, the grass, all of which are Walmanstadt, made him feel as if he had been walking at night, and suddenly found out that it was day. Themba felt naked.

What do people mean when they say the Movement works underground?

This question, which came often to Themba, conjured memories of photographs he had taken of miners. The mysterious light which glows on their foreheads; their thick shirts and trousers, crowded by patches sown in haste; the sweat and bewildered eyes and smiles as the miners posed for the pictures when they came out from underground. The meaning of underground, Themba told himself, was hard work – hard work until the sweating flesh shone like a star. That is what the faces of the miners coming our of the hole looked like. They were shining. Their eyes were shining. The dust and dirt on their clothes, and the smell of water and soil, was like the dust and dirt on the clothes of the people whom Themba found himself amongst during his stay in Walmanstadt. The people here carried with them the smell of water and the smell of the soil. They seemed to come from underground.

'Snakes don't go out looking for people to bite,' Mmaphefo said, wiping her nose.

'You have said that so many times, and so many times I try to believe what you say,' Themba said.

'A snake has a feel for sound. When you walk, it feels the sound of your footsteps while you are still far away. It runs, it gets out of your way . . .'

'But it has bitten people, has it not?'

'Yes . . . '

'Did it not hear them come?'

'That is just accident. It is like two cars hitting each other and causing the deaths of the occupants. Are you going to ask if the occupants did not see the car?'

A snake, in motion, looks like flowing water. It slides, it glows. It seems to defy the sense of touch. If you cannot touch it, how can you fight it? It has this ability to strike at lightning speed. It is not as if Themba did not know much about snakes. He even knew that once he was confronted by a snake he would kill it. But how could he, if it defied touch?

Themba was lying on the floor. Mmaphefo was curled on the floor. It was late morning. The sunlight, weak, a winter-sunlight, spread from the hills in

Jerico down to the village, to the house where Mmaphefo and Themba sat, drinking morning tea and waiting. Themba laughed. 'Everything seems to demand that I learn it again. I've felt like that all the time since I came here.'

'But you understand what I am getting at, don't you?'
'Well, I think there are those snakes which will attack you, whether provoked or not, accident or not, but I know what you mean,' Themba said. Mmaphefo began to struggle to stand up. Themba was watching her, struggling. At last she was upright. She picked up her mug. She began to walk towards the door which led outside.

Mmaphefo's house consisted of four thatched rondavels. All of them were joined by a knee-high wall which also formed a circle, within which she made fire for cooking and for warming the home. Similar houses spread over the length and breadth of Walmanstadt. The distances between the house gave Themba a feeling of bountiful space. Mmaphefo sat on the wall and began to wash dishes. Themba slipped his overalls down to his waist and walked to where Mmaphefo was sitting. He got some hot water and began to wash himself.

'When are you seeing Makgatho?' Mmaphefo asked.
'I was thinking that I should go there now,' Themba said, wiping his face.
'Yes, I think there will be word from Johannesburg. It has been some time since we heard anything from them.'
'I think that means things are going on as planned,' Themba said.

In his green hat, faded overalls and boots, Themba walked the now familiar footpath, embraced by silence and the sunlight. Clothes had nothing to do with being underground. It was being underground which shaped the clothes, and accepted the person.
'This is Charles,' Makgatho said.
'Haai, how are you?' Themba said, looking at the tall, smiling man.
'I am fine, and you?'
'Okay,' Themba said. 'When did you come?'
'Oh not long ago. Tuki says to say haai to you,' the man said.
'I did not catch your name,' Themba said.
'Charles,' the man said.
'Charles, yes. How is Tuki?'
'Tuki is healthy,' Charles said, staring at Themba. They looked at each other.
'I see,' Themba said.
'How is Mmaphefo?' Charles asked.
'She still eats snuff,' Themba said.
'Comrades, I have to be on my way,' Makgatho said.
'Thanks, comrade,' Charles said.
Charles and Themba were walking back to Mmaphefo's house.
'One of our comrades has been captured,' Charles said.
'Who?'
'Oupa.'
'Oupa?'

'Yes,' Charles said.

'Oupa,' Themba said. It was a way of trying to summon his mind, his memory, his knowledge, from the past to the present.

'When?'

'Yesterday.'

'Where?'

'Alexandra.'

'How?'

'It is not clear yet. Tuki said to say he is healthy.'

'I see, I see, yes,' Themba said.

'We have to prepare to receive Oni and Dikeledi . . .'

'Tuki is healthy,' Themba repeated.

'Yes.'

'So the change is with Oni and Dikeledi?'

'Yes, I will take care of them.'

'When are they coming?

'Any time now.'

'Can you show me Tuki's health?

'Yes, yes,' Charles said, and he took out a .38 police special and gave it to Themba.

'I see,' Themba said, his face now clear. 'This is the blue Granada,' he said.

'Yes.'

'Comrade,' Themba said, 'Russia is waiting for you. You see that house there with huge stones on the roof, the red one?'

'Yes.'

'He will be there,' Themba said. 'He will bring you to where we are. I will see you then, comrade.'

'Okay, comrade.' They parted. The weight of the .38 pulled Themba's overall down, dangling in rhythm with his movement. He was walking fast, a way to keep his mind clear of Oupa's fate. He had work to do. When he arrived, he found Mmaphefo still washing the dishes.

'Yes, I got the news. Oupa has been captured. And here is something.' He took out the gun and showed it to Mmaphefo.

It was late at night when the car stopped. Themba went out to meet them. Oni came out of the car and hugged Themba, kissing him. Dikeledi, smiling, held his hand. John came out last. In the dark, which turns eyes into holes, they stood speechless for a while. 'Come in, come,' Mamaphefo was saying from the door. They filed into the house and soon they were all seated on the floor eating.

'Tuki got the word first,' Oni said. 'Oupa's contact who lives in the same yard saw the police take Oupa's mother. He heard the police talk to her about Oupa. Tuki picked this up and when he checked another comrade told him that Oupa did not come to him as arranged. Now we have confirmed it. Oupa has been picked up. Word came from John Vorster Square.'

'Yoooooo,' Mmaphefo said, her hands on her head. 'Jaaaa.' She looked away from them. There was silence.

The Movement is old. It is as old as the grave of the first San or Khoikhoi who was killed by a bullet that came from a ship which had anchored at Cape Town to establish a stop station. The Movement is as young as the idea of throwing stones, of hurling one's life at the armed men who believe in God and shoot with guns. The Movement is the eyes which see how poverty is akin to a skeleton. So white. So dry.

'Who is this Willy, that you are talking about?' Mmaphefo was staring at Oni.

'Dikeledi, you know the details — may be you can tell Mme-Mmaphefo.' 'Yes . . . ' Dikeledi looked at the poles and zinc of the house, as if they were to relate who Willy was. 'Willy was one of the students,' she said. She looked at Mmaphefo. 'Willy Diale, he was eighteen. You know that it has been a while now since the Power days . . . ' She paused and a quiet settled on the house. She could go no further. The dozens of eyes in the house were on her. For a while no one did anything. 'I am sorry, I am sorry,' Dikeledi said, and wiped her eyes. 'Willy was shot during a demonstration. He was taken to the mortuary alive. An old lady who had gone to collect her son's corpse says Willy pulled her dress and asked for water. He was among the many, many dead. She looked at him and recognised him. He asked for water . . . '

Mandla and Tuki arrived in Durban early in the morning. Glenda met them at the station. A thin Indian girl with a warm smile, she shook their hands, still looking at Mandla. Glenda and Mandla had known each other when Mandla was a teacher and she a student at her school. Mandla and one of her teachers who was now in exile were good friends. Then, Glenda did not know how to react to Mandla. Not that now she knew how, but she had been on the road and had met many, many people.

Charles got off the ox-wagon. Mmaphefo, who was sitting at the back among the many watermelons, extended her arm to him. Charles held it and helped her off. It was as they were walking towards the labourers' compounds that Charles, walking side by side with Mmaphefo, felt as if he had done this before. The Le Roux ranch reminded him of some place he could not really place, in Sekhukhuniland. The old lady next to him, in a strange way, reminded him of an old man he used to work with on his arrival in Sekhukhuniland. Hlase, in his seventies, was still a strong man. Hlase, like many and most of the people of Sekhukhuniland, had a face that spoke of their fight against the law. There is something called Resettlement. It has enabled the people of the villages to break with their past and hurl themselves into a troubled and angry present. Villagers defied chiefs and the guns which protected them. Or chiefs defied the white law and the guns which represented it. The latter was the case in Sekhukhuniland. The people of this village had stood against the guns, had spilled their blood to say no to the white man's law. Hlase was one of those people chosen by fate to go to jail rather than succumb to the law. Fate is not an abstraction. Fate is a thought, is life, is experience. It is the ability to say no, when the consequences of that may be sweet or sour. It is a conscious decision.

Mmaphefo and Charles were warmly received by the labourers at the Le Roux ranch compound. The cattle were outspanned, the ox-wagon parked with others which belonged to Le Roux. In its time the ox-wagon had rolled through Pretoria, the uniformed city whose word is supported by the gun.

It was late at night when Le Roux got the word that there were strange people on the farm. His instinct took him to the phone and then to the radio, and both were out of order. He became desperate. He and his son went to the compound, to ask. They were met by silence.

Charles and a few other people met him and his son at the gate as he was driving out. Charles asked him to hand over the keys. He refused. Charles took them from him after a struggle. He was tied to a pole and watched as his house was set alight. The farmers nearby came to investigate and were met by machine-gun fire.

Several farms went through that experience on the same night. In Natal and the Orange Free State, cattle were set loose. Prisoners who were working on the farms were set loose. The papers said that it seemed as if the terrorists were switching from urban to rural targets.

Themba parked the truck, Mmaphefo and Charles climbed out of the passenger seats. Walmanstadt was asleep. Themba drove down the footpath to Makgatho's store.

'No old lady, you listen to me,' Charles said. 'From now on, I want you to rest. They and I will cook and make tea for you, and clean the house. All you do, at least for a few days, is rest . . .'

'Has there been word from Oni and Dikeledi?'

'But we have just come, how can I know?'

'Your mother's head, who are you talking to like that?' Mmaphefo said.

'But I am telling the truth, we have just come . . .'

'We must know how those children are. You telling me about rest, how can you rest when thinking about the unknown?'

'But that is what I mean. I am saying, leave all that to us. We will do everything we can to find out. But in the meantime you must rest, that is all I am saying.'

'How do you rest with worries in your head, tell me that. Do you call that rest?'

'I know what you mean,' Charles said, unlocking the door.

'Here comes Themba. Maybe he has news,' Mmaphefo said. Charles lit the paraffin lamp. He went out to the stoep to make fire.

'Did Makgatho say anything about Oni and Dikeledi?' Mmaphefo asked.

'No word yet.'

'No word?'

'Nothing.'

'I was just telling Mme-Mmaphefo that we would like her to rest,' Charles said to Themba.

'Girl, how is that?'

'Girl is your mother,' Mmaphefo said, busy with her snuff tin.

The news did come. It took Oni, Dikeledi and Mmaphefo away. It was early in the morning when they entered Sekhukhuniland. Oni let the car crawl towards Hlase's house.

'It's your little girl,' Oni said, after tapping on the window.

'Awu, mother of the children, you are here?' Hlase said, looking at Mmaphefo.

'Yes, yes, I am here,' Mmaphefo said. She was feeling very tired.

'I am glad to know you. We welcome you here, we hope we will be able to make you rest.' He shut the door. 'Heh, mother of the children, the land is up and groaning heh? Sleep has become foreign to you, heh mother of the children?' Hlase sat down after serving tea.

'The land is up on its legs, it knows no rest,' Mmaphefo said.

'Dogs are groaning, having nightmares,' Hlase said. 'Heh, you say the land is on its legs. Heh, I hear you,' He leaned forward.

'We have had to move, as you see. One of us was captured,' Mmaphefo said.

'Heh, a soldier. You have had to move, I hear you.' Hlase was staring at the flames in front of him, his old face stern and thoughtful. 'That is part of us now, mother of the children, the times say so. That is part of us. I think all of you want to rest,' he said. 'You have been on the road a long time, you must rest now.'

The morning after John arrived in Zimbabwe, the planes came. Flying low, their shining round black bodies looked like fish swimming in a tank. The thunder came. The fire came. And then the smoke came. And then there was a terrible silence.

On the third day, the planes and armoured cars reached Botswana. A week later, the Prime Minister of South Africa said again that those countries which harboured terrorists would be dealt with in no uncertain terms. On the same day, the planes went to Tanzania.

Mandla was fast asleep in Umlazi. As he woke, jumping out of bed, he saw the door fly open. He had only managed to bend when the bullets hit him.

Fourteen

The last time I saw him, Oupa met me at the door, wearing shorts. He had a book in one hand and a cup of coffee in the other. He looked at me, standing aside to let me in. 'Uncle,' he said with a mischievous smile, 'are you lost?'

'Lost?'

'This is your home, you know!'

'I know.'

'No you don't. How come you stay away so long if you know?'

'Oupa, I am here now, so let me in. How are you?'

'Fine,' he said. 'You know, Mary was talking about you this morning.'

'What did she say about me?'

'She wondered where you were.'

'Where is she?'

'She has gone to help at Willy's,' he said.

'Willy?'

'Yes, the boy who was shot and . . .'

'Oh, Willy, Willy,' I said, 'how could I forget Willy?' Does that say anything about where I have been?'

'You must promise that you will go to the funeral,' Oupa said.

'I will.'

'Shall I make tea or coffee for you?'

'I would like a beer,' I said.

'But you cannot get beer anywhere,' Oupa said. 'All shebeens are shut today.'

'To respect Willy,' I said.

'Yes.' I looked at him at that point. His eyes, his nose, his face, his hands, even his voice, told me he was a young man, a boy. But the way he stood there, cup in hand, book in hand, looking at me, smiling, also told me that he was not a boy. I sat down. He took my coat. He asked me to take off my tie, or at least loosen it. I did so and felt fresh air, a sense of newness come to me. He took the stuff into the other room and came back.

'How is Aunt Lily?' he asked, looking straight into my eyes.

'She is fine,' I said.

'How come she does not come here?'

'Why don't you come to see her?'

'You are never home,' he said. 'I have stopped many times at your place and you were not there.' He offered me tea. I was amazed by Oupa's broad shoulders. His sharp eyes and the way he seemed so relaxed. He sat at the edge of a chair, looking at me as if to ask something.

'A lot has been going on around,' I said.

'What?'

'I mean, good lord, railways are being cut, buildings are bombed, police stations are being attacked, there are guns and guns all over wherever one goes,' I said.

'The people are claiming their history,' he said.

'The people?'

'Yes.'

'I see.'

Silence.

'Are you still writing?'

'When I find time, I try.'

'You don't sound as eager as you did the last time I saw you.'

'I would really want to do it, but I don't seem to have time,' he said.

Like an old tree, the Movement spreads and spreads its roots. It entrenches itself in the soil, issuing root after root, to spread and spread and spread. Some roots end up on rocks, baking in the sun. Some end up in sand. The roots spread and spread and spread. The tall tree, spreading its branches all around, gives shade to the weary.

Tuki turned and lay on his back. The grass had been soft when he first lay down. Now he could feel the hard earth and the little stones firm against his side. He fixed his eyes on the dark sky. There was no moon, only the stars twinkling forever in their distance. The breeze was blowing a little cold. Tuki tucked his arms between his thighs and stretched his legs straight. He could feel the pistol tucked into his belt. He felt calm now.

The settlers had settled. Their settlement, inspired by an ingrained will to make profits, had pitted itself against the simple nomads, hunters, pastoralists and land cultivators, in the midst of vast space. The settlement was an impatient and brutish force when it was resisted. This same sky watched as battle after battle led to defeat, and the loss of land, of freedom as enslavement followed. Why? Why was it that when the settlers arrived, the people here were not able to meet the demands of the time? The present says, Tshaka's army lost. The present says, the nation could not meet the demands of that time. Yet a nation never accepts, nor can live with, defeat. This is the point which the world, which now relentlessly plans the defeat and subjugation of the Movement, will never understand. There is no way that it can understand that, since its life is based on the fruits of defeat of the people of these regions of the world. The Movement is an idea in the mind of a people; a resolve that it will never accept the process of defeat. Since the settlers first settled, all their laws and wars have succeeded in only postponing the real issue – that the people want and need their land.

Tuki yawned. He must try to sleep. He thought about Umlazi. He turned again, and lay on his stomach. He folded his arms under his head and made them a pillow. He must loosen his shoes. He sat up. He untied the shoe-laces. He pulled out the pistol and held it in his right hand. It must be about one now. He must move within an hour. He lay on his stomach, spread his legs, his arms, and tried to rest. He had walked since six. He must try to make Colenso by daybreak. And then, Ladysmith by next night. From then on, he was going to break the rules. He must get a car. No, the best really would be to try a lift with a white person. That way, the scales would tip in his favour. White people are not easily stopped. Even if they are, they are white. At the garage in Ladysmith Ndlovu could organise a lift for him, so he could cross the Orange Free State. Tuki laughed at himself. So he feared the Free State, heh? In the Free State, where the boer-farmers are, every black is a potential prisoner and every white a potential policeman. It would be dangerous to take the Free State easy. Fear or no fear, he must move with extra caution. It was safe, absolutely safe, to try and get a lift with a farmer, sit at the back of the truck; that would erase him from the face of the earth. He must try to reach Ndlovu.

He yawned again. There was no way he was going to sleep. His mind was too active. So what must he do? Perhaps reduce the distance, use the hour.

How many people had had to lie low, in the thick of the night on the vast empty veld of this country? There must have been millions, starting with the San and Khoikhoi; in these parts, the amaZulu had had to hide, as the battle for the land raged. The issue then, as now, was power. That stern and staring tree, the dark grass, the earth, the flowing river, all these must have been witness to what happened then, as they were now.

Africa had known terror. It had been the raw material first, shipload after shipload; then the raw material had included people, shipload after shipload, piled with raw material, women, men and children, chained and at gun point; the trek of millions and millions of people to unknown lands; it had been cotton, cocoa, silk, diamonds, gold, people, crossing the mighty oceans, destined to profit the lands which now day and night planned to defeat the will of the people.

Without being emotional about this, what did it really mean? The people had been forced to leave their land. They were then forced to work, to toil in foreign lands. The stolen raw material was used in those lands; today, those same countries wanted to dictate to the people the meaning of freedom. It was quite understandable, yes it was. Africa had gone through a chain of eras, been torn by it; now it had holes, holes everywhere where the wealth was dug out and taken away; holes, fathomless holes which now whistled and whistled with their emptiness: gold, diamonds, coal, uranium, asbestos, copper, manganese, you name it.

The silence here was really amazing. He wondered if Jully had managed to go back to work. Long after her detention, she had stayed home. Jully must make her mind up. He, Tuki, could not decide that for her – that she must now leave the country of her birth for an unknown destination, perhaps forever. No, she must make that decision herself, though perhaps he could discuss it frankly with her. He had had that decision to make, too.

What had gone wrong? He began to tighten his shoelaces and put the pistol into his belt. Oni, where would she be? Themba? The many other fighters of the Movement? Something had gone wrong. What? He thought about the last farm they had been to. The Afrikaner farmer who was also a dominee told him that the whole world would hunt them down and punish them surely for that. The whole world! The children of the house, boys and girls, had fought back with the parents, shooting from all the windows, it had seemed. After the first intense few battles every farmer in that region had been waiting, gun in hand, to shoot them. He remembered the face of the dominee as the man realised that the alarm was not functioning, that they were not only trapped, but that they were going to have to take orders from this gun-wielding black terrorist. Fear had taken over, his eyes had shot out, his mouth had hung open: drop the gun, or else your son, wife and daughter are going to be killed. He did not drop it voluntarily, it fell out of his hand; perhaps his hand had lost its strength. 'My skat, my skat,' he had cried, and hugged his wife. Tuki hit him on the chin, with a full cross-cut, and the man staggered. He put the gun right at the back of his ear, and told him to face the wall. The dominee was crying like a small boy. That is when he told Tuki the story of the world.

Tuki pulled himself up. He must get on the road. He would have to enter the Free State by car. Colenso. Ladysmith, the last town before the Free State, then Harrismith and he would be in. He began to walk. Yes, that dominee was right. He was right because for him the world was the 'civilised' world, and indeed, it would do everything in its power to punish its enemies. Tuki felt alone and terribly small when these thoughts flooded his head. For over four centuries we have fought, man after man, woman after woman, fought with everything we had, for what seemed to us a very simple and easily understood reality: this is our land, it must bear our will. South Africa is going to be a socialist country, this is going to come about through the will, knowledge and determination of the people. Tuki was walking fast now. His legs, swift and swinging to and fro, slid over the grass, over pits and stones. He needed to get out now, find a safe zone, everything was closing in around him.

He must be exposed to other ideas. Not long ago, not so long ago, minutes ago it seemed, were those days when he used to criss-cross the country, now in Cape Town, now in Port Elizabeth, when the slogan was: Black man, you are on your own! So many of his friends of those days, so many of them, had paid so dearly. South Africa became, in no time, a different country. It was no longer a personal knowledge, a private knowledge for anyone, that the only way to win back the country was to fight. How? That was the big question. Those were the student days. Today the papers declared: Police crush terror onslaught. Tomorrow it will be another story. There is no looking back now. It was as he thought this that Tuki felt tears come to his eyes. He had become used to going through time, with other people. Now, he was so alone. Indeed, the toll had been very heavy. Without his comrades, all by himself, in the middle of a vast, empty, now hostile land without his AK47, Tuki felt almost lost. No, that was not true. There were thousands on thousands of people who could come to his rescue. He had only to get himself there, intact. That was his responsibility. He put his hand into his shirt and felt the butt of the pistol. He would try to get through this journey, but if it came to it, he would be taken dead.

Suddenly Tuki felt that he was not the only one walking in the vicinity. Every nerve and muscle listened. It was dead silent. His eyes pierced the dark. Nothing. He began to walk, slowly this time, listening and looking. Something moved. He stopped; there was again the light of the stars, and the dark of the night and its silence. He was dead still. His hand was firm on the pistol, finger on the trigger. He heard the movement, and placed its position. He glued his eyes in that direction. It was not only a movement, but a great deal of movement. He pulled the pistol out, cocked it, held it in both hands and waited. A cow coughed. He looked around, sighed and relaxed. He walked towards where the sound of the coughing had been. Many cattle were sitting on the grass chewing. They stood up as he approached them. He touched one as all of them were moving away.

'Where the hell do you come from?' Tuki heard himself say. There would be many cattle roaming the fields. He remembered how, at farm after farm, after taking care of the owners they had set the cattle free. They destroyed the kraals, and sheep, goats and cattle were set free to roam the veld; fields and orchards were destroyed. The paper had said, though, that the situation was once again under control. What had gone wrong? From where he was standing, he could see the headlights of a car, speeding in his direction. He sat down. He must have made over ten miles now.

When, in the morning, he hit Colenso, after lifts on a horse-cart and a dairy truck, he went straight to the hospital there. He joined the long queues, first for a ticket, then for the doctor. He talked to the nurses and clerks there. It was three o'clock before he was through. He sat on the bench. He had tablets and a bottle of medicine. He did not feel that he needed them really. His ears and head were filled with the crying of children, and his nose had absorbed the smell of methylated spirits. This was the only way he could while away time. The doctor had said something about flu. So the nurse had told him; the doctor had said nothing to him.

The doctors hardly spoke to their patients, nor did they really look at them. The nurse spoke on behalf of the patient, and the doctor listened. Then the stethoscope kept doctor and patient apart, moving to the chest and back, and the doctor said to the nurse, tell him to say *heh*, and the nurse told the patient. The doctor wrote something on the card, and told the nurse to call another patient. End of examination. When they were through with Tuki he asked the nurse, what did he say was wrong with me? The nurse read the card and said, touch of flu. Tuki had then gone to join the long, long queue at the dispensary. He got his medicine and then, since he had time to kill, he sat on the bench. He had learnt from one of nurses that a bus for Ladysmith would be leaving from the hospital.

In the bus, Tuki made good friends with one of the nurses. She knew Ndlovu. And, as soon as she had said so, Tuki realised that the nurse was looking at him strangely. She kept looking at him, and when he looked at her she quickly looked away. Tuki was becoming uneasy.

'What shift does he do, night or day?'

'I don't know. I really don't know.'

'Have you seen him lately?'

'I can't remember, but I last saw him, god, I don't know.'

'But do you know him well?'

'I know him yes,' she said, stretching her hands out. 'Do you know him well?'

'Yes, very well, very well,' Tuki said, and thought, I am really taking a chance here. 'Why do you ask?'

'No, I am just asking.'

'Do you know where he lives?' The nurse, pretty, young, bespectacled, looked at Tuki, steadily.

'Not really.'

It was then that Tuki decided he was not going to get off at the garage. From now on, this nurse was going to be right under his nose. She was going nowhere, not until he knew where Ndlovu was. And this woman knew where he was. She knew too much about Ndlovu.

'You don't speak Zulu well,' she said. 'Where do you come from?'

'Umlazi.'

'Umlazi?' She was really saying, you can't come from there if you don't speak Zulu well. But Tuki ended the story there. She started a conversation with another nurse who was sitting in the seat in front of them. She was talking about some patient and some doctor.

'Are people allowed to smoke here?' Tuki asked her.

'Yes,' she said. The other nurse looked at Tuki and then at her.

'He wants to see Ndlovu,' his nurse told the other. The other nurse looked Tuki straight in the eyes, but said nothing.

'But why don't you tell me where Ndlovu is, he is a very good friend of mine. It will help me a lot.'

'But who are you?' the other nurse asked.

'My name is Dan.' Tuki took the card from his pocket and showed it to her.

'Where do you come from?'

'Umlazi.'

'Thuledu, where did you meet this man?'

'At the hospital.' Tuki watched the two women. This Thuledu was a cool person. But her friend could cause problems at any time. She gave him the card back and twisted her body to look at Thuledu and Tuki.

'You are not from Umlazi. Where are you from, before Umlazi?'

'Johannesburg.'

'What are you doing here?'

'Now, why are you asking all these questions?' Tuki said.

'You are asking about someone who is related to me.'

'He may be related to you but he may have friends you don't know, right?'

'I know all his friends.'

'You don't know me. At least that is what I gather from the things you have been asking me.'

'I don't know you, and you can't ask me about him,' she said.

'Please don't talk so loud,' Tuki said. It was as he said it that he saw her catch her mouth like a child trying to keep the words back. 'I am a very good friend of Ndlovu. If you know him, you know me now. He will be very displeased with you if he learns that I tried to get help from you and you became impossible.' Tuki took Thuledu's hand. 'I need your help,' he said.

'Shh,' the other woman said. 'Get off with us.'

'Look, I don't want to come with you if you won't tell me where Ndlovu is. I need your help as I said, but if you can't help me, there is no point in my coming with you, moreso if you are unwilling to help.' The bus stopped. Many people got off. The two women remained seated. The bus began to move. It was now a little quieter inside it. Tuki looked around. He thought about the buses from town to Alexandra with loads of workers going back to their homes. The same tired-looking faces. The same buzz of talking and laughing people.

'What help do you want?' Thuledu asked. Tuki looked at her.

'I want to meet Ndlovu, he is the only one who can help me.'

'So you want us to take you to him?'

'Yes.' He touched her hand again. 'That is all I need, my sister.'

Thuledu shrugged, and buried her face in her arms. Tuki could feel that the other woman was watching him. He faced her.

'What are you to Ndlovu?'

'He is my cousin.'

'Do you believe me when I say I am a good friend of his?'

'I think I do.'

'I need your help, then. Take me to him.'

'Ndlovu is not there.'

'What do you mean he is not there? Where is he?' Tuki looked at her. She looked away.

'What do you mean?'

'But who are you?'

'I am not a policeman. I am Ndlovu's good friend and I need your help.'

'Ndlovu is dead.'

'What?'

'Yes, he died.'

'What of?'

'He was fetched by those people and when he came back, he was a corpse.'

'Which people?'

'The police.'

'Ndlovu is dead!'

'Yes.'

'I must tell you then, that the police are looking for me. If you can help, you must say so. If not, say it now,' Tuki said.

'Are you in the Movement?'

'Yes,' Tuki said.

'How did you come to the hospital?' the nurse asked.

'I met him this morning,' Thuledu said. 'He asked me for the queue to the cards, then later he came and told me he was a stranger in Colenso. He was going to Ladysmith, and I told him about this bus. Then later when I met him again I asked him if he was hungry. I gave him food. It was only when we were on the bus that somehow we started to talk about Ndlovu.'

'How did you know she knew Ndlovu?'

'Well you have a small location there, and I am sure you know each other.'

'Ndlovu is my brother: his father and my father are of the same woman.'

'I see. When did Ndlovu die?'

'Last month. We buried him on the sixteenth of February.' Tuki thought, God a month after we had met.

'What kind of help do you want?'

188

'I wanted to stop at the garage, and I needed Ndlovu to advise me. I need transportation. Do you think it is safe for me to come along with you?'

'Not with me,' Ndlovu's cousin said, 'it would be totally unsafe. Thuledu, do you think you can help?'

'Yes.'

'Thuledu gets off a stop before me. The best is that you go with her. Tell her what you need. She can then send a child to me, and we can meet later and combine heads.'

'I thank you my sister,' Tuki said. He must move fast, really he must move fast. The net was gradually tightening. He now had no way of checking what was happening behind him, nor could he check what was waiting ahead. Something was not holding. That night, as soon as he had rested and gathered the information he needed, he would have to move, get a car, get through the Free State. The bus had stopped again. There were fewer people now.

'Tell me, are the police active in the location?'

'Yes, very active.'

'Do you think it is wise to get off with you?'

'Yes, come with me,' Thuledu said.

'Look, my journey is still very long. I need to move fast, and as you know it is dangerous to try and get in touch with people in the Movement, for they may be closely watched. What advice can you give about how to move?'

'For now all I can say is, come with me and we will see.'

'Sister,' Tuki said to her friend, 'I am sorry about Ndlovu. He was one very brave man among us and I knew him well. What he stood for will come true.' He saw tears in the nurse's eyes. He sat back. The bus stopped again. Thuledu stood up and Tuki followed suit. 'Please be consoled,' he said, 'be strong.' He held the other nurse's shoulder, then without looking back he followed Thuledu out of the bus.

The location was alive. It was already dark. They did not have far to walk, but for Tuki an age seemed to pass as Thuledu stopped to greet people and chat along the way. When they were inside her two-roomed thatched hut, she immediately switched the news on. She made Tuki tea. And while she was cooking they talked. Thuledu suggested to Tuki that he should get in touch with one of Ndlovu's friends. She would fetch him.

When he came, the man told Tuki that there was a Boer, a Mr Koos, who often travelled between Colenso, Ladysmith and Heidelburg. He had not been this week, and since it was Thursday, it was likely he would be passing through the next morning.

Tuki reached Heidelburg. From there he travelled by train to Johannesburg. David Horwitz drove him to Zeerust, and from there he crossed into Botswana. Sitting in the bus from Lobatse to Gaborone, his face glued to the window, Tuki gazed again at space after space, vast veld after vast veld. The bus was noisy. Men and women were talking at the tops of their voices. The music, whatever it was they were playing, was loud. The speaker was just above his head. It was about ten in the morning, but the bus was full — women, men, and children, their endless baggage on and inside the bus, which seemed to stop everywhere and anywhere. The mountains, the trees, the grass, the stones, everything was silent. The sun was already very hot. From the station in Gaborone he took a taxi.

He felt very tired now. What next? It was best, he had heard, to report at the police station. But before that, he thought, he must first have something to drink. He went up the stairs into the President Hotel, up other stairs and into a lounge. There were a few people there. He sat down at a table and called for a coke. What must he say to the cops?

Yaone got off the train. She was there to meet him, the train still hissing. Women, men, children, girls and boys, all were coming out of the train, onto the gravel platform. There were crowds on the platform, with blankets, suitcases, and boxes, waiting to board the hissing train. Yaone had a pair of trousers, unwrapped, in one hand, and a jacket over his shoulder. Onalenna stood, hiding in the throng, watching Yaone as he too searched the crowd with his eyes. She was smiling. He had not changed. No he had, he was almost yellow now. And bigger? Yet she knew, he had not changed. There he was, with his tired-looking face, his slightly tilted head which made him seem to be thinking or watching. Now he was searching. She watched from amid the crowd. This was the man she had thought about, wept about, laughed about, got angry at, the man she sometimes wished she had never known, and sometimes felt to be the only man she was to know; she watched this man, whom she had last seen so long ago. She had learnt, since the time when they saw each other at the airport in Cape Town, that tears were useless. She walked out of the crowd, slowly, towards where he was standing.

He seemed to be looking at nothing in particular. This empty gaze struck Onalenna. She knew it so well. It was this empty look which used to hurt her. She felt scared now, she felt like crying, she did not want to see him, she felt as if the eyes of the crowd were laughing at her. No, she did not want him to change. Did he know how much she longed for him, how many times when she was on her own she had wished to be with him, him, not anyone else? Did he know? She kept walking at an easy pace, knowing she could not go back now. She was going to walk towards him, to look into his eyes. He too began to walk. His eyes were still searching, he walked as if he would stop walking any time. He was heading towards her, but it was clear to her that he was not seeing her. She stopped and waited. Their eyes met. He smiled. He seemed very happy, she thought.

He saw her face, the huge eyes which he had longed for with such pain, he saw them, and the bewildered, sometimes mischievous, sometimes terror-stricken face she had. It was as if she was the only one on that crowded platform. He walked towards her, and when he reached her he held her hand lightly as they stared at each other, not smiling, with a sternness like that of judgement day. They both laughed, and she began to walk. He followed her, still holding her hand. She had a tall, straight, confident gait. He thought of a tigress walking in the bush alone.

'Onalenna, how are you?' he said, with a bright smile, a terrible quietness.

'I am happy to see you,' she said. They weaved their way through the buzzing crowd. He wanted to stop and look at the people, she kept walking. From across the road, opposite the station, came loud music, which he recognised. There was a bottle store. There was a hotel. There was a bar. There was a whole row of shops out of which came people, into which people walked, at ease as if owning time; some people were on bicycles, some came out of cars, others were on foot; the red, dry earth seemed very busy, over-burdened.

'We will come here. You have your life to be here, so why don't we just walk, Yao?' She did not smile. Their eyes met. He nodded. She took her hand out of his, and began to search her bag. She stopped to make a thorough search, peering into the bag. He stood, waiting for her, watching, watching her. She took out the keys, and they began to walk again. She stopped at the Nomad, unlocked the door, got into the car, and opened the door for him. He kept watching her, as if they had never known each other. She started the car. It purred and began to move.

'That is an expert take-off!' he said.

'Thanks,' she said, concentrating on her driving.

'You did not say anything about this in any of your letters,' he said.

'About what?'

'That you can drive.'

'Ah, Yao!' she said, and touched him lightly on the hand.

'No, you did not.'

'I know, but I have become so used to driving, I have even forgotten that you do not know that I can drive.'

'Who the hell am I with in this car?'

'Your woman,' she said. He looked ahead of him, seeing the red earth road; people, people walking to and fro. There were many trees, green trees. The sun was gentle with its heat, gentle on his flesh. The sky was blue, so blue, it looked transparent, confirming his belief that it was empty, as empty as a deep whistling pit.

'Yao, how are you?'

'Fine, love, fine, happy to be back here.' He looked at her. She was holding the steering wheel with both hands. He touched her on the thigh.

'Whose car is this?'

'Ours,' she said. He took his hand off her thigh. He clutched both hands and looked straight ahead of him.

'Onalenna, can you park right there.' He pointed toward the side of the road.

'Why?'

'Will you?'

'No problem, but why?'

'Because I want to kiss you,' he said.

'No, not in the street like that,' she said. 'We'll soon be home.' Their eyes met.

'What do you mean, home?'

'Exactly that,' she said. There was silence in the car.

Oni parked the Nomad in the yard. Briefly, they were both bathed in the heat of the sun. Then they were in the house.

'Is this our house?'

'Yes,' Oni said.

Yao closed the door behind him. He held Oni, pulling her towards him, looking into her eyes. Oni cupped his face in her warm hands. They embraced. Her grip got tighter around his neck. It was a grip strengthened by the nights and days of waiting. They sat on the sofa.

'It's been a long, long time,' Yao said.

'I know,' Oni said. 'So many things have happened.'

'Yes, so many things.'

'Many people are waiting to hear from you,' Oni said. 'I have to fetch Themba, Tuki and Fidel.'

'I will have a bath in the meantime,' Yao said.

'No, let's get there together.'

'Okay.'

I had to leave in a terrible hurry. The train took me. Rattling and rattling forever, having embraced me with its steel arms, it was the only sanctuary open to me in the whole world. It was also the most exposed since it was so public, and when it moved and rattled, I felt it was conspiring against me. It seemed the slowest thing in the world, slower than the tortoise itself. When it stopped, it seemed it would never move; that the mountain would move before it did.

I watched every face. I stared into every eye. I sensed any and all the movements coming from behind or from in front. I watched every hand movement. I watched every foot movement. I heard almost every whisper and deciphered every loud voice. I was in the third class coach, where nobody sleeps. People are packed on top of each other. Those who have made such journeys often before, like the mineworkers, bring radios and gramophones and play them at peak volume. The train guards, really prison warders of the train, walk up and down all night, shouting, screaming at passengers, beating them up, swearing.

I sat in a corner, and lost count of how many times I was asked for my ticket. I learnt to keep it ready in my hand. The wooden seat I sat on was for three people. I don't know how many of us sat there. Whenever I started to fall asleep, my sleep would be shattered by a nightmare in which I had fallen asleep on a baby, and it had died. There was a baby on the seat, its mother and two men. There was a third man, drunk out of his mind, who kept coming to offer liquor to the woman, and to us men. Sometimes he came with friends, who were dead drunk too. They always found somewhere to sit on this seat; they staggered, sat, drank, talked and talked, fell about as the train swung this and that way. We braced each other, whichever way we could. The baby was fast asleep. Three radios, playing three different stations, yelled at us. Dancing, the train sung its own song as the wheels turned. It was taking me away. On this journey, I thought a lot about Oupa's death.

We buried Oupa. I was the spokesman for the family at the funeral. I don't know what I said at the cemetery. But when after two days the police fetched me from my home, read to me what I had supposedly said at the funeral, and wanted to know what I meant by it, I told them, I told them a lot more. The death of my nephew, I said to the Captain, had made me stop and look at South Africa, face to face. The country had gone mad. 'By 'country', I meant the government, those who protected it, those who lubricated it with money, wealth, oppression, violence and their lives. They had had no choice but to go mad. We had no choice but to stop the madness. Oupa was just one of many, many children who were dead. I felt ashamed that the madness had had to hit so close to me, to rage into my home before I realised fully that South Africa had gone mad. Had I not always known this? I knew that my country needed to be saved by us, its people. Oupa had told me so. He had told me this with a clarity which had sobered my drunken escapism. I had known this before. I had seen it. I had heard it. I had experienced it. Now I knew that it was not only important to know. The most important thing was, what does one do once one knows? I would not talk about the tragedies which my people had learnt to live with. That would break my heart, and I didn't want to break my heart before them. I could do them a favour. I could make them believe that they were victorious. They were not. There was no way that they could be. All those people in my country to whom they had given no choice, whom they had turned into enemies, were plotting their defeat every day.

I did not know what to say further than that. I knew I could say more. I could put it more clearly to him. But I realised that I was only wanting to tell him that his time was over. There was no point, really, in repeating this. I stopped talking. He told me that a long, long jail sentence was waiting for me. He said it would be like locking me in and throwing the key away. He said take heed, I warn you. I have warned so many of you before; some listened, some did not. Those who did not are rotting on Robben Island. He stood up. He hovered over me. We stared at each other. I did not care. I felt he was wasting my time. There was nothing in common between us. We disliked each other intensely. Certainly I did. I asked him whether he wanted to throw me out of the window. He sat down. He wanted to talk. I said, look, please don't waste your time, there is nothing that you can tell me that I can listen to. He kept talking. I don't know what he said. He called others. They mocked me. They said something about go, and the next time you come back here, you will find out what happened to your communist nephew. The Captain, playing the kind one, told the others to leave. When we looked at each other again, I thought God, you bastard, I have nothing for you but my anger. I sat back. I asked him, why don't you remove me? Lock me in. Throw me out of the window. Pull out my fingernails. Shoot me. He started talking again. I sat back. I began to plan my departure from South Africa while sitting there in John Vorster Square listening to this mad man talking. I will never know what he was saying. I knew that as soon as I walked out of that building, I was going to the border. I was going to get onto a train and leave.

So the train took me. It took me from Johannesburg on a Friday night. Saturday morning I was in Mafeking. I walked, took a taxi, walked some more, got a lift. Finally I arrived in Gaborone by Tuesday night. One day I will talk about that. The train took me away from Seventh Avenue and London Street. It took me away from Alexandra. It took me to Botswana. I was just one among thousands who had taken this journey. Some were still going to take it. South Africa keeps vomiting. It vomits and vomits. I am just a drop in this vomit. So now I walk the Gaborone streets by day, sometimes by night, sometimes very early in the morning. I have said nothing to those I left behind. I met Yao one day. I met the others on other days. I had become something called a refugee. At first, that is what I called myself. Then I said, I am a political refugee. Then I did not want that tag. I said I was an exile. Then I said how can I say I am an exile when I am in Africa? No, I am not an exile. What am I then?

It was my second week here. It was deep in the night, perhaps very early in the morning. I was sitting on a cold cement slab. I kept looking at it, and at others like it. Some were white, some were black. They formed a large circle, a circle the size of a park. At the centre of the circle there were trees, grass and flowers. The streets were deserted – no cars, no strollers. I was alone, my buttocks feeling cold. I looked at the moon. I looked at the stars. I looked at the sky. Then back at the black and white slabs. The tar. The circle. The trees, grass, flowers, and the silence. I sat back. I leant on the wire fencing. What was I then? A political refugee. Right. What did that mean? Not what I thought it meant. What did the world think it meant! I thought about Palestine. What had I heard about the refugees there? I could not remember the details. I knew that whatever I had read about them, it was nothing favourable. Zimbabwe. Namibia. I thought about planes rushing in on their hot pursuit missions, bombs and bombs! Is that what I was then? A target for bombs? I heard a car screeching somewhere in the centre of town. How do the people in Mozambique feel every time a jet sounds in the distance? The people in some villages in Zambia? Angola? What do people mean when they say, in fifteen minutes, perhaps even less, six hundred people in these countries lost their lives while the jets swept back to the countries they had come from: South Africa, Rhodesia, Israel. What did this mean?

I thought about Jesus Christ. Okay, he and I had not been talking for a long, long time. I said, come and sit next to me now, on this cement slab, and let's talk about bombs. Maybe that is too far-fetched. Let us talk about the Captain. Captain Slabgat. Or Koekemoer; or Major Swanepoel. No, that too is far-fetched. Let us talk about the fact that I am drunk now, that I have been drinking since morning, and now my head is buzzing and I am thinking about bombs. They are real. I am read. Where are you? I thought about my

194

mother. She called on Jesus Christ the day Oupa came home in a coffin. I thought about Mary. I thought about my wife. I thought about the people who drive jets. I am being an idiot. First thing is, I am a political refugee. Right. What next? The refugee council takes care of me. The UN has all sorts of programmes for me. They give me thirty pula a month to live on.

My mouth was foul. I needed to wash somewhere. My legs were aching. I was still a bit drunk. Where did I go from there? I wished I could go back to Lily. It was unfair. I might never see her again. Crowds of people were coming out of Bontleng. Bontleng reminded me of Alexandra. The houses. The untarred roads. The dirty water in the streets. The people, the way they walked, like people in Alexandra. I found a fifty thebe piece in my pocket and decided to buy ginger beer to take away the bad taste in my mouth. I walked on, sipping the drink. Now there were people around me. They were walking as if they knew where they were going. They hardly looked at me. I saw a girl in blue, a bank teller. Standard Bank teller, from her uniform. She was tall. Something about her looked very familiar. Oh yes, she walked like Lily.

Another morning. It was not silent. Thee were many cars outside, roaring as they went up and down the main road. I could hear women talking, and men too. If it were in Alexandra, I would get out of the blankets round about now. I would walk up Seventh Avenue, up Hofmeyr Street, buy a newspaper at the corner, then begin to count down the avenues to Second. Then my day would begin. Or I would put on a Dollar Brand record, which would help me pace the day, carry it through like everyone else, able to understand that we were all trapped, but were not going to weep about it. But then, I was not in Alexandra now. Alexandra seemed so many hours away, a fathomless distance away, a distance which with every day grew deep and deeper and, becoming bottomless in its depth, seemed to whistle and laugh at me. Now it seemed that no matter what I did, or where I went, I would be a stranger, a stranger everywhere and forever.

I was done with Alexandra now, that I knew. I was done with it forever, and I had known this long, long before I left. Then, everything had become deadly. Every step, every word, every friend I made, any street I walked, every minute, made me understand death. Death ceased to be the large thing, the elusive thing which I had grappled with, which had frightened me, which had made me wonder why – if death was so tall, so loud, so powerful, so endless, so final – why life then?

I understood death because everywhere there was no life. Then who was I, if I had rejected – assuming that I could – life and death? I had seen so many eyes flicker and glitter with life, as if these eyes knew something about hope. Did they know something about how they could pay so hard, so endlessly for drinking water, eating bread, finding out how they could search and destroy their ignorance, how they could learn how to hold the hands of those they loved, how they could learn how to handle hatred? Yet their eyes began to glimmer.

I found myself near the refrigerator. My hand shook as it reared for the bottle of cold water, for the glass which stalked my mouth. Last night's music was still ringing loud in my head. I could also hear the voices, pitched high, battling with the loud, formidable music which had taken control of our bodies until men and women got so close that only the sharpest blade could pass between them. Yet they were so far from each other that even the ocean could not fill the gap. Now they were vulnerable, now all-powerful, now their eyes whistled with love, now with hatred, now with fear, now with a certain knowledge. The music kept pounding, pounding, leaving nothing unknown, revealing so many things which we did not know about each other; and all of us danced, hard, with all our strength, with our hands, feet, eyes, ears, with our stomachs and buttocks; we danced and danced, crushing the might of night beneath our feet.

The music, now dull, kept hammering. The water, very cold water like a long flexible needle, zig-zagged its way down my throat, and then found its way to my stomach. I felt it sing in there. My feet were cold against the shining floor. I saw my plate of food on the stove, covered, sweating a little. I started to make tea. It was when I entered my room again, looking for a cigarette, that the smell hit me in the face. I held my mouth with both hands. There was this weight in my stomach. My eyes went blank a while. I don't know why, but I thought of Oni. What had happened to Yaone while the music pounded last night? What had happened to everyone who was there? I had to get out of that room. I took a cigarette from the back pocket of my trousers which lay sprawled on the floor. The packet felt as if it had been resuced from the mouth of a cow. Not a single cigarette was unbroken. I heard a dog barking, and other dogs began to bark outside. I heard a car hoot. I heard the squeal of brakes. I lit a piece of cigarette. The kettle was whistling. I switched on the radio. Some bullshit music came out of it, music which might have been sung in Setswana or Sezulu, or sung in a 'pop' accent in either America or England. The announcer said it was sung by some children from Soweto. I walked outside. The sky was bright blue, the trees deep green. There was a cool breeze blowing. Again, my eyes went blank.

It was when the vomit hit the stoep that I thought of Oupa. I thought of Mary, the two of them always inseparable in my mind. I thought of the little boy, wearing a grey cap and black boots, clutching his mother with both hands and then, awkwardly obeying her, stretching his hand out to shake mine, looking straight into my eyes. We were under a bus shelter. We were summoned by the roar of the traffic that was carrying thousands of my people past us — maybe, even, carrying the man who pushed Oupa one night, one terrible night, out of a tenth floor window. When that happened, I thought, Oupa must have been long dead. I thought of Mary at the graveside. She had held my mother's hand as she stood there, looking into the hole where her boy lay, now lifeless in a box, even in death hammering out a truth to us as we stood there, that a new chapter was finally being added to the history of our country. It was being written in the ink of life and death. It was being written that way because, as soon as they were born, the children died. They died before they could handle their cocks correctly for peeing. They died. They died, not having known that there was something called life.

The last time I saw Mary was at our home in Alexandra. For days, for months, I had fought for Oupa's clothes, the ones he was wearing when he died. I came out of that place and she looked at me. She was dead still, her eyes staring straight at me, watching me, having put all their hope in me. I gave her the parcel I had.

'Are these Oupa's clothes?' she asked. I shook my head. She dropped the parcel on the ground. I heard the thud. She began to weep. I picked up the parcel. I held her hand. I took her away. I wanted to throw the parcel away, leave it in the middle of the road. I did not. I knew I had to take it home. In the taxi Mary sat very close to me and held my hand tight, as if she was afraid she would get lost. I could feel her tears wetting my shirt. I paid the driver and we got out of the taxi, went through the gate, entered the house. My father was there.

'Are those Oupa's clothes?' he asked, his voice terrible, frightened, pleading. I said nothing. I put the parcel on the table. My father walked a few paces nearer and stopped. It was as if he expected to see Oupa himself emerge from the parcel. I cut the string and undid the paper. A new pair of jeans, a new shirt, prices and all on it, socks, and a pair of clean polished shoes lay on the table staring at us. I will never forget my father's silence, his sigh as he stood there and looked at that shit. Mary had walked away and was weeping in the other room, calling on the God of my mother and father, and perhaps on her God, who took Oupa, who bought Oupa a new pair of jeans and a shirt, who polished my nephew's shoes.

Shit. I backed away from the sun and the sky. I backed away from the breeze. I made tea for myself. I switched the radio off. If I could find Yao, we would raise the money and then he and I would go some place, sit there, talk and drink together. I gulped the tea, made up my bed, left the house. Yao and I met as I was going to his home, and he was coming for me. I felt bitter. I did not care.

'Tsi-Tsi boy, hoozet?'

'Okay. What happened last night?'

'You would not have found me home this morning, so let's leave it there. Let's not make things messy. What happened to you – did that little girl take you home?'

'That is where I woke up this morning, so I guess she did.'

'I have a Ten. We can put in some time at Hilda's, right?'

'Beautiful.'

We sat at the table. I pulled the ash-tray nearer to me. Thousands of sorrows were dancing with all their strength on my heart. I kept reading: Lion Beer, Lion Beer, Lion Beer, which was what was written on the plastic cover of Hilda's table. The smell of whisky hit my nostrils. I remembered that I had not cleaned the stoep. I took the glass, and swallowed.

'That was a good get-together last night, but I didn't like the way it ended,' Yao said.

I did not want to talk. I kept my eyes in the glass. I got hold of the bottle and poured me some whisky. I enjoyed the feel of the thick glass in my hand.

'People don't live like this,' Yao said. I heard Hilda talking to someone in the kitchen. I could feel Yao watching me. 'What's this, hang-over or blues or both?' Our eyes met. He looked down. He sighed.

'I am all right,' I said. I did not know what else to say or do.

'Fine,' he said. We were silent. Yao sat still. He sat there on the chair, playing with the stick of matches, his legs dancing against each other, and yet he was still. I knew it was hard, extremely hard for him to lift his head, for then he would not know what to do with his eyes. So he lept them on the table, twisting a matchstick this way and that. I was watching him. I knew he was feeling terrible, that maybe he needed my help.

'I am all right bra,' I said.

'You bastard,' he said and laughed. Then, 'Do you think it is possible to love two women?'

'It is possible to fuck them, one at a time. I don't know about love in that context,' I said.

'Hey, now look, I am asking you, as you well know, if it is possible to care for them both. You know what I mean.'

'No I don't.' I took a gulp.

'Don't be mean now.'

'I love you, so I am going to be mean.'

'No, but I am serious. I mean what I am saying.' He shot his eyes at me, wearing their wise expression.

'Just don't, please don't waste my time,' I said.

'I left with Molly last night and came back from there this morning,' he said.

'Don't waste my time.' I felt like screaming.

'You are not all right then?'

'I am.'

'Don't give me shit then.'

'Not a single person is surprised, or would be surprised by what you are saying you and Molly did last night, especially not you and her, so don't give me empty big deals, that is all.'

'Bra, be my mirror, that is all I am saying.'

'I know, and I am saying don't waste my time.'

'If you insist, all right.'

Hilda came into the kitchen, a nauseatingly huge and untidy woman, wearing a wig and yesterday's fading face cream and lipstick. I felt my stomach roar again.

'Are you paying, or what?'

Fuck you, I thought. Silence.

'Yao, heh?'

'I don't owe you, right?'

'No, I have just checked my books.'

'Exercise book, not "books",' I said.

'What?' She looked at me.

'Don't play big and talk about "books", say exercise book,' I said, as mean as I could. 'You are such a foolish bitch.'

'Heh? What?'

'Fuck you,' I said.

'Tsi, haai, drop that shit,' Yao said. 'Hilda, don't talk to him. Look, I will pay you tomorrow.'

'He says I am a bitch?'

'Forget him,' Yao said, laughing.

'He says I am foolish?' She had this nauseating smile on her face.

'Don't worry, Hilda.' Yao stood up and held her by the arm, leading her to the kitchen.

I was getting drunk. My stomach was empty and my head was heavy. The room began to dance. I could see Lion Beer dancing on the table. I knew from the way Yao was talking that he was drunk, or getting drunk, and that wherever he was in there, in Hilda's kitchen, he was hugging her. I could be mean if I wanted to, but I didn't want to get up from the chair. I thought of Molly. She was a beautiful girl. They could twine in each other's arms, she and Yao, and never separate, but, well, I did not care to know about it. I knew Oni well. I mean, I knew she loved me, she cared for me, that she would bury me, so — where did Molly come in? Yao came out of the kitchen, another bottle of whisky in his hand. I felt very hungry now. Yao sat opposite me. He looked at me as if he had never seen me before. He kept staring at me. Then he poured himself a drink.

'I am thinking of my sister,' I said.

'Who, Puso?'

'Yes, Mary,' I said. Silence.

'She is nice and sweet, like a peach.' He brushed his nose. 'She is a sweet pumpkin, like something you enjoy.'

'That's true.'

'She had a lamb, and it died, got killed.' Yao was looking straight into my eyes, not even blinking. He cleared his throat and shifted on his chair, settling down. I watched Yao drinking from his glass, sipping and sipping, holding his glass with both hands all the time, as if it were something that might melt and disappear, holding it in his tender careful hands outstretched before him towards me, relaxing, at ease, now and then the golden contents of the glass dancing as he said something, gestured lightly, without forgetting to nurse the glass. Yao had changed, but only in the sense that he could be silent for long periods. In most other ways he had not changed. His eyes would still stare, stare and penetrate, like the edge of the sharpest spear, penetrating, settling, waiting for a response. He still laughed in his old way, revealing himself as a very vulnerable man. Then he would stop suddenly after laughing uncontrollably. Sorrow would strike his mouth and eyes, write a chapter there about his journeys. He laughed now, and speaking softly said: 'When last did you see Mary?'

'Long ago. I hoped never to see her again.'

'Oh yes, you did say.' He looked down.

'What do you think is going to happen?'

'No, that is not the question. The question is whether we are still able to love, you know.' His eyes were glued on the glass, which was now miles and miles away from his mouth. He was staring at it, making its contents dance, nursing it gently at long range. 'Now I am talking about something which I have thought about many nights and days. You see, when we love we cannot forget, and this means that we know a lot about hatred. We cannot give birth to children like Oupa, and have them thrown out of windows or killed the way Oupa was killed. But that did happen, and we know it happened, and we loved Oupa — shit, now we know too much. You and I know about Fix, about you, about me. And that means that kids like Fidel will know this too. You and I, let alone your father and my father, did not know anything compared with what Fidel now knows at his age. So we love, that is what we still have to do, and now we can take any storm that comes and we can make storms, because we love . . . so okay, okay, now you sit there and weep.' He sat back, still holding his glass far away from his mouth. 'Now you sit there and weep, weep boy, weep, you can't fool me, no you cannot fool me, you think I don't know that Oupa, on that day, that night, took a terrible journey? You think I don't know that when he got into the hands of those people he had everything a person has, and that when he was put into his box he was toothless, he had no nails, there were parts of him missing? Don't try to fool me. I know these things. I know that they kicked his teeth out, and that there were a lot of them in his mouth as he tried to scream. I know all these things. Fidel too knows them.' He looked at me. 'See?' He laughed. I saw the calendar on the wall. It was an old calendar, kept there because of the nudes on it. Fat nudes. Hilda came out of the kitchen and disappeared into the other room whose door was visible to me. I wondered how many men had disappeared into that door with her. I saw for the first time the little boy who sat by the door, making sounds like those a donkey makes. I saw him and realised that he looked like Hilda, like someone else too, and that he had ginger skin-colour, curly hair and brown eyes.

'Well, I hear you.' I did not know what else there was to say to Yao. He had worked the revelation of his life, well, that was it. I knew about the many, many journeys he had taken. I knew him a long time.

Fifteen

The Movement, like the sea, is deep, is vast, is reflective. It can be calm. It can be rough and tough. Like the wind, it moves and moves and moves.

The incident started at a small school in a small township near Springs, near Kinross, in Leslie. The children at this school told the teacher, who came to teach Maths, that they could not learn if he had his holster on. They told him that they thought he should go to the operational area and teach the people there the Maths of Life. That there were no longer any borders to protect. That if terrorists had crossed the borders, or never actually been outside the borders, then there was no point in guarding them. When he did not listen, they told him they were walking out of class. At this point, he threatened that anyone who left the class would be arrested. The government could not allow lawlessness and disorder to rule. Whose government, one pupil asked. The man said that this pupil was marked and would regret the question. The class stood up and was walking out, when, out of frustration, the teacher pounced on the boy who had asked, whose government? The whole school joined in the protest. The women, who heard about this soon after, joined in the protest. The police came. They were stoned. They opened fire.

The other schools in Springs joined the protest. Benoni joined the protest. Boksburg joined. Brakpan joined. Germiston. Maraisburg. Johannesburg. Cape Town. Durban.

The agitators from outside who are instigating the students are cowards. They stay outside and send students to fight their battles. So said the Prime Minister. The government was ready, with all the might as its disposal, to crush this unlawfulness.

The system of discriminatory education must be scrapped, the students said.

If the government does not listen, we resign. So said the teachers in Cape Town. Johannesburg. Durban. Springs. And now even towns whose names had never been heard of, like Paul Roux (probably a farm school) joined. The streets of South Africa's cities were again filled with two types of uniforms, both feared: camouflage dress and school uniforms.

The parents of the children — domestic servants, street sweepers, bus drivers, gardeners, everyone — joined. Some white teachers joined the boycott. Discriminatory education must be scrapped. In Leslie, the children disappeared. Trucks were coming for them. The trucks did not find the children the next time they came. They took the mothers and fathers instead.

From the main cities came demands that they be released.

The mineworkers joined the strike. The trucks came for them too.

The Churches came out, saying they would disobey the government.

TERRORIST ATTACK ON HEIDELBURG MILITARY BASE, the newspaper headline declared the next day.

Oni looked at Yao. He was fast asleep. She closed the door behind her and disappeared into the dark. Before daybreak, she had reached Derdepoort. Three days later she was back in Walmanstadt.

'I am sorry my child's child, but your father is silly,' Mmaphefo said.

'How come he is silly?' Fidel asked.

'He does not talk nicely to me,' she said.

'I was joking with her, then she threw this tin at me,' Themba said, and gave the tin of snuff to Mmaphefo. 'Dikeledi said to greet you,' he said to her.

'Oh, how is she? Is she still fat like a fatcake?'

'She works hard. She does a lot of good work in Europe.'

'Yes . . . and fat?'

'No, slim.'

'Really?'

'She works hard.'

'She reminded me a lot of Mike Ramono. Hardworking people, those.'

'How have you all been?' Themba hugged Fidel.

'Fine. Granny came to see me and granny Mmaphefo,' Fidel said.

'How was Granny?'

'She, she . . . she said you said she must not come and join us.'

'I never said that.'

'How come she does not join us then?'

'Didn't you ask her?'

'I did. She says you said she must not,' Fidel said.

'No, I did not.'

'Fidel, I think you must go to see Mpho,' Mmaphefo said.

'Why?'

'Why, because I say so. Also, I have to talk to your father.'

'When will I talk to him?'

'Soon as I am through.' Fidel walked away.

'They fed you well where you were, heh?'

'I did not like the food there at all. It is full of chemicals,' Themba said.

'Chemicals?'

'Yes, when you eat an apple, it only reminds you of an apple. It tastes like rubber.'

'Where is that?'

'Especially in America.'

'Why do they do that?'

'Mass production, for sky-high profits.'

'I see.'

'The place is decadent,' Themba said.

'Did you travel well, though?'

'Yes. People send their greetings.'

'So what have you decided about the boy?'

'He belongs to the Movement,' Themba said.

'Meaning?'

'The Movement must take him through school.'

'Where?'

'Can you discuss that with the relevant people?'

'I will if you say so.'

'I am leaving today. Send word through the usual channels. It will reach me wherever I am,' Themba said.

'What message?'

'About the boy, where he is, and all that.'

'I see.'

'How is your health?'

'I am old now. I can feel that.'

Themba got into the Nomad. He headed back to Gaborone.

'Yes, you can see him, but you must use either English or Afrikaans,' the policeman said. Georgy lifted his head. He saw Granny and smiled.

'How are you?' she said in Afrikaans.

'Fine. Fine, but I feel weak,' Georgy said. Granny looked at the policeman. Around her there were many beds. Their occupants, faces pain-struck, tried to give her a smile.

'It's terrible,' Georgy said.

'I know,' Granny said.

'They are going to cut off my legs.'

'You are not the only one,' she said. She looked away and held her breath.

'I am not the only one?'

'No. We will get artificial legs,' she said. She looked at the ceiling: the huge lights stared back at her. She sighed. The smell of clean sheets and blankets, and polish and death and urine and shit, hung in the ward. She took out a handkerchief and blew her nose.

'Why are you crying?'

'I am not crying,' she said, her voice shaking.

'Did you bring cigarettes?'

'Yes.'

'Thanks.'

She lit him one.

'You have to go now,' the law said.

She looked at the cop. She looked back at Georgy.

'We will be all right,' she said.

'Yes.' He looked at her. 'Yes, we will be all right.'

'You must not be so thin,' she said.

'Am I?'

'Yes, you are.'

'Time up now,' the cop said.

'I will make you fat when you come home.'

'Yes,' he said. 'Tell me, have you been to see Fidel?'

'Yes, he is a big boy now.'

'Where?'

She looked at the cop and then at Georgy. She said nothing.

'I see,' he said. 'Did you see his father?'

'No.'

'Woman, I said it is time up now,' the cop said.

'How do you feel about it all?'

'I miss Fidel, but I will be all right,' she said. 'They said they will talk to his father to allow him to come and see us now and then.'

'You feel all right about that?'

She looked at him. She looked at the cop.

'I think it is best if they look after him. They have taught him many things now.'

'I hear you,' he said. 'You must go now, come tomorrow.'

'Okay.' She leaned towards him and kissed him full on the mouth. The sun fell on her face. She saw the many people coming out of the wards, people who had come to see their sick, their wounded, their dying. She became part of the crowd.

Charles had told her that, because of the many victims of war in Zimbabwe and the other countries there was talk of building a school for the handicapped. He would keep her informed. He would keep in touch.

She got into the bus. She sat by herself and watched the houses, the similar, cold-looking, grey houses of Tembisa, running backwards as the bus sped by. The bus was full, but Granny did not see all these people. Her head supported against the window pane, her eyes glued to what was now a blur of houses, she was lost in thought. She must ask Charles for more details.

JAN SMUTS TERROR BOMB EXPLOSION – so read the morning placard.

Somewhere else at this time, Jully was boarding another bus.

Charles arrived in Durban early in the morning. He got off a milk truck. The man gave him two pints of milk and drove off.

Jully arrived in Walmanstadt in the afternoon. She and Oni embraced and kissed. She went into the mud house. A man was lying on the bed in the semi-dark house.

'This comrade just arrived,' Oni said. 'He was shot in the leg and the shoulder.'

Jully went to look at the man, whose eyes were semi-closed. She could smell the familiar smell of blood as she took off the blankets. His thigh was a mess and his shoulder had been shattered by a bullet.

'It looks as if his leg will have to be amputated,' she said to Oni. She was standing by the basin which was on a drum, washing her hands. Oni looked at her.

'Tuki said to give you this when I see you.' Oni gave her a piece of paper.

'Where is he now?'

'I don't really know.'

'When last did you see him?'

'Four or five months ago.'

'Where?'

'Botswana.'

'Comrade, revolutionary greetings! This is to say I am all right and thinking of you. I do not know when I will see you. However, the struggle continues.' So the letter said. Jully looked at it again, then burnt it.

DARING TERROR ATTACK ON DURBAN OIL PLANT.

The planes arrived in Mozambique. Thunder. Fire. Smoke. Silence.

The Prime Minister declared a news blackout.

Themba arrived at the gathering. The woman, short and fat, her face framed by an enormous Afro, met him at the door.

'How are you, Themba?'

'I am fine, I hope I'm not late.'

'We haven't started yet. Since you are here, do come in,' she said, 'and meet the people before we begin.' There were many other Botswana women present. Themba shook their hands. The fat lady was by his side, murmuring the names of the women. When Themba was through, she asked him to follow her. They went out into the yard at the back.

'This is what we have managed to collect since the last time we met,' she said to Themba. Themba looked at the arsenal of artificial legs and arms.

'We will dispatch them home,' Themba said. He held the wheelchair bar, pushing it backwards and forwards. They went back into the hall. People began to sit down and silence fell. Themba stood right in front, hands folded in front of him. He cleared his throat to speak.

He got to Gaborone airport in time to see Fidel and the ailing Mmaphefo off. It was to be the last flight. The following day, jet fighters circled over the airport. It was ordered that no further flights would leave Gaborone.

I saw people queuing for bread for the first time at the Corner Supermarket in Gaborone.

It has become hard to say anything now. All I know is that besides being a loss of safety, change is also a promise. These planes cannot bomb us forever. Nor are we going to queue for bread for the rest of our lives. I am sure about that. I saw the women and the children come with their bundles. I saw their eyes. I saw their faces. I know that this cannot go on forever. The first leg of the journey is now well and truly in progress. There is no safety anywhere – not for anyone. The pilots who fly the planes – like these mothers and their children and their bundles – stare and stare and stare, in the way that only a human can, in the only way that a human fears. At a certain point, the stares of fear and of hunger look alike. It does not matter whether one flies a plane or stands in a queue. Now and then we look at the mighty planes with their mad speed, hovering and swooping above us. But we also know that, while we fear them, they also are in great fear to fall. We know – as they roar above our heads – that since we are human and they are not, we can wait and they cannot. They cannot fly and wait. In the same way that we cannot wait and starve for a long time. We can fall, and they will fall. We see their huge shining bodies whizz past and roar afterwards, and before we know where they are they come back. But that is because they do not see us, or know us, or want to know us. The strongest will win this game. It is costly. But the strongest will win it.

Who is the strongest?

The woman lay on her back. Her vagina, open like the lip of the earth, the lip of the sky when the sun pours out, was red with blood.

'Push, push, push,' Jully kept saying to her.

'Hoooo, hoooo, hoooo,' the woman kept saying, holding her head, holding her huge stomach, holding her thighs. 'Mama mama we, hooo, jooo, mama!'

'Push, push, push,' Jully kept saying.

Blood like the sun's rays spilled from the lips, the now-red lips, to the thighs, to the mat, onto the newspapers.

'Push, push, push.' Jully walked towards the woman from the bed where a man, with a silent groan, clenched the pain around his guts. She looked at the woman, whose legs were in the air. 'Push, push, push,' she said. She walked back to the man.

I got my half-loaf of bread after midday. My knees were wobbling. I could hardly see. It felt as if, anytime, I was going to fall. I stopped at the corner and leaned against the wall. I must get back. Lily and our four children are waiting for the bread. The children are looking at their mother, with eyes asking how come you can't give us bread. She knows I am coming back. I must get back. The road seems long. I must get back.

'Push, push, push.'

New York – Gaborone – Kanye   *1975 – 1980*

206